Short Fiction of

William H. Coles

2000-2016

SHORT FICTION

of William H. Coles

2000-2016

This book is a work of fiction. Places, events, and situations in this story are purely fictional. Any resemblance to actual persons, living or dead, is coincidental.

First edition

Published June, 2016

Story in Literary Fiction
99 West South Temple #1802
Salt Lake City, Utah 84101

www.storyinliteraryfiction.com

ISBN: 978-0-9961903-9-8 (softcover)
ISBN: 978-0-9976729-0-9 (hardcover)
ISBN: 978-0-9976729-1-6 (ebook)

Contents

The Gift

illustration by Peter Healy

The Gift

In 1959, a week after her seventeenth birthday, Catherine missed her period in February, and then in March. By late April she was not sleeping well and most of her waking hours were spoiled by nausea and hating everything she ate. Her mother, Agnes, made an emergency appointment with Dr. Crowder.

"Stay here," Dr. Crowder said to Catherine before he left the exam room. The receptionist had brought Agnes into his private office, where she sat in the wing chair for consultations.

"She's pregnant," he said.

Agnes's face paled with the accusation. "She's a child," she said.

How often mothers would not let their children grow up. He gave her time to absorb the truth. "She's a young woman who is going to have a baby," he said.

Agnes wept, her hands to her face. Dr. Crowder handed her tissues from a desk drawer. After some moments, Agnes blew her nose and breathed deeply with a long exhale.

"Have you told her?" Agnes said.

"I've told only you. But she's not stupid."

"Can something be—you know—done?"

Dr. Crowder stared. He had been the family physician for more than thirty years. He had delivered Catherine. "You might find someone. But never ask me, Agnes." he said. "I do not approve."

Agnes flushed. Now she was ashamed. "It will ruin us," she explained.

Bullshit, thought the doctor. Birth is a miracle. Oh, yes, life was fragile, dangerous, and loaded with inexplicable injustices, but he still loved humanity. And he stayed in practice well beyond retirement to marvel as his patients juggled life's inflated minutiae in their own creative ways.

"I'll send her away," Agnes continued.

"Let her make the decision," Dr. Crowder said.

"No. I'll make up an excuse."

"Think about it. There would be gossip if she stayed. But if you and Harold were supportive and proud, the gossips would cease caring after a while. And life would go on."

"It's a sin," Agnes said.

"I doubt having a baby is a sin," Dr. Crowder said.

But Agnes could not trust the advice of an idealistic doctor who she thought was immune to reality, nor the judgment of her errant child who was too young and too stubborn to know what her slip-up would do to a prominent family.

At home, to her husband, Harold, who knew otherwise, Agnes dismissed Catherine's nausea as tummy upset and refused to discuss the baby with Catherine for hours. She blamed Catherine's problem on Harold's family, all of whom were pig-headed and arrogant.

After dinner, alone with Catherine in Catherine's room, she demanded to know the father of the child. She shouted the most likely possibility. But Catherine refused to answer. "So many you don't even know?" Agnes asked. Then Agnes sent Harold into the bedroom for a one-on-one (she hoped he would beat the crap out of Catherine). Agnes leaned with her ear against the bedroom door so she could hear every word. She was appalled: he felt lucky to have a grandchild. Birth was God's gift to each of us, and how lucky this baby was to have Catherine for a mother. Not one word of condemnation. It was typical of her husband to turn disaster into a conspiracy against all she had accomplished.

Agnes kept her plan simple. After the birth, far away, an immediate adoption was the only solution, and after the town no longer remembered or cared, Catherine could return to live out her penance.

Dry-eyed, Catherine lay on top of her bedcovers on her back, which was already the most comfortable position for her. Her father's visit had renewed her confidence. She was a good girl, a girl who made love to only one and with a sincere passion and respect that justified her action. Even with her first suspicions, she could not destroy her lover's future with burdens he could not yet handle. There was virtue in a love baby, far different from sluts who made love to anyone, and whores who got paid, a fact she had shouted to her mother when her mother had used the word.

In the days after the doctor's appointment, Catherine endured her mother's frequent side glances and wet hissing sounds, and turned away when her mother reminded her how evil premarital sex was. But soon her mother's unpredictable outbursts became so irrational that Catherine ignored her, and turned to prayer for her baby. Her mother then developed a distracting twitch under her right eye, loud speech, short sentences—and long, cold silences.

In due time Agnes found the priest, who was hesitant at first to help. Agnes made him admit he had arranged clandestine solutions to similar problems, saying she knew, at least secondhand, of a girl he had protected. He soon admitted compliance. He said infant victims of accidental pregnancies deserved a life away from the debauchery of their mothers, who must spend their lives seeking full-time repentance to receive grace. He would help.

Two weeks before school let out for the summer, Agnes took Catherine to the airport. She gave Catherine numbered instructions on a folded piece of notepaper tucked in a paper-bound English-French dictionary. Agnes cried briefly at the gate, but she felt only relief when the plane finally took off. She was profoundly afraid of flying, but she felt no apprehension about Catherine's trip, and although she had hated the pain and discomfort of her own pregnancy, she did not worry about Catherine's delivery in a foreign country. Whatever happened, good or bad, Catherine had brought it on herself. All was in the hands of God now. She could not be expected to do more, and she was confident that many parents would have done much less, and much less effectively.

The convent school looked like a fortress, with a high stone wall around the buildings that were set next to a wide, rapidly flowing river at the northern edge of the town in the south of France, where the trees were already full with spring and the air warm even at night. From the hill, visible from the school and anywhere in town, a thirteenth-century buttressed cathedral jutted two spires toward the heavens.

The Mother Superior was cool and distant but not mean or dismissive, and Catherine, after a few weeks, liked her authoritative efficiency. Catherine began school and attended mass daily, but understood almost nothing. To help, a novice taught her French in private sessions after atins and after the evening meal.

For weeks, Catherine's sickness came on her at unexpected times. But the Sister in the infirmary gave her medicines and arranged special foods from the kitchen, and soon Catherine felt fine.

Catherine's best friend was Sister Mary Margaret, an impish little nun who rarely thought of God outside of church, but who was eager to be involved with Catherine's delivery of God's gift. Sister Mary Margaret listened to Catherine's fear of dying when the baby came out. "It is impossible," Sister Mary Margaret said confidently in French, although she had never seen a birth. "What if God punishes me with a hairy monster?" Catherine asked hesitantly. "God does not always seem to care, but He is not mean," Sister Mary Margaret said. Then Catherine told her of her fear of being stoned by French peasants—she had seen that in a film, for other sins, with Boris Karloff. Sister Mary Margaret gave her lyrical bubbly laugh that Catherine loved and frowned as she tried to find the right words in English. "C'est fou," she said.

Agnes did not write to further emphasize her indignation at her daughter's sin. Catherine sent only rare postcards to her mother, but sent long letters about her new life to her father at the office. Catherine counted the days for her father's return letters about home that he faithfully wrote.

And Catherine wrote to her priest.

Dear Father O'Leary:

The Mother Superior speaks English okay and spoke of you at both my meetings with her. She smiles with her memories of when you met. She introduced me to the people who want to adopt. The woman put her hands under my blouse on my bare belly to feel her "petite poupée." I didn't like it but I try to be Christian.

Except for Sister Mary Margaret, one of the nuns, I still can talk to only a few here. The novices laugh when I use French words and they don't try to understand my English. But I take walks through the town with Sister and visit the cathedral daily that is half a mile from the school.

The women here sew beautiful clothes that they sell in Paris. They have taught me and I now make baby booties and soft nightgowns for my baby. I crochet lace for the sleeves and the hem, even though Mother Superior says new parents will be waiting to take him … or her, away. She says it is best for all that way. As time grows close, I want to keep my baby, but I will not go back on my word.

I help the groundskeeper herd the goats that graze on the lawns of the school. He is a gentle man who sings lively songs in a high voice while he works. He makes goat cheese to give to the poor that tastes awful. But I pretend to like it to please him.

Yours in Christ,
Catti

When labor pains started regularly, Catherine went to the convent infirmary, where there were two iron beds with mattresses. Sister Teresa, the midwife, gave Catherine a draught after the delivery. Catherine slept. When she woke, Sister Mary Margaret sat on a chair next to the bed, her back six inches from the splat. The sheets were clean. Catherine accepted a glass of apple cider from her friend. Catherine's body hurt when she rose up to drink. She returned the glass and fell back, exhausted at the effort.

"Well?' Catherine asked Sister. "Did you see my baby?"

Sister was silent.

"Is it a girl?" Catherine asked.

"A little girl," Sister said in English.

Catherine found her friend's hesitancy unexpected, and she turned on the bed to see her friend better. Sister was sobbing.

"What's the matter, Maggie?"

Sister stood up and turned so Catherine could not see her face, then she hurried out the door.

"Please don't go," Catherine called. But Sister did not stop.

Catherine slept that afternoon. Sister Mary Maggie returned in the evening. Catherine was glad to see her.

"I want to see my baby," Catherine said again.

"The baby is gone already."

"So soon?"

"It was Mother Superior's plan."

"What's gotten into you? I thought you were my friend."

Sister Mary Margaret cried again.

"You're useless," Catherine said, immediately sorry when Sister turned her head away. "I want to talk to Mother Superior."

"It is not possible," Sister said.

Catherine threw her feet over the edge of the bed, wincing with pain. "I will go to her," she said.

"No! I will be punished. I was not supposed to tell you."

"Tell me what?"

Sister began crying again.

"What? Tell me, Maggie."

"The baby."

Catherine knew her friend too well to not fear the worst.

"Is the baby dead?" Catherine finally asked.

"Oh, no, not dead."

"What then?"

"She is—alive good."

"What is that? What is not right about a baby? Tell me!"

Sister did not speak but squeezed her eyes shut, helping Catherine stand and holding her arm as they went to Mother Superior. Twice Catherine had to sit on a bench to rest. Her friend could not speak for her sobs. "Run ahead. Tell Mother Superior I'm coming," Catherine said. Sister hesitated. "Go," Catherine said, disturbed by her friend's crying.

Catherine was surprised that Mother Superior hugged her for the first time ever, firmly and long. Mother Superior stepped back. "The family would not take her," she said.

Catherine looked to the floor away from Mother Superior. "Why?"

"The baby is not well. They were afraid."

"What is wrong?"

"I didn't see her. But she has no feet."

"That is ridiculous," Catherine said. "I must see her."

"I had the baby sent to a special hospital for children near Lyon. She will be given special care."

"And the parents?"

"They have refused to be involved."

"I must go," Catherine said.

"No. She will have the care she needs to grow—and serve Christ."

"I must see her. I will pay the way. Father has sent me more than I need."

"It is not the money."

"I will go. I do not need your blessing."

"You always have my blessings, child."

"I must go too," Sister Mary Margaret said, looking directly into the eyes of Mother Superior.

Catherine used her savings and she and Sister, with the now-silent gardener and cheese maker driving, took a wagon to the train station in the next town. With stops, the train took six and a half hours to the city. To save money for the return trip, Catherine and Maggie walked two miles from the station to the hospital.

At the hospital, Catherine looked down at the baby, covered in a nightgown. Catherine had already decided her name was Patricia, not Audrey, as the nun dressed in a black-and-white starched habit had told her. Patricia was in a little nightgown with buttons on the back. One arm in a sleeve waved. The other sleeve partially covered a short arm that ended in three finger stubs that jerked up and out. The nightgown hem lay flat. Catherine retracted the edge. The right leg ended in a smooth knob above where the knee should be. The other leg tapered to an end above where the ankle would be—with no foot. The corner of the baby's mouth tried to smile in a strong effort with unsure results, and the eyes wiggled and waved, sparkling as if sharing the irony of trying to make everything all work right.

"You have seen enough?" the nurse said. Her harsh accent was difficult to understand.

Catherine removed the little nightgown. She smiled at her child, and the child's roving eyes seem to fix on her, at least for a few seconds, until they wandered off, but they came back again. And how soft her skin was, her red hair so fine. Her eyes were faded of color, but inquisitive and sharp. Her lips continued to wiggle at times in an uncoordinated smile.

"She is mine," Catherine said.

"She must stay here with us," the nurse said firmly.

She put the nightgown back on her daughter. She touched the side of her cheek. The little arm waved. She touched the chest with her index finger. There was a little passage of gas with a squeeze of the face.

Searching for French words exasperated Catherine. "Tell her Maggie," she said to Sister Mary Margaret. "Tell her who I am. And get some milk and food for the trip."

Maggie explained in French. The nurse listened intently without response.

Catherine began to take off her sweater to use as a blanket, but the nurse, with a gentle hand on Catherine's arm, let Catherine know to keep her sweater—and then wrapped little Patricia in a hospital blanket. "It is for you," she said in broken English. When Catherine was holding Patricia against her breast, the Sister leaned over and kissed the back of Patricia's head. "Elle est miraculée," she said.

At the convent every nun and novice was immediately infected with motherly instincts for Patricia. Even the gardener and goat-herder, as the pater familias, made daily visits with milk and fresh-cut pansies. Sister cooked while Catherine fed Patricia, and she rocked Patricia when Catherine needed rest to regain her strength. And Catherine took Patricia to church, to market, to herd the goats. She sewed, after many trial designs, a special sling that supported Patricia. Patricia was comfortable when carried on Catherine's chest or back, and she could face in or out, and sleep when she wanted.

Catherine with Patricia became a common sight in town and the surrounding fields and wooded paths. Strangers to Catherine waved with pride and familiarity. Catherine loved Patricia's laugh as she jiggled her in the sling; loved her intense stares at new flowers they found in the gardens or in the wild; loved the "ooh" of watching a worm on a stone, or a hawk circling in the sky.

Patricia became adept at getting around the house, using her stumps all together to scurry like a tilted crab. But she was limited outside, and Catherine could see that Patricia would need some upright means of mobility.

Catherine visited veterans who lost limbs in the war, and talked to them about support. They used limbs usually provided by the army, premade, and not specially designed. But she learned unique problems for each disability, and studied the principles of various prosthetics. She found a furniture maker and explored different woods—ash and yew and oak—for strong support for Patricia's shorter leg. For the other leg she needed a sturdy foot. At first, a foot replica in walnut was tried, but eventually, a functional design looking like a miniature toboggan with laminated woods from saplings was found to be best. Catherine used her sewing skills to attach and brace the prosthetic legs with shoulder straps and snug waistbands. These were attached for stability to the wooden prosthetics by threading through multiple holes. And Patricia, with a laugh, toddled around for a while, tumbling often, and then adapted with the speed of the young until she could walk, albeit stiffly and with a tilt backward. This worked for almost a year. But it was not enough. In the leg without a knee, Catherine knew she needed a hinged prosthesis. She wrote Father O'Leary and received a quick response.

Dear Catti,

I was pleased to discover our own Dr. Crowder went to school with a world authority. Poor Dr. Crowder has had a stroke and cannot walk and he speaks so slowly we can barely understand him. But his mind is sharp and his wife now writes letters for him, and records drafts he dictates for his memoir. I am sure he would help in any way he can.

God Bless,
Father O'Leary

She received a reply from her letter to Dr. Crowder in two weeks.

Dear Catherine,

How nice to hear from you. You are one of my favorite patients. And I was also glad to hear your little Patricia is saying her first words. I imagine they're all in French, which is a beautiful language.

I do know about artificial arms and legs. But you must come home to see the best. She will need to be refitted often as she grows, and you will have to travel to Boston. But it is a very good idea.

I am a mess with this stroke. But I love my memories.

Sincerely,
Amory F. Crowder

When Catherine and Patricia left for home, more than a hundred people from the convent and town came to wish them well. Even Mother Superior cried and Sister Mary Margaret had to be pried away from her hugs of Catherine and Patricia.

Harold and Agnes were at the airport terminal gate when Patricia and Catherine arrived.

Little Patricia took her first look at Grandma and howled.

"Is that any way to treat your grandmother," Agnes said curtly.

"It's not you, mother. The trip has her constipated."

Catherine picked up Patricia and snuggled her on her shoulder. Patricia's footless longer leg poked out below her dress.

"She doesn't look so bad," Agnes said.

"Let me show you, Mother." Patricia loved to be touched, and loved to be moved. She gurgled with pleasure. "Your grandchild."

"I didn't mean she wasn't perfect."

"Dis 'bon jour,'" Catherine said to Patricia.

Agnes frowned at the French. Although she thought she knew what it meant, she was always suspicious that there was some meaning in foreign words that might be against her.

"Say hello," Catherine said, sensing her mother's feelings.

"Lo," Patricia said, and waved her arm at her grandmother, and she smiled. "Lo," she said again.

Agnes gasped at her impulse to reach out and hold her grandchild, and she took back her hands before she had extended them too far, slipping them in the pockets of her sweater.

"Take her," Catherine said.

"Oh, I'll scare her."

"I'll take her," Harold said stepping forward.

Agnes reached out quickly. "I'll do it, Harold, " she said.

As Agnes took Patricia, clutching her chest under the arms, Patricia smiled. "Pooh bear," she said with a little spittle.

Catherine handed Patricia small brown bear with one button-eye missing, and Patricia held it out to her grandmother.

Agnes held her face rigid in resistance to revealing any pleasure. Catherine tensed. But Patricia could not contain her natural affection for people, and she grinned with a warm bubbly sound. Patricia held out her bear again to her grandmother, who smiled, taking the bear and giving it a big hug. Catherine relaxed as her mother jiggled Patricia from side to side, and thanked God for Patricia's magical gift of making others happy.

Agnes held Patricia in her lap on the ride home.

Patricia discovered Catherine's toys in a trunk and in dresser drawers in Catherine's room, which had not been used since Catherine left. Harold had bought a child's bed, but everything else was the same. Agnes found energy she had not had for years: she baked and swept, she arose early before the alarm, and she took daily photos of her family. Catherine got a job as a receptionist in the office of a doctor Dr. Crowder knew. And the newest advances in jointed prosthetics were fitted to Patricia in Boston; they were waiting the new limb any day.

Three times a week Catherine took Patricia to the YMCA pool and taught her to swim dressed in a one-piece red bathing suit Catherine had sewn herself from a design she had seen in a magazine. Patricia learned to swim quickly, smoothing out her first awkward movements, and Catherine was pleased to think it toned muscles in new ways that Patricia did not normally use and would prepare her for heavier, more complicated prosthetics.

One evening, after Patricia was asleep, Harold and Agnes sat with Catherine in the living room after dinner.

"I don't like you taking Patricia swimming," Agnes said. "People will stare."

Catherine had sensed her mother's disapproval weeks ago. "Why should she not go swimming?"

"It will make her feel different."

"She is different, mother."

"But you shouldn't make her feel bad."

"She has to learn to accept the stares and not feel bad."

"At least you could cover her. That skimpy bathing suit doesn't hide anything."

"That skimpy bathing suit is what most of the children wear."

"But they're different."

"She's not ashamed, mother. She's pretty and very smart. And she has every reason to be proud."

"I didn't mean that, Catherine. Don't twist my words. I just don't want her hurt by those who think her differences should not be exposed. That's all."

"They are curious, mother. People do stare. But for most it isn't mean and it doesn't last long. And Patricia can be seen for who she is."

"She'll never go out on her own if you keep it up."

"I want her to go out on her own able to handle anything that she might face."

"Be quiet, Agnes," Harold said.

"Don't talk to me like that, Harold. This is important."

"It's not your business. Stay out of it," he said.

"You're always against me. I am not pleased, Harold."

Harold folded his paper, running the dull edge between his forefinger and thumb until it was sharp and then placing it on the footstool. "Take her swimming," he said to Catherine. "Take her everywhere she wants to go."

"That's not what I meant and you know it," Agnes said.

"Be quiet," Harold said as he left the room.

Six weeks later, for Patricia's birthday, they had a party in the kitchen with a cake and candles, balloons and presents. Harold gave Patricia books. Catherine gave her a necklace with a garnet single-stone pendant. And Agnes went to the garage and carried in a small wheelchair with a leather seat support and shinning chrome spokes on thick rubber-tired wheels.

"Look at that!" she said to Patricia.

Patricia smiled.

"Can you say thank you?" Catherine said.

"Thank you," Patricia said to her grandmother.

That night, after Catherine heard Harold finish reading one of Patricia's new stories, Pinocchio, to Patricia in bed and she had fallen asleep, Catherine approached her mother in the living room. "You must take the wheelchair back."

"Nonsense. I had it specially made," Agnes said.

"She doesn't need a wheelchair," Catherine said.

Harold came down from the upstairs and sat in his armchair.

"She can't keep up," Agnes said. "I almost lost her in the store."

"She does very well, mother. Just slow down a little."

"The new leg has been good," Harold said.

"She'll be going to school soon. She can't always be strapping on legs." Agnes said.

"She is not a victim, mother. Ignore what she can't do. Help her do what she can."

"How unloving that is, Catherine. How selfish," Agnes said. "You are making her life miserable. You've always been selfish. From the beginning."

Harold's jaws were clenched, and his hands balled into fists. "I will not allow this, Agnes. Take back the chair."

"Ridiculous."

"Take back the chair!"

"It's all right, Daddy."

"No, it's not all right." He stood.

"Don't you walk out on me," Agnes said.

He went into the kitchen. Catherine followed. He had the chair in his hands.

"What are you doing?"

"You're right. She is not a victim, Catherine. I don't want this around."

She had never seen her father this angry.

"I'm taking it to the office for now. Tomorrow, I'll be sure it's returned—or destroyed."

Agnes came into the kitchen as Harold left through the back door, taking the wheelchair to the car.

"Don't you dare—" Agnes began.

"Say one more word and I'll explode." He shut the door.

Two weeks later, Catherine went to her father's office at the bank during the lunch hour. She had brought sandwiches and sodas for both of them.

"We have to go back," Catherine said to her father.

"Because of Mother?"

"We both miss Maggie, and all the nuns."

"But it's your mother, isn't it?"

"I hope to find work. But could you help with our trips to Boston?"

"Of course," he said.

They ate in silence for a few moments.

"Your mother loves you both, you know."

Catherine thought for a moment. "She seems ashamed of Patricia sometimes. And she's always been ashamed of me. I don't think shame and love can mix."

It was some time before he responded. "After I married your mother, I discovered that what she wanted most was to love, but she never knew how," he said while stuffing his sandwich wrapper in a bag. "She didn't know what she was searching for. A true disability, I think."

"Do you still love her?" Catherine said.

"She gave me you—and Patricia."

They finished eating in silence and then arranged return to France within the week.

Patricia returned to the States fifteen years later when Catherine, who had established a clothing design business in France that gained worldwide attention, moved to New York to expand her designs to the American market. Patricia went to Stanford the same year. She wore knee-length dresses or pants when she wanted, her choice based on what was appropriate for the occasion. Harold died of a heart attack, and Catherine and Patricia returned home to visit Agnes on Thanksgiving and Christmas holidays. Pleasant times for all, except for Agnes's silences smoldering with unstated resentment about how life and her family had treated her unfairly—silences punctuated by biting remarks about how Catherine and Patricia's choice of apparel failed to meet her approval.

Speaking of the Dead

illustration by Betty Harper

Speaking of the Dead

After a six-hour drive north from Toronto, John Hampton arrived at the family home of his wife, Grace, and her daughter Candy, both dead six days. The house was dark. His sister-in-law, Ruth, greeted him in a nightgown and robe, and knee-length woolen socks. She led him toward an attic room. He hadn't seen her in more than four years.

"Henrietta's in the bedroom attached to yours. You'll have to share the loo. You know her, don't you? Candy's roommate?"

"I don't think so. I didn't see Candy often."

"Oh, you'd remember. Tall, slim girl. Round face. Crystal-blue eyes. Black hair cut in a pageboy. Unusual, so you can't forget."

"Is she nice?"

"You don't even have to talk to her if you don't want to. People call her Henri. I don't like her much. She's silent in a standoffish way. Definitely not shy. And I don't think she was happy about saying a few words in memory of Candy at the funeral when I asked her. I think she almost said no."

"An adventure in the attic," John said.

"She won't bother you."

"Especially if she doesn't talk."

"Roger will be coming to the vigil and the funeral," Ruth said. "I'm so sorry."

Roger was Grace's first husband, father to Candy, and a lawyer—general law—whom Grace had left during their first year of marriage, three months pregnant, for good schools and a life in the city.

Ruth went back to bed.

The attic air was frigid, fed through cracks under the eaves. Exhausted, John lay down on the single bed to await the slow coming of sleep, the corpses of Grace and Candy brought to Barrow and awaiting burial invading his thoughts. He felt the generations of dead that still occupied this austere, two-story, insulation-deficient frame farm house, as the living impatiently survived the bitter, long-winter cold to see the sun and its yearned-for relief in the spring.

At 2:24 AM, someone stood in the door that separated the two bedrooms. Henrietta! She wore a flannel nightgown with a hem that came to just above prominent knees. She stood motionless; her arms by her sides looking awkward, as if they were hastily attached as replacements.

"What are you doing?" he asked, throwing back the covers and sitting on the edge of the bed. "Are you all right?"

She began to walk slowly, her arms angled out purposelessly in front of her, her glazed eyes staring straight ahead. She was asleep. She turned toward the hall, quickly out of sight. He slipped on his untied shoes and followed her. Without holding onto anything, she started to descend the stairs that led to the garage: twenty narrow, steep steps to the first landing. He rushed to her, taking her elbow and gently leading her back to her room and bed. She did not wake, and he returned to bed. But two hours later a crash of glass and metal followed by a moan came from her room. She'd knocked over a lamp. John rushed to her, tried to help her, but she pushed him away.

"Where am I?" she asked with fear.

"In the attic at Ruth's. Candy's aunt. I'm John Hampton."

She understood and calmed a little. He guided her back to bed and pulled up a chair, determined to watch at least for a while until he was sure she was asleep again. But she remained awake, agitated at times.

"I'm worried," she said, "about the eulogy."

"You'll do fine."

"I'm not worried about performance. I speak well before others. It's what to say."

"What about Candy at school?"

"Students don't seem to know her as you would expect. And many didn't seem to care."

"There must be things about her past you could use."

"I didn't like her," she said. "There were times I stayed with a friend rather than go back to the room where she'd be."

"Think of adjectives."

"Self-centered, mean, lazy, directionless." She smiled with self-deprecation. "Selfish, and not too bright."

"We need to think about it a little more." He smiled.

"She used recreational drugs. I think to addiction. The papers didn't say, but I think that's what killed her."

"Grace died on the way to the hospital to see her before she died. A friend was driving."

"How can I find positives in that scenario?"

"Why do it, then?"

"I promised. Ruth really wanted testimonials the family could cherish. How could I turn her down? The family didn't feel competent to do it right. I didn't know it would be impossible."

"You didn't know her well enough. Ruth is the most understanding of the lot of them. Talk to her again."

"It's a matter of integrity, of my word."

"It's not a moral issue. You just can't find the right material."

"I'll think about it," Henri said.

He suggested they get some sleep.

Henrietta was waiting for breakfast in the living room with four family members when John descended from the attic the next morning. She stood when he introduced himself. She said nothing but nodded her head slightly, with servant-like civility so pronounced that he actually waited for any hint of a curtsy. She retreated to a sofa, picking up a magazine from a side table, never looking back. She seemed tired, and she gave no sign that she recalled her sleepwalking, or their conversation.

At the table, Henrietta sat next to Jason, Ruth's youngest son.

"Do you like your school?" she asked Jason.

"Not much."

"Where do you go?"

"Barrow High."

"You like it at Hursthaven?" John asked Henri.

"I don't," she said.

The sputtering of bacon grease crescendoed as Ruth added more rashers for new diners coming in from outside through the front door.

"I'm sorry about Candy," Henri said to Jason. "Were you close?"

"Naw," Jason said. He was large, about sixteen, and spoke slowly with a lisp.

"What will you miss most about her?" Henri asked. Jason continued eating. John doubted Jason even remembered the last time he saw Candy, who rarely came this far north, and when she did, she stayed with her father, Roger, and not the family.

"I'm giving a eulogy at the funeral. What do you think I should say?" Henri asked Jason.

John didn't wait to listen to the response. Henri was doing for Candy's eulogy what he needed to do for Grace. What in the name of God could he say that was good about a wife who had just spurned him? Ten days before her death, she had confessed to him a four-year affair with her boss at the university. She was moving out to live with her lover. John was shocked and angry and quickly despised her for her deceit, her dishonesty. His emotions frightened him in their magnitude, emotions that suppressed caring she was gone. He did not care in the least! He never spoke to her again, and moved to a hotel so he could dull the humiliation of her abandonment.

And Grace's family and friends might carry his words to their graves. The family did not approve of Grace's first divorce and her contact with family had been limited to letters to Ruth on the holidays.

When John tuned back into conversations at the table, he admired Henri's determined interviews with family members. Once, her blue eyes locked on his, glittering with a porcelain luster and incandescence in stark contrast to the statuesque immobility of her features, appropriate for the gravity of the moment. Her facial features had a unique incongruity that was magnetically attractive. And she was obviously smart.

"Was she your favorite cousin?" Henri asked a young man in coveralls. He shrugged.

Henri left the table to sit in the living room and read, legs crossed, her head bent in concentration.

"I'll go over the list for the vigil with you if you like," Ruth called to John as he stood after half-finishing servings of flapjacks buttered and flavored with maple syrup, and bacon and sausage.

"Thanks," he said with real gratitude. He would know few; he was married to Grace for twelve years but he met the family only twice, and had never visited here at the family home.

"There are pictures and memorabilia in the living room," Ruth said. "Upstairs in the guest bedroom, too. Take anything you fancy. She would have wanted you to have them."

After breakfast, hidden away in the sewing room where a horizontal rug loom dominated the center of the room, convenient to hide comfortably in an easy chair near the window, he reviewed, as chief librarian, two books for presentation at the Library Society meeting next week. But his mind skated without direction. He had to pretend grief, having not experienced it, and never let the family know that Grace and he were no longer soul mates, or even friends, when she died.

He went to bathe and dress for the visit to the funeral home where the vigil would be held, and to reluctantly pay the bill for Grace's interment. She had no entitlements as an adulterer in his mind. But he had no choice; Ruth and her siblings, with few financial resources, had convinced Roger of his commitment to Candy's burial, and after pointing out the mounting expenses for the vigil, presumed John's responsibility for Grace's burial. Their thoughts were just and he could not refuse.

On return from the funeral home, after dinner and before bed, John looked at pictures and mementos as Ruth had suggested. There were photos of Grace alone before marriage, and with Roger, her first husband, and Candy, their only child. And there were many photos of Grace with John, mostly on vacation to the Galapagos, Machu Picchu, the Outback, the Great Wall, the Lake District. On the mantel over the fireplace, photos of Grace's graduation, summa cum laude, and of her with her fellow psychology department faculty members at the university were displayed. Her lover was there, but he was not standing close to Grace. One five-by-seven showed Grace in a circle of children at Toronto Children's, where she methodically volunteered and donated. She was generous. But the memories irritated him, reminded him of her deception and his humiliation. He would never take mementos of Grace to haunt him, and he left them untouched for Ruth and the family.

The vigil was at the funeral home. Both caskets were displayed, exactly the same in color, so that it was impossible to know which was Grace's and which was Candy's unless you went up close and read the engraved brass plates on the ends. Grace's family and friends had, as tradition dictated, baked and cooked, peeled and chopped, sweetened and salted relentlessly to contain their grief.

The room was crowded, overheated, and loud, as family greeted friends and acquaintances, almost all of whom they had not seen for many winters. John saw Henrietta standing alone. She had on a plaid wool skirt with a thin black belt and a collared off-white blouse that buttoned down the front. She looked expensively au courant in a traditional way. John overheard her talking to Roger, Candy's father.

"Did you see her often?" Henrietta asked Roger.

"Once or twice a year. She came to visit. Always in summer," he said.

"Candy was so accomplished. What were you most proud of?"

Roger hesitated. He seemed lost for an answer. "I don't want to talk about it," he said.

Henrietta leaned toward him slightly. "I'm so sorry."

"You're not family."

"I didn't mean to pry."

"You're giving the eulogy tomorrow, aren't you?"

"Ruth asked me."

"I wasn't asked."

"Why?"

"This family doesn't like me. We've barely spoken for two decades," Roger said. "They took Grace's side. She left me when she was pregnant with Candy. Did you know that?"

Henri stayed silent.

"Without a thought of anyone but herself," he continued.

"Did you seek reconciliation?"

Roger's eyes were hard. "On my knees, for Christ's sake. And years later. I begged her not to marry him." He waved his hand toward John.

Henrietta expressed condolences and walked to join others. A few minutes later she approached John.

"How's it going?" John asked.

"It's going miserably. It's as if Candy touched no one's memory."

"What did Roger say? At least he seemed to have some caring for Candy."

"I didn't see it."

"You'll find something to work with."

"I'm having doubts."

John smiled and changed the subject. "Do you find vigils unsettling?" he asked.

"This is my first. It's more social than I expected."

"Lacking a certain gravitas of respect for those departed?"

She smiled. "I guess there is a caring. The industry of the preparation and consumption seems to block thinking about the reality of the day."

"Did you expect tears?"

"Maybe reflection in silence. A reverence in stance. A control of motion." She was mature to three times her age, as if she'd been too intellectually busy to have a childhood.

"You're religious, then?"

"In my own way," she said.

Ruth approached. "You two surviving under the eaves?" she asked.

"Is there anything I can do to help?" Henri asked.

Ruth replied that she could use some help with cleanup. "And again thank you both for saying a few words tomorrow," she said. "It must be hard, having been so close to Candy and Grace for so long. But it will mean so much to the family."

Henrietta's glance to John conveyed her growing lack of enthusiasm at being trapped by her impulsive acceptance to speak. "Is it time to start picking up empties?" she asked.

"You could start bringing in plates and glasses from the entrance hall. Put them in the kitchen."

Henri walked away.

A few minutes later John left to return to the farm to read in his secluded spot in the sewing room. He went to bed just before nine.

His room was especially dark this night, the light from the single dormer window almost extinguished by low-lying, dark, snow-impregnated clouds. Chilling wind gusts swiped the side of the house, disturbing him with their crisply tactile, inhuman echoes.

Henri shook his shoulder to awaken him just before midnight. He sat up with his feet on the floor, pulling the covers over his lap. She'd pulled a chair up to within a few feet of him.

"You were sobbing and moaning," she said leaning slightly toward him, concern in her eyes. "Are you all right?"

He was unaware of what he dreamed while he slept. The cover of his pillow was wet, his throat tight when he tried to speak.

"Is it about your wife?"

"Definitely not!"

"Why do you say that? You loved her?"

"Married twelve years. Our marriage changed over that time."

Even in the dark shadows he could see concern in Henri's eyes, definitely not just curiosity.

He took deep breaths to relax his chest and his extremities. "In the early days, we traveled worldwide together. And we thought the same about a lot of things. We could talk late into the night—thinking together."

"It sounds idyllic."

"It wasn't perfect. She was busy with her teaching and lecturing, and we were often apart. And she worried about Candy, who lived a while with her former husband, then went to school in Ottawa, and almost never visited Grace."

"Candy rarely spoke of her mother while we were roommates," Henri said.

"It bothered Grace at first. Later, she didn't seem to care as much."

"Do you still love her?"

"Grace had an affair with her chair at the college for four years before she confessed. It hurt me."

"Were you able to forgive?"

"I don't know. It hasn't been long. But I think so, at times at least."

"But you didn't love her at the end?"

He closed his eyes. He was calmer now than when he awoke,

although his soul ached with almost a burn to it. After a few minutes it eased. "No," he said.

"Was it the deception?" Henri asked.

John thought for a few seconds. "It was discovering she didn't love me—when I never doubted her love."

"Because she loved another didn't mean she didn't love you."

He hesitated. "No. It was gone. She didn't love me."

"Does that mean you can't grieve her death? The good times?"

"What's to grieve?"

"Will you be able to speak tomorrow?"

"Of course. I'll think of something. Mention her promotions. Her publications. Her charitable works."

"But you're angry."

"Anyone would be angry, their wife leaving them for another man."

A barn owl screeched behind the house, faintly.

"You loved her once."

"Yes. I did. But it faded, even before she left."

"It seems her need for change would never go away. Almost inevitable."

"I don't want anyone to know she wasn't living with me at the end. Her new lover was driving her to the hospital; they'd heard Candy was close to death. His blood alcohol was .15. Think about the folly. She'd be alive today if she'd been faithful, stayed to rediscover what we'd had."

"What will you say at the funeral? How can you avoid the circumstances? You don't love her the way you did when you married."

"Those early years were good," he said. He felt a rush of deep sadness never before experienced, a flood released after these eight days since the accident. He had an unbound urge to weep. He squeezed his eyes shut and set his jaw until his anguish eased enough so that he could speak.

"Is it always there or does it come in waves?" Henri asked.

He lay back down on the bed, turning his pillow wet side down. A minute passed and he seemed to regain control of his breathing.

"It just came on," he said, staring into the darkness that obscured the details of the ceiling.

"It's not easy to forgive," Henri said.

"I am the resurrection and the life," saith the Lord; "he that believeth in me, though he were dead, yet shall he live: and whosoever liveth and believeth in me shall never die." John 1:25–26

The one-room church had a single steeple and oak pews. The congregation shivered in coats and gloves, the cold unrelieved by the single electric heater in the back. At the front right, a minister spoke from a raised pulpit. Nine choir members sat in metal folding chairs to the left, an upright piano against the wall behind them. After the gathering, with the coffins placed end to end in front of the congregation and the greetings complete, Henri was introduced to speak. She ignored the podium, standing between the two coffins. With assuredness, she negotiated Candy's short, checkered life. She enhanced memories of the family she had so doggedly sought, which revealed the good in Candy's life that no one had ever seen before. Henri swerved away from Candy's lack of connection to others by naming the few people she'd had ties to, and making those tenuous ties seem to be remarkable accomplishments for Candy. Throughout, her poignant gaze gave every mourner a sense of profundity in her words. She painted Candy's valiant struggle against life's fears that all humans face, the temptations, the needs. "Candy didn't evade life's inexplicable perils. She never shunned her responsibilities even when faced with injustice and impossible choices. Candy became a Joan of Arc for her own survival."

Her words were tasteful and truthful—though never addressing the negatives—and beautifully rendered. John wished he could have led a standing applause.

John followed. Henri's position between the coffins had been so effective that he likewise chose not to mount the pulpit and stood in front of the congregation, although with more distance from the caskets. He breathed slowly and deeply. He paced his beginning with silence, looking out over family and childhood friends of Grace, whom she had never really nurtured.

Anger surged as he thought of her treatment of him and others, anger that constricted his thinking to her betrayal. He lost control of his thoughts and feelings and fought to regain them. God, he couldn't let his aggrieved anger corrode his opportunity to make the family proud, give them the satisfaction of kindred respect. The effectiveness of his silent pause was waning. “We have gathered—” he began, and he searched for the forgiveness that had released his grief last night. And it was there. Grace was who she was and she could not help herself, always moving on and searching. She had loved him. And he forgave her.

He spoke from the depth of grief for the woman he had loved for years, not the woman who died eight days ago. He spoke of their intellectual compatibilities. He described discovering nature together, and how it would have never happened without Grace. He spoke about Grace's need to mold her thinking to address the hard metaphysical questions of life, how she searched for answers in science and social work. “‘Why are we here? What is our purpose? How you answer forms the essence of who you are,’ she'd say, always with kind advice and direction. And she would work hard for long hours rather than ask someone to do something for her.”

Then, with intimate expression, John explained how humor surprised Grace, warming her to others. He could see every mind before him following his thoughts, see them appreciating the severity of the loss of Grace. Never did he let anger misdirect his thoughts from an ever-present pride of having Grace in their existence. He ended with his head down, exhausted from his effort, and absorbed the depth of the silence inside the church that told him of the emotions he had stirred.

He moved slowly to sit in the front row next to Henri. Out of view of others, she took his hand and squeezed it gently without looking at him. He felt a lasting peace and thanked God for strength to overcome his weaknesses.

After the service and goodbyes, John was standing at his car, packed and ready for the drive to Toronto. He saw Henri about to get into the passenger side of a white Honda across the parking lot. She stopped when she saw him and stood still looking at him, and he at her, for many seconds. His heart ached. She was going back to Ottawa with a friend of the family.

Her gaze mesmerized him. How lucky the man would be if Henri ever decided to marry.

She waved. She smiled. He lost sight of her as she got in the car. Faintly, he heard the door close.

The Honda carrying Henri turned onto the highway, disappearing in a couple of minutes into the spurned intensity of the persistent storm. John did not move. Snow layered his world, spotting the velvet collar of his Chesterfield. Cold penetrated his clothes as if spring might never arrive.

Homunculus

illustration by Peter Healy

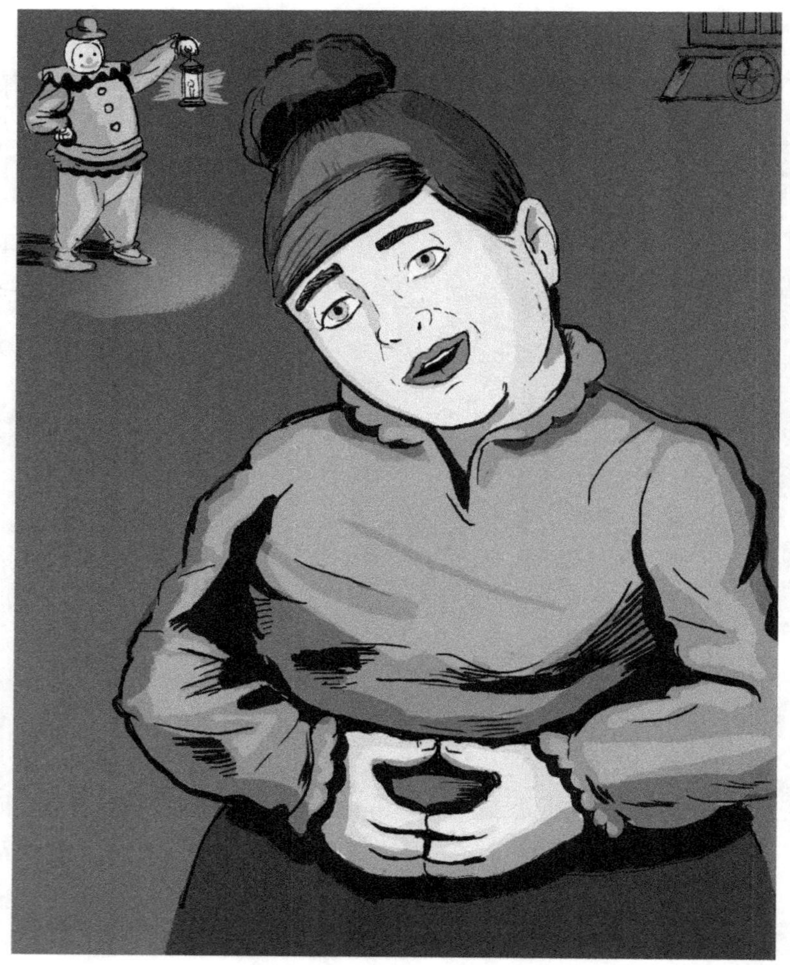

illustration by Peter Healy

Homunculus

Didi sits on a three-legged stool on the stage in a sideshow tent. It's the third show of the night. She listens to the barker, Captain Withers, as he gathers a new crowd outside. "Didi, the Dynamic Dwarf! The doll of the midway!"

Onstage, Didi is hidden behind the wooden facade of a miniature house with a hinged door, two fake windows, and an angled roofline bent on each side of the peak. The tent air is hot and stuffy, and sweat trickles from her armpit down her side. She wonders if it is due to nerves or the weather.

"This tiny morsel—born of ancient royal heritage—is the reincarnation of Cleopatra, an Egyptian goddess. The smallest woman in the world. Thirty-two inches low. You will see every detail of God's amazing work right here, tonight, gentlemen, and for two nights only."

Didi's real name—Gloria Pinkham—is rarely used, a smudged memory from the real world. After eight years with the circus, she barely remembers the shape of her mama's house on a side street in Lewiston, Maine. She carries a scratched daguerreotype of her mother sitting in a chair; her father, stiff as a cigar-store Indian, stands by her side with a hat in his hand. The war killed him when Didi was four; he faded away in some Georgia prison. He left her no memories.

Captain Withers yells until he fills the first four rows of the twelve benches with customers. Didi doesn't care how many; she gets food, shelter, and a few dollars every month if there are two, ten, or twenty. These farmers and farmers' boys are like fish in a pond—different sizes and hard to tell apart. They've never been more than twenty miles from their mothers or wives, and they clump together like curdled cream to gawk at something from away. She sees in their gaze how they undress her, their curious glares often speckled with desire. She loves to be wanted and she wants to be loved. But she hates pity; when she sees it in a sucker's eyes she looks away and pretends it's not there.

Captain Withers signals those inside when he yells, "You're lucky, my friends, the show is just starting," and blows his whistle. Didi opens the hinged door in the house facade and steps out onto a stage that dances with the shadows of four flickering torches. Wisps of smoke cloud the air. Growls, shrieks, and cries pulse from the midway and dampen the scattered applause. The eighteen-by-twelve-foot stage with collapsible support beams rises three feet above the ground. The front is slightly lower than the back, and there is barely enough room for the miniature dogcart in front of the dollhouse facade. To make Didi look smaller, the cart has oversize wheels and a single seat on a small frame. Didi mounts the single step, and sits on the seat and waves. She wants them to enjoy her. She watches the faces of the men and boys with the same intensity as they watch her. Men mystify her. Didi wants a husband to pamper, children to correct, a house to come home to even if it is just during the winter when the circus doesn't travel. She dreams of Lazlo the Hungarian trapeze artist.

Rudy, the Daring Dwarf, handles Terry the Terrier, who is harnessed in front of the cart. With a leash, Rudy leads the dog through a tight figure-eight journey around the stage. Then Didi steps down. Rudy picks up a half-size banjo from behind the house facade and strums. Didi sings a song, "Wandering in the Garden of My Mother's Withered Roses." When Rudy signals with his hand, Terry wags his tail. Didi unhooks her gown and it falls away; Rudy dashes to collect it. Terry barks. Didi wears a see-through costume, over white undergarments, that resembles a nightgown and glitters with sequined trim. Her breasts swell in the golden silk of the fabric. Didi pulls up the hem, shows her baby-like ankle, part of her stubby leg. She climbs back into her dogcart carriage, holding her nightgown so that much of her backside is exposed. Seated, she crosses her legs so her dress rides up her thighs and Rudy comes over and kisses her on the cheek. Off they go. Off the stage. Behind the facade. The act takes less than five minutes.

As Rudy and Didi leave the stage, Billy Batton, the full-size sideshow buffoon, walks up and down the rows of spectators whispering, "You want to see Didi's thing? Her woman stuff? Over there." Billy collects additional money and points to the tent flap where gentlemen go, one at a time, into a booth the size of a one-hole outhouse. In the dark, a two-inch diameter hole glows weakly from candlelight on the other side. It's on the back wall, about four feet above the ground, and easy to find.

With one eye pressed to the hole, a customer sees Didi's feminine parts. They are perched on a table covered with purple-red velvet drapes mounded to suggest that Didi is lying on her back with her knees raised and her legs spread apart. The edge of the drape can't quite cover a little piece of gold cloth with sequins—the same cut of cloth as Didi's gown. Between the two leg mounds is a slit the size of the spine of a small hymnal that reveals moist flesh poorly illuminated by two candles in glass hurricane shades on a side table. These are really the private parts of a freshly killed lamb.

In the dressing tent, Didi is folding up her white dress to place it in the trunk with her golden gown when Captain Withers grabs her by the arm. "Tell Rudy one more show."

"We ain't finished?"

"You talk too much for a runt."

Didi wishes Captain Withers would drop dead. She hates his voice. She hates his yellow teeth and his breath that stinks like the floor of a chicken coop. And she hates what he makes up about her. About her savage beginnings. About how all the dwarves crave her. And she's thirty-four inches, not thirty-two. One time in Indiana, when Didi tried to run away to marry a barber's son, Captain Withers whipped her.

Rudy stamps his feet when she tells him about the show. It's something a full-grown man wouldn't do, and she feels embarrassed for Rudy—and for herself. "It's not fair," he says.

"Of course it's not fair. It's not fair being some shrunk-up freak either."

After the last show, Rudy helps Didi fold her costumes. He walks her back to the wagon where six of the thirteen circus dwarves sleep. Rudy touches Didi's bare arm and tries to hold her hand, but she takes it away.

"Let's get out," he says. "You and me."

Didi laughs. He is a funny little man, always dreaming the impossible. His only skills are making Terry the Terrier do its tricks and making people smile with his curious thoughts. And he wants to hold her in the night, he says, forever, and keep her warm when the drafts sneak through the boards of the wagon.

Rudy stops her near the utility wagon. He grabs her shoulders and turns her small body toward him. His wide face is round with teeth that are too big and lips too small to hide them. His eyes are wide apart and give him a dull-witted look, although Didi knows he is very smart. He writes letters for her, and reads the ones that come from her mother.

"I'm going. With or without you."

"Poof," says Didi.

"I mean it."

"Where would you go?"

"I'll figure it out."

"And you'll starve. You'll be eaten by wolves."

"You'll see," says Rudy. Didi hears a resolve in his voice. Would he really leave without her? She has assumed that he will always be there for her, always leading her wagon. But she says nothing, and they turn to climb the small, closely spaced steps into the wagon where four dwarves play cards and a fifth is playing "Oh! Susanna" on a harmonica, a sweet and lively tune that makes Didi happy and sad at the same time. "It rained all day the day I left, the weather it was dry / Susanna, don't you cry."

That night Captain Withers dies. He does not drop dead exactly, but he is found on his cot in his wagon, twisted at the waist, his legs in a grotesque pose of writhing. Most of the circus people think it was some sort of fit. He lost all control of his bowels and bladder and snot hangs out his nose. With her low vantage point, Didi gets a direct peek at dead Captain Withers's open eyes. He looks afraid. She whimpers to impress the other circus people who are near, but she wants to laugh and clap at the same time.

"He did the best he could," says Rudy.

"You're crazy," says Didi. A crew from the animal wagons takes Captain Withers out near the river and buries him and his soiled nightclothes in a damp, shallow grave. Some sideshow people watch.

Didi doesn't go, but Rudy tells her about it, and she worries that the hasty grave is too shallow to bury the mean spirit of Captain Withers. She dreads his image in nightmares, and fears wicked spirit visitations from his black soul. She asks Rudy about the grave.

"Graves don't matter. I'll take care of you," he says. But Didi wants Lazlo the trapeze artist, not Rudy. And she doesn't want the ghost of Captain Withers to haunt her.

The next morning the new barker, Colonel Phister, who is part owner, starts to make changes. "To not go broke," he says, "not to belly up." He does not like Didi's act. "Never have," he says. He wants an act that will make the farmers and their boys come back the same night to see it, as he puts it, "again." Pay more money. At first Didi is excited; she dreams of a better position on the midway, with new costumes. But Colonel Phister wants to double-bill her. "We'll make more money with the giant," he says.

"Gargantuan does his own act," Didi complains.

"He's a dud. There ain't no surprise. No one pays to see a giant in a tent when you can't miss seeing him outside on the midway. We got to do something original."

Colonel Phister thinks Gargu the Giant should be the one to unloose Didi's dress. Fumble a little. Build some tension.

"What about the dog?" Rudy asks.

"No dog. Just play that goddamn banjo. And change that stupid song. Get one of them nigger tunes."

Gargu the Giant is slow to think. "Why you want to change the act?" he asks, looking down on Didi, Rudy, and Colonel Phister. Didi thinks that if she's got to share billing, she'd rather it be in the big tent with Lazlo.

"I could work with Lazlo and the trapeze family."

"That's stupid. Ain't no runts in the big tent."

"We work with the clowns," Rudy replies.

"That's different," says Colonel Phister.

"Can't we wait for winter quarters?" says Didi. "Take some time to work things out?"

But Colonel Phister sees economic potential. "Now," he responds. They change the act on the road. Didi has new billing: "GARGU the

GIANT and DIDI the DYNAMIC DWARF with Rudy the Daring Dwarf playing BANJO."

They decide to have Didi enter on the dogcart after all, and do away with the dollhouse facade, which needs painting anyway. When Gargu the Giant tries to pick up Didi, he grips her waist so hard she cries out. She refuses to let him touch her. So they get an eight-rung little ladder that they prop against Gargu's chest. Rudy holds the base of the ladder steady. Didi climbs up, and when she is almost to the top, Gargu kisses her and puts her on his shoulder. Rudy takes the ladder away. It is from there, holding onto Gargu's hair on the back of his head for support, that Didi sings her new song, "Oh, Susanna."

"The sun so hot I froze to death / Susanna, don't you cry."

Colonel Phister wants Didi to show her body. He gives her a shorter see-through gown and has Gargu hold her up and look up under her dress. "Make 'em want to pay to see," Colonel Phister says. To dismount from Gargu's shoulder, Colonel Phister thinks Didi needs to have a whiz-bang ending. "Jump."

"I'll kill myself," Didi protests.

"We'll borrow a trampoline from the Wondrous Polenskys."

"You can't make her jump. It's too dangerous. She's the star," says Rudy to Colonel Phister.

"She ain't no star. She's a runt on the midway."

Because the Polensky trampolines are too big for the stage, Colonel Phister has the carpenter build a circular wooden frame with a diameter the size of two barrelheads and stretch a canvas over the top. Didi jumps to fall on her back and spring up so she lands on her feet on the stage. She can't get the timing right, and she bounces crooked and lands in a heap.

"That's great," laughs Colonel Phister. But it hurts to fall wrong and Didi practices every day to get it right. She jumps off the water wagon onto the new special dwarf trampoline to practice landing on soft grass. Then she climbs back up an iron ladder bolted to the side of the wagon and jumps again. And again. Until she can land standing up almost every time.

Rudy is a pest. He finds flowers in the fields or next to the rivers, and brings them to Didi to celebrate the new act. In the mess tent, he offers part of his apple pan dowdy to Didi. He says he loves her. She smiles at his passion, but thinks he is short and ugly. She is ashamed of him; he is a joke of a man no one could love. And she resents his advances because he could never be Lazlo the Hungarian trapeze artist.

Lazlo wears white tights trimmed with sequins. Although he is barely five feet tall, he has wide shoulders and strong arms that hang down, each bent like a tightly strung bow. On each arm, a bicep bulges big as a potato. His black hair is cut short, and his small ears are low on his skull. His eyes are dark and close together. He is clean-shaven except for a thin mustache, and he has a big smile and good teeth that are only a little uneven in spacing. He flies through the air and the crowds hush so that Didi fears they might hear her heart racing. Every unmarried girl likes him. A lot of marrieds too. Many give themselves to him hoping he will marry them. Didi knows that Khatooma the Cat Woman and Rhonda, who is second billing for the Flying Rolands' horse riding act, both had to get their babies stopped. Lazlo's babies.

Didi is sure that Lazlo could love her if he knew her. Big people have loved little people. She's heard of long, happy lives together. And Lazlo isn't that big. He just needs to get to know her. And isn't she pretty? Doesn't she have long hair that flows to her waist? He could comb it for her. She could sew his costumes. They could have a house somewhere with china plates.

She has a plan. She hopes to talk to Lazlo alone, as if by accident. She will meet him after a show when he is going back to his family's wagon. She is smaller than a wagon wheel so that she can fit under many wagons without bending. She waits hidden in the shadow of the tent-pole wagon every evening for a time when Lazlo might walk by alone on his way from the main tent. For two nights, he is with someone. Then the third night he is alone, and she pops out and acts as if she is walking the other way.

"Hi, Lazlo. You did real good tonight."

"You think so?" Lazlo says. And he smiles. "You're mighty cute down there on the edge of center circle," he says. When she goes back to the wagon where the dwarves sleep, she smiles to herself and hums her new tune, "Oh, Susanna."

Each night, Didi goes back under the wagon to wait for accidental time with Lazlo. When Didi and Lazlo are alone, she tells him how accomplished he is, and she makes him laugh with stories about little Rudy and Rudy's silly ways.

In the tent where Madame Fortuna does her séances to talk with the dead, Didi climbs into the red velvet upholstered chair used for soul seekers. Madame Fortuna is Didi's big friend, and Didi talks to her often about Lazlo, about making a family.

"I love him," Didi says.

"Ah, vat eeze luf?" Schenectady-born Madame says in her European accent that Didi wishes she could learn. Didi practices alone, away from the others, dreaming she might have a real speaking part in the act someday. Lazlo has an accent.

"I want to be his wife."

Madame Fortuna takes off her turban and shakes out her thin hair. It is black, streaked with gray. Hidden in a wash of French perfume, Didi smells a mixture of sweat, mold, and dead shellfish.

Didi tells her about her meetings with Lazlo.

"You've got to make him want you," Madame Fortuna says.

Didi thinks for a moment. "He likes me. I know it."

"He's got to crave your body. Wake up in the night hot for your wares."

"You mean down there?" Didi nods to her private parts.

"Do you know a man can fit?"

"I've heard."

Madame Fortuna unties the sash that holds her robe. Her large breasts hang loose, ballooning her undershirt. "I mean did you make love to a big man? Did it work?"

Didi doesn't speak. She does not want to say she has never made love to any man. Big or small.

"Being with a man hurts me, Didi. And I ain't small by a long shot."

Didi squirms in her chair. She believes that when you love someone it can never hurt.

Madame clears her throat. "I'd forget it."

"I can do it," Didi blurts out.

"Look, honey, don't get mad. It just ain't possible."

"I'm a real girl. It ain't just lamb parts."

"Well, he's had every girl who would let him. He'd be glad to add you. With women, he's like Bill Cody shooting buffalo."

"I know he's not like that."

"He's an uncaring bastard, Didi. The worst kind of man."

"I could make him want me," Didi mumbles.

Madame Fortuna has not said what Didi wanted to hear. Now Didi thinks Madame is too old to know of these things about love, although she has been helpful before. Does she have a man? No. Besides, her tea leaves are tobacco, and she smells bad.

Didi is so angry with Madame Fortuna, she goes directly to Lazlo. She finds him practicing on a bar propped between wagons. Didi says she needs to talk to him.

"Of course." He smiles.

"Alone," says Didi.

Later that night, she meets him behind the laundry wagon. She is there early and he comes late. He slides down on the grass beside her and sits with his ankles crossed and his knees apart.

Didi tells him about the new act. She talks about Captain Withers dying before she says, "Do you think I'm pretty?"

"Exquisite," Lazlo says, and smiles down into her eyes.

"Could you love me, Lazlo?"

"I love you. Naturally." His accent seems thicker now.

"Really love me. Like a wife?"

"Ah. That is the question?"

"Of course it's the question, you oaf. It's what's important to me."

"You're a very pretty woman."

"But I'm too small." Didi pouts.

"No, you are very attractive. Desirable."

Didi takes his hand, feels the calluses on his palm, rough like cured leather and harder than amber. "Make love to me, Lazlo."

"Here?"

"No. We'll go over near the edge of the woods."

Lazlo squats to look into Didi's face. "You mean it?"

Didi nods. She looks up into his eyes. He still grins, but she is sure he is not making fun of her. He seems interested. Curious, maybe. She wonders—wasn't this what she wanted? She reaches out to put her finger on his lips. She feels the scratch of his waxed mustache.

"It is not possible?" Lazlo asks.

"Of course it is. I've known lots of small people who love big people."

"We must be quick."

"Of course."

"Be sure no one knows."

"Absolutely."

"I'll get a blanket," Lazlo says.

"Yes. Hurry," she says.

As Didi waits, Lazlo finds a washed blanket on a line strung between two wagons. It is dark among the wagons, and he touches the blanket's lower edge to see if it is dry. He yanks it off the line. Together they walk. Didi hurries to keep up. He reaches down and grabs her by her shoulders. Lifts her.

"Put me down."

Lazlo laughs. He walks a little faster. Didi twists out of his grip, sputtering, and when she is free she has to trot to keep up.

Lazlo finds a dark spot and throws the blanket onto a grassless patch of dirt under a tree. There is a late quarter-moon and a faint glow from the cooking fires of the circus. She sees the mussed blanket. From each corner she works to the center and smooths it as best she can.

Lazlo has taken off his pants. Didi looks away, embarrassed and afraid, and sees the low branch of a tree move. It could not be the wind.

"Lie down," she says.

"No. You." He still has on a tight shirt. He has kicked off his slippers.

She fears his weight. Her bones are easy to break. "I can't." When he bends slightly, she thinks it is to find his pants to leave, and she is surprised that she feels relief. But Lazlo moves his pants off the blanket and lies down on his back. His member looks different—still hard, but pointing to his chin and pulsating a little. Didi smiles because it looks silly.

She takes off her dress, but keeps her shoes on. She presses her palms together to keep from shaking. She pulls her undershirt over her head and stands next to Lazlo, who is looking at the stars with his hands locked behind his head. She straightens her back so her breasts jut out a little more, and she moves a few steps toward him.

Lazlo reaches up and touches her left breast, scratching her nipple with his rough skin. Didi senses his disappointment as he pulls away his hand. Did he expect more?

She reaches over to take his organ in her right hand. Her stubby fingers can't get around it so she uses both hands. It is warm, but not as hot as she expected. And she can feel the surge of Lazlo's heart pumping the blood into his organ. "Damn it. Be careful," he says.

"What happened?"

"It's tender sometimes," he says. "Ain't you had it before?"

Didi wonders why she feels dread instead of excitement. She tries to touch Lazlo carefully, standing next to him, barely needing to bend. She strokes his member with the tip of her finger.

"You jump on," he says.

"Do you love me?" Didi asks. But he doesn't answer.

She strokes him a few more times and he moans. He breathes hard. He tries to grab her breasts, but he can't get a hold of the little mounds. He grips her arm, draws her closer to him. His member is still between her palms, and it squirts like a cannon—three times, she thinks, but maybe four. She is so surprised she squeezes. He swats her hands away.

"I didn't—"

"Shit," says Lazlo.

She wipes her hands on her hip, then picks up her nightshirt and cleans off each finger of her left hand.

Didi tries to take his hand, but he jumps to his feet, puts on his pants, pulls the blanket from under her so fast she tumbles down, hurting her shoulder.

"Lazlo," she says softly, but he is too far away to hear. "Lazlo."

She stays on the ground, rolls onto her back in the same position Lazlo waited for her. She rubs the sore shoulder until the pain is dull. She looks to the sky and the stars. Follows the outlines of the Big Dipper and Orion's belt. Some stars twinkle in pairs, like eyes watching. In a few minutes, she is cold, and she rises to put on her clothes. Then she lies back down, still chilled, but not wanting to return to the cluster of wagons and tents. She watches the sky change, the moon covered by swirling clouds. She waits to go back until the sky is black and the fires among the wagons die to embers. From the woods, she walks slowly, her arms stretched out in front for protection, but she still trips on an unseen tree root. As she approaches the circus tents and wagons, the light is better, and she moves without stumbling. The sounds of the circus are muted, and she hears only the snorts of sleep and the restless pacing of animals in their cages. She opens the door and enters the dwarves' wagon. From the way they breathe, she knows they only pretend to be asleep. In the frail light coming through the open door, she sees the twisted blankets near the door where Rudy sleeps. He is not there. His satchel is gone. The nail where Terry the Terrier's leash hangs is empty. She feels the urgency in the way every dwarf is holding his or her breath, trying to be silent. She closes the door and gropes her way to her spot on the floor. When she lies on her pallet and closes her eyes, she hears a train whistle, a discharge of steam, and the stutter of steel wheels on iron rails, and she does not know if it is real or imagined.

She sits up. "Where is Rudy?"

"He's gone. We don't know," someone says.

"We can get someone to fill in for the act," whispers another.

"It's not the act," Didi cries, surprised at her anger. She lies back down, facing the bleak silence of harried dwarves, and the dark. Her shoulder throbs, and the pain seems to march into her chest, toward her heart.

Suchin's Escape

illustration by Peter Healy

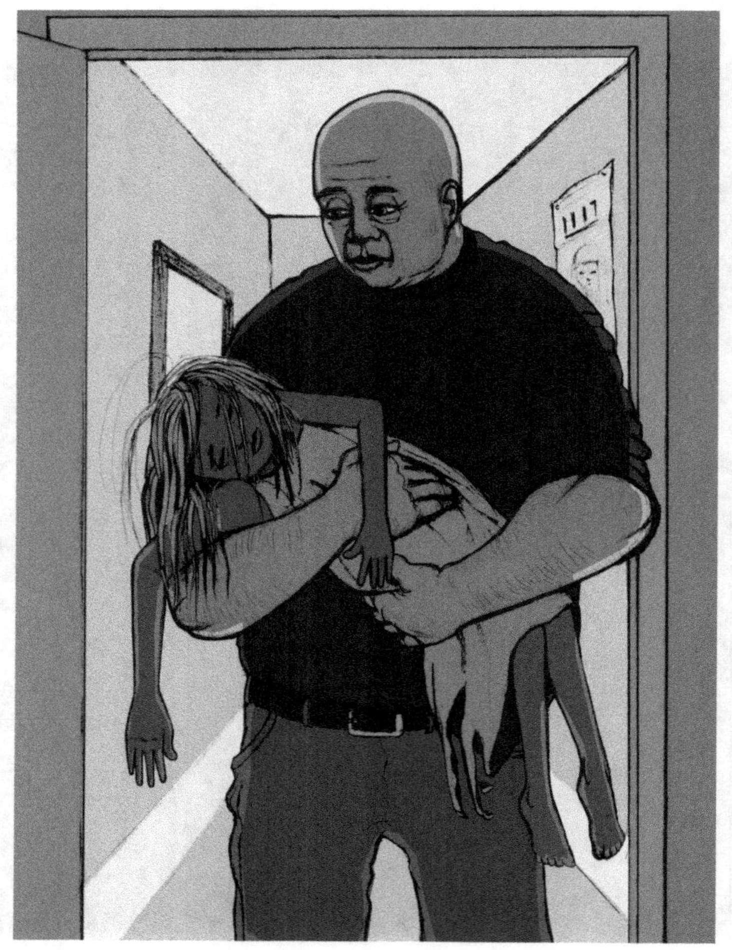

illustration by Peter Healy

Suchin's Escape

Antoine lit a cigarette with the lighter from the dash of the twenty-seven-year-old 1976 Lincoln Continental and leaned forward with both forearms on the steering wheel. Harry beat out a rhythm on the dash with both hands—BOOM chee CHEE di di BOOM—and sang a song of lost love. Antoine liked the tune, liked the way his cousin could make it flow.

Antoine watched the green two-story frame house across from where they were parked on a side street in Gretna. The image of the thin child Suchin, the eleven-year-old Chinese girl, materialized in the dark, narrow alley between the houses, the blurred outline of a man blocking the alley behind her. She was naked except for a pair of patent-leather Mary Janes. She stopped before stepping into the glint of the morning sun and slid a lace-trimmed white dress over her head, pushing her arms out the sleeve holes. She smoothed the fabric in front with both hands and the hem fell to her ankles.

"She's done," Antoine said. Harry stopped his rhythm and got out of the car. He met the girl still in the shadows, grabbed her arm, and brought her quickly to the car, her moving feet barely touching the ground. Harry opened the back door and shoved her into the backseat.

"Don't push me." Suchin said, kicking out, her shoe heel glancing off Harry's arm.

The girl made money and this guy in the shadows was one of her many repeats. But Antoine didn't trust her. Something about the way her eyes held his, hard and cold in their darkness, and the way she never flinched if he had to cuff her.

"Tape her," he said. "I got a bad feeling."

"We ain't going that far," Harry said.

See! Even Harry was ornery now, started about the time this girl arrived in a shipment of twelve. Strange, too, because the kid was all girl—not anything womanly—like a twig in a forest of leafy branches.

"That Paradise Motel near the airport," Antoine said.

"Tape hurt," said Suchin.

That proved it. Pure trouble—the way she'd just butt in like she belonged.

"Ride with her, then," he said to Harry.

Harry shoved Suchin over to one side of the backseat to make room. He slammed the back door as Antoine cranked the motor.

"But don't put them locks down," Harry said.

Harry was a goddamn two-year-old trapped in the body of King Kong sometimes. Antoine undid the childproof locks on the back doors.

"Don't like the door locked," Harry said, feeling foolish even as the fear of being closed in grabbed him.

The Lincoln Continental rolled down the expressway. Antoine kept in the right lane, five miles an hour below the speed limit. Harry's big head blocked half his view out the rearview mirror. He checked the side mirrors for cops. He was clean but Harry had a prior for assault with a parole violation.

The kid wasn't in the mirror. He glanced back over his right shoulder. Nothing. She was either lying down or she'd slipped over next to the door. He reached for a rumpled cigarette pack wedged between the windshield and the dash, squeezed out the end of the last cigarette, extracted it with tight lips, and lit up.

The silence from the back seat mounted.

Then tap … tap … tap … tap. The kid was beating her shoe against the doorframe, grooving on the beat like a pro, the pulse asking for more. Sure enough, Harry's big hands clapped soft but firm with emphasis on the late off beats. Tap tap CLAP tap CLAP tap CLAP CLAP.

Without thinking Antoine beat his thumb against the steering wheel. He tucked the Lincoln in behind a bakery truck.

Harry started singing, his voice filling up the car, and the kid making ooou-ooous like a real backup.

"It's down" tap tap

"In Pascagoula" tap tap

"Where the women" tap tap

"Do the hoola" tap tap

"And the men" tap tap

"They the ones" tap tap.

"They the ones, whoooo—-oooooooooooo"

"Wicky … wicky … whacky—whacky—woo."

For a few bars Harry and Suchin clapped and tapped almost perfectly in their shared drive. Then they shifted in unison to a slower groove, four to the bar. Harry's voice fell off a minor third.

"Ohhhh, ohhhh," he wailed.

"Ouuuuu, ouuuuu" the kid chimed in.

"It's my woman, …ohhh, yeah,"

"That cheating woman," …

"ouuu, ouuu,"

"It's my woman, ohhh, yeah,"

"That done me wrong." Harry finished.

"Soooo wrong," the kid added. "Ouuuuu …"

Harry chuckled.

Then, smooth as a river running, the two of them were back working on and off the beat, setting up for another verse.

Goddamn her. She could work Harry like a dog jumping through hoops.

"Tolls," he said.

Harry shoved Suchin down in the footwell to hide her as Antoine held bills out to the collector. "Be quiet," he said. The engine strained when the Lincoln started up the bridge incline over the Mississippi. Two minutes later the car slowed in traffic. Suchin stiffened, her teeth clenched.

She yanked the door handle, shoved the door open, and rolled out headfirst, flipping on her back. In seconds she was up running toward the guardrail, the river, so much bigger than the stream that ran near her village in China. Horns blared. Fast cars moved in the opposite direction. Harry yelled behind her. How close was he? A sports car hit her, throwing her up on the hood, screeching to a stop. The girders above her weaved like dragons' tails.

Harry grabbed her before she slid off to the pavement, held her so close his hot breath smothered her face.

Her leg began to throb, she could barely see out one eye, but her heart squeezed fast and strong. "Shouldn't a done that," Harry whispered to her. "Antoine going to kill you."

The sports car guy came running up, screaming about his innocence. With one arm still holding Suchin, Harry picked him up and threw him against the side of the car so hard his head flew back on the roll bar with a crunch. Harry grunted satisfaction as the guy slumped half-conscious.

Suchin moaned when Harry put her in the car.

"Stay with her," Antoine said. He blew the horn, waved at people. He had to get moving before any cops came. He'd have to switch the plates again, find something in the Marriott parking garage from Ohio or Indiana this time. In a couple of minutes they were at the exit ramp. He was out of cigarettes.

The kid trembled, her head in Harry's hands, her shoulders on his thigh, her legs out on the seat.

"She breathing?" Antoine asked into the backseat.

"Blood coming out her mouth." A trickle of dark red mixed with spit-foam dripped on Harry's thigh. "Her leg getting big," he said.

Antoine caught a red light. He looked back. The girl's chest moved with quick in and outs. Her dress was torn. Her upper leg a sick purple. No one would pay for sex with a bleeding, moaning kid. He hated to stiff the guy on Airline Highway but he headed for Claiborne to get on the I-10.

"She bad," Harry said, "She real bad."

Suchin heard Harry's words as if the volume had been turned to maximum on a set of headphones. She did not think about dying and she wondered if she could run with her leg hurting.

She coughed.

"What was that?" Antoine said.

Harry saw a bloody tooth on the seat. "She bad," he repeated.

Well, shit. Antoine was going as fast as he could without putting them behind bars.

"Her eye look crooked," Harry said like he blamed Antoine.

It was Harry's fault she got out. No locks! Harry had jumped at the click of a deadbolt sliding home since he was in Angola for two years five months. Like he caught a phobia and now we can't lock the back doors.

Antoine wasn't being unreasonable. Okay. He didn't like kids. But he wasn't a monster. And he never let a guy down. Or a kid, for that matter. He was taking her to the doc, for Christ sake. How many guys would do that? "How many?" he said out loud.

"What you say?" Harry said.

But he didn't explain. Harry was slow to understand sometimes. And too soft to keep rules.

Antoine pulled into a mall and parked. Harry followed him, carrying the kid through the door between a liquor store and a Goodwill clothing outlet, marked in faded yellow letters:

OFFICE HOURS 10–2
M, W, Th

The doc sat alone at a desk in a single room. Harry laid Suchin on a bare examining table with metal stirrups on one end.

"That's repulsive," the doc said, swiveling back and forth in his chair, his short-sleeved tan shirt with yellow brushlike swirl patterns unbuttoned halfway down the slope of his hairy chest. He was a hundred pounds overweight.

"Hit by a car."

"Take her to Charity."

"She's illegal."

"I don't do trauma."

Suchin's leg spasmed for a few seconds.

"The big man pays you damn good," Antoine said. "Too much."

"Not for this." The doc belched; Antoine was close enough to whiff the scent of decayed oranges and cheap booze—like the man's insides needed to be flushed down a toilet.

The doc stood up. He took a wooden tongue blade from his shirt pocket. He lifted the kid's dress fabric with the blade, careful not to touch anything bloody. Still with the tongue blade, he pushed up a swollen eyelid and stared at a pupil.

"She'll live."

"Aren't you going to X-ray or something?"

"Do you see an X-ray machine?"

"She could die."

"She isn't going to die!" he said.

The doc picked up a wallet off his desk and left through a back door that went straight to a service alley. "Office is closed," he said as he slammed the door shut.

Antoine pointed for Harry to get the kid.

"Where we going?"

"Auntie's," Antoine said. "She'll do something."

Suchin felt the big arms cradling her again, her mind clear. Her stomach churned. Her tongue probed the sore little craters where her teeth were gone. Her leg ached but she thought she could walk if she had to. With her non-blurred eye she searched from habit for locks on the doors. Then, when the sunlight glared on her, she squeezed her good eye closed and went limp to let Harry think her mind had shut down her body for a while.

The Lincoln got to Auntie's in Plaquemine Parish just before five, a rooster tail of almost-white dust pluming up behind that monster car. Auntie went downstairs out of the farmhouse, stood there waiting as they drove up, her arms crossed. She was heavy, big boned, and barren, her blood Indian, Creole, and black, and every corpuscle heavy with this love-hate feeling for kids. It was a mystery why she took care of them at all after being in the trade for thirty years.

"You whack this one?" Auntie said to Antoine as Harry worked at getting Suchin out of the car so she didn't hurt.

"Watch your mouth," Antoine said.

Auntie's hands probed Suchin's thigh while she was still in Harry's arms. Suchin cried out. She pushed on Suchin's belly. Suchin moaned. She looked under Suchin's swollen eyelid. Suchin's eye was seeing well now and she locked on Auntie's gaze. Auntie frowned and turned away.

"Put her to the right of the door in the bedroom," Auntie said to Harry, and pulled Antoine's shirt to move him a few feet so no one could hear.

"Cash up front." she said.

"She's big money. Next to top in the convention trade. She good for it. We ain't got cash."

"Out of where?" Auntie asked.

"Mere Bull. In Kenner."

"Tell Mere Bull she to bring that cash down here personal."

"You got my word," Antoine said sincerely.

"Ain't that a lot of slippery shit?"

Suchin lay on her back on a cot with no mattress. The only window had a yellow shade pulled down and the dim light from the filtered sun wasn't strong enough to define the floral details on the scruffy wallpaper. Two bunk beds were stacked as a unit against the opposite wall. On the lower bunk a lump of a girl bulged under a sheet, the ends of her straight long hair—shiny as a black lacquered piano—hanging over the edge. The upper bunk didn't have a mattress.

Harry was gone, but his words stayed with Suchin. "Give it up," he said, his breath tickling her ear. "The beat don't work good." He didn't touch her.

Suchin dozed to the sounds of flies chasing each other around the room. She woke just before all the light faded. The girl under the sheet hadn't moved. Suchin could hear Auntie bumping around somewhere down below, on the first floor.

Suchin ached all over, but less now. Her leg throbbed but when she stood and pressed down, the pain eased.

"Who you?" she called to the lump on the bed.

She waited a minute. "You living?"

She hobbled over slowly and peeled back the sheet. She sucked in a rush of air.

"You beautiful," she said, suddenly aware of trying to use her very best English. The girl had the delicately sculpted features of a porcelain doll and her eyes were wide open, the whites showing all around irises so brown they seemed almost as black as the pupil. She stared straight through Suchin, deep into some other galaxy.

"My name's Suchin. From China. Six months. Came on a ship."

The girl didn't change.

"You sleep like that?" Suchin asked. "Your eyes open?"

She thought the girl's eyes focused a little, her lips parted slightly.

"You like it here?"

The girl closed her eyes slowly, breathing faster, and turned away. She wasn't a druggie, Suchin thought. Her eyes were too hard for that.

Auntie's mountainous form filled the open door behind Suchin. Auntie came into the room, light from the hall making a faint halo behind her.

"She talk to you?" Auntie asked.

Suchin didn't move, keeping her back to Auntie.

"Well, don't you be bothering her," Auntie said. "She's having some time to herself until she talks again."

Suchin stayed stone still, not knowing how to feel about Auntie. But she wasn't afraid.

Auntie gave Suchin a bowl of red beans and rice with a plastic spoon stuck in it and pulled up a chair next to the girl to begin feeding her soup from a Campbell's can. "Mushroom only thing she'll eat. Don't like tomato," she said, mostly to herself.

When she finished Auntie turned to take Suchin's empty bowl. "You moving better than I thought. You scamming Auntie?"

Suchin stayed quiet.

"Well, you pick up that chamber potty and empty it in the bathroom down the hall before I lock up again. Wash it out good too."

For hours after Auntie closed the door and turned the key in the lock, Suchin lay on her cot, but no sleep came. She wondered where that girl's eyes were looking, what they saw. She wondered if she was thinking about the men. How men treated girls. She wondered if the girl thought too that if you did right, maybe someday a man take you away and be good to you. All the girls had heard of that happening—a nice man. But they never knew anyone it happened to, only knew by the storytelling that skipped from girl to girl like a flu bug.

It was still half dark when Suchin woke. The lump girl was sitting on the floor cross-legged, her hands on her stomach, and she was rocking slow—front, back, front.

Suchin eased off the bed and stretched, watching the girl. Suchin's leg and chest hurt less.

Two glasses of water and a saucer with two oven-cooked rolls sat on the floor inside the locked door. Suchin drank and ate a roll. "You want this?" she said, tempted to eat the second roll. But the girl said nothing and Suchin left the water and the roll close enough for her to reach.

Suchin's leg didn't bend easily, and she lay down on her side on the floor, her legs straight out to one side, her head propped up on her hand with her arm bent at the elbow.

The black-haired girl rocked. Forward. Back. Forward.

"My mother's dead. Father dead, too," Suchin said, staring under the bed as if to find some hidden non-person in the dark recess.

Back, forward, back, the girl went on, her eyes never blinking.

"Yours too? Your parents?"

Forward, back, forward, about as fast as a pendulum on a giant clock.

"It's okay. I know you're like the rest of us. Sometime you need to get away."

The girl still rocking.

The door unlocked and Auntie came in. "In the name of God, leave that child alone. You too healthy and she too sick for you to keep bothering her." She yanked Suchin up to sitting, then grabbed the girl's shoulder to stop her rocking and held a glass of water to the girl's mouth. The girl swallowed a few times.

"Now for you," she said, grabbing Suchin. "I'll take you to the bathroom to wash that dried blood off. Then I'll sew up that dress and give it a good wash."

That night after Auntie put them both in bed, Auntie came back in with a flashlight because the light socket for the screw-in bulb in the ceiling was empty. She sat in a chair next to the girl's bed, her back to Suchin. She opened a book with a torn red cover. Suchin was lying on her cot, looking at the ceiling.

"'It was Toto,'" Auntie read in a low, singsongy voice.

"Who was Toto?" Suchin asked.

"Shut your face," Auntie said shining the light straight into Suchin's eyes. "This is Helen's story."

Suchin turned away but not far enough so she couldn't hear.

"You don't need storytelling," Auntie said to Suchin before turning her flashlight back to the book again to read.

"'It was Toto that made Dorothy laugh, and saved her from growing as gray as her other surroundings.'" Auntie paused. "'Toto was not gray; he was a little black dog, with long silky hair and small black eyes that twinkled merrily on either side of his funny, wee nose. Toto played all day long, and Dorothy played with him, and loved him dearly.'"

"Who's Dorothy?" Suchin couldn't keep from asking.

"She's an orphan. Now hold your tongue." But the meanness was not in her voice.

Auntie continued loud enough that Suchin could hear. "Today, however, they were not playing. Uncle Henry sat upon the doorstep…"

Suchin wondered what Uncle Henry would do to Dorothy, then listened all about Kansas and Oz, a world that, as Auntie continued reading, Suchin imagined might be the real America.

The lightning bolt lit up the room bright as day just after two AM. Suchin sat straight up and in the after-flash, the room seemed pitch black; even the thin strip of pale yellow under the door from the hall overhead bulb was wiped out. Suchin stood up, limped to the window, and raised the shade. The sky swirled with gray clouds. Sheets of rain streaked across the yard and lightning pulsed the pewter sky.

The girl was sitting too, her eyes fixed on Suchin.

"It's okay," Suchin said, recovering quickly. She had survived too many nights in the open hut of her grandmother—or more recently the lean-to she shared with her uncle for a while—with storms raging around her to worry. She sat next to the girl.

"We got to get away," Suchin said. "You understand?"

The girl stared at her with eyes black in the darkness. She turned her head and her black hair flowed around her face.

"Now!"

"No," the girl said. Her voice was deep and raspy.

"We can do it."

"No!" She shoved Suchin away, took a deep breath, and screamed.

"What are you doing?"

"You go!" the girl said.

"You too."

"I can't," she said. "I don't think right sometimes."

The girl's eyes had shifted from terror to fierce determination. She screamed again, getting off the bed. She took the chair that Auntie had been reading in and smashed the window twice so all the glass was gone.

The key in the lock turned and Auntie rumbled in. The girl, after a quick glance of clear-bolt sanity thrown at Suchin, headed for the window, throwing herself half out, but not far enough to fall.

Auntie lunged across and grabbed the girl by the legs. "You crazy!" she said. "It's a long way down."

The door was open. Suchin slipped out, felt her way down the stairs, out the front door, across the porch. She could see orange groves outlined against the sky. Rain swept across her face until she reached the protection of the first line of trees. She stumbled on, running as fast as her sore leg would allow. It would be many minutes before Auntie could follow. She heard Helen still screaming, demanding Auntie's attention. Even hurting, Suchin knew she could keep her distance from someone as big and slow as Auntie. In minutes she reached the river and headed downstream, looking for something that would float. Soon the rain stopped, the wind died, and an almost full moon threw glints on the surface of the water.

Antoine and Harry arrived the next morning to take Suchin back. Auntie didn't offer them anything to drink.

"Last I saw of her she was headed for the grove, toward the river. It was a hell of a storm."

"We got to take her away," said Harry.

"Jesus," said Antoine. "Did you go after her?"

"I don't go looking for runaways."

"Mere Bull transferred her to Houston," Antoine said. "They got tight discipline down there. And she's a moneymaker."

"That girl full of Tabasco."

"There's only one road out. That's where she'll be."

"She don't know the road or the river."

"You think she's hiding?"

"Maybe. But she's smart as they come. Might be long gone by now."

Antoine signaled Harry to move to the car. "Road's the only way out."

"Where's my money?" Auntie asked.

"I ain't paying for letting the kid get away," Antoine said.

Antoine was out the door, following Harry to the car.

Auntie grabbed her shotgun from behind the kitchen door, stepped back outside.

"Cocksucker," Auntie yelled. She was waving the shotgun, holding it with one hand in the middle. "You ever show up here again, I'll blow your head off."

There was a white girl standing in the doorway behind Auntie. Even from a distance she was ghostly beautiful, with her white skin and long black hair glistening like black silk. One of the nut cases Auntie was famous for bringing back into the world for service. Antoine slammed the door and drove off.

"That Auntie's one weird bitch," he said to Harry. "Probably let the kid go."

Antoine and Harry used up a tank of gas cruising the only long road that led out of the parish, but they didn't see the girl.

"You think she all right?" Harry asked.

"She's got to be alive or we're gator meat," Antoine said. "She's worth a lot of money."

Antoine had to poke Harry to keep him awake, keep him looking. You big dumb gorilla, he thought. But Harry was good kin. Shit. They'd drawn women's tits on the bathroom walls at school together. They'd buddied up with whores. Harry had saved his life too, once on a B&E when the owner tried to kill him with a shotgun, and once in a knife fight in the Ninth Ward.

At night they slept in the car in a truck stop parking lot, then headed south in the early morning. They changed their approach, asking in the towns for anyone who'd seen a pretty, barefoot Chinese girl about four feet high wearing a ripped-up white dress.

It was just after eleven o'clock they cornered Suchin in the storeroom of a convenience store just north of Venice. The woman owner had let a Chinese girl sleep there for a few hours after her daughter found her down near the river and brought her home.

Suchin awoke, startled by an outside noise. The windowless room was black until the door opened and light from the store's fluorescent overhead bulbs outlined Antoine's silhouette coming toward her. Framed in the door behind him was the bulk of Harry. Antoine gripped her arm, with the force she knew and dreaded, and pulled her upright. In seconds, he'd dragged her into the store toward the high counter where the woman owner stood watching. Suchin looked around. Through the glass door on the front she could see two gas pumps with a red pickup truck parked in front. The tailgate was down and long lengths of lumber stuck out a few feet, a red flag hanging limply on the end of the longest board. A door to the restroom opened. She watched a man come out, go through the door toward the pickup. Harry went into the restroom.

Antoine let her go and turned to buy a lighter and cigarettes. She slipped down the aisle between the motor oil and the potato chips, out the door. She grabbed the lumber on the back of the truck and pulled herself up as the truck accelerated and lurched without a stop onto the road. She was in the truck and lying face down, the truck bed vibrating under her as it went through gears to reach cruising speed. She stayed low. Within two minutes, looking back, she saw the Lincoln, the headlights flashing. It gained on the truck, the horn blaring. The pickup slowed. Antoine pulled up to the side of the truck. He was yelling for the pickup to pull over. The pickup stopped. Antoine parked the Lincoln in front of the truck, off the road. Suchin slipped down from the truck bed and limped up a drive toward a house, but Antoine and Harry reached her before she could hide.

Harry was breathing hard.

"What a way to make a living," Antoine said as he and Harry took Suchin back toward the Lincoln.

The pickup truck driver was explaining that he didn't know she was there.

"I'm cool," Antoine said.

"Why are you chasing her?"

"Wise up, man. Forget you ever saw her."

While Harry held Suchin, Antoine emptied the trunk of the Lincoln—a bag of golf clubs, a Styrofoam cooler, fishing rods, a small outboard motor, and a five-gallon can of gasoline. He put them in the back seat. Then with two-inch tape he bound Suchin's arms to her chest with around-the-body passes from shoulders to waist. It was hard for Suchin to take a deep breath.

"I could keep her up front," Harry said.

Antoine lifted Suchin's dress and made seven passes of tape around her thighs. "I ain't taking any chances. We got a long way to go." He made seven more passes of tape around her ankles. She was still standing when he picked her up and put her in the trunk. "Damn if she can get out of that."

Harry held the trunk lid open when Antoine tried to close it.

Antoine wanted to belt Harry, but he held back. They needed to be moving. "Be sure it's locked," Antoine said and went to the front.

Harry turned Suchin on her back, took a loose tire iron out from under her and put it next to the back of the seat where it wouldn't hurt and shut the lid. In minutes they were on their way to Houston, back through New Orleans because that was the only way out of the delta.

Antoine smoked continuously as he drove. Harry slept with his head against the door until they reached Port Sulfur. Suchin had cried out a few times, but there were no sounds from the trunk now.

"Maybe she don't need to go to Houston," Harry said.

"And maybe Mere Bull and the big man will just be happy that all that money to get the kid bought in China on top of the cash to ship her and slip her in will never be returned."

"Houston not a good place."

"Maybe they send her back when she gets broken in," Antoine said.

"She got the beat."

"They're kids, for Christ's sake. You got to learn not to care, Harry. They ain't like regular people."

They stayed quiet, passing through Algiers, then New Orleans, then up on the I-10. Soon they were near the airport.

Suchin was yelling.

"See if you can tell what she wants," Antoine said.

Harry leaned over the seat and pushed the motor and gas can aside. "She needs to pee."

"Shit. Tell her we ain't stopping till we get to Houston."

Harry told her loud so she could hear through the backseat.

"I got to go bad!" she yelled. Antoine heard that.

Harry came back in the front seat. "We got to let her pee."

"Okay. Okay!" Antoine pulled onto the breakdown lane where it was dark. He popped the trunk lid. "Go get her."

Antoine opened the front and rear doors on the right side. "Bring her in between the doors. No one will see."

Harry set her down on her feet between the doors and had to hold her upright; she was too tightly taped to bend.

"I can't sit," she said.

"Do it standing up then."

"I can't."

"We got to cut the tape," Harry said.

"We ain't cutting the tape. I've only got a couple feet left."

"Let it go," Antoine said to Suchin and hit her lightly on the head. Harry still held her, afraid she'd fall over.

"I can't." But in a few seconds her dress went dark, and then a puddle formed in the dust.

"I'm wet."

"That's so terrible," Antoine whined.

"We should have cut the tape," Harry said.

"Put her in the back. I ain't touching her."

"We got something to wipe her off?"

"Some paper towels under the seat."

They were back on the road. Harry rested against the door but didn't sleep. Antoine turned on the radio.

"What if she calls out or something?" Harry said.

"Won't make any difference."

"We won't hear!"

"Okay, I'll turn it down!" Antoine turned the music down a little.

Harry reached forward and turned it off.

"Hey, asshole, I'm not going all the way to Houston without music," Antoine said.

Traffic was light. Antoine drafted behind an eighteen-wheeler in the slow lane to avoid attention.

Suchin called out about half an hour later. "I can't breathe!"

"Did you hear that?"

"She must be breathing. She's yelling, for Christ's sake."

"We got to check."

"We don't have to check. I'm not stopping until we need gas."

"There might be no air back there."

"There's enough."

Harry stared straight ahead for a few minutes. "She ain't said nothing," he said.

"We got an hour, Harry. An hour before we need gas!"

Harry growled as he turned to shove Antoine on the shoulder, shoving him up against the driver's-side door. "We got to check."

Antoine looked at Harry in surprise. "Jesus, Harry. Don't ever do that again. I'd have to whack you." He kept driving.

Harry was breathing fast, his eyes wide with anger. He drew back and threw a right fist at the side of Antoine's head. Antoine blacked out for a few seconds, his hands slipping off the wheel, the cruise control holding steady. The Lincoln left the road. Antoine came alert in seconds, realized the danger, turned the wheel, jammed on the brakes; the car swerved to the left and the right, then hit a low bridge abutment head-on. Harry moaned.

The engine hissed but had stopped running, pushed back against the firewall by the impact. The dashboard was crumpled, the steering wheel inches from Antoine's chest, the front window cracked and mostly gone. Night air floated into the car, damp and oppressive, mixing with the stinging smell of gasoline from the tipped gas can in the back seat.

"Can you move?" Antoine asked Harry. Harry worked to open the door.

"Get out!" Antoine said. Antoine's door was crushed and he slid out Harry's side.

He could not let the kid be found, or any evidence remain in the car.

"Run," he said. He reached in his pocket, lit a lighter, and threw it in the back seat. There was a burst of flame. He pushed Harry. "Run. It'll blow."

"The key." Harry said. "The kid."

"Leave her!" Antoine said. But the keys were to many locks and could be evidence, and they were in his hand. He slipped them in his pocket. "It's going to blow."

Antoine started running.

Harry went to the trunk, pulling up on the lid. Nothing budged. He kicked, once, twice, three times. Fire flared in the open doors. Finally the trunk lid rose. Harry grabbed Suchin, her skin pale, her eyes shut.

Antoine was thirty yards away. The explosion, loud enough to hurt the ears, shot flames above the trees into the night sky. Metal and glass propelled with bullet speed. Harry didn't stop running, Suchin cradled in his arms. The clothes on his back burst into flame. His right carotid artery had been severed by a piece of glass that still glinted on the side of his neck, but he stumbled on, finally falling forward. Suchin hit the ground face first. Harry fell just behind her.

Antoine reached Harry in seconds and stomped out the few burning cloth fragments that remained. Then he rolled his cousin over. He was breathing.

Harry coughed on his own blood. His eyes opened. "She okay?" he asked.

Antoine swore. The flames threw flickering shadows on his face and pinpoint, wiggling reflections glowed on his eyes.

Antoine turned Suchin over. She'd been dead a while, he could tell from the bloodless facial wounds.

"Antoine," Harry gasped, "She okay?"

"She'll make it."

"You take care of her."

"Sure, man."

Despite the burning glow on his skin from the fire, Antoine shivered. He crossed himself.

Harry stopped breathing. The fire died in his eyes, the spirit shimmered out of him.

God bless you, you big dumb gorilla. The danger is in the caring—not the cops, or the FBI, or the syndicate. You cared too much. Like you ever listened.

Antoine knelt down and closed Harry's eyelids. He picked up the kid and tossed her into the flames of the Lincoln's burning trunk. Then, as cars stopped and people were closing in from many directions, he blended into the dark to zigzag a course that would take him away from the city for a while.

The Wreck of the Amtrak's Silver Service

illustration by David Riley

The Wreck of the Amtrak's Silver Service

Heinrick Clever, MD, FACS, asked his wife, Agnes, to have a special anniversary dinner. Thirty-two years. They never ate together anymore. They rarely even talked after his affair with nurse Penny Pram, even though Agnes fully understood and had forgiven him years ago. Agnes still loved life, God, her dog, and her bridge parties. Her ecstasy seemed limitless. She was always too much about everything. He hated the unwavering joy that kept her brain from generating even the slightest blip on the EEG of life's battery of significant ideas. She had been the sea fog around his ship of opportunity, happily obscuring his chances for advancement, cheerfully diverting any choices that could have made him great. She had, insidiously, buried him in this godforsaken town with her mundane acceptance of everything with excessive good humor. He could have been a Parchlick Scholar, or a CJ Beatty in-house surgeon, for Christ's sake. He was that good.

At dinner, in the silences between them, he revisited the weekly cycle of her habits: church on Sundays, grocery shopping on Mondays, gardening on Tuesdays and often Fridays. She volunteered at Goodwill on Thursdays. Saturday, without fail, she walked the country roads with one or two of her good friends. Wednesday evenings were always for her bridge club. He was tired of thinking about her routines, as regular and irritating as a loose bowel movement. It was at that moment that he began to plan, slowly and meticulously—generating a delay in his decision to act alone, which proved prudent—on the perfect solution for Agnes.

Heinrick had an emergency call to the hospital. For weeks thereafter he tended Billie Bob, who was charred and half-crazed after he almost burned to death in a car wreck following an alleged, but never proven, bank robbery. Under Heinrick's care, Billie Bob improved, although his thinking zigzagged at times. Heinrick became obsessed with the man's past, and how it might fit into the future.

In one of Billie Bob's lucid moments, the doc pulled down the hospital gown to where some good skin had survived and exposed a tattoo just below the left clavicle: a clock the size of a half-dollar, the hands frozen at the twelve o'clock position but no number twelve, and only the numbers for hours one through seven along the dial edge, some light, others darker, as if they had been done at different times.

The doctor questioned with a frown. When Billie Bob didn't respond, he asked, "What's that?"

"It's a clock."

"I don't get it."

Billie Bob cackled. "You don't really want to know."

"But I do. Did you commit—"

"Stop!"

"Wha—?"

"Don't say that word, doc. Never say that word."

"Accidental, wasn't it?" Heinrick smiled knowingly and noted that Billie Bob didn't see the humor in the antonym. That frightened him a little. "You'd never do that on purpose," Heinrick said to ease the tension.

"Don't know what you're talking about," Billie Bob said.

"You do. It's important to me."

Billie Bob kept quiet but the doc studied his face. "I can read you like a book," Heinrick said.

"It's a living, doc. I never done nothing that I didn't think was deserved."

Heinrick was slightly ashamed of the thrill that surged through him when he knew for certain Billie Bob was the man he needed. And Billie Bob owed Heinrick for healing him. So, day by day, Heinrick slowly presented his plan in oblique, vague installments. It took a long time for Billie Bob to be convinced of Heinrick's misery and to get the plan right—and agree. Then they finally settled on a price. One hundred thousand dollars.

"You're a little odd, doc," Billie Bob told Heinrick.

"But I'm the best at cutting 'em open and sewing 'em up," Heinrick said with a laugh.

Billie Bob was against complexity. Heinrick had wanted to shoot Agnes on his first thought, or, as a second possibility, poison her. Not for Billie Bob, who didn't like up-close blood and didn't do knives. But Heinrick insisted that Agnes must suffer. God had spoken to him, Heinrick added for emphasis, although he despised the thought of God. He wanted to never see Agnes exhale again, he said repeatedly, with clarity, but reverently following Billie Bob's insistence about not saying the forbidden word.

It took months for Billie Bob to fully heal and for the time to finally come: a cold, windy night with a light snow cover. Visibility was low. Billie Bob unzipped his parka and pulled down the collar to show—with a pocket flashlight—the clock tattoo.

"I got me a little needle work," Billie Bob said.

The doc stared. There were two numbers freshly added to the clock, eight and nine.

"I got the eight. Why the nine?" he asked.

Billie Bob laughed. "This is a tough one for me," he said. "Complexity."

"I still don't get it."

"Lot of integrated stuff. Deserves a nine." Billie Bob zipped his jacket back up with a smile.

Heinrick eased the family car onto the railroad tracks. Agnes was sitting bound and gagged in the back. He killed the engine. Billie Bob parked his car on the road. Even when they untied her, Agnes did not struggle or speak. Billie Bob put her gently in the driver's seat. Agnes remained still and Billie Bob put the can of chloroform he'd used to knock her out back in his pocket. "Good," Heinrick said. Billie Bob secured the doors from the outside. Heinrick stood behind him, breathing hard and fast. Agnes had regained her senses and stared straight at Billie Bob, nonjudgmental, without a hint of fear, and a faint smile that disturbed Billie Bob but inflamed Heinrick all over again.

In minutes, the Amtrak engine whistled around the bend; both Billie Bob and Heinrick were sure the train would not slow for the remote crossing. The headlight pierced the darkness. The barriers descended, the warnings lights flashed. Heinrick stood near a tree by the roadside and watched the express bear down on Agnes, the definitive object of his vengeance. Billie Bob stayed down near the barrier to the last minute to be sure Agnes didn't get free of the car somehow.

A hundred yards from the car the engineer reacted and braked; the train skidded on the tracks toward Agnes. Sparks flew with a screech of steel on steel. Heinrick saw Agnes, her face pulsing red, then white, from the blaze of the crossing lights. She sat motionless, and he was sure she still smiled. He pulsed with anger. Whap! The train threw the sedan fifty feet into the air to land away from the tracks, upside down. It was ripped open, windows smashed, and a fire flickered under the rear axle near the gas tank. Agnes lay in a ditch, her severed head resting right-side-down on her breast, attached only by a piece of skin.

Heinrick raised a fist into the air. "Yes!" he cried. "We did it."

Billie Bob approached, carrying the crowbar. "I sort of admired her sitting there, like she was taking a punch in the face standing up without moving," he said.

"She was scared out of her mind!" That was what Heinrick hoped, after all the years he suffered her bland, water-drip torture. But deep down he was enraged at her serene acceptance. Her smile at the end had already begun to haunt him.

"No, doc. She was …uh … like she didn't care. I liked her spirit."

Heinrick could not comprehend Billie Bob's thinking, and frankly found him crazier than he originally had thought.

With one swing, Billie Bob hit the doc in the neck with the crowbar. Heinrick, frozen with surprise, sank to his knees.

"What's this?" he asked, looking up at Billie Bob with wobbly eyes, his neck broken in two places. "I got the money," Heinrick wheezed. His hand weakly patted the money in a satchel by his side. "Why?"

"She was a better soul than you," Billie Bob said.

"You made a deal," Henrick said.

Billie Bob hit Heinrick with a direct whack to the head. The skull cracked.

"What kind of man are you?" Henrick said on the edge of incoherence and death.

"You one crazy dude," Billie Bob said, pounding the doc's head with two more blows. Then he tossed the crowbar into the withered weeds that stuck up through the snow blanket waiting for spring.

Heinrick took a last breath, gurgling with blood.

"It ain't all about money," Billie Bob said to the doc. "You ain't got no sense about what's good in people."

Billie Bob took the satchel with the cash from Heinrick's right-hand death grasp and disappeared, well before the first emergency personnel arrived.

The Indelible Myth

illustration by Anna Sokolova

illustration by Anna Sokolova

The Indelible Myth

Leesville perched—and clung—to the banks of the Percumsah River, as did Natchez, on a much grander scale, on the Mississippi River at the opposite side of the state. Citizens of Leesville were born and raised within twenty-five miles of the town center and it was rare for a family to leave for the outside world; no people from afar that I remember ever permanently settled in Leesville when I was growing up. Although a few tried, they always moved on.

Leesville had its own way of thinking in the 1960s. People didn't celebrate Lincoln's birthday, even when it was its own national holiday, but closed the schools to mourn the death of Jefferson Davis. Above my school a Confederate flag was raised at sunrise and lowered at sunset, not the stars and stripes. It wasn't protest, just habit.

When I was in the fourth grade, my art training was with Miss Patchett in a Thursday-afternoon session with students from many different grades. In May we were creating Mother's Day gifts; I drew a bird. It took a full two hours, and Miss Patchett stopped by often to see my progress. Then, before the bell rang, she singled out my bird as the best accomplishment of the day. She held it in front of her, the top edge gently squeezed between thumb and index finger, and rotated it side to side for all to see. Most of the kids my age frowned and wished their art had been chosen. The older kids closer to high school smiled at what they thought was a lack of sophistication. But it was special, everyone knew it in their hearts—a narrow snipe-like bill, long legs and three-toed feet, a perfect circle for a head with a yellow eye, alert yet kind. The thrush-size body had reds and yellows and tilted forward, the tail fanning out behind, the wings with greens and deep blues of the peacock.

After school I headed home alone. My mood was buoyant. School was exciting and my parents loved me. I was their only child. My sister, my only sibling, died at birth at the hospital and I never saw her.

I walked steadily, eager to see my mother. I had my book bag strapped to my back and carried my drawing in one hand so there was no chance of smudging the surface. I held it facing out and tried to be casual, but I wanted the world to see what Miss Patchett had been so proud to display to her students, and what I was going to give my mother.

As I neared the corner to my home street off Elm, I saw Ruth, a girl who was a grade above and lived near the river. Usually her brother walked her home, and except for a few taunts, they usually ignored me. Her father was a doctor.

Today Ruth sat alone with her back against an oak tree, her books at her side. She was looking down at something in her hand. She was big for a girl, with strong, muscular legs and thick upper arms. She had short dark-brown hair and a wide, thick-lipped mouth with spaces between the teeth in front—not ugly really, but it held your attention. I circled around so as not to come close.

"That's a stupid bird," she called to me without looking.

I began to cross to the other side of the street, away from her. She stood up. She was in my art class. She knew what Miss Patchett had said about my bird.

"A really stupid, stupid bird." She stood, leaving her books, and came toward me. I moved quickly but she was too fast and snatched my drawing and backed off. She had torn the bird into small pieces by the time I reached her.

My rage empowered me. With my fists I pummeled her, pushed her down. I did not kick her, but I hit her again and again with my book bag, the brass buckles cutting her face and neck. Blood oozed from her forehead. She cried out and I hit her in the mouth with my fist, felt the pain as her teeth broke skin on my knuckles.

Two adults came. They held me back. I tried to explain about the bird, but they saw me as unreasonable and out of control. I quieted and waited until Ruth's parents were found to take her to the hospital, and my mother came to get me.

Through tears I told Mother about my bird, and she held me. I told her about my rage at Ruth destroying my gift without reason. And Mother said she loved me. But Ruth's parents demanded I be punished. The school was contacted to impose penalties. Ruth's parents thought I should be sent to reform school in New York. But I was put on probation and required to attend counseling sessions with my mother with the local pediatrician, who had majored in psychology in college. The pediatrician was intent on reconciliation, and in time included Ruth's mother in some sessions with himself and my mother. My mother and Ruth's mother came to an understanding, and, I believe, liked each other in addition to gaining a mutual, if at first hesitant, respect.

I survived my probation and my counseling. My family began to share family gatherings with Ruth and her parents and her brother, who was much older than me. One Saturday Ruth's parents invited our family over for an afternoon barbecue. Ole Miss was playing LSU, away, and a radio had been propped on a windowsill of the house with the volume at maximum. The adults sat in folding lawn chairs around a brick-lined barbecue pit with a pig on a spit that Ruth's father, the doctor, pasted sauce on every few minutes. Ruth's brother went to shoot squirrels with a twenty-two near the dump, refusing to take Ruth and me. Ruth decided to fish on the river, a skill her brother had taught her, usually on the oxbow about a mile north. Ruth's mother insisted I tag along. Carrying her rod and tackle box, Ruth went to where the river narrowed, the surface white with froth swirling in eddies. I followed. There was a floating dock with a planked walkway that tilted up slightly now that the river was high from recent rains. The flushed river grumbled and swished. She stood at the dock's edge in her bare feet and cast a lure awkwardly upstream.

"Are there fish here?" I asked.

"There are millions of fish," Ruth said.

"Like brim?" I asked.

"All kinds. Like every kind in the whole world."

After that, she did not speak to me. I soon walked away, back to the house. I threw a tennis ball for Ruth's father's black lab to retrieve.

When it was time to eat, I was sent to tell Ruth. But there was no one on the dock. I returned to tell the adults.

"Where is she?" Ruth's mother asked.

I didn't answer.

"Have you done something to her?"

"I'm sure she'll be here soon," my mother said, coming and standing close to me.

"You're an evil child," Ruth's mother said to me.

"That's not fair, Martha," my mother said. "He's done nothing."

But Ruth's mother, breathing fast through clenched teeth, was already sending people out in different directions to find Ruth.

"I'm sure everything is all right," my mother said, taking me with her as she followed Ruth's parents to the river. My father tended the grill.

An hour later, Ruth's body was lifted from the water a few hundred yards downstream from the dock. I stood back at the edge of the crowd, but I could see her face was scratched and her leg was bruised. Her fishing rod was never found.

The sheriff questioned me that day. Then later, twice, once for three hours. I sat at the police station and we went over every second of that afternoon. But nothing happened, and I went back to school in the fall. I thought life was as it should be, except that Ruth's parents never spoke to me and walked away when they saw me, even at school.

But life was not as I expected. Little things happened—things that now seem unimportant, but that were etched into me. Adults looked over me when they talked, and teachers rarely called on me in class. In gym I was passed over when teams were chosen, and even at church in the children's choir, where I usually sang lead in "Down by the Riverside" from the front row next to the sopranos, I was told to stay in the back next to tone-deaf Arthur, whom no one liked. Later that year "Just a Closer Walk with Thee" replaced "Down by the Riverside," and I had no solos.

My mother became my only confidant. I told her how I was treated. I told her I didn't care what people thought, but I did care and couldn't sleep well. I was haunted by formless nightmares with sensations of falling that were prolonged, and slow to wake me. On weekends I often went alone to sit, motionless and silent, by the river, near where Ruth died. Mother had conferences with my teachers and the principal, who seemed sympathetic and said I was a good boy and a hard worker. They trusted me, they said. They definitely thought Ruth's mother's tirades against me regarding her daughter's death would stop and soon be forgotten.

I graduated from high school in the top half of my class, but at the ceremony, when the principal handed me my diploma and shook my hand, his eyes never connected with mine as they did with those of my classmates, looking instead beyond me to someone in the audience. My mother died when I was away in my third year at a Birmingham college. My father retired and moved to Florida with a woman he'd known since high school.

I did well enough in college to win a scholarship to pharmacy school. I've been in practice now for four years and manage a drugstore in Dayton, Ohio. I never speak of my past and I can't remember when, or if, anyone here has ever asked.

But I must tell my story now. I have a decision to make. A woman, Robyn Welter, loves me. She is a small, frail woman of thirty-five, two years older than me, quiet, gentle, and shy. She is a school librarian and teaches English to fourth graders. I love her, too, and we want to marry. A date has been set. But as the time has come closer, I cannot find it in me to want children. Robyn wants a family. It is what will fulfill her life. And it has become a source of contention, and many tears. And I have come to wonder if marriage is right for me. I do not want children. I do not want to see them have to grow up through unpredictable dangers.

We have come for a consultation at the church office of her minister. Robyn is religious, and I believe in God but have little faith in the church. She and I sit in chairs in front of the minister's desk. He is a young, unmarried man with glasses and a nervous glance that lands on people at odd times, disjointed in some way, avoiding eye contact as if he couldn't face the realties he might see. Robyn and the minister discuss our incompatibilities and, after an awkward silence, I dread telling my story when they hint at the need for catharsis. Robyn is adamant about children. I comment that a child is a slice of potential reality that I cannot take on. That I cannot cope with offspring. Robyn urges me to tell my story, leaving nothing out. The minister insists, too. I tell it directly to him in every detail. When I finish, Robyn expresses her love for me again, and looks immediately toward the minister who smiles and nods, as if she'd just spelled the winning word in a spelling bee.

The minister mumbles something about perceptions and justice. Then his voice strengthens. "I must be honest," he says, not looking at me. "You show an urgent need to address guilt. It seems to have consumed you. For a successful marriage, you must confront your inner demons."

I stare at him, not exactly sure of his meaning. I say nothing. I am not demonic.

He continues. "Your guilt frankly seems excessive for what you describe. Is there something that day by the river you might have repressed? Some nudge? Some hesitation to save her? Something to distract her?"

I look to Robyn. It is, for her, the moment when she can make our marriage whole by believing in me. A marriage with children, too, I now am willing to believe, if she has faith in me. In her soul, she must know that even as a child I was incapable of murder, or even assisting in an accident. And that is what she must communicate to me.

She stares at me. At this instant I look into her eyes, tenuous in their lock on mine, then she looks to her left, toward a table with framed photo of a modern painting of Jesus in a romantic pose holding a shepherd's crook. I continue to stare at Robyn, despair sweeping over me. And she looks back to me. Now her eyes do not hold the sparkle and desire of our lovemaking. They hold pity. She has brought me here to confess the sins that she perceives I have committed. Her look deflates me, voids me of emotion and self-worth. I slowly rise, button the front of my white lab coat, and bow slightly to both of them.

"Don't run," the minister says.

"Please," Robyn says.

"Hypnosis," he says. "To explore your unconscious."

"You were a child," Robyn adds. "You cannot be held responsible."

A child who did nothing wrong, I want to yell at her. But I've told her many times and the well of doubt, once discovered, can never be abandoned.

"We could discover the facts," the minister says.

But we know the facts!

I exit to the street. I am surprised at how calm I am, still unaware of the weight of my resolution. I refuse to believe there is an evil memory inside me that will satisfy the omnipresent suspicions. I will bury myself in the demands of my profession. Alone, I will make my contributions to the world. But I do not find any comfort in these resolutions.

I pace away from the church until I am sweating, even though dark clouds swirl above and the chill of winter is already on us. I sit down on the low wall near the air force base. The street traffic is heavy. A near-freezing rain begins to fall and the cars' windshield wipers slap from side to side. I tremble, then sag, my arms limp.

The minister is a fool. It is only Robyn, whom I love, who could pierce me with my own doubt regarding what I remember about that day. And she has coated her love with impenetrable suspicion, and I'm left with the truth that now, with inescapable doubts, her feelings would dwindle, and force her to a separate world, a prisoner denying how love is destroyed by uncertainty in the mind.

"I am without sin," I say aloud to a passing stranger, who looks at me oddly without breaking stride.

The Stonecutter

illustration by Peter Healy

The Stonecutter

I was fifteen, never yet in love, and yearning to leave home when a red two-seated convertible drove up to our gate. The driver's door opened, and a girl of twenty-two with a perfectly shaped, light-skinned body emerged in a see-through dress that showed almost everything. I imagined the rest.

My father, a tall, imposing figure of a black man with bulging muscles from carving statues and grave markers for the dearly departed, tried not to look. He felt strange around women, I assumed because my mother had left when I was two. He never talked about her or much of anything, and we lived alone on a twelve-acre plot of half-swamp property where I suffered his long silences, broken only by the sharp blows of a hammer driving a metal chisel into stone.

Well, this girl was a treat for both of us. She closed the door and looked to our been-here-forever, two-room shack raised two feet off the ground by concrete blocks, with only a screen door on the front and all the windows up to catch a breeze. My father worked on, but slipped a glance when he knew she wasn't looking.

She walked through the opening in the iron fence that stood on the front line of the property. That gate had never kept anything in or out. My great-grandfather had installed it in the time of Calvin Coolidge to let people know he had made some cash farming, and my father was too proud to recycle it. Neither the shack nor the fence impressed the girl.

"You lost?" I asked, walking up to her, smelling the freshness of soap and perfume seeping through the humid air.

"I'm looking for—" she turned as if she might go back to the car to find the name.

"Ephraim Picard. Graveyard Stones and Statues?" I said.

"Yes. But I expected—" she paused, looking at me with soft, deep-water eyes that made me want her so bad I thought I might explode.

"A sign that say the business here?" I said.

"A professional building. Displays of the work."

"Papa don't do things up 'head of time.'"

"I know that. I just expected examples."

"I show you something in the barn might satisfy you some," I said, and waved for her to follow. We headed for our barn, not very big and without doors on the front or back so birds flew through without landing. A rusted, out-of-gas forklift half-blocked the door, and I put out my hand for her, which she took, and helped her wobble in her spike-heeled shoes over the two prongs of the fork into the barn.

"Quite the gentleman," she laughed.

Inside on the dirt floor sat blocks of stone and marble randomly stacked, mostly by me. I led her to one corner that was in shadows, but with enough light to see the only sample I could think of showing her. I pulled a tarp off a marble sculpture of a woman's head propped up on two stacked wooden crates.

"Why has it got all those lines through it?" she asked.

"It got smashed," I said. Her hands lightly touched the surface, like a blind person trying to remember someone.

"What happened?"

"Nothing," I said quickly. But Papa had made it and destroyed it.

"Can I see the rest of it?"

I pointed to a rusted tub filled with marble chips, most smaller than an egg from being smashed with a hammer.

"Takes time—gluing it back together."

She stood back, walking from side to side to see the whole head.

"Does he always do Negroes?"

"Not always."

"Well, she must be beautiful in person," she said.

"She is," I said, but I didn't really know. I had only been two.

"You Ephraim?"

"I'm Willie."

"Well, I'd like to talk to Mr. Picard, then."

I led her out of the barn, helping her again over the forklift, but she said nothing about my manners this time.

We approached my father, carving a marble angel. She stared. It wasn't a typical graveyard cupid-looking angel made by Italians and chubby with fat as if it couldn't fly. That wasn't Father's way. This angel had a small body with huge, muscular wings stretched out on each side. It looked like a hawk in a dive, the smooth-topped head cranked back as if catching the full force of the wind, the legs bent back at the knees. My father didn't put clothes on his angels, and I wondered what this woman thought about male private parts hanging down.

"You needing something?" Father didn't stop working.

"My father—well, my stepfather—was killed in Statesville, Georgia. At a rally. Maybe you heard of him. Reverend Al Jackson?"

"That was your daddy?" I said.

My father and I had seen the Reverend once, in a church we rarely attended upriver about a mile. He was campaigning for senator or governor—I don't remember. People yelled and cheered. He had a fat stomach and bulgy eyes, and his solid-black capped-toe shoes were polished so they reflected the sun like the mirror surface of a still pond.

She spoke past me to my father. "His will said he wanted a graveyard statue done by you. He made special arrangements with a cemetery near New Orleans that takes Negroes."

"Takes time," my father said.

"He got special permission from the committee because of who he was, and he wanted it to be bigger than real. Will you do it?"

It wasn't his busiest time, and I thought he'd be eager. But then again, he wasn't a man to jump at anything fast. I, of course, wanted to see this girl as much as I could. With time, I knew I could get her to like me. I was full-grown for fifteen and packed with muscle from lifting those blocks for my father.

She waited for an answer. My father had an infuriating habit of not talking when the silences between him and others clearly demanded some words.

"He do it," I said.

"Will you?" she said to my father.

"Bigger than life takes time," he said again, in his deep voice husky from not talking often enough.

"It's in the will I should oversee the progress."

"Why you?" I asked.

"A prerequisite for my inheritance." She added, "Every day that I come, you'll have to sign and date my book. For the judge."

"I do the writing," I said proudly, "He don't write." Father had worked cane; then he was cleanup boy for a white tomb maker near Lafayette for a while. He learned to carve by watching. I guess he never even thought about school; he'd worked steady and hard his entire life.

"When will you start?" she asked my father. "I need to know when to come back. To keep the terms of the will."

"Pick the stone tomorrow," Father finally said, still working.

"Not today?"

"You need to bring all his pictures," he said to her.

She sighed and walked back to her car. I ran to catch up with her.

"You miss him?" I asked. "Your stepdaddy?"

"I hated his guts," she said, with so much anger I stopped short. I couldn't think of questions to keep her hanging around, and she got in her car and drove off.

The next day I stayed home from school, eager to be with her, and she brought photos and newspaper cutouts of the Reverend for my father to work from. The sky was heavy with gray clouds and a thin gentle rain came down.

Father led her to the barn; I followed. He waved his hand at the blocks available. She went straight to a slab of marble veined with copper-colored lines the shade of her skin, but my father shook his head and pointed to a huge block of granite.

"I'm supposed to supervise," she said loudly. "I like this one."

"You ain't doing the carving," he said. "That marble ain't big enough."

She walked away fast to let him know she wasn't pleased. Father went back to the angel. She sat on a gravestone already finished and inscribed for a Baton Rouge preacher. I sat down beside her.

"Don't know how to call you, seeing as I'll be the one to do the signing," I said.

"My name is Annatilda Jones. AnnaTee."

"AnnaTee," I said. "He'll make it real good."

"The marble's more elegant," she said sharply.

She didn't know the granite gave power. "You can see the man come out of the big block," I said. "It's cool."

She held her head in her hands. "I can't believe he made me do this," she said.

"The Reverend must have trusted you something hard," I said.

"He was cruel. Arrogant. Thought only of himself," she shot back. "That's why he made me do it."

"What happened to your real daddy?"

"He left my mother early. She was Reverend Al's third wife."

"Me too," I said.

"He's not your real daddy?"

I told her fast it was my mother who had left. And when she asked, I told her how I had never seen her or heard from her.

"You miss your mother?"

"Don't miss her," I said.

The rain came thicker and we moved under the overhang to the barn, away from where Father still worked.

"Why does he work outside?" she asked, her voice soft and friendly for the first time.

"For the light. We ain't got electric out here in the country." Of course, in the seventies, electricity was available everywhere in Louisiana. But my father didn't see a need for it.

"I hope all his statues of people don't come out looking as angry as that angel."

"Naw," I said, "Don't worry." My father was famous for his carving.

Even after a few weeks, AnnaTee didn't gain any interest as to what the Reverend was going to be in stone, but I was like a frog waiting on a fly watching my father finding the man with his hammer and chisel. It is still is a mystery to me how he knew what to chip off and what to leave on.

One day, AnnaTee and I were talking. She was sitting on a rough stone block, leaning back with her hands behind her, her head slightly back. I had my back against the barn wall with my feet out.

"You got a boyfriend?" I asked.

When she stared at me, I couldn't tell what she was thinking and my heart dropped like a stone. I'd screwed up. Then she grinned.

"Why are you asking?"

"Just wondering."

"You wouldn't have a crush?" she said with a little laugh.

"I ain't got no crush," I said, but my heart pounded and ached at the same time. I went into the house and sat on the floor next to my bed. I picked notes on a rusty dobro my uncle had given me, but I couldn't make music. I refused to go out, even when I knew it was time for her to leave.

I waited every day before going to school to see if AnnaTee would show. I missed her some days when she came late, but not very many. The more time I spent with her, the more curious I became about why she hated the Reverend so much. At the time, I saw hating the Reverend the same as hating God. And I worried about what God's thoughts were about me. The more I spent time around AnnaTee, my shame about my father's ignorance and poverty seemed to keep growing.

"You go to college?" I asked.

"Morehouse."

"What you doing now?"

"Don't know what I'll do. But I was travel secretary for the big man."

"The Reverend?"

"He wasn't reverend. He was base. The whole world was blinded by his smooth tongue." Her anger surprised me again.

"He did good for the ordinary folk. I read it in the paper at school," I said. I had stayed after school to learn about the Reverend. I saw pictures of him with the president, the secretary of state. In one photo, he had his arm around Martin Luther King Jr.

"He was a crook. He spent the money for the poor."

"I can't believe it," I said. The Reverend was a great man! He had died for all of us. He didn't give a damn about bad people hating him, trying to hunt him down like wild boar.

"His bodyguards cost a quarter of a million dollars a year! He flew in a private jet that my mother can't sell for a half of what he paid."

"He must have been good to you sometimes."

"Of course he was good to me sometimes. Of course."

"Then I don't see why you hate him so much."

She glared at me. "You wouldn't know what it means to a woman. He put moves on me! Twice. Even with my mother in the same house thinking he was God's disciple!"

She was shaking, and I felt bad for causing it. I searched for a word to soothe her, but I was lost.

"Maybe he didn't mean it," I said.

"Of course he meant it!" She hung her head and closed her eyes, and I just watched her for many minutes. Then she looked at me, her forehead ridged with lines of determination.

"You don't know about your mother, do you?"

I shook my head.

"Come with me," she said. She was breathing hard and walked with long strides like she was on a freedom march. She led me straight to Father.

"What happened to the boy's mother?" she said. Father kept working. "I know you know. Tell him."

The sound of the hammer striking the metal quickened a little.

"She left you, didn't she? She left you."

"Shut your mouth," my father said, moving the chisel to a new sight, starting to strike again even faster.

"You destroyed all this boy had left. Her statue."

"Ain't your doing," he said, his voice seething.

"It's not much to give!" she said. "Ease this boy's longing with the truth."

My father dropped the chisel and raised his hand. I lunged at him, grabbing his arm. He shoved me to the ground. I moaned from a pain in my leg.

"Ha!" AnnaTee said, backing away. "Is that what you did? Is that why she left you?"

My father picked up the chisel and went back to working. He was trembling.

"Come," I said, grabbing AnnaTee's arm. I moved her toward her car.

"You'll lose him," she called to my father. "You could at least tell him it wasn't his fault!"

"Don't say no more," I whispered.

She broke away and ran back to my father. "You're evil," she yelled.

My father threw his tools to the ground within inches of her feet, his tight fists at chest high.

"Loosen up. Let the good times roll." AnnaTee laughed.

My father glared. "She loved another," he said.

"Oh! That's so sad. Boo hoo," she said.

"Maybe. Maybe not," he said. Slowly he opened his hands and lowered them to his sides. He headed toward the house.

She hissed. "I hate men," she said as I walked with her back to her car.

Soon after, AnnaTee stopped coming. She told us she had argued to the court that she would come on and off for three months and that was enough. The judge had agreed. It took Father another two months to finish the Reverend, and when the statue was washed and treated, my father said for me to call and tell AnnaTee when he'd have it installed.

I walked toward the state route, then turned up the levee road to go to Aaron's Shell and Grocery store, where there was a pay phone nailed to an outside pole. I dialed AnnaTee's number and knew her voice when she answered; I'd been cursed to remember it in my lonely times often enough.

"This is Willie."

"Who?"

"Stonecutter's son," I said speaking too loudly. "He's setting it up Tuesday. Doing the unveiling on Wednesday."

"I'll see if I can make it," she said.

Then I called my father's cousin Arno in Morgan City, who hauled trash in a truck big enough to lay the Reverend down for the trip to New Orleans, and who owned the unbroken pulleys and intact chains to get him upright again. I skipped school and rode in the truck the eighty miles to New Orleans between Father and Cousin Arno, and helped them bolt the Reverend—after dark—in his final resting place above the tomb, which was no easy task since he was more than eight feet high and weighed more than half a ton.

I stayed the night with Cousin Arno's sister-in-law, who lived in the Treme, and I got to walk the streets of the French Quarter.

The next day, Father, Cousin Arno, and I went to the cemetery about an hour past sunrise. AnnaTee was there waiting! After a few moments, her mother came, and then friends of the Reverend, and even two crews from TV stations in New Orleans.

The Reverend was covered by six sewn-together bedsheets that were held tight at the base by a rope. A minister of God climbed up on the tomb, with my father's help, to speak about the Reverend, and to God. I went to AnnaTee, who stood off from the crowd a little.

"Hi." It was not what I wanted to say. I wanted to tell her how much I'd missed her, how I wished daily she'd come to see the Reverend—and me. She stared at the fluttering sheets. A breeze gusted, and the sheets flapped.

"You want to see him?" I asked.

"I dread it," she said. I was inches from her, and I could sense how tense she was.

My father walked over to her.

"I brought my checkbook," she said.

"The Reverend Jackson pay me last year he visited. Told me about you."

"He paid you for his statue?" She sounded as if she thought my father was lying. It was all news to me.

"Enough for Willie's college."

"Bought his own monument!" she said mostly to herself, shaking her head.

The minister had finished his words to the crowd, and Cousin Arno cut the fasteners and the sheets fell. AnnaTee's face didn't change one bit. It was like her features were in stone.

From a distance, I looked up to the Reverend, standing straight as a tree, his arms crossed over his chest and resting on his stomach. He was in a suit and tie; his feet, in fancy tassel shoes, were set together, and were small like his hands. The pale stone made him ghostlike, and at first look he seemed angry, mostly in the way he stood. But as you studied the lines in his face and his granite eyes that looked down, the anger faded: he showed fear as plain as if he'd been alive and ready to speak. He'd been alone in the world.

AnnaTee felt something too. As if the Reverend himself was talking to her mind. She cried.

I'd had little experience with women, and I turned to Father, standing behind us. For the first time I could remember, my father's face softened and his mouth turned up a little, not much at all, but a lot for him, and like a bolt of lightning from a gray sky, I was proud of him. Proud of his work. Proud what he'd done for the Reverend, who was, as promised, bigger than life. And for AnnaTee, who had her inheritance. I smiled back.

"What you think?" I asked AnnaTee.

She didn't try to speak for a minute or so. "It's so big. I think that's what hit me."

"I think he was a great man," I said.

"It's not what I expected to feel," she said. Her face softened with a little less hate than before.

Then she hugged me, long enough for me to hug her back. "You're sweet, Willie," she said. "You'll do just great in college."

Being sweet wasn't at all what I wanted to hear, but I formed an immediate plan. I would stay with my father on the property until I finished school. I would grow up and be educated. AnnaTee would learn to love me.

But the truth still hurts, even after these many years. Papa died when I was in college, and the letters I wrote to AnnaTee came back unopened. I never saw her again.

The Necklace

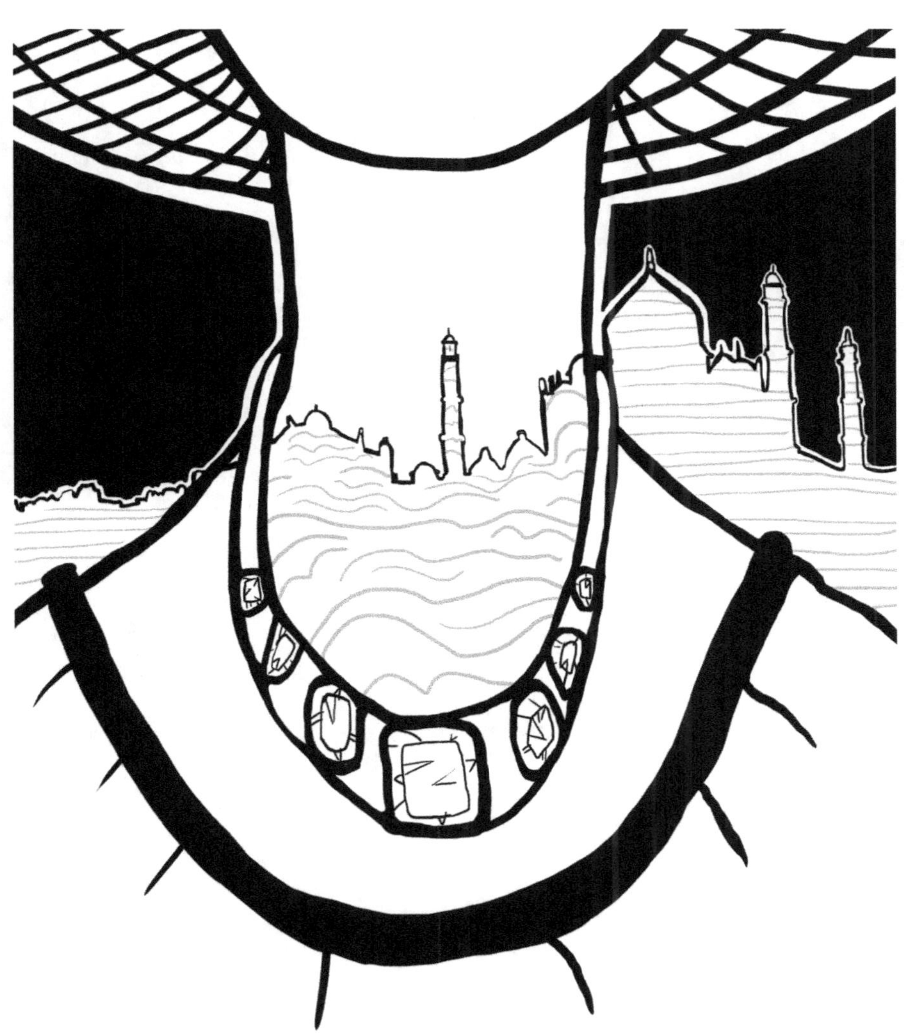

illustration by Peter Healy

The Necklace

On our first night in New Delhi, Helen and I ate dinner in our hotel with our new acquaintances, Betsy and Anwar, from Birmingham, Alabama, where Anwar practiced orthopedic surgery and she kept house.

"You two married?" Betsy asked Helen and me.

"We live together," Helen said. She didn't want to explain that we lived together most of the time in my cramped condominium facing Lake Ontario, but that she still had her house from her divorce, where she spent time during the week.

"Well, I declare," mooned Betsy. "An arrangement."

"A little more than that," Helen said, bristling.

With canny insight, Betsy had cut open the conflict between Helen and me—conflict we had not planned to share with strangers on an Asian tour.

Helen wanted commitment—meaning us married and settled in her seventeen-room, early-twentieth-century house in town with tennis court and three-car garage. She believed that if we changed the furniture and decorated with art we chose together, we could be happy newlyweds. But every time I stepped into her house, memories of her ex-husband rustled around me in the walls like trapped rodents. He was a sixty-four-year-old famous and successful neurosurgeon who was cavorting around Florida with his twenty-four-year-old office receptionist, who Helen and I thought too overweight and shaggy to be attractive to anyone but a lecherous older man still in a midlife crisis. I was convinced I could never replace her ex in his former home even though Helen insisted she had erased him from her life, which I thought was probably true. But I suspected she longed for the life they had created together, a life of almost constant in-home entertaining and guests' admiration for the uncramped comfort of her echo-filled interior, shelved walk-in closets, and eight-burner stove surrounded by acres of counter space. Although I never confronted her, I knew she wanted legitimacy for our relationship and to re-create her previous high-society life.

Despite our lack-of-a-forever-marriage commitment, Helen and I were intimate good buddies, and we leveled our friendship canoe pretty well by stroking carefully in unison on opposite sides. She was an eager traveler—we loved tours—and she rarely complained as she followed routes on maps with her clear-polished fingernail and tirelessly read guidebooks where she marked pages with dog-ears and pieces torn from in-flight airline magazines.

In Delhi, on the next night at dinner at the hotel, we learned that Betsy and Anwar had been married for sixteen years. Helen gave me a raised eyebrow. When we were alone in our room, she expressed her usual suspicions about how happy couples really were in their marriages. She pointed out blaring incongruities about Betsy and Anwar. Even on tour, Anwar was our best-dressed traveler and wore beige Italian silk suits, dark blue or maroon Egyptian cotton shirts, no-pattern ties of magenta or gold, and narrow hand-cut shoes with pointy European toes that looked painful. "That is one uptight dude," said Helen. In contrast, Betsy wore plain cotton dresses printed with flowers and insects, or swirl patterns in pastels, and serviceable cross-trainer running shoes. "A real homebody," she added. And both Helen and I had been puzzled by Betsy's one consistent ostentation: a necklace of seven diamonds graduated in size on each side of a central more-than-one-carat stone, all mounted in platinum.

"Zircons," I said to Helen, who was an expert from frequent expensive purchases from Tiffany jewelers in New York.

"The real McCoy," she said.

"Who'd wear a real necklace on a tour?" I asked.

"Only the socially insecure," she said.

"Why take the risk?"

"Beyond comprehension."

So the very next evening at dinner I asked Betsy about the necklace.

"Aren't you afraid you might lose it?"

"All the time," Betsy said. "I love it so much. Anwar gave it to me."

"I hope it's insured?" I said. Helen threw me her you're-out-of-line look.

"Of course, but it could never be replaced," said Betsy.

"Women shouldn't have possessions that are not used," Anwar said emphatically.

Helen frowned. She hated sexism and inflexible pronouncements. But despite her many ingrained opinions, she was socially adept and completely capable of hiding her real thoughts. She tilted her head slightly as if in agreement with Anwar. But after dinner, when we were alone at the bar, Helen turned irritable. "I'm sick of that goddamn necklace."

"You've got prettier ones," I said.

"It's just not appropriate," she said.

"Low-class?" I asked.

"Nouveau riche," she said. "Ridiculous."

That night, I fantasized out loud to Helen about Betsy shielding her necklace with her washcloth in the shower as she lathered up, clutching it with both hands while Anwar made love on top of her, refusing to remove the prized possession when she went for a mammogram. Helen said my imagination was out of control.

For three days we toured, shopped, and ate spicy food. On the fourth day in India we waited for our special tour to the Red Fort. Helen and I were drained of energy from jet lag and often sleepless from uncomfortable foreign beds. The group felt the exhaustion, too. Anwar's laugh, a measured breathy monotone, cut among the tour group as he busied himself reloading film into his camera. Betsy felt the group's irritation with Anwar's pithy apercus she glared intently at guidebooks without reading or speaking, her lips pursed, refusing to look at Anwar. Finally the bus arrived that, an hour later, delivered us to the Red Fort.

The hot, humid air clutched our skins as we stepped down one by one from the bus interior and beggars swarmed around us, desperately reaching out.

"It's so sad." Helen said, looking at one emaciated woman with a toothless smile and vacuous eyes.

Most of our group stayed within a few feet of each other as we walked—except Betsy, her diamonds sparkling, lagging behind to give a few coins to a child, and Anwar, who stayed in front next to the guide, a place he preferred so he could ask questions.

"I'm not sure I'll ever love India," Helen whispered to me. "There's too great a difference between the haves and the have-nots." I squeezed her hand.

We trudged on behind the guide and Anwar until Betsy's yell stopped us all. A thin woman with sores out on her arms and leathery skin with a yellow hue clutched Betsy's knees. Betsy struggled, her arms flailing, but she went down, the woman on top of her. Betsy struggled to get up, pushing the woman away. A shoeless man knocked Betsy forward facedown to the ground. He yanked the necklace from her neck before she could get her hands free. The two thieves disappeared into the crowd that opened and closed to swallow them. I ran to Betsy. Others followed. She sat on the ground, whimpering.

"Are you all right?" someone asked. Betsy sobbed.

Helen found a tissue in her bag and dabbed at bleeding, dirt-encrusted scrapes on Betsy's arms and knees .

"Get the police," Anwar yelled at the guide. Within minutes uniformed officials wrote notes for reports. Our group fidgeted, openly afraid of the crowd, and demanded our return to the hotel.

Anwar stiffened. He thought he saw the thief. A grinning old man with something sparkling on his neck stood maybe fifty feet away from us.

Anwar bolted away from where Betsy still lay.

"That's not him," I yelled. "It's metallic."

Anwar ignored me. The old man's eyes widened as his mouth dropped open.

Once in full stride, Anwar was a quick as a leopard. "Thief," Anwar screamed, his face flushed. He closed the gap and threw the man to the ground, kicking him in the ribs with his pointed shoes. Once, twice. The man howled, pushed up on his knees, lunged to his feet and ran for his life, his malnourished and arthritic frame swaying to the right in a grotesque limp.

Anwar surged after him but the natives closed in a protective clump around the man, who disappeared.

"It probably wasn't my necklace," Betsy said, still in tears, when Anwar returned to the bus.

"Oh, shut up," Anwar said.

"I just meant—he didn't look the same."

"Betsy, it's the principle. A thief is a thief."

Anwar's teeth gleamed in a sudden smile as his eyes swept over each of our stares. His face softened. Helen shivered at his transparent goodwill. He hugged Betsy briefly. "That's my little pumpkin. Sorry, honey. It's all so unfair," he said. But I could see—and Helen was looking too—how he could not hide his anger-induced trembling.

All but a few refused the tour of the Red Fort, eager and thankful to get back to the comfort of the hotel. Helen and I felt hopelessness for Betsy and, with the window drapes tightly closed, tried to rest in our room. Later we retreated to the hotel shop to look at faux-ivory carvings and Hindu masks.

At dinner that night, only Anwar joined Helen and me at our table.

"Betsy's not feeling well," he said.

"I'm so sorry about Betsy's necklace," Helen said, looking to me for support. I looked appropriately sad, but it was damned hard to be sincere. Earlier, alone with our analyses, Helen and I agreed. Betsy had asked for trouble. We were not unsympathetic, but the necklace had been a stupid idea.

"These beggars are animals. Barely human," Anwar said. Helen tensed and was about to say something contrary but I touched her leg with my hand under the table.

After dinner Helen and I settled on the two-person sofa in our room. Helen shook her head. "I had a little trouble with the animal bit. These are desperate human beings."

Helen read out loud the details of our trip to the Taj Mahal. My eyelids were heavy and I fought to keep my head from nodding. A noise, like a scratching, was outside our room. Helen stopped. I jerked fully awake. Faint rapid raps came from our door, too timid for maids. I moved when Helen threw me a demanding glance. I opened the door cautiously. Betsy wore a white T-shirt and capri pants, her hair in disarray.

"Sit on the sofa," Helen said to Betsy. "I'm so sorry. That necklace was beautiful on you."

Tears rolled down Betsy's face again. "Oh, it's not the loss," Betsy sniffled. "I never really liked wearing it. It's that Anwar blames me!"

"You?"

"For not keeping up with the group. It wouldn't have happened if I had been careful."

"You weren't that far back," I said.

"He's crazy sometimes. He thinks I'm a silly woman too stupid to do anything right. You don't know how small I feel around him."

Helen shot me another of our private glances that Betsy could not see.

"You can find another necklace, " I said. "Helen could help when we get back."

"We can never replace the necklace of his dead mother. That's why he insisted I wear it all the time. To remind him."

Helen gave me a so-there nod. Anwar's fault, she was saying. I gave her an exasperated glance.

"Can I sleep here tonight?" Betsy whispered. "You could close the bedroom door for privacy."

"Of course you're welcome," Helen said.

"You don't want to be in your own bed?" I asked.

"I'm afraid," Betsy said. "Anwar is a stubborn man. His feelings get buried inside."

"I don't understand," Helen said.

"He hit me. He didn't mean to. It just came out." Betsy said. "The first time ever."

"Are you hurt?"

"It wasn't hard." But even though the light was low, I thought I saw a faint purple of a beginning bruise near her temple.

Helen helped Betsy settle, then came to bed. "Call out if you need me," Helen said. Helen quietly closed the bedroom door and we whispered for an hour about Betsy and Anwar. "It's as if he possesses her," Helen said angrily. "Like marriage is bondage."

"She's really kind," I said. "And she's not stupid."

"Not at all. She's the real jewel. If he only knew," Helen said before her eyes closed and her head snuggled onto my shoulder. "He had the chance to do her right," she whispered, "but he failed."

"I don't understand."

"To forgive her. At least not blame her. There's not a drop of evil in her."

I agreed.

The next morning Betsy looked exhausted but was cheery to a fault. She did not mention Anwar or the necklace. She refused to take a shower in our bathroom, and went back to their room determined to greet the room-service maids who brought morning tea.

"It's as if Anwar loved that necklace more than her," Helen said after Betsy left.

This was our free day before the Taj Mahal excursion. I had decided we would visit the museum of historical artifacts.

"You go," Helen said. "I'm going to ask Betsy to go shopping. She'll need me."

"I'll ask Anwar if he wants to go to the museum," I said. Anwar had plans to join another doctor on a tour to visit a hospital to claim the trip as a tax deduction. But on reflection, he decided to go with me. "I can go to the hospital earlier," he said.

At the museum, Anwar and I learned more of Asian culture in the endless halls of glass-enclosed objects—decaying authentication of past generations' existence. But I missed Helen. I liked sharing thoughts with her.

When we were walking down a hall between display rooms, I said to Anwar, "If you have photos of the necklace, I'm sure Helen has the connections to replicate it exactly."

"Jesus, John. It's the sentimental value. It was passed down in my family for generations."

"Betsy is strung out about the loss."

"I told her, John. Over and over. Stay close to me. She didn't listen."

"It might not have made any difference. She was only a few feet away from us."

"It was her responsibility. She failed. I can't forgive that."

We split up when we reached the end of the hall, and I did not see him until we met at the exit to find transportation back to the hotel.

Helen and I did not sleep well, but the next day we joined the tour for the Taj Mahal with Betsy and Anwar and most of our group. The road to Agra stretched through fields with dung, garbage dumps with human scavengers, and polluted rivers too thick to flow. Human adults and children stood roadside and stared at the passing traffic, an entire population seemingly abandoned by humanity. Then we saw the Taj Mahal, an ostentatious jewel glimmering in the refuse-packed, ravaged landscape.

We toured the Taj with the group. Anwar assertively maintained a distance from Betsy, who stayed close to Helen. Helen and I separated from the group upon leaving the Taj to sit on benches and discover the symmetrical elegance of the architecture. Light from reflecting pools threw shadows on Helen's face, and my gaze stayed fixed on her beauty, marred only by her painful thoughts of the ubiquitous poor.

"We have so much," she said. "And we never value what we have. The gods are angry."

"You think the theft was divine vengeance?" I asked with more incredulity than I wanted?

"The money that necklace would bring could feed a family of ten for years. We have responsibilities to our fellow humans," she said.

That seemed a little too much, but I got her point. "Wearing a necklace isn't a sin," I said to relieve her guilt.

"When it's worth thousands," she said, "who knows what's a sin?" Helen's faith held a creator with more than a touch of retribution, and she held complex beliefs in cause and effect. I slid closer to her on the bench and touched her hand. She cared so much it became a burden at times, but how could I comfort her with careless council?

We returned with the group to the bus. Fifteen to twenty beggars surged toward us. "I don't think I can take much more of this," I said. Helen elbowed me, pointing to a gaunt woman wrapped in a torn sari who held out a naked male child in her arms. The woman begged with unrecognizable words.

"What does that mean?" I said to Anwar.

"She just wants money," he said. "The kid is for sympathy."

The woman held up the child.

"It's dead!" Helen sobbed and clutched me as if she might slip into an abyss.

The corpse was skin and bone, head back, legs bent, and already in the rigor of death. "It's okay, Helen, get on the bus," I said over the clamor of our fellow travelers.

"They pass that body around for days," Anwar said authoritatively, as if that might ease our outrage.

Helen grabbed our touring bag that held our stuff and her wallet. She broke away from my protective grasp, ran toward the beggars. They froze, unsure. Then, seeing no danger, they moved around in a swarm.

Helen dug in the bag. From her wallet she took all her currency: Indian, American, and a few other foreign bills and coins. She was dropping money into any close hand. Beggars dissolved into frenzy. She placed a ten-dollar American bill on the chest of the dead child now on the ground. A hand from the crowd scooped it up before Helen stood up.

Helen ran out of money but she gave them tissues, candy bars, peanut butter and cheese crackers, anything that was in the bag. The crowd grew to more than fifty with mystical rapidity. Helen seemed not to care. When she finally turned her dazed eyes to me, I saw her confusion, her pain. I waded into the crowd to retrieve her. I worried for her health and safety.

"It's not enough," she said.

"It's a start," I said.

It took a few minutes for everyone on tour to calm down and find a seat on the bus, and we began the trip back. We found seats together four rows back from Betsy and Anwar. "They have nothing," Helen said, still gasping. Our fellow travelers said little and seemed divided in opinion about Helen, between admiration and suspicions of insanity.

The return was silent except for the drone of the bus's diesel engine, whining with braking and acceleration. Helen sat rigidly staring ahead. Before we reached our hotel, the guide announced the scheduled stop at one last gift shop. "Half an hour," he announced.

Helen was spent, her mood sour, unwilling to look at one more expensive souvenir. "I can't," she said. She was selfless with worry in a way I had never noticed before. She seemed about to cry. "I can't do it."

"I'll take a look," I said, wanting to buy a gift to surprise her. She stayed on the bus with a few of the other weary travelers.

Inside the shop I looked into glass jewelry cases and at rows of shelves of carved Hindu gods with strange clothing and in awkward positions. A sparkle of reflection from a dark necklace of polished jade, vibrant with the living colors of a new-growth leaf and the plume of an exotic bird, caught my eye. I flagged a saleswoman. The necklace wasn't expensive, and I paid cash. I refused to have it gift wrapped, liking the red velvet draw sack it came in, and put it in my pocket.

That night Helen dressed for a cultural show of music and drama with Betsy and mostly other women in the tour group. Anwar and I had decided on a leisurely dinner and early retirement.

"You run today?" I asked.

He nodded.

"Dangerous?"

"Who knows? Lots of evil-looking characters but most either too malnourished or close to death to be able to do you any harm."

"I bought a necklace yesterday for Helen." I reached in my pocket to show him. "I'm going to surprise her." I thought it might give him some ideas for Betsy.

"Jade?" he asked, as if weighing the differences between jade and diamond with disdain.

"Good value," I said and showed him the price.

"My mother's necklace had been in the family for three generations. My grandfather was a Syrian diplomat. He bought it in London. My mother could only wear it when she traveled with my father, but she was very proud."

"Betsy loved it. You could see it in her eyes," I said.

But Anwar's eyes turned opaque and then he looked away. I pocketed my necklace for Helen, dejected that Anwar had no interest and had turned sullen. He said little for the next few minutes and we returned to our rooms to read.

I was reading in bed with the nightstand light on when Helen returned in tears.

"Betsy's sick. I thought she'd die," she said. "We were in the theater. She had a terrible headache. When I touched her she was burning with fever. She vomited. She fainted as I was getting her to the bus."

"Where is she?"

"The hospital. I went with her. Anwar came. He went crazy. Accused the doctor of not using the right medicines. He told me to leave." Helen's eyes squeezed shut with the thought of Anwar's exclusion.

"What was wrong?"

"Infection, I think. They didn't know exactly."

I held her. "We've got to go. They'll need us." I dressed quickly.

The hospital elevator glided two floors up, the doors parting smoothly. The door to Betsy's room was open. "Be careful," Anwar said to an ambulance crew as they lifted Betsy's writhing body roughly onto a gurney. "Don't drop her," he said.

Anwar saw us. "Fucking blockheads," he said to us.

"What's happened?" I asked as he held an IV bottle in transfer.

"Meningitis maybe." He didn't look at me, collecting a syringe with a needle and empty vial and putting them in a bag that he tucked under the gurney mattress.

"Will she be okay?" Helen asked.

He glared at us, as if we didn't exist. "How could I know that, Helen?" Anwar said with disdain. "Look at her. Why don't you tell me?"

Helen gasped, unable to respond.

"What can we do?" I asked.

The attendants tucked sheets around Betsy. Anwar hung the bottle on the end of a metal support pole at the corner of the gurney. Betsy's open eyes showed no recognition that we were there and were now searching without pause.

"There's nothing to do, John," Anwar said. "This hospital isn't worth a shit. I've hired a private jet to get us to Tokyo. If I can keep her stabilized, I'm taking her home." Now his voice held fear and concern.

Anwar and Betsy were on their way out the door. At the elevator, Anwar turned as Helen and I caught up.

"Can we make any calls? Send anything?" I asked.

"Just enjoy your trip," he said.

"Please let us know how she is?" Helen pleaded.

"When do you think I'll have time to call you?" he said. "You have a good time."

"We'll be worried," Helen said.

"I can't help that," Anwar said. Helen winced. "She might never come back," he said. "Even if she lives, she'll never be the same."

Helen cried silently, hurt by Anwar's rebukes. Anwar had reached under the covers to hold Betsy's almost lifeless hand. Just before the elevator doors opened, he cried silently.

In the elevator, on the gurney, Betsy now lay still, her eyes closed, her head turned. The attendants positioned necessary equipment under the gurney. Betsy's skin was drained of blood to the shade of alabaster. She retched once, her arms and legs jerking then her body relaxed as she went unconscious again. The doors closed and they were gone.

Helen paced in our room.

"If she lives," Helen said to me about Betsy, "maybe Anwar will finally appreciate her wonderful qualities."

"He seemed to really care," I said. "I'd never seen that in him before."

"I hope so. But too late. I hope Betsy knows he cared."

"I think he loves her—in his own way."

"I hope he gets the chance to tell her."

Finally, I got her to sit on the sofa and she held me tightly.

My last image of Betsy surfaced; she'd never be the same. I didn't think she'd live. But I said nothing to Helen. Still, she read my thoughts.

"She's a goofy good person," Helen sobbed, "loyal, devoted, caring. God, I hope she makes it."

The next evening after dinner, a faxed message waited in our inbox at reception. Betsy died in a Tokyo hospital. I searched Anwar's handwritten note for meaning, but the words—starting with "Dear friends,"—were cold and distant.

Helen read the message sitting on a lobby bench as I stood beside her. She carried deep concern for Betsy's soul. A moment of fear pierced me; I never wanted Helen to ever doubt that I loved her. I reached in my pocket and placed my gift necklace around her neck. Fixed the clasp. With the back of my hand, I touched the damp skin on the side of her face, smoothed a wayward strand of hair. I'd never seen her more beautiful.

"Am I possessed?" she asked with a dubious smile.

"Never possessed," I said. "Valued forever."

"I'll sell the house," she said with a wistful smile.

"We'll live wherever you choose," I said. I bent over and kissed her lightly on the ear. "I love you," I whispered.

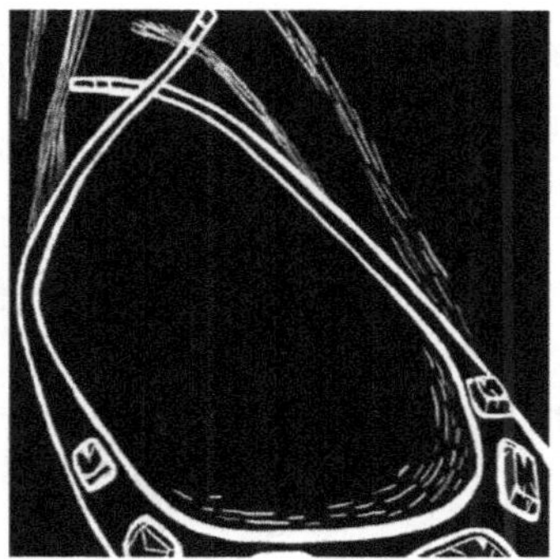

Nemesis

illustrations by David Riley

Nemesis

More than a year before his divorce, Fred Bean had a confrontational day at work and lost his job of twenty-two years. He was born in Clinton, Iowa, and attended the university in Ames, where he matriculated one year but due to low grades did not graduate. He worked as an audiovisual technician for the department of business administration at the university. For meetings, he made slides for projectors and charts for easels, maintained equipment, adjusted microphones, and fiddled with controls on tape recorders. He took photographs, too, of visitors, students, and faculty, for publications, yearbooks, brochures, portraits, and Christmas cards. He'd held his job through the tenure of three chairs of the department, and two governors of the state of Iowa.

On the day of his career's demise, he was the audiovisual support for the annual national conference for businesswomen, a tradition for the department and a pride of the U. The audience numbered more than three hundred. The slide projector was midway down the center aisle and projected the speakers' slides onto a giant pull-down screen at center stage. A podium stood at stage left.

Computer projection would soon be the established norm, but Fred still struggled with computer-based electronics and stubbornly held onto his area of expertise. In truth, he feared losing the considerable control slides gave him over faculty and guests' presentations. He fantasized about his leadership role over his intellectual and hierarchical superiors—a fantasy that gave him the confidence to direct, ignore, and demean professors, distinguished guests, and students.

Eleanor Sampson, a national leader for women's rights in the business community, mounted the stage, gripped the podium microphone, made extended introductory remarks (which Fred thought were boring and not well received), and called for her first slide.

"Push the button," Fred yelled out from his metal folding chair situated near the projector—loud enough to turn heads.

"I am," Dr. Sampson yelled back into the microphone, with considerable irritation.

Fred, tall and lanky, lumbered down the center aisle to the stage and mounted the podium, took the slide changer from the frowning Dr. Sampson, and punched the right button, illuminating on the screen the state seal of Iowa with the state bird, the Eastern goldfinch; the state rock, the geode; the state tree, the oak; the state flower, the wild rose; and the inspiring state motto, "We will prize and we will maintain our rights and our liberties." As Fred regained his seat, Dr. Sampson, after suitable rote praise for the state of Iowa, activated her next slide. The image of the backside of a prize bull with a glimpse of considerable genital volume filled the screen.

"These are not my slides," Dr. Sampson now screamed into the microphone. "I cannot proceed without my slides."

Fred cut the switch to the projector and ran to the back of the auditorium, where slide carousels were laid out on a table. Each carousel had a speaker's name in black magic marker written on a torn-out notebook page that protruded from an empty slide pocket. Fred found Dr. Sampson's slides right away, and began a sprint back to the projector. Tripping on the leg of the rear corner seat, he fell, sprawled out. The carousel with Dr. Sampson's slides propelled itself four rows ahead, hitting the metallic back of an auditorium seat. The loosely applied circular slide fastener flew off and all but three of the twenty-four slides fell to the concrete flooring.

The audience gasped with collective distress. Fred righted himself and ran to pick up the carousel, trampling many of the dispersed slides. On his knees he fumbled to reinsert the unnumbered slides in the tray, but had no idea of the order, and many were now bent and distorted. Three were too severely damaged to even position. He did the best he could and placed the carousel back on the projector.

"Try now," he called weakly to Dr. Sampson.

A slide image loomed in front of the participants with a smudge that with only a little imagination could be viewed as dirt from the tread of his shoe.

"It's not the right slide," Dr. Sampson called out.

"Try the next," Fred stuttered.

The next slide had wavy streaks and a linear tear.

"That's wrong," Dr. Sampson said. She pressed the remote again. A damaged slide jammed the projector. "I will not proceed."

"Just try," Fred pleaded. "Describe the slides as you remember them."

"Ridiculous," Dr. Sampson replied. She scanned the audience. "My sincere apologies to all of you who have traveled so far to receive so little. Thank you." She left to stage right behind the side curtain, rather than descending the steps and walking through the audience.

Twenty minutes later the chair of the department dismissed Fred and gave him three hours to clear out his few possessions from his office in the basement next to the boilers and massive heat-duct fans.

"You're making a mistake," Fred said to the chair before he left. I'm indispensable, he thought.

"You're a disaster," the chair said.

"I built this department," Fred said. "You would not be seated in that chair if it were not for me."

"I've dreamed for an opportunity to get rid of you," the chair said.

"You are pea-brained dope," Fred countered.

"Get out," the chair said.

Fred demanded early retirement, threatening to sue, and received sixty percent of his salary. A pittance of what I'm worth, he thought. He decided to wait until the right job offer came along, something with better pay and leadership potential. He watched television during the day and formed opinions about politics and sports that he shared with his wife, Veronica, who had worked as a bank teller at First National for more than twenty years and knew everyone in town. Fred's dismissal humiliated her. "Get a job," she said, irritated to have him perpetually at home.

"I think I'll start writing a syndicated column for the newspaper," Fred said, emboldened by his recently acquired comprehension—through his intent study of extremist TV news—of how seriously deficient America had become.

"You're lazy," Veronica said.

"Lazy people do not reach my levels of success," Fred replied.

Veronica left Fred a year later, on a Thursday in the third week of February; she vowed never to see him again. Fred's self-absorption with the perceived injustice of his dismissal had made him impossible to tolerate. She would face the rest of her life alone, and she felt, if not happy, at least a sense of calm assurance of her own worth, without Fred's acidic assaults on her ideas and beliefs.

"You're incompetent and arrogant. A crummy combination," she yelled at Fred. She sat on the two-seater sofa in the living room of their two-story clapboard house, with its deteriorating, flaking white paint and exposed wood discolored with age. She was thin and had a nervous tic that shut her left eye and made her right eye widen, exposing the white of the globe as if in unilateral fright. "You're a fucking idiot," she added. "Everything you touch turns to shit."

"Oh, my. Isn't that shocking?" Fred mocked.

"You're a jackass."

"Don't be your unreasonable self, Veronica. It only demeans you."

"A half-wit," she said.

"Now it's down to name calling, is it?" Fred said.

"It's not a name, asshole. I'm not addressing you. I'm telling you the reality about your pitiful self. What everyone knows. You are an incompetent, unemployed, self-absorbed nincompoop. You're the only human I know who takes pride in his failures. And I hate you."

In an instant Fred assessed the entire scene as some hormonally induced, paper-lantern feminine crisis not worthy of his attention. She'd come around. She always did.

But Veronica put her head in her hands and cried, sweat beading on her forehead. She hated her loveless life in this loveless house with this loveless man. She'd feel guilty to break the vows of marriage she sworn to in the name of God. She was honest and religious, and always responsible. But this was the end. She refused to negotiate, went to Montana to live with her sister, and never returned to see Fred again, even during the divorce proceedings.

Months passed. Fred hadn't thought of starting another career since

Veronica left, and although he continued to believe he had an army of friends, only one secretary from work came to visit, and it was only once to sit for coffee. She never returned. Fred began talking out loud to himself and, without Veronica to absorb the sound, his voice seemed to echo, cave-like, in the empty rooms of the house. With insidious intensity he began to crave human contact. So he started going to church. The First Presbyterian.

How the services dragged on and on; he felt the constant urge to make comments and disagree with the sermon sentiments. He soon stopped Sunday church but attended Bible studies instead on Tuesday nights, purely on an exploratory basis, and there he met Minnie Carver, whose husband had died mysteriously in a hotel room not his own on a gentleman's getaway to Las Vegas. Minnie inherited the fortune her husband had made from selling slightly used, "lovingly cared for" cars with innovative no-cash-down financing and aggressive repossessions when qualified buyers didn't pay. With no children, no in-laws living, and an estranged half-sister, Minnie wallowed in reserves that cried out for excessive luxury.

Fred stood close to Minnie near the table that held a coffee urn and plates of cookies and cold pizza slices.

"I was indeed sorry to hear about your husband's passing," Fred said, staring down at Minnie's plump being.

She looked up. "Did you know Harry?"

"Only by reputation," Fred said. A potbellied philanderer, he thought.

Minnie half-filled her cup with coffee and topped it off with three packages of creamer and two pours of sugar from a glass container with a pullout metal spout.

Fred stared at her wedding rings as she worked. The diamonds glittered value worth a year of his salary when he was at the U.

"I'm so sorry, but I don't think I know you," Minnie said. "Are you a church member?"

"I'm the Lenny Brice of the U," Fred said. "Fred Bean. I'm a professor," he lied, feeling the title justified with the time he had spent at that detestable institution.

"Oh my, that's so intellectual. Do you teach?"

"I can tell that you have an exceptionally insightful gift of perception." Fred smiled. "I was in business and marketing. More than twenty years."

"Do you have a business?"

"I consult," Fred said vaguely, avoiding any truth of his brief college time and subsequent audiovisual career.

"Harry was a good businessman. He started with nothing. He sold dustpans door to door when we first got married."

"How coincidental. I sold vacuum cleaners for my start in the summer when I was in school," Fred said, basking in his assurance of the superiority of vacuum cleaners over dustpans.

"Everyone liked my Harry," Minnie said.

"Do you have children?" Fred asked.

"I always wanted children," she said. She looked ready to cry.

"I'm sorry then that you don't have them. Wanting them and all."

"How does your wife feel?" Minnie asked.

He hesitated. "We're divorced. I don't think she ever thought about it much."

"That's strange. I would think all women think about children."

"She was a hawk among songbirds," he said. "A thorny weed among blooming pansies."

Minnie took a deliberate sip of her coffee. "That's so poetic. You must be lonely," she said. "I heard poets are always lonely."

"Not in the least," Fred responded instantly. "My horizons are unlimited. My career has yet to peak. And I have a Boston Whaler on the lake. I can say without exaggeration, I am envied for my skills as a fisherman."

"Fish?"

"Brim. Bass."

"I miss Harry," she whispered to herself after a moment of reflection.

Fred refilled his coffee cup and followed Minnie when she went to retake her seat. She said nothing as he sat next to her. The social secretary introduced the speaker, who owned a hardware store in Ames and had had intimate experiences with God through his skydiving hobby.

Fred felt he had not impressed Minnie. But he sensed her need for companionship and saw … well, frankly, opportunity. Believe in yourself! his mother had insisted throughout his life, until she passed. The echo of her words careened inside his head.

After seeing Minnie at church two more times, the attractive features of her round face settled in his memory. Her only wrinkles were smile lines near her eyes and the corners of her mouth. She is agreeable to almost everything, in such contrast to Veronica, who agreed about almost nothing our entire marriage, he thought. He took Minnie to a church social. She wore a colorful print dress with red and green stylized flowers on a white background. She had amazing dancing skills for her two hundred pounds, her lumpy legs moving with grace and agility. She had a jade necklace that swung to and fro as she dipped for the oyster, dug for the clam—worth a few thousand at least. He fondly thought she looked a little like the exquisite, brightly colored, porcelain teapot his mother had cherished throughout her adult life. How proud he was of Minnie's company, and he introduced her to former friends and faculty in his former department at the U.

Within the month, Minnie was cooking dinners for Fred three times a week either at her place or his. After another month, Fred spent all his waking time with Minnie. She was the soul mate he'd never discovered—guileless, soft-spoken, persistently striving to please. Soon Minnie depended on Fred to guide her through life's precarious widow decisions, a dependence so unwavering he felt the true value in his abilities he always known he had.

Fred enjoyed touching Minnie's round form—soft, pliant, malleable. One evening after dinner cleanup she came to sit next to him on the sofa. He surfed the web on his laptop, his feet up on the coffee table. Minnie adjusted his arm with both hands—carefully, so she wouldn't impede his surfing—and put her head on his shoulder.

He was reading about Plimlico, a pop star with a newly disclosed eating disorder.

"You like it here, don't you?" Minnie asked him.

He thought she meant in Iowa. "Of course," he said.

"I mean in this house. Here with me."

He was on to the girl kidnapped, held captive in a basement room, and raped daily for ten years by her abductor.

"Look," Fred said, holding the screen for Minnie to see the girl. A pretty face but with eyes of the living dead. Minnie shivered at the pain the photo induced.

"They ought to hang the guy," Fred said.

"That wouldn't be Christian," she said.

"Capital punishment is the only deterrent society has to prevent these horrible crimes."

"Thou shall not kill," Minnie whispered.

"Without a death penalty, America as we know it would sink into chaos. Murderers and rapists without fear of justice, attacking at will."

Minnie released his arm and moved slightly away. Fred continued surfing, "Look at this," he said pointing to a picture of a legless soldier competing with artificial limbs in a marathon.

Minnie's sobs startled Fred; she was no longer touching him, and for the first time he panicked at the thought that he might never feel her soft skin again. He sat motionless for more than a moment. Slowly he put down the laptop on the coffee table and shut the lid.

"It's wrong to kill," Minnie said. "It's against the will of the Lord. And your thinking the death penalty is good will make you a lesser person in God's eyes."

That's stupid, Fred wanted to say, but he held back, still not moving or looking at her. He knew not to correct her by an instinct he'd never experienced before. In the silence, his need to comfort shocked him. He'd never felt this way about anybody.

"You really think that?" he finally asked.

"No human should every take the life of another," she said, decisively.

He quashed his desire to argue. I love her, he thought. He reached over and put his arms around her, moving close so his huge skeletal form enveloped her smaller round self.

"I'm so sorry," she said. "I didn't mean to …"

"Shhh," he said. He kissed her closed, damp eyelids, then her slightly parted lips. Even with his new desire to please her, he carried pride in his restraint to set her straight about capital punishment.

She collapsed into his arms by turning on the sofa and bringing her legs up. "Come live here with me," she said. "I can't do without you." With her knees up, her dress slipped down, exposing her round thighs spattered with faint fuzzy-hair stubble.

Fred flushed at this freshly reaped and previously unexperienced intimacy. Wordless, through the tenderness of kisses, he let her know he would be hers forever.

Over a few months of concentrated effort, Fred convinced Minnie to start a new life together in Maine, where she purchased an ocean-view cottage near Black Point that Fred had picked out from Influential Real Estate magazine. He had been overwhelmed by her financial resources, and with his partial degree in business, he gladly offered his expertise in financial planning. Without a frown, Minnie bought him his dream of a Morgan 55 Fast Commuter; its maximum speed was thirty-five knots, with twenty-three tons' displacement. It slept six and was fitted for ocean trips. "A terrific investment for a great price," he told her. He bought yachting clothes in Boston and spent nights standing on the bridge looking out over the harbor. Although Minnie was often lonely without the familiar surroundings of Iowa and descended into extended blue moods, they existed in newfound comfort with each other. His only irritation was Minnie's occasional mention of husband Harold, but that stopped after Fred insisted she never say the name again. After all, he reasoned, did he ever say Veronica's name? Ever?

Seven months later Minnie and Fred married in a private ceremony and departed on an around-the-world trip, first class, on Pristine Cruise Lines. Minnie's estranged half-sister, Pearl, whose husband had done time after a fraud scandal in a gambling casino where he worked as a floor manager, flew from Louisiana to the East Coast to see them off. Gold digger, Fred thought, and he winced as Minnie embraced Pearl, clearly unaware that Pearl might be a pig sniffing for truffles.

Fred and Minnie honeymooned with Minnie confined to the cabin suite after she took a tumble climbing the vertical exterior ladder from the pool to the bridge, her flip-flops still wet and slippery. Her leg bone broke in two places and caused her so much pain Fred cancelled the Monaco leg of the honeymoon six weeks before the scheduled end to take his ailing Minnie back home to Maine for health care. While under treatment for the fracture—complicated by osteoporosis—Minnie ran a low-grade fever from infection and further examination revealed a cancerous breast mass.

Distraught, Fred denied the truth. He sought second opinions while doctors scheduled chemo and radiation to start as soon as Minnie could be accommodated. But the doctors irritated him—the greedy charlatans, most of them anyway, he thought. You couldn't tell the good from the bad.

When Minnie returned home between treatments, she turned sullen with her prognosis and took to watching videos of old movies alone—Laura and Singing in the Rain.

"What's wrong, honey?" Fred asked.

"Leave me alone, Fred. I want to be alone."

"It's not good for you."

"Stop telling me what's good for me."

Minnie's half-sister Pearl called from Louisiana for a confidential discussion with Fred. He resented Pearl's continued interest in Minnie's health and saw no sincerity in her curiosity. Was Pearl trying to solicit a change in Minnie's will without his knowledge?

"Why's Minnie so sullen?" Pearl asked.

"She's not better," Fred said. "I don't think the new treatments are working."

"It takes time. I've had friends …"

"We should see some improvement!" Fred said.

"I've checked with Oschner in New Orleans. They're the best available."

"All doctors are quacks. I'll find a better way." Fred seethed at Pearl's intrusion.

"I'll make arrangements. Don't do anything rash," Pearl said, with a newly forced sympathetic tone.

"Don't do anything. I'll get her the best," Fred said.

"Love you guys," Pearl said with cool distaste as she hung up.

Fred still saw no signs of progress in Minnie's condition. He was horrified. For days he surfed the Internet for cancer cures—testimonials, scientific articles, clinic recommendations, experimental treatments—andeventually came across an ancient remedy that used apricot pit reductions orally and subcutaneously: a remedy backed by tens of thousands of cures, the Internet ad said. Patients stayed at a clinic in Mexico for a minimum of a month where a controlled diet included

Peruvian spring waters ingested during ten hours daily of sun exposure followed by sleep on a firm mattress packed with pulverized nutshells. Daily group meditation gathered positive energy from all patients in cure at the moment. Invariably, patients felt better during their cure—no nausea, no hair loss, less debilitating fatigue.

"You've got to go," he told Minnie. "For me."

"But my doctors …"

"They're money grabbers, honey. Expensive treatments. And they give you a fifty-fifty chance. In Mexico almost everyone is a cure."

"Well, why don't they do it here?"

"This system is all about profit, Minnie. It's expensive treatments looking for patients. I've studied the business of health care. It's appalling." He paused. "Put your trust in God's natural way."

"But the insurance?"

"We can afford it. And it'll cost less in the long run. With the deductibles and limits, it's way cheaper to do it right and just pay for it. You'll be well in no time."

Minnie was not at all comfortable with anything that was happening to her and she prayed, asking Fred to kneel and join her. She knew her professor loved her, and he had checked this treatment out. He always seemed to know about everything.

But then she had moments of doubt. "Shouldn't we check with Dr. Cranfield, too?" she asked after meditation.

"He's nice, honey. But he'll always be skeptical of someone else's success. Believe me. You can listen to one of the patients on a toll-free line."

"Those are actors."

"No, they're not. They say so. 'I am a grateful patient, not an actor.'"

"Dr. Cranfield's been so good to me." Tears ran down her face.

"He can't promise a cure, can he?"

She put her head in her hands, her mind in confusion. Fred brought water with ice from the kitchen.

Finally she agreed, and within twenty-four hours, without beginning her radiation and taking only two sessions of her chemotherapy, they were on their way to Mexico.

The cure was beyond Fred's wildest dreams.

"Oh, it's so expensive," Minnie moaned.

"There is nothing expensive in regaining your health," Fred said as he maneuvered her wheelchair to their couples massage session.

"What's that smell?" Minnie asked as the door to spa was opened by a barely five-foot, overweight woman in a pale-pink uniform.

"It's the oils, honey," Fred said, "apricot, I think," although he had no real idea.

"You're so smart," Minnie cooed. They were pressed, pinched, and kneaded on side-by-side tables close enough to see each other.

"It hurts," Minnie said after an enthusiastic squeeze by the male masseuse on the back of her thigh.

"President Harry Truman said, 'No pain, no gain,'" Fred said.

"He never had a massage."

A month went by like a summer evening in a rocker on the back porch of a vacation cottage in Florida. Minnie complained less—it seemed to Fred—and he loved the ministrations of the spa staff. He arranged for a second month of therapy.

On the trip home, Minnie came down with flu symptoms and by the time they were home in Portland, she was coughing and sniveling. She had a fever of 102. Her doctor made a house call and sent her to the hospital. A complication! A patch of pneumonia.

"I told you, never touch the inside of those back-of-seat pockets in airplanes," Fred said.

"I'm so sorry, honey. I dropped my earring in there when I took it off to use the headset for the movie."

That's no excuse for carelessness, Fred thought, but offered no sympathy, even to the woman he loved.

Antibiotics reduced the fever, but the cancer was worse, the doctors said. They recommended immediate transfer to the oncologists, who advised internal treatment even though they were pessimistic about cures in the late stages and reluctant to pinpoint a prognosis. Fred and Minnie discussed it together, alone, with the consultation-room door closed.

"They don't know what they're doing," Fred said.

"I don't feel good," Minnie said.

"Temporary. You know how you recovered in Mexico."

Minnie did not respond for many minutes, her eyes closed. Fred watched. Then Minnie's eyes snapped open as if frightened by a bad dream. "Tell the doctors I want to start the treatments."

"Honey—"

"Do it, Fred!"

"It's not the way …" Fred began.

"And call a minister, I want to pray," Minnie interrupted.

"Not the one you went to before Mexico."

"Just call him, Fred. And you, too. Go out and find God. Ask him to save me."

There is no God, Fred thought. At least, no God that cares about folks like you and me. But he loved his Minnie. "Okay, Minnie. I'll get started right away."

Having disdained God his entire life, Fred now felt hopeless. He studied religions and reasoned that the Catholics were the closest of all religions and sects to God. They had statues and icons, and rituals that seemed to give them special incentives and favors. He'd try the Catholics.

He went to the nearest parish church. It had a bucolic New England setting and a cemetery spattered with Mainers going back two centuries. The priest was attentive and urged Fred to join the church. "I don't have time to join the church. This is urgent. I need to talk with God."

"You must be a believer."

"I am committed to Christ," he said. He did not know what commitment would feel like, but he felt piety just saying it. "Now teach me to pray."

The priest hesitated. Fred insisted. The priest started with "Hail Mary" and "The Lord's Prayer."

"I want to speak to God," Fred said.

"You will know when you can. Keep thinking of Him in your meditations."

"And what about the Virgin? Could she help?"

"I believe she is often sympathetic to those in stress."

"Should I try them both?"

The priest shrugged. "As you wish."

After weeks of prayer, Fred resented God's failure to connect with him. The key to opening a conversation was never clear to Fred, although he sought the priest's advice frequently and attended mass. He thought communion might be the way to reach God but was denied access to the sacraments by the priest. Fred intensified his prayer offerings.

Dear God. Let me know if this gets to you. My wife Minnie is dying of cancer. She's a sweet woman. The best. There is no reason for her to die. Save her! I know you can do it. You've done it for so many others. Do it now. For me, please. Your adoring servant, Fred Bean

God doesn't hear, or even listen, he thought. But he kept trying.

Minnie lived three months and twelve days from her start of therapy that had, in the last month, turned palliative. Before her weeks of unconsciousness, she had insisted on being buried in Iowa near her lifelong friends. Fred arrived days before Minnie's coffin. The weather was good enough for a graveside ceremony. More than a hundred mourners attended, each a thread in the carpet that had been Minnie's life.

Minnie's Iowa Presbyterian minister conducted the ceremony. A portly pompous asshole in black, Fred thought. What has he ever done for Minnie? The minister began: "We are gathered here, dear friends, in grief for our dearly departed. A woman of fortitude, exceptional kindness …"

Fred could stand no more. He stepped up from the front circle of friends and pushed the minister away from the head of the casket. The minster fell on his face, his arms outstretched to break the impact. He was helped to standing by those close by. Fred had taken the minister's place. He addressed the mourners; grief fueled anger in his words.

"You're all to blame. Minnie dies. Who cares? Minnie cried out to doctors who failed her." Callous slimeballs, he thought. "When she moved away from your idyllic little town, friends forgot her." Bloodsucking worms. "And God scorned her. Never heard her pleas after she dedicated her life to Him. You're all to blame. Don't wallow in self-righteousness. Weep for your souls. You killed the best woman in the world." His mouth was as dry as a river bottom in a summer drought. His heart burned with outrage, his soul was punctured with grief.

The stunned crowd stayed silent. "Have you no respect?" Fred cried out.

"You're insane," a voice yelled from the rear of the crowd. Two men, business associates of Minnie's former husband, grabbed Fred by the arms and, assisted by others, dragged him toward the iron gate of the graveyard fifty yards away from Minnie's casket. The minister recovered and began saying something to the crowd. "Forgive … "

You fraud, Fred thought.

Alone, walking away from where Minnie was being lowered into eternity, a leaden silence of lonely isolation enveloped Fred, and he wept uncontrollably.

The Bear

illustration by Peter Healy

The Bear

We left our two snowmobiles and crossed a frozen river that I knew wouldn't carry the vehicles, with my brother-in-law Errol weighing 340 stripped and riding his twelve-year-old stepson, Sean, my sister's kid by her first husband. I led the way, shouldering my Winchester 70, Sean with a 22-rifle, his legs spread wide trying to keep in my snowshoe tracks, and Errol with a Savage 110.

We checked traps. Two snares were empty. One of the spring loaders had a small hind leg in the clamp claws but something had ripped off the body.

"Coyote did it," Errol said.

"Bigger than that," I said.

We began to circle back to the rigs. Sean's tw22 discharged.

"I'm hit!" Errol moaned to scare the kid.

Sean started to cry. He didn't think good and had no schooling.

Errol slapped him on the back of the head. "Grow up," he said. "I was joking."

Sean stood. "Bear," he said, pointing to the edge of the clearing. The sun was low and the shadows long over the snow cover, and the trees in the forest seemed welded together.

"He's big," Errol said.

Sean fired a shot. The bear reared back on its haunches.

"He's government protected. You hurt him, the boogeyman put you in jail."

The bear had dropped to all fours and was walking toward us in a squiggly line.

"Let's move." Errol said and broke into a run. But Sean fell. I stopped. Earl reached his rig and took off. I got the kid standing.

"Don't run," I said. "But move fast." We only had a hundred feet to go when the bear hit full stride on all fours.

We mounted, and I got the rig moving, Sean straddling a gas can.

We caught up to Errol.

"You left the kid," I said.

Errol shrugged. "He's your blood kin, not mine."

A cloud cover rolled in and we had to camp early. We rigged a nine-foot-high platform on four sturdy pines for me and Errol to sleep. Within reaching distance, I strung a hammock high up for Sean.

The moon reflected pewter patches of light on the snow. We were unable to sleep. After midnight we heard limbs cracking. The bear was on us. Errol reached for his gun but his weight shifted and he tumbled to the ground, his gun trapped under him. The bear tore at him. Errol screamed, then gurgled a moan. Then nothing.

"He going to eat us?" Sean asked.

I could see the whites of the bear's eyes, his snout slashed with Errol's blood. He swatted at us with his claws and the platform rocked. I clutched a tree trunk and looked for a gun.

The bear turned from Errol and roared. The kid whimpered. I needed a distraction. I unsheathed my knife and cut the rope to the kid's hammock, thinking he'd be a momentary diversion. He fell. "Run," I yelled.

But the bear caught the kid in the air. The kid screamed but was silent by the time I shinnied down the farthest pine and ran for my rig.

I drove twenty miles and dismounted at the top of a ridge. First light painted me with warmth I knew was imagined. In minutes the sun broke the horizon, blood red with an orange halo, and the distant cloud underbellies turned purple. I'd never seen such beauty.

"Thank you, dear God," I yelled as the sun exploded into the sky. I was alive. I was special. "You the man," I yelled to the heavens. My echo faded. Behind me, a coyote howled in the landscape. Then I heard the cracks of a dead tree limbs … something big, something heavy.

Gatemouth Willie Brown on Guitar

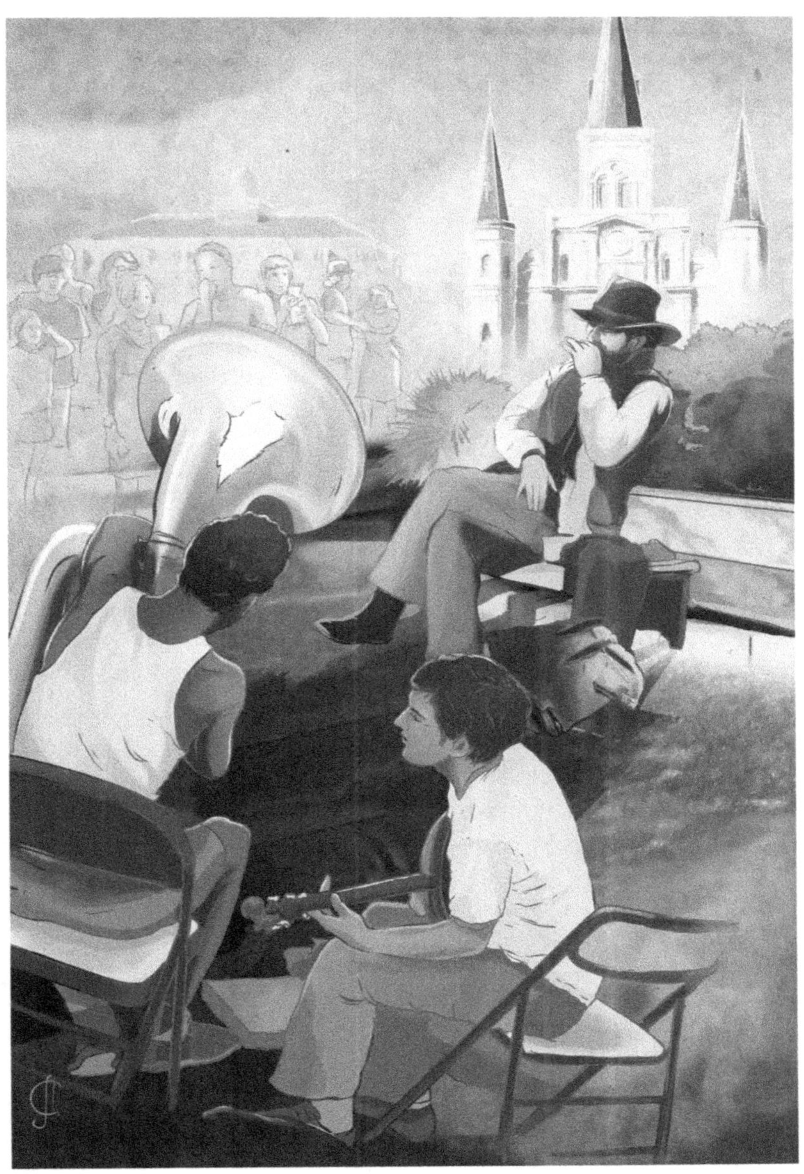

illustration by Anna Sokolova

Gatemouth Willie Brown on Guitar

New Orleans.

Gatemouth Willie Brown coughed into the microphone on a boom that poke out horizontal from a chrome stand with a black painted metal base. He ease out smoke he breathed in from the lit cigarette in his left hand, his right hand gripping his battered Gibson electric guitar by the neck to keep it steady. A small easy-grab speaker at his feet amplified a short, screechy, inhuman sound.

Willie sat alone on a city bench in Jackson Square, on the Cabildo side. The gray sky blocked the sun and trickled a light, misty drizzle, more relief from the heat than a pesky bother. Tourists were sparse. Willie quit playing until he might gather a crowd, make a few music lovers put a little something in his Cafe du Monde coffee can for playing something they thought was New Orleans special for them. But it wasn't much New Orleans jazz what he play, it mostly Delta, some folk tunes, a lotta just strumming what he felt like at the moment. White tourists weren't special to him and he didn't really care what they thought about his music, but he did care whether they might give up a little change, sometimes a one, and maybe even a five or a ten on a good day. But big bills like fifties was like charity, which he take but don't like, and he don't cotton to white folks treating him like charity. But this week he low on cash and he take anything. His wife bad sick and need a doctor.

Blacks rarely roamed around the French Quarter, except the punks; the punks don't have nothing to give that wasn't stolen. No, sir. Nothing for Willie from blacks. Even black got-the-stash never put out a dime for bro Willie. Willie's life tied to the whites when it come to money.

Piss him off, too … ever since he first learn about whites when he about six years.

But this white dude come into his life. Arrogant son of a bitch, too, like he is superior.

This white guy all bearded and bushy-headed come toward Willie out of Pirate's Alley wearing pants with holes in the knees and a plaid shirt with buttons missing —like he come out of a dumpster—and a wrinkled Panama hat with the brim down in the front so you only see his eyes when his head tilt back. He'd been in the alley for a while, leaning against the cathedral-wall fence, just staring. With all that hair on his face you never tell what he feeling, but he had these piercing eyes, cold like he don't be liking black folk. He don't say nothing, just hold up a harp, a Big River.

"Split the take?" the man say. He don't talk like a crazy or even a down and out. He got some schoolin'. Probably be chased by the law.

"Don't need no sidemen," Willie say.

The dude sit down on the bench, no more than a couple feet away.

"Said I don't need no help," Willie say strong.

"No law against me sitting here."

"You on my spot, my man. This my spot for a long time."

"Not on your 'spot.' I'm on my spot next to your spot. And I'll put my hat out in front of me to collect money if you don't want to work together."

"Look, my man. No playing. This is all I got."

"Don't bullshit me," the man said.

"I'm straight with you."

"You're on welfare. Probably got social security. Maybe a pension. Maybe got a woman turning tricks. Living in the Tremé and liking life just fine."

"I don't like you," Willie said. "I be's young, I whup you ass."

"Don't think so," the man said.

A tour group walk down from the corner of Chartres and St. Ann. Willie turn the knob to up on his amp and begin playing, kicking his money can out into the path. The white dude next to him put down his Panama a little farther out in front and a few feet from Willie's can, turning the hat-hole to the top to make a place for coins and bills. Then the dude put on shades he take out of his shirt pocket; they sit crooked on his face cause they bent and cracked, like he sit on them.

Fucking honkie, Willie think.

So Willie's got the thumb on the downbeat on the low string in open tuning, and he's using his first and second fingers to carry an upbeat for rhythm, changed in with a little melody and a slap on the heel of his hand that with the amplifier sound like a gunshot. He ignore the white guy best he can but he see'd him out the side of his eye sucking in on a note here and there on his harp, getting the pitch. He change his harp then, taking another—a Horner blues—out of his jacket pocket. Willie start playing quick. The tourists is getting close. The crowd slow to a stop, like blackbirds swooping in for a roost, all gathered round looking at Willie, so Willie ups his energy a little. But the tourist be looking through Willie after one chorus, eyes jerking around like they lost where Willie was. So Willie sing a song, and for a moment the group look back at him … but not for long. A few people in the back of the clump of music lovers already start leaving with nothing in Willie's can.

Shit, the white dude get ready to play; he going be blowing over Willie's guitar and the white dude start tapping his foot hard so his beat crush out Willie's faint slow pulse and the dude start wailing, sounding like a fast train's wheels clacking at a spur crossing. Then he put in fill, bending notes easy as a willow branch. Damn if them tourists don't freeze like they wax figures in that fake history museum on Bienville. They stare at the dude. The folks that start off going away from Willie turn back, come to take in the dude. Now the tourists give bad looks to Willie, rattled at Willie's sound chopping up the dude's, looking like to bust Willie's guitar and turn it to ash. Willie stop playing. The dude's not bad, goddamn it, Willie think. Willie ain't heard many like him. Piss Willie off, white man play a beat like that and make it sound joyful-sorrow like a colored parade band coming back from a funeral. The white guy stop, then pick up a slower tune, tourists throw green into his hat like he collecting for the church. So Willie ain't in tune with the guy's harp, but he don't like being outshined, and he start slapping out a rhythm on the strings with the heel of his hand, and in seconds he lay the guitar flat on his lap so he can use both hands to pound out a shuffle with that slow Mardi Gras Caribbean beat. He kick his can a little farther out.

Shit. The dude never look at him, never even give him no apperceived eye-glance. And the tourists still reaching out them arms and dropping paper into that dude's hat. In two tunes Willie's sure the guy make fifty bucks. Fifty! Some blimp of a woman drop two quarters into Willie's can. Clunk, clunk, on the bottom. No one else. Nothing more than two quarters for Gatemouth Willie Brown.

The dude play maybe a half hour making money. The crowd growing. Then he put the harp in his right side pocket, reach down to take the cash out of the hat and stuff it in his left pocket, then take off his shades, then put that hat on top his head and walk off. Goddamn if he don't never look back. Not one time he give a wave or call thanks to Willie for backing him on a couple tunes. And Willie wants to drown that white man in the Mississippi, push him into the wheel of a paddle steamer. Yes sir, that dude don't deserve no mercy.

Next day, Saturday, after the flow of drunk guys in town for the Saints game slow down a little, Willie slide around the corner onto Saint Ann where Tuba Fats playing with Henry Thibodeaux on clarinet and some sixteen-year-old kid outta the Ninth Ward blowing a valve trombone. Stupid kid. Tourists don't like no valve on a trombone. They like the slide, the growl, even when it sound like shit.

"You see that white dude on harp before?" Willie ask Fats. Fats shakes his head no.

"Well, he playing on my spot."

"He fucking know how to blow that motherfucker," Fats say.

"Well, he ain't s'pose to be taking my tips."

"He talk to you?"

"Maybe three words full."

The next day the white dude back midafternoon. The fucker sit the same place next to Willie's spot. Willie kick his can a little farther out. Today Willie is bent on turning some bread when the dude playing. He going to back the white dude no matter what, keep him from hogging. So Willie pull out his bottleneck slide and slip out a little melody on a top string where he don't need to change tuning, just slide on the string in the right place trying to make it sound good. The dude never look at him. Don't even glance to say he like or don't like.

After a half hour, the dude clear his hat and cram cash into his pants pocket Damn. Must be seventy-five dollars. But nothing for Willie. It be racist cash. White folk prying on the black. No count 'bout the dude's playing. The dude is a fuckoff racist. Hating negroes. Taking advantage. Playing to the white crowd like they his.

The dude come back three days in a row. After the first day Willie keep putting out his can. He get a little, but the tourists still giving most to the dude. And that ain't the usual for a white guy crowdin' in on a black man's gig in the Quarter. Them tourists pity the blacks playing the street; they always give Willie plenty when he alone. Them tourists give to black music men like they give money to five-year-old pickaninies dancing and singing for coins. It's about feeling sorry.

Dude still don't talk much. Willie's sister-in-law say the white man murder someone. Escape from prison. She think she seen it on television a year ago but don't know nothing else. But Willie don't see that in the dude. Maybe he steal, but Willie don't see him killing nobody. Not a guy blow harp like that.

So Willie decide to talk the guy. "Hey, mister, how about you splittin'?"

"You said you didn't split," The dude say.

"I changed my thinking," Willie say quick.

The dude shrug. But he don't share nothing with Willie, whose can still only get a few coins and rare green, nothing higher than a loner.

On a Friday, Willie take the wife to the doctor early in the morning. They got to ride the streetcar to City Park. "Come on, Hermonie," he say, but she sitting in her wheelchair, staring out like her skull gone empty. "We going to the doctor," he say. That git her and she begin wailing and moaning. She saying something like "Nah" but only Willie know she upset 'cause he been listening to her crazy talk for so long. She got "dimension" since Hurricane Camille and that be hard to take care of 'cause Willie ain't got money for the doctors she need.

But the next day Willie back on his spot. Well, the dude, he don't show. And then Willie get confused 'cause he like the dude's playing, even though the honky ain't generous with his take. And in truth, lately Willie been making more with his can when he's playing next to the dude collecting with his hat than when Willie making all the sound himself with his tin coffee can.

After lunch crowd, Willie take a smoke break with Tuba Fats. "That hairy white guy ask 'bout you," Fats say.

"What you tell him?"

"I tell him you take Hermonie to the doctor."

"None a his business."

"He ask. Like he want to know you do drugs, steal from the church collection plate. Stuff like that."

"What you say?"

"I tell him I don't know you real good. But I tell how sick Hermonie be."

"Don't be telling him no more. He not like a bro."

"But he blow good," Fats say.

Well, the dude come back. Willie decide he's going sing a song while the guy wipe out his mouth with a tissue over his finger before blowing his harp, like cleanin' shit out the stable before puttin' the horse in. Then the dude just sit back and listen to Willie, the dude's hat still on his head down over his eyes, his legs stretch out.

Willie finish his song and light up a joint he been saving.

"Sing that again," the dude say.

"I just done it."

"Just sing it again."

So Willie knock the glow off the tip of his joint and put the butt in his shirt pocket for later and start singing again. The dude's got the right Eb harp out of his pocket and he play along cross harp, not like he want to solo, but like he toting a cotton bale delicate down a wharf with some wharf rat, bale be heavy and need to be tipped just right to ease the weight between them, and the feet need to set just right on each step testing the wood planks for cracks and holes to keep from falling on yo' ass. It take feel can't be learned. The dude's got feel for the blues. And the tourists come like a swarm of roaches drop off banana-leaf trees in the Garden District. And they looking at Willie, who's trying his best to look like a lead. Willie kick his can a little further out while he singing and the dude back Willie for maybe only the second time in as many weeks. Damn if the greens don't start almost flowing over the side of Willie's can. And from that song on, for many days, Willie sing and make money, and the dude back him. And when the dude leave, he divvy up equal the bills from his hat and give 'em to Willie no matter how much them tourists put into Willie's coffee can.

Every few day the dude come for more than a month. He might teach Willie a song, or tell Willie how to play one of his standards better than he doing. Tuba Fats bitch at Willie making money cause it cut down on Fats's take, Fats being the big draw on the square for more than a decade, and Fats don't take to being second best.

A week later it still hot, and Willie hear the word pass and creep through the Quarter—through the artist vendors hanging them pictures on the fence around Jackson Square, pictures of the cathedral and the Cabildo, and them drawings of famous people that no one knows who they are 'cause they all look drawed the same, and the tarot card readers, the living statues, the tap-dancing seven-year-olds with beer can scraps sewed on the soles of their sneakers and scamming tourists for tips: "Hey, mister, I bet you a quarter I can tell you where you got them shoes." "Okay." "They on your feet!" "Jesus."

The whisper come through all them folks like a wind before one of them whiplash storms. "Undercover cops on Royal off Esplanade," go around the square in a flash, then up and down Decatur, out to the park across the streetcar track. Willie and the dude hear the word. They look around. Few minute later Willie spot 'em first. Then dude see 'em too. The cops got jeans and open-neck shirts with a collar. Not tourists. And blue sports jackets with a bulge near the heart; they carrying heat.

The dude take cash from his hat and put it in Willie's can. Then he reach into his jacket inside pocket and pull out an envelope he give Willie. Willie hurry to hide the envelope in the lining of his guitar case so the cops don't see nothing when they walk from the tarot-card reader, who smiling like she ain't never had dope in her possession since Christ be born in Bethlehem. In seconds, before the cops see him, the dude disappear in the shadows of Pirate's Alley. The dude hold back long enough to see if the cops leaving. He can't see them. He look to Willie. Willie give a thumb down and look down, shake his head when the two dickheads be asking him a question. They not locals. Feds, maybe. Willie see the dude shoulder his pack and with a wave of his hand he's gone when the cops move on to jaw on Tuba Fats. Fats just smile and say he don't know nothing.

Willie never see the dude again. In the envelope is enough money to add to Medicare and welfare and get Hermonie into a nursing home where she be watched 24-7 so she don't hurt herself. And Willie's coffee can still doing good filling up on its own now without the dude, like the dude left some good vibes in Willie's axe when he disappeared. Soon, Willie playing bring swarms of tourists that throw money his way, like he's a healing cave at that Lord's place in France he want to take Hermonie when she get better.

The Golden Flute

illustration by Peter Healy

The Golden Flute

Most of the lawn-party guests at the country club were Jean's friends from childhood, and we knew from her brittle greeting and fixed smile that she was upset. My God. Most of us would have been weeping behind a locked bathroom door. She welcomed us alone–although the invitations read "Hosts: Jean and Tim"—without a word about Tim's whereabouts. We knew the essential: Tim hadn't returned from a surgical meeting in south Florida. We were curious. Who was he with? What did Jean know? But she looked too fragile, and we'd been friends too long for me to ask.

Near the open-air bar my distant cousin, Patrick, talked to three women. He'd been one of Tim's surgical partners for twenty-five years. I waved at him and pointed to a giant oak where we might have some privacy.

"She's devastated," I said. "Where's Tim?"

His look scolded me.

"She's flying solo here to save her self-respect," I said.

"She's embarrassed," he said.

"She sees it as demeaning."

"No one knows what goes on behind closed doors," he said, as if he might smirk.

I cringed. "She doesn't deserve this, Patrick."

"I find that disingenuous, Carole."

Patrick would never believe the friendship Jean and I had over the years. He couldn't forget or forgive the brief, secret affair Tim and I had when Jean was pregnant with her second. What had happened was in the past. Let it go!

I grabbed his arm but he pulled it away.

He scowled.

"Tell me where Tim is," I said.

He laughed. "You want to go to him? Is that what this is about?"

"I care, Patrick. She needs me. I need to bring him back, make her feel whole again."

"You don't need to bullshit me, Carole. I'm not telling you where Tim is." He backed off a few inches, shaking his head.

"I only want to help Jean. I don't give a damn about Tim," I said. "We were only friends."

Patrick laughed again.

"It's true," I said.

"I don't know why Jean puts up with you." He stared into his glass and swirled straight scotch around a lone ice cube. "Stay out of it, Carole. As best friends go, you don't rank very high."

"Damn you," I said. Kin or not, he had no right to insinuate that my wanting to help Jean was devious. It was totally unwarranted.

He left, and after a minute or so of silence I walked back to the guests by myself.

Even after an hour, guests still avoided eye contact with Jean, uncomfortable with the unstated knowledge that was now in the collective consciousness. I asked friends what they knew about Tim's leaving and whereabouts, but they changed the subject, unwilling to voice opinions or facts. One of my ex-husbands, who was a partner with Tim and Patrick, kept his distance and never acknowledged me. Conspiratorial cohorts of feminine denigration, every one of them. I'd paid my dues for my past fling with Tim, and my long friendship with Jean proved it.

By the second hour, Jean knew her party was failing. She tried to whip up innovative activities. Finally, ahead of schedule, she herded people toward a croquet-patch of lawn for the traditional three-legged race.

I quickly paired up with Rubin, who, since his wife had died two years ago, had been a growing romantic interest that I'd pursued cautiously, since he had always been on the edge of social acceptance and, by Jean's standards, close to poverty. Rubin and I went to concerts and movies. He'd been over to dinner at my house a few times. He seemed interested;

we laughed a lot. I'd needed male companionship since my last divorce and Rubin had filled that need for the past few months.

Jean announced that race pairs could not be spouses or significant others; I was sure the rule for significant others was new. It was unclear why until she grabbed Rubin's hand and didn't look at me as she enticed him away. She'd not let her famous allure be tarnished by Tim's defection. Rubin was capable of adoration of anything feminine, and Jean used it as a display that her skills of enchantment with men had not faded.

Rubin seemed pleased. He had played classical music duets with Jean for years, and had intensely courted her before she was married and in college. I watched the race with the twenty or so other guests. The manager tied Rubin's massive right leg to Jean's thin, muscular left leg with a strip of torn-off, white sheet. Staff assisted other pairs to the start line.

"Three, two, one … go!" yelled the manager and seven leg-bound couples started off. Jean strained—excessively, I thought—pulling Rubin forward. Rubin's head bobbed as he tried to insert some common rhythm into their progress and strands from his full head of white hair fluttered in the air.

"Concentrate," we heard Jean urge him. But they were the last couple to stumble over an imaginary finish line between two folding chairs. He fell, gasping and wheezing, to the lush country club grass, dragging her down with him, trapping her under his heavy thigh. She looked in pain and moaned, unable to reach the bedsheet knot to free them. If Rubin sat up he'd crush her. The manager rushed over to untie them.

After prizes were awarded, Jean circulated and I went to Rubin, who was exhausted. He managed the local life insurance agency and didn't exercise.

"You gave it a good try," I said.

He laughed. "I was tied to the best. She's strong, that one."

We talked about his not-publicly-announced estranged daughter, who was off at college, the source of much grief. His smile faded when he talked of happier times, and it touched me.

By afternoon, the sun burned in a cloudless aquamarine sky and a gentle breeze rustled the oaks; it was a perfect setting for the outdoor buffet dining the club was famous for. After dessert, staff rolled an upright piano onto the lawn before a three-row-deep semicircle of folding chairs. Jean introduced Rubin–whom we all knew—as he stood with his flute behind the crowd. Rubin joined her to stand proudly next to the piano as she sat down and adjusted the stool.

With tender respect, he raised his nickel flute, a used instrument flecked with indentations and scratches. Jean was an accomplished pianist, and president of the symphony board, and she played well even though she tended to drown Rubin out in the fast passages. Still, his sound was so breezy soft, his melody so pure, that the performance pleased everyone, even me–I preferred Frank Sinatra. Jean jumped up to lead the applause of the awed guests; Rubin bowed. Then the crowd wandered away, back to party anxieties such as to how to leave without appearing ungrateful. I left early and drove home alone. Jean had invited Rubin to her place, not only to pronounce that her self-perceived charm was still intact, but also to irritate me. She was well aware of my interest in Rubin. I didn't deserve her disdain.

I was in bed asleep when Tim called from Florida–just after six the next morning.

"Carole?"

I couldn't speak.

"Carole?" he repeated.

I'm here, I almost said. Had he called for advice? Comfort?

"Yes?" I said.

"I thought I had the wrong number."

I turned over, pulling the covers up around me and cradling the phone close. "Are you back?" I asked.

"No. Of course not."

"We missed you at the party."

He laughed. "She should have cancelled."

"That's not Jean."

"Tell me about it."

Words failed me.

"Look," he said, "I call the house and she hangs up."

"She's angry, Tim."

"I talked to Gary. He said separation is legally tricky. That Jean won't let anything out of the house."

He paused. I waited. His voice pleased me more than I wanted to admit.

"I want my golf clubs," he said. "The signature Palmer ones. They're irreplaceable. Could you ship them for me?"

"You want me to … to steal them?" He should have taken them with him. All of this was more impulsive than I had thought. I tried to figure out a way to say no.

"Just take them to that UPS store on Genesee. They'll pack them. I'll mail you a check."

My chest ached. I wondered if his companion was close by.

"I didn't know who else to ask," he said.

"It's okay," I said, and I couldn't suppress a laugh. "Everyone thinks you've left for good. But she's acting rock solid in public, as if there's nothing wrong."

He made a derisive sound. "She's indestructible."

"She made moves on Rubin. At the party."

"I couldn't care less."

"I don't believe that."

"Hey. No need to dig in the crap, Carole."

I clutched the phone. "I'll think about it," I said.

"I want to play a reciprocal-club tournament here."

I let him wait. I could get his clubs somehow. I wanted him to call again.

"Okay," I said. "It'll take time."

"Send them express when you get them," he said.

With phone in hand, I went to my desk near the full-length bedroom window that opened onto a patio where I tended my roses. I wrote down his address: Sunset Retirement Villas. I listened, but I didn't hear any sounds from a bimbo in the background. And I was afraid to ask.

I went to Jean's house before eight the next morning, earlier than usual. We played tennis with our group at 9:30 on Mondays as regular as sunrise. She was already dressed in a crisp white outfit, with a new fluffy white sweatband on her right wrist, her hair shiny from a morning wash. She always looked good but on the court her timing generally wasn't, and she was obsessed with self-recriminations. Our group tolerated her mostly for the energy she put into every match.

"You're early," she said.

I poured coffee from her silver urn into one of her antique Limoges porcelain cups.

"I need to find Tim's golf clubs."

Her back was to me as she put dishes from the sink into the dishwasher.

"You talked to him?" she said.

I didn't answer.

"How could you, Carole?"

"He wants his clubs. I told him I'd ship them."

"The separation is official. Nothing leaves the house until we've settled."

"These are special to him. You'll never use them."

She'd taken out a toaster and was separating English muffins with a fork. "I want to do something nice for Rubin," she said. "His birthday is coming up soon. We've been friends for so long."

I looked away.

"He said they were in the garage near the Porsche," I said.

"I'm asking friends to buy him a new flute. Would you start the giving? A few hundred dollars?" Requesting a donation I couldn't socially turn down, it seemed as if Jean was deliberately flaunting her desirability over mine by feeding Rubin's puppy-dog but lifelong attraction to her.

I sipped my coffee, concentrating. "Is the garage open? I could put them in my car?"

She still had not looked at me. "That thing he plays looks like a drainpipe," she said.

"Is it open?" I asked.

"I want to give him something elegant. He plays so well, don't you think?"

I placed my cup firmly on the porcelain tiles of the center kitchen island. It clanked and chipped at the base. Jean made no move.

"I'll be back," I said. I went out to the three-car garage. The side door was locked. I peered through a window. I saw the clubs in a bag propped against the wall next to his car.

"Muffin's ready," Jean called from the kitchen door.

Two toasted English muffin halves were on a bread plate with preserves in a small, matching bowl. My cracked cup had been replaced by a Styrofoam to-go cup, which I preferred anyway.

"Would you like orange juice?" she said. "I may have a grapefruit half."

I declined. I took a bite of muffin.

"Maybe a few hundred dollars?" she asked. "To get things rolling?"

I paused. "This isn't right," I said.

"You're his friend," she said.

The air was tense. Rubin had probably spent the night consoling her.

"I'd like to present it to him at the annual symphony donors' dinner next month," she said. "He's playing Mozart with a string quartet for the entertainment. You'll be there, won't you?"

I always attended this dinner, as she well knew. I sat on the symphony committee for marketing and promotions. She had appointed me, a social coup for me a few years back.

"We'll be late," I said, removing my racquet from her kitchen closet, where I stored it between games.

She put the toaster into a cupboard and stacked the dishes in the sink.

"He's down there fucking some bimbo," she said without looking at me.

My thoughts scattered. "Do you know that?" I said. But from the start, I'd seriously wondered who his bimbo was.

"I called the office, Carole. The plump receptionist with the frizzy hair? She's gone too. 'On vacation,' they said."

"That doesn't mean she's with Tim," I said hesitantly. But I hoped it wasn't the receptionist. How tacky.

"Don't be naive. She's not his first," she said. Of course, I didn't look at her, afraid to know her true meaning.

The dishes clattered in the sink as she cleaned up.

"Can I count on you?" she asked. "For Rubin?"

"I'll think about it," I said.

Under stress, Jean defaulted to fundraising, her most accomplished skill. It was no surprise that raising money was her plan to snatch Rubin, and in two weeks she had more than fifteen hundred dollars. It was not enough but she would make up the difference. She could easily afford it, and she enjoyed appearing generous.

She asked me to go with her to New York to pick out the right instrument, and with my still-present-but-waning interest in Rubin, I didn't turn her down. Deep down I knew her leech-like attachment to him in her moment of stress would not last.

The woodwind shop was on Thirty-Ninth Street near Broadway.

"I've heard of Rubin," the proprietor said, standing behind the counter and opening a purple, velvet-lined case. "This golden flute is handmade by Patronelli. Drawn tone holes with an offset G."

It looked expensive. And ostentatious.

He handed the instrument to Jean, who looked it over.

"Shouldn't Rubin pick it out?" I asked.

"He can try it," Jean said. "If it isn't right, he can always exchange it."

"Of course," the proprietor said.

"It's so personal. Maybe he wants another color," I said, suddenly realizing there weren't many choices in colors of flutes.

"I doubt this would not please any player at any level," the proprietor said, obviously offended at my suggestion that flutes might be preferred by color.

"What's the rush? Let him come here," I argued to Jean. This gift had become a proclamation of her feminine attraction, intact and functioning.

"It's a surprise for the gala. He's to be honored, Carole." Jean said. "There needs to be a tangible object. It's the way to raise money. Trust me."

"Excuse us a moment," I said to the proprietor and tugged on her arm until she reluctantly joined me on street.

"You can't do this," I said. "He won't refuse your gift but he loves his old flute. You can see it when he plays."

"Nonsense."

I was getting red. "Give him a gift certificate or something."

"That won't do, Carole. This is part of the ceremony."

I was turning ugly red, I was sure.

"You're too nosy," Jean said, "Keep out of this." She returned inside, leaving me on the street, and spoke to the proprietor, who nodded. I left.

Two hours later I met her at her seamstress's shop, where I knew she had her usual periodic appointment. The flute glittered in its velvet case, which bore a gold-plated brass plate with Rubin's initials, resting on a chair for display while she discussed fabrics.

On the trip home, on the thruway, I was silent. Jean enjoyed her conquest. My irritation mounted. Rubin was not glamorous enough for her. And he was poor. He was a temporary salve. I wondered if he would ever show an interest in me again. We'd had some good times together.

The next morning, when I arrived for tennis, Jean announced that Consuela would take her place. She was no longer playing tennis.

The Armory was a relic from the early twentieth century, now listed on the historic register, and with vast open spaces once dedicated to military ceremonies. In the Grand Hall I was assigned to one of the sixty-plus linen-draped tables at the left rear, a spot roughly determined by the average yearly total of my donations to the symphony endowment as related to others, almost all more generous and capable donors than me. Rubin and four others sat around me amid hundreds of formally dressed "Friends of the Symphony." The main course had been cleared and the dessert bowls were being placed in front of us.

On a portable stage with a floor mic, Jean thanked us for our support. She glimmered in a sequined, off-the-shoulder, form-fitting dress. She spoke without notes, always confident in her achievements: philanthropist, revered socialite, and incredible fundraiser, with three perfectly mothered, difficult-to-manage children.

Jean had made the secrecy of Rubin's gift my responsibility, and when she gave me her signal, I weaved among the tables to hand her the golden flute, which had been hidden in a decorative sideboard.

I handed it up to her on the platform. She presented it to Rubin, who flushed when the weak applause quickly dissipated. I was pleased that the patrons had not been overwhelmed with enthusiasm by the presentation. It was exactly the opposite of what Jean had thought it would be. She had succumbed to honoring Rubin as a way to heal her own wound by hog-tying Rubin's ever-present devotion to her when she really didn't give a damn about him.

The guests were served dessert wine. I followed Rubin into the green room, where the quartet musicians and Jean waited. They congratulated Rubin. He handed the golden flute to me, then unpacked his old one.

"What are you doing?" Jean asked.

Rubin stared at her.

"You have to use it." She was breathless. "People gave. You can't disappoint."

"I've never played it," he said.

"Use your lip plate. You've played others like that."

The musicians and I fell silent; we waited for him to refuse. But after many seconds, he nodded. "Of course, you're right, Jean," he said.

She smiled. The cellist glanced at the first violinist, but no one spoke. Rubin played a few notes, fidgeted with a key. His brow creased.

The musicians left for the stage. Jean went to the table for dignitaries, and I returned to my seat.

The music started. Even with a tin ear, I knew the essential unity was lost. The usual gazes of admiration in the audience shifted to uncomfortable glances. A few serious listeners walked out. I feared others were about to do the same when it was finally over. The spotty applause ended quickly and the guests left.

I returned to the green room. Only the musicians and Jean were there. The snaps of latches on instrument cases were as sharp as rifle shots in the tense air.

"I'm sorry," Rubin finally said.

"Nothing you could do," said the first violinist.

The cellist touched Rubin's arm. "Not your fault," she said. "It wasn't our night."

Rubin left the room without looking at Jean or me, his lips in a tight line, carrying his coat and the golden flute. He'd forgotten his old flute and I picked up the case to give it to him when I next saw him.

Jean stiffened. "I'm not responsible," she said.

The musicians stared.

"No one is blaming you," I said.

"Of course not," said the violist.

Jean left flushed with anger at her failure to evoke the sympathy she thought she deserved. I sat alone, silently, as the musicians dressed to go out in the cold.

I went out into the walkway that surrounded the main gallery, ready to go home. At the end of the corridor Jean stood motionless with her back to me. The golden flute lay deeply scratched and beat into bizarre angles on top of a metal radiator.

"They'll never take that back," she said with strange dispassion.

"He was humiliated," I said.

"Ungrateful," she said.

"If you cared for him," I challenged, "you'd hurt for his pain."

She paused. "You're jealous."

"You led him on, Jean."

"He's always wanted me, Carole. He didn't love his Wanda. It wasn't just the cancer that took her."

Blaming Wanda's death on lack of affection was hard to believe.

Jean remained silent and rigid for a few seconds, and then she sighed. "I'm so sorry, Carole." She was crying. I didn't move. She wrapped her arms around me in a hug I didn't return. "I need a friend," she said. She let me go and stood back. "Don't turn on me after all these years."

I looked away. She was a stranger, and she did not follow as I left her alone with Rubin's destroyed golden flute.

The next day I made no attempt to talk to Jean and she didn't call, but I worried about Rubin. He would not take the performance failure lightly. I could use the excuse to return his flute, which was still in my car, and see him. Just after noon I went to his modest bungalow in a declining neighborhood. He did not answer my knock. I tried the knob. It was unlocked.

He was lying on his back, in boxer shorts and a V-neck white undershirt, on a sofa in the living area. He looked half-dead.

"Rubin!"

His eyes snapped open to look at me. He focused. "What are you doing here?"

"Are you all right?"

He closed his eyes without changing his position.

I scanned the area for signs of whisky or beer, but saw nothing.

"Should I call a doctor?" I asked.

He still didn't open his eyes. "You curious?" he said. "Or have you come to collect some compensation for that trashy gold flute?" His eyes were still closed but he was obviously thinking: Jean's little lackey.

"I came to see if you were okay." I put his flute case on the coffee table. He didn't acknowledge the favor I had done.

"Why would you not expect me to be 'okay,' Carole? What am I missing here?" He sat up with his elbows on his knees, his head in his hands. "I'm sick of Jean. I don't want to talk about it." He smiled, "But I'm not suicidal."

I flushed. He had no right to belittle my concern. "I don't care now," I said. "Die for all I care."

"I've got a hacksaw under the couch. I'll cut my head off. You'll always carry my death on your conscience." He laughed again.

"I came to help," I said.

"Help with what?"

"Yesterday. I didn't think it was right. What Jean did."

"Jean is Jean."

"She said you've always loved her."

He paused and I waited.

"Typical. Jean thinks everyone is in love with her," he said.

"She said you cared for her, not Wanda. That Wanda wasn't cared for."

"She died of cancer."

"It's obvious you've always loved Jean," I said, spiteful at his guarded responses. "Even at the party. And then at the concert, putting up with her demands."

He stood, reached for his pants on the floor, and began to dress.

"You don't deserve to know how I feel about her. What you did to her—with Tim." He spoke with restrained anger.

"That's unfair."

"Right. Unfair. Her best friend." He shook his head.

"Years ago," I blurted out.

"Carole. No one respects you."

"No one knew."

"Everyone knew." He slipped on a shirt with effort.

I was breathless. "Don't trash me with your own guilt, Rubin."

"Jean survived despite you. You and your fake guilt and meaningless regrets. You made her what she is, Carole. You made her feel worthless. She's been trying to feel good about herself for years."

"You're an asshole."

He sat now, fully dressed. He sighed. "I have loved Jean. And she's needed me. She doesn't love me, or anyone, but she did need me."

"You're sick," I said.

"Go," he said. He stretched his arms upward then lay down again, on his side, his face to the back of the sofa. "You'll never be a Jean for me."

"I don't want to be."

"Thank God you've cleared that up."

How pathetic. This bulk of an old man.

"You're insane," I said.

"Go." His voice muffled in the upholstery.

I stood, my heart pounding. He turned and belched with such force I could smell the sour acid.

"I won't feel guilty about your suicide," I said, pushing open the front door. "Don't comfort yourself with that."

"Slut."

"I am not a slut!"

When he didn't answer, I backed out onto the porch. I imagined him smiling behind the closed door. I drove around aimlessly for more than an hour before going home.

That night, I was alone in bed but awake with the lights off. My red digital alarm displayed 10:14 in a steady glow.

Tim called. "You got the clubs?" he asked without a greeting.

"Not yet," I said cautiously. "I saw them."

"They would make my isolation more tolerable, Carole. I'll give you the alarm code so you can get in when she's not there."

I hesitated. "What about your friend?"

A silence, short but significant. "Friend?"

"The receptionist, Tim. Jean knows. Everyone knows now. Please don't deny it."

"I didn't run off with a woman, Carole. I left Jean."

I weighed the possible truth for a few seconds. I had never known him to lie to me.

"Sorry," I said softly. "It's the rumor."

"Spread by her."

"I don't think it was only her."

"Those clubs would make my life happier," he said.

I stood up. Something in his voice moved me.

"Are you still there?" he asked.

I paused. Was this what I'd always wanted?

"I'll bring them myself," I said, almost as a question.

A silence pervaded.

"Is that okay? My coming down?" I finally asked.

"You're Jean's best friend," he said.

"Do you have room?" I asked.

He paused again for what seemed like an eon. "Of course," he said.

Dilemma

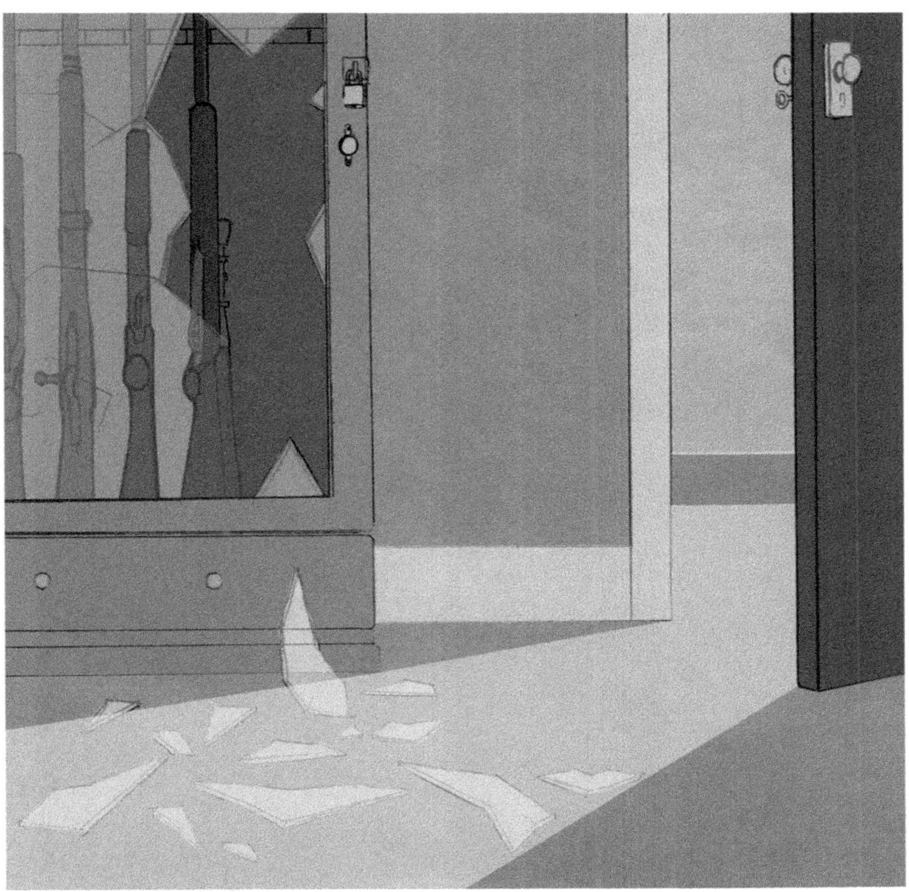

illustration by Peter Healy

Dilemma

His sweet, troubled son, alone in his room; he and his wife sitting downstairs, irritated by the bass thrust of the loud music emanating from the second floor. They knew he had taken drugs, they'd had taken him to a psychiatrist, had paid for the Prozac that insurance didn't cover. But they didn't know that he had taken a loaded shotgun from the locked cabinet—a gun whose stock he put on the floor and, while sitting on the bed, placed the barrels under his chin and pushed down on the trigger.

After the explosion they were quickly inside the room. The gun had fallen to the floor. His son had fallen to one side, his face gone: the lower jaw blown away, a few upper teeth haphazardly clinging to flesh. Nose and lower lids gone, deflated eyeballs wrinkled like a fallen soufflé. His son's legs, then his arms, went into spasms; he was alive but without air.

I'm a surgeon, he thought. Focus. Think like a doctor and not like a father.

His wife had crumpled to the floor, hands over her eyes, wailing.

He held his son's head with both hands; straightened the torso. "Get up," he said to his wife. "You've got to do this." She stood. "Slide the pillow under his shoulders."

He let the head fall back, hoping to find the glistening end of the trachea. There were no landmarks, only flesh and blood, and bits and slivers of bone.

"Bring me a razor, a toothbrush, towels." He needed tools … and he needed to keep her busy.

His wife was sobbing now. Her bare feet made a dampened sound on the wooden floor of the hall.

He supported the head, trying to find a position so his son might suck in air. He pressed the chest, to see if expulsion of air could show him the trachea. Should he let his son die? He saw no air. If he lived, he'd have no life. He'd be blind, unable to eat or taste, never smell, might be deaf. Never talk. He'd be trapped in the dark with no way to communicate.

She returned. He swabbed with the towel, told his wife to press, to stem the ooze. He used the smooth end of the toothbrush to separate tissue. "Bring me some dental floss," he said.

It would be a blessing for his son to die. But he refused to wish his son had been more thorough, not left him with these decisions. He saw the glint of the tracheal cartilage. He slipped the handle of the razor behind it. His son could live, at least to get to emergency. There was the swoosh of the intake of air. It would have to be now, before she came back. He still had time. How crucial for her. It could allow her grief to shrink to a memory with time.

His wife handed him the dental floss. Now he could firmly isolate the trachea, knot it gently, hold it in a position until a cannula could be inserted when help came. "Bring wet towels," he said.

He looked at the head of the son he had loved, a head he would never recognize again. His heart ached. He leaned forward and kissed the one ear that was left. Was there movement? He touched the ear again, running his finger along the pinna. Yes. The head seemed to move, as a bee is attracted to a flower. He could not let his son die.

He adjusted the trachea opening to ensure that air would pass.

At the sight of his son, the ambulance crew froze with an instant perception of what the future might bring.

The Amish Girl

illustration by Dilleen Marsh

illustration by Peter Healy

The Amish Girl

Peter Pisano failed computer science and Russian literature at the state university, credits he needed to graduate, so he took courses at Hunchett College in Ohio in the summer of '06. He lived on campus but often took his meals in the only restaurant—the Whispering Maiden—in the small town of Raspier, which hadtwo cross streets and no traffic lights and was juxtaposed with the campus entrance like the cap on an acorn. On many days, especially on weekends, the Amish set up a table or two on the grassy central island on the main street to display food and furniture they made for sale. Usually a buggy or a wagon was parked nearby, the horse tethered to a parking meter or a tree. One evening, Peter saw a lone girl sitting next to a table with baked goods. His meal had been more tasteless than usual, and he had eaten little. He wanted dessert.

The girl wore a gray, ankle-length wool dress and a white bonnet that covered her head, and that tied under her chin so that only wispy dark strands of hair showed above her brow. She looked down and away as he approached.

He studied the table. A hefty assortment: apple, cherry, and mincemeat pies; muffins; shoofly and whoopie pies; and cookies with raisins and oatmeal. On a small wooden display shelf were loaves of wheat bread, and tall, round chocolate cakes frosted in white.

"Do you sell a piece of the pie?" he asked. "Say, maybe the apple?"

She had still not looked at him and did not respond.

"Look," he said. "I live in the dorms and I have no place to keep a pie, so I can't buy the whole thing."

She looked at him briefly, her warm, intelligent eyes clear and bright as if carved from diamonds. Then she looked away.

He took that as a no. He went back to examining the baked goods for smaller items.

"This whoopie pie. It's small. What's the price?"

She stood gracefully, the folds of her dress straightening and covering her ankle boots with brass lace-holes and hard, steel-reinforced toes.

Her hand reached out, her fingers long, the nails short but trimmed with care. The perfection of the pale skin on the back of her hand was marred by a recent abrasion scab. She pointed to a slip of notebook paper with "whoopie pies, 29¢," on it.

More than reasonable. He picked up a small sample of whoopie pie, one of many that had been cut into half-inch irregular squares to entice customers. The chocolate taste was bitter and the crème inside, between the two exterior cake layers, was a lumpy, bland paste. He made a face in spite of himself. He decided to find a candy bar at the general store that was only a few hundred feet up the street.

"Another day," he said, walking away. The girl ran up to him, touching his arm and leading him back toward the table. He saw her eyes up close now. A deep, enigmatic ocean blue without the coldness he imagined in these people. With a stainless steel bread knife she cut a triangular piece of apple pie, placed it on a paper towel, and handed it to him, stepping back.

"How much do I owe you?" he asked.

She waved her hand dismissively as she shook her head no.

"I'd be happy to pay," he said.

She shook her head again.

"Thank you," he said. With his feet together, heels touching, he gave a little bow.

She smiled.

"Goodbye," he said.

She did not answer.

He ate the pie with his fingers as he strolled back to his room, down the wide, tree-lined gravel path that bisected the campus. His spirits lifted and he found he was uncharacteristically smiling at people he passed on the way.

In the morning on Saturday he tried to study in his room. The morning sun blazed well above the horizon. Lacy high clouds moved lazily across an azure sky. He decided to drive to Columbus, catch a movie, and hang out at a bar where he knew he could get served and meet people from the University—maybe a girl, although most of the women available in Columbus were bar girls who didn't excite him much anymore. He'd lately been eyeing college girls he might take home to his parents. He drove with the top down in his two-seat, deep-red, imported sports car.

The road snaked over hills and through fields and copses. For four miles he saw no traffic. He came over a small hill and braked, gearing down with loud swell-whines of the engine as he closed in on a farm wagon with two large wheels in the back and two smaller wheels in front. A man wearing a brimmed straw hat and coveralls, with a boy dressed the same next to him, loosely held the reins attached to a team of horses. In the back, with the tailgate down, two girls sat with their legs dangling. He pulled out to pass but visibility was blocked by another hill. With irritation, he tucked back in behind the wagon, staying in second gear and riding the clutch to meet its pace.

The older girl was the one who gave him the piece of pie. He eased the car a little closer. Her dress today, although still plain and frumpy, suggested a trim, feminine body. He could see glimpses of her ankles as she flexed and extended them in time to the wagon's movements. He imagined her in a short skirt, a dark blue maybe, showing her legs. Her blouse would be plain, glinting with the luster of opal buttons, and well tailored, the way he liked women's clothing, with a deep color, and open to show her neck and suggest the curve of her breasts.

The younger girl touched her arm and said something that made her laugh. Her head tilted slightly so that her lush hair obscured the lower part of her face. He pulled out to see if the way was clear. The man waved to him to pass. He downshifted to gain speed quickly. She waved before he lost sight of her.

No college girls were at the bar, but he met a high school grad who was working temporarily as a waitress until she could find a career in singing. She was watching a soap on the TV above the bar. She was fake blond, plump, and easy to giggle, an outgoing girl but with an air of desperation in her banter that wiped out the usual attraction he would have had for her. When she wanted to go to her place, he refused, saying he had to study. He felt bad; she looked ready to cry, but he could not imagine any enjoyment at being with her. He went to a movie before heading back to campus to sit in his room and stare blankly at his assignments.

On Monday he failed the midterm exam, missing the cutoff by two points. One question! He argued with his professor, who finally agreed to allow a make up. If he passed the make up, he could finish. If not, he was out. The repeat test would be Thursday afternoon in two weeks at five o'clock.

The next weekend he devoted to study at the library. The air was hot and stuffy, filled with musky smells of sandwich remnants and the lingering perspiration of students doomed to failure. From a third-floor window he saw the distinctive shape of an Amish buggy on the street in town. He tried, but it was impossible to read, and he decided to take a break.

She sat alone on a three-legged stool. She watched him approach, gazing not at his face, but at his chest, as if she'd discovered a shirt button that needed tidying up.

"Hello," he said.

She looked away.

"Do you speak?"

She turned on the stool so her back was partially toward him. He sidestepped so he was in front of her.

"Why not say something?" he said, looking down on her.

She turned back to her original position, her back almost completely to him. He did not move.

"This is ridiculous," he said. "You could say hello."

With her elbows on her knees, she put her head in her hands. "Please," she said. "Go away." Her voice trembled.

He laughed. "I knew you could talk." He sidestepped to be in front of her again.

"You selling much?"

She shook her head no.

"You must have sold something."

She shook her head no again, more emphatically.

"You look intelligent enough to speak," he said.

Her eyes turned hard with anger. “I’m not stupid,” she said.

“Did I say stupid? I said you looked intelligent.”

“I am not allowed to talk to strange boys.”

“I’m not strange. What if I was married? Could you talk to me then?”

“That would be permitted.”

“I’m married,” he laughed. “And I have nine kids.”

He expected she would smile, but she looked away, flustered and angry at his condescension.

“Was that your sister on the wagon?”

She did not move.

“You don’t look like sisters.”

“She is my cousin.” She still did not look at him.

“You take care of her?”

“She does not need to be taken care of. She is a competent young lady.”

She still would not meet his gaze. He sat down on the grass in front of her, his legs out, leaning back on his hands.

“Do you like sitting out here? No customers. No one to talk to.”

She turned her head to stare at him.

“It is not for me to like or dislike. It is what I do.”

“Do you go to school?”

She turned her head away again. “I am not to talk about myself.”

“You ashamed?” he challenged.

Her head snapped back to look at him. “I am not proud.”

He looked off into the distance as he spoke.

“I’m stuck in this know-nothing town with a roommate who won’t talk to me, students gone for the summer, teachers who think I’m too distracted or dumb to pass. And I have to pass to graduate or my father will kill me. He’s rich but never went to college. I’d be the only college graduate in my father’s family for three generations. That’s what he tells me.”

She leaned slightly toward him, studying his face intently. “Did your mother go to school?” she asked.

He nodded. “She works in a pharmacy. She’s pretty smart.”

She looked away again.

“You people don’t go to college, do you?” he asked.

"Of course."

"Women too?"

"Some."

"Do you want to go to college?"

She still looked away.

"You do, don't you?"

She was silent.

"I'll bet you read all the time."

She said nothing.

"You don't watch TV, do you? I heard that. You don't have electricity."

"We do have electricity."

"Do you have lights in your house?"

"We have power tools. My father has a milking machine."

She was sitting stiff and proper now, her hands on her knees that were together. Her chin was up, her head tilted back. He uncrossed his legs and looked away from her.

"Seems dull to me. Like you're missing a lot."

"That's not true," she said.

"How would you know? You never tried to live out in the world, have you?"

She looked down, staring straight at him now. "I don't like talking to you."

She stood and he watched her go to the wagon for boxes. She carefully wrapped each of the baked goods one by one, and packed them. When a box was full, she placed it in the wagon and returned to pack more.

He stood up before she was finished.

"How much is that pie?" he asked, pointing to an unwrapped pie.

"The mince?" she said. She picked up the pie. "One dollar and forty-two cents."

"I'll take it."

She covered it and placed it in a plastic bag. He handed her two dollars from his wallet.

She frowned. She handed back one dollar. "I don't have the change."

He held out the dollar to return it to her.

"It's worth two dollars," he said.

She shook her head.

"Take it," he insisted.

"It would not be right."

He shrugged and put the dollar back in his wallet.

"Nice talking to you," he said, and backed away.

Walking toward the dorm with his pie in its bag swinging at his side, he could still see the remarkable blue of her eyes, like gazing into a clear mountain stream that reflected a cloudless morning sky.

The next day he awoke before dawn and sat down to study. After two hours, he had read fewer than five pages. He looked through his pockets for change but found none. He shuffled through papers and books on his roommate's small table that served as a desk. He found scattered coins and carefully, with his finger, slid a quarter, a dime, a nickel, and two pennies off the edge of the desk into his open hand. He walked to town.

She looked exactly the same as before. Probably the same clothes, he imagined, washed and dried overnight as she slept alone, maybe on a pallet on the floor, or, at most, a cot for one in a room with her siblings and maybe her cousin.

There were three women today. He walked up to them.

"Hi," he said. The girl turned away.

"May I help you?" an older Amish woman said, walking toward him.

"I owe that girl money."

"I can take it."

"No. I came to pay my debt."

The woman hesitated and decided not to interfere. "Hannah!" she said.

The girl turned.

He reached into his left pocket and held out the five coins to her.

"I don't want that," she said.

"No," he said. "I owe you. Take it."

She hesitated and then held out her hand.

"Thanks," he said. Her hand touched his in the transfer of coins.

She shifted her weight awkwardly from her left leg to her right. She looked down at the dust at his feet.

"Did you like the pie?" she asked softly, still looking down.

He wasn't even sure where the pie was. Somewhere in the room, still in its bag, untouched. He hadn't even thought about it.

"Did you make it?"

She nodded.

He smiled. "It was great," he said.

But she turned abruptly to stare intensely at him—and coldly. She trusted only honesty, he saw that plainly.

"Could we talk?" he whispered so only she could hear.

She walked to the display table and said something to the woman who had first greeted him. The woman picked up a whoopie pie with a piece of waxed paper and approached him.

"Here," she said.

"I didn't buy a pie," he protested.

"No, it's yours."

He was about to say no again, but over the woman's shoulder he saw the girl staring at him impassively. It was her doing.

"Thank you, ma'am," he said, taking the pie, stepping aside, and then nodding to the girl.

He carried the whoopie pie palm up and walked back to campus. He took a bite. Heavenly. The pie was gone when he reached the dorm. He tried to study in his room but he wasn't in the mood and went to the gym to hang out.

Every day at his mealtime walk to and from the Whispering Maiden he looked to see if the Amish were there. Four times he saw someone, but never Hannah. No one in town knew the Amish well or where Hannah might live. Twice he drove the roads that wound through the local Amish countryside. Although he retraced the routes over and over, he saw no sign of Hannah, or very many women—only men with straw hats working the fields or tending cattle.

On a Wednesday he received a note from Mrs. Mangrove, who owned the Whispering Maiden. The envelope was sealed and had only "Peter" written in pencil on the front.

"Where did this come from?" he asked Mrs. Mangrove.

"Amish girl comes all secretive like and asks if I know you. She describes you, tall, dark hair, college student. I said of course I know you. Peter, I say. You eat here five or six times a week. Then she writes your name on the envelope and says soft, like a dove cooing, would I give this to you and you only. So here it is."

He put it in his pocket.

"Ain't you going to open it?" Mrs. Mangrove asked.

"It can wait," he said casually, going to his usual table in the corner where he could see the TV screen over the bar at the front of the room.

He waited until he was in his room. The note said she would be in Ambiance. The booth would be set up there on Saturday. Her father would leave in the morning about seven-thirty.

He slept poorly that night and the next day, Saturday, just after dawn, he drove to Ambiance to see Hannah. She was waiting, expecting, and smiled with pleasure at seeing him. She took his hand. He tried to hold her but she backed away. "Not here," she said. "I can't."

And with the impact of a meteor, his heart was aching as he had never known before.

"When can I see you? When can we talk? I want to talk," he said.

"It is so hard."

She sat down on the stool, glancing around for anyone near. But it was early. She patted a chair for him to sit. She wiped her eyes with her dress sleeve.

"I am to be married in the fall," she said.

His heart sank. Married! "So soon?" he blurted out.

"My dress is being made. Only a few know. It will be announced soon." She looked away. "He is a nice man. We will have a nice family together."

"But do you—love him?"

She turned her head back to him, glaring. "Don't ask that."

He searched for words. "But that's what marriage is about."

"What do you know about a woman's love?" she asked, irritated. "The scripture teaches us love is selfless, love is giving. Love is an open heart and mind."

He paused. "Love is how you feel," he finally said.

"Oh, how selfish that is." She looked down and held her face in her hands.

"I know how I feel," he said.

She cried again, her body trembling.

He saw a woman in Amish dress approaching from the north, walking down the path. "Someone's coming."

"Jumping Jehovah," she said, "It's mother." She wiped her face. "Go. Before she sees you."

"When will I see you?"

"Go," she said. "Hurry."

Two days passed. He didn't see her in town and waited for some sign. Finally, he received another note. She would be at a crafts fair in Cranton. Alone. Early in the morning. She prays he can come.

The tent with furniture displayed had its side flaps down and the front flap opened only partway. Her face showed her joy at seeing him. She had arranged two stools in the back. She reached out and took both his hands. He felt the warmth of her palms. They sat facing each other.

"I'm so glad you came," she said, withdrawing her hands. "I think about you."

He hesitated. He had never opened his heart to a woman. Never. He was afraid he would lose something, some essence of his strength, like Samson. Her stare spoke of her love for him, and he needed to speak. Finally he said, "You're very pretty." She held his hand. It was a touch of desire and caring, selfless, without guile. He wondered what it would be like to be with a girl like this—so unaware, so pure.

"I failed my test," he said. "I don't want to go home. My father will find out what's happened."

"Oh, no."

"There is no make up this time."

They sat silent for a minute. She looked at him. "Ely knows something is wrong in my heart."

He looked puzzled.

"He's my fiancé. I didn't say anything, of course. He said, 'You're avoiding me, Hannah. Have I done something to offend you?'"

They sat, silent; she did not look at him for more than a minute. "I'm going to take some time off before I have to go back home," he said. "I thought I'd go to the beach."

"Is it far?"

"Myrtle Beach. In South Carolina."

"It is good, Peter," she said. "To take time off. Do not feel guilt."

He hesitated, mulling over the other part of the idea. Finally, he said, "Would you come with me?"

She gasped and put her head in her hands. He could not tell what she was feeling. "I didn't mean anything—" he stammered.

She was crying.

"Really."

"Oh, no," she said, looking up. "Oh, no. You don't understand. I mean it is my prayer. Dear God. I feel so guilty thinking I must get away. To be me. In my heart I believe it is what God wants for me. But I cannot make Ely miserable. That's not God's will. And Mother is so against any of us doing anything away from home."

He was confused.

"It would be a sin," she said.

"It would be time off."

"What would we do? Where would we stay?"

"I'd get you a separate room. We'd be like friends on spring break. All the college kids do it."

"Mother wouldn't allow it."

"Couldn't you just leave her a note? Tell her you're all right and you'll be back soon."

"Father would be so angry."

"I could talk to him."

"Never. Never do that."

Her eyes moistened. She paused to contain her emotion. "You are never from my mind," she said softly. "I miss you when you are not in sight."

He was sure she spoke truth. He had never had any woman feel this way about him. It frightened him a little.

"I want to be with you," he said. "I can't just keep buying pies and seeing you at dawn."

She didn't respond for a moment, and again he was afraid he had offended her.

She reached out and took his hands again. "It would be so enjoyable. And it's not a sin. It's not, to go with friends to the beach."

He was pleased. He started to embrace her. She pushed him away. "No. Someone might come." She kissed him on the cheek.

They sat back down with an acceptable distance between them.

"Will you come?"

She sighed. "Oh, Peter. I'll try."

"When can we go?"

She didn't know. But she would find out and tell him.

The next day Mrs. Mangrove slipped him another note with a conspiratorial smile. "The Amish girl," she whispered unnecessarily. He opened the note as Mrs. Mangrove stared. Hannah would be ready at four in the morning on Friday. She gave a spot at a country crossroads where she could be concealed in bushes by an abandoned farm shed.

She was there when he arrived eight minutes early. She ran to the car and got in, carrying her belongings in a laundry sack. He ran the stop sign in his eagerness to get her away from her heritage. She was giddy, asking questions about Myrtle Beach, how long it would take. She didn't have anything to wear. She wanted to eat at a Burger King. She'd been to one before, she assured him. It was great.

"What did you tell your parents?" he asked.

"I wrote Mother a note. I told her I was going on a trip with a friend for a few days." She looked at him. "That was okay, wasn't it? I mean I didn't know how long we'd be gone or when you had to be back home."

"Fine," he said. "I can stay as long as you want. I don't want to go home yet."

She was silent for some time. "I'm so lucky. That you've come into my life."

He smiled at her. She'd taken off her hairnet and her hair cascaded, freshly washed, around the sides of her round face. Her full lips were a vibrant, deep red. Her eyes glittered with expectation.

"You're very pretty," he said.

She blushed, her cheeks and ears the shade of a ripe apple.

"I want to buy you some new clothes," he said.

"A dress?"

"If that's what you want. Two or three if you find what you like."

She glowed in the reflection of the early morning sun. He was fascinated by her.

Peter made it to I-40 and in a few hours found a shopping mall near Raleigh. She picked out frilly, little-girl dresses, nothing above the knee or open at the neck. But he smiled at her joy.

In twelve hours they were in Myrtle Beach. He found separate rooms on different levels at a motel on the beach. She ate a hamburger and a milkshake at Burger King. Then, in bare feet, they walked the beach. She let him hold her hand, so delicate, yet substantive and strong. After their stroll, he took her to her room and knelt with her by her bedside when she prayed for her family and for him. He wanted to kiss her, but he decided it was not the right time.

The next morning she was up long before he arrived at her door. She was sewing. She had rearranged the room, storing the lamps, the coffee maker, and the TV in the closet. At breakfast in the motel lobby, she told him of discovering how the shower worked, and how she usually bathed in a round copper tub with heated well water.

He bought her a bathing suit that she chose: loose fitting, one piece. When she modeled it for him, she felt comfortable only with a towel wrapped around her. But he still could detect small breasts, and a firm, cute butt. To him she was unique and beautiful. Now he held her hand and wanted to do so much more, to hold her in his arms, stroke her, sweep back the hair from her face and look into her eyes, but she seemed oblivious to the extent of his passion. She loved him, but she did not know his need to possess her, to culminate the expression of love he wanted to deliver to her.

The next day they went to movies, and the local formal gardens the following day. Then the amusement park. She was afraid of the roller coaster but did bumper cars—keeping her eyes shut—and gripped his arm with both hands. She liked the water rides. He won a teddy bear at a shooting gallery; it was only six inches tall, and she smiled and held it to her heart when he gave it to her. But at the end of each day she retreated alone into her room before dark to read her Bible. Once, after sunset, when he hesitated outside her closed door, he heard her quietly singing familiar hymns in a clear, pure voice. He wished she wanted to be together, and went to the beach to sit alone.

With her first—and also the last—time swimming, she was not comfortable in her bathing suit; "someone will see" she said, and she wore his blue sweatshirt with the long sleeves the entire time, in and out of the water. So they walked the beach the next few days fully clothed and sat in the sand side by side and talked.

She worried about Ely and what he was going through; she hoped her parents would forgive her; she loved her cousin, the one on the wagon, and she wondered if her cousin's feelings about her would change. He began to feel her sadness at being away, even though she gushed her gratitude for his bringing her many times a day. What captured his heart even more was her seeming inability to have an evil thought. She freely talked of her frustrations and dislikes, but she did not hate, or seek revenge, or feel jealousy. And when she told him earnestly about what she felt, the wind on the beach swirling her hair around her face, her eyes intently holding his, he wanted them never to part.

When he went to see her to start the fifth day she was crying. She missed her family. She wanted to go back.

Her distress pained him. "I'll pack," he said. "We can leave tomorrow before eight." They'd be home after dark but before midnight.

She nodded but did not say anything as he closed the door to her room.

As they traveled back to her home, he began to broach the future. Could he continue to see her? he asked. Of course, she said, but she could not say how.

When they were on I-77, he put the top up on the car at a rest stop so she could hear him speak while driving. For the next hundred miles he talked, she listened, her eyes moist, her breathing faster than normal. He told her she was the most beautiful human being he had ever known. That she was beautiful outside, but even more beautiful inside. That he was going back to learn his father's used car business, and he knew they were ready for each other at this moment in their lives. He wanted to be together. He wanted to spend his life with her. Together they could be more than they would ever be apart. He hoped she wanted the same. To be together.

He knew his sincerity, his inability to look at her more than a few times while he poured out his inner truths, had affected her. He was the man who could make her happy. She would learn no man could desire her with so much love. And surely she'd never seen such love among her family and friends. Ely probably had a genuine interest in her in a paternal way, but different—distracted, even. He knew his time with her had made her feel alive and special. His heart began to ache again with the need for her. He wished they were back at the beach, and they could lie on the bed full-length and she could lose herself in the touch of him.

She undid her seat belt so she could reach him over the gearshift console and she kissed him on the cheek close to his lips.

He looked for a place to pull off the interstate. He needed to feel her next to him.

She settled back down in the seat and fastened her seat belt again. "I have to get back. I've got to work things out," she said, undoubtedly sensing his want to stop, and fearing her loss of control for something she did not really understand.

"I'm afraid I'll never see you again!"

"You will," she said.

"I don't mean at the baked-goods stand."

"I have to plan. I have to talk to Mother. She's the only one who might convince Father. But I will work it out, Peter. I will."

He heard the determination of an adult in her voice for the first time. But his aching need for her was suddenly coated in a deep sadness.

"Can I talk to them?" he asked.

"Maybe later," she said. "I'll need to talk to them first. It will take time for them to understand."

"How much time?"

"I'm not sure."

Two hours later he let her out about a half-mile from her house. She did not want anyone to see him or the car. She wanted to tell them about her trip and her friend, and then tell them about her love.

He agreed because he felt her need for him was starting to move closer to his infinite need for her. And he loved her all the more; he knew she had changed for him. He knew, before he had come into her life, she would never have withheld the stark truth from her family. Now she was scheming to change them. Risking the honest comfort in her life.

He got out of the car and kissed her. She was crying.

"When can I see you?" he asked. "Tomorrow?"

"Come the day after tomorrow. Two o'clock. After midday meal. Father will be in the fields. I'll have my chores done. I want you to meet my mother first. She'll understand."

He spent most of the next day in the gym. Exercise lessened the pain of missing her. But in spite of complete exhaustion, he could not sleep well that night.

At two o'clock the next day, he stopped his car in front of the farm just to the side of the unpaved path that led from the road to the house. Near the barn, a man worked on a horse-drawn iron tilling machine. Cattle grazed in a pasture to the right, and on the left mature corn swayed in the brisk breeze. He waited, unsure what to do, hoping Hannah would see him, come to him. But there was no activity. He got out of the car, straightened his tie, and buttoned the second button on his dark-blue sports jacket.

He knocked on the solid wood door and waited. On the repeat knock the door opened. A man in coveralls stared at him without speaking.

"Is Hannah here?" Peter stammered.

The man glared for a few seconds.

"She told me to come," Peter offered.

The door slammed.

He knew she would be here. He hadn't misjudged her caring for him. He waited a few more seconds and knocked again.

The door opened quickly. Only a few inches. A small woman in a gray dress and a white bonnet looked up at him.

"I came to see Hannah," he said.

"That is not possible."

"She said to meet her."

"She is no longer living here."

Words failed him for a few seconds.

"I must see her."

"She is on her way to live with my husband's cousin."

"Where can I find her?"

"You can't. She is far away."

A new tall man with broad shoulders moved to stand behind the woman and looked down on Peter.

"Are you Ely?" Peter asked.

"It is of no consequence to you who I am."

"Go," the woman said. "You are not wanted." The door closed.

He went to the car and waited, sure that Hannah was close. The two windows at the front of the house had the blinds drawn. He watched, but no one looked out. By late afternoon two men walked toward the barn, looking over their shoulders at him for a few seconds, but without stopping.

He got out of the car, took off his coat and tie, and walked to the barn. They were feeding cattle lined up for milking. They did not acknowledge his presence.

"Where is Hannah?"

They continued working.

"You know where she is. I want to see her."

"She will not see you," the older man said.

"Let her tell me that. I want to know that is what she wants."

The older man dropped his pitchfork to come to him. The man was taller than Peter and when he stopped, they were almost face to face and only a few inches separated them; Peter stepped back.

"Hannah has sinned," the man said. "Against God and her family."

"She did not sin," Peter said loudly.

"God bless you, young man. For your caring. But she is gone."

"Tell me."

The younger man Peter was sure was Ely walked to stand beside the older man. "You will never find her," he said, his tone angry and bitter.

"Go," the older man said.

Over the next few months, Peter asked for news of Hannah in many Amish communities. People listened but either did not know or would not say. In the fall, one old woman, vending quilts near the Pennsylvania town of Cadmium, said, "You mean that Wisconsin girl?"

"Could it be Ohio?"

"You're right. It probably was Ohio, come to think of it. "That girl was sent to Belize. There was a heap of trouble."

Peter described Hannah. About five feet five. Unique close-set eyes the color of an early morning sky that turned deep-sea dark when frustrated. A quick, ready smile, a musical laugh. Auburn hair. A narrow waist and long, straight, shapely legs, thin like an adolescent girl younger than her seventeen years. And beautiful hands that would, when she got excited and the words tumbled out, spring and circle in the air like swallows in flight. "Is that the one?"

The woman shook her head. "Wouldn't know, really. Saw that little girl only once when she was a baby, and then only from afar."

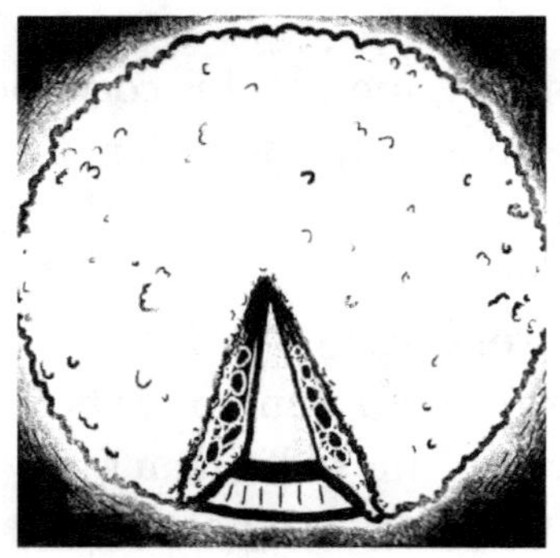

Dr. Greiner's Day in Court

illustration by Peter Healy

Dr. Greiner's Day in Court

My Auntie Caroline drove my dead mother's plum-red van on the way to the courthouse. Aaron, my older brother by two years but not quite as tall as me, sat unstrapped on the passenger side in what my mother used to call the death seat; Patsy, my seven-year-old younger sister, and I were in the back. We were dressed up to go to Dad's arraignment, but no one was exactly clear on what an arraignment was, except maybe Auntie.

The van was soooo warm; Auntie had set the temperature knob in the red. We didn't know about our dad, and I was afraid to talk about him—or anything—until I started sweating.

"It's hot back here, Auntie," I said.

"Shut your face," Aaron snapped. I wished the death seat would do its job.

"I don't want half-moons under my armpits," I said. It was a silk blouse my mother gave me.

"That's not from heat," Aaron said.

"What is it then?"

"From being so friggin' screwed up," Aaron said. Without Auntie around, he would have used the F-word.

Auntie was my dead mother's younger sister, and she was taking care of us this month. This was her second day. The family members drew straws to assign responsibility for us. No one was eager to take on three orphans.

Patsy and I missed Mom, but having Auntie in the house suited Aaron just fine. He was crazy for her. He followed her around like a puppy dog and his eyes searched up and down her body as if her clothes had dropped off.

Before the arrest Auntie and Dad had jogged together and when they returned, she would shower and dress in the guest room and Aaron would hang around outside—as if he were there by accident—for a glimpse, I knew, of her nude through a partially open door. After Auntie caught on and shut the door I saw Aaron on his knees looking through the keyhole. He said to shut up or he'd kill me.

Aaron talked back to Auntie now, but he still liked her. He was just messed up because she acted like a parent. He would have liked to screw her. Believe me, it would have been his first time, although he said he did girls all the time. No way, Jose.

"I'll turn down the heat, Sandy," Auntie said. "It's hard to tell how hot it is in the back from up here." We had at least an hour before we got to the courthouse.

My sister, who saw Auntie's adjustment with the heat knobs as a victory for us in the back, stuck out her tongue at the back of my brother's head. She was young enough to still do that. I would have given him the bird but Auntie had a clear view of me in the rearview mirror.

I hated my brother. There was talk of him going away to school again. I prayed that someplace would accept him. But none did. I knew him for the devil he was and every school discovered it sooner or later. He'd been expelled twice from preppy schools and now had to go to public school. Aaron hated public school. He hated me, too.

Aaron was furious that Auntie made him go to court. Aaron shouted and told her to mind her own goddamn business. But Auntie was like Mother was, steely willed, and she stared Aaron down and told him to get dressed, that our father needed us and she was not going to be a part of his son not being there. Aaron said it was the last time. She didn't answer but there was a firestorm in her blue eyes that were usually glacier cold.

Next to me, Patsy leaned forward, straining against the seat belt to be heard. "Do you think Daddy did it?" Patsy piped up with innocence, but there was nothing innocent about Patsy. She could be twice her age if you measured in craftiness. Aaron and I were dead silent. I wondered what Auntie Caroline thought about Dad. They were always best friends.

Did she blame him for Mom's murder? Everyone on the TV news acted as if he was guilty.

Auntie Caroline waited. She made an extra fuss over turning left against traffic but I could tell she was finding her words. "Of course your father is innocent. How could you believe anything else?"

That's exactly what the papers said about us. We had to believe. I saved the stories in an oversize envelope. Some had pictures of us, old and new, with lines underneath like "Children of the deceased" or "Family of local doctor charged with wife's murder." The posed studio picture of Mom was taken before we were born. I don't think she looked pretty even then—just more determined and intense with a round face, cocker spaniel eyes, and light reddish hair. I would look like her. Not like gorgeous Auntie Caroline.

"Has it been hard at school?" Auntie asked, to all of us and none of us.

"No," said Aaron. Aaron's friends were geeky, pimple-assed weirdos. They probably thought it was cool to have a dad arrested for the murder of his wife.

"What about you, Sandy?"

"Oh, they've been just great," I said. The kids my age shunned me, as if I had the clap or AIDS. When I went back to school for the first time a week after Dad was arrested, girls who were once my best friends suddenly wore frumpy frowns and ran into the restroom to avoid me. Groups of kids I used to hang out with would split up like exploding stars when I approached. I said screw it. It wasn't my fault. My dad isn't guilty. I don't need you fartheads anyway.

"They asked me what it was like to be famous," said Patsy.

"What did you say?" asked Auntie.

"I dunno."

Patsy was acting like a four-year-old to make Auntie think she didn't have a purpose. But Patsy wanted to know what Auntie thought. Auntie merged the van into the fast lane.

Mom called Patsy a mistake. I was never sure whose mistake Patsy was—Mother's, Father's, or God's. Maybe that's why Mom was always lecturing me about safe sex. I haven't done it but I think Mom thought

I did. She called me a slut once and said nice girls didn't pierce their navels. I had wanted to but she wouldn't let me.

"Who killed Momma?" Patsy said.

"Someone in the park," Auntie said. We rode in silence.

"Why do they think Dad did it?" Patsy finally asked.

Auntie didn't answer, so Aaron said, "Don't be stupid, Patsy. They don't know Dad like we do. He's too smart to be guilty. If he were going to hammer Mom to death he wouldn't stab her with a knife, too. That's psycho stuff."

Patsy said, "Eeeyouuugh."

Auntie said, "Aaron!"

I didn't like Aaron's talk, either.

"They found the hammer in the garage," Patsy said, "I saw the picture."

I was a little pissed that Patsy, who had been reading my clipping collection, was acting like she knew it all.

"The papers say it's only circumstantial evidence." Aaron said.

"What does that mean?"

"No witnesses, no confession."

I read the columns over and over. This week's Newsweek and Time had pictures of Dad in an orange prison jumpsuit holding his handcuffed arms up to hide his face. Dad was a famous surgeon. He lectured and taught other doctors. He had a clamp named after him.

"Will Daddy come home today?" Patsy said.

"He might if the judge sets a reasonable bail," said Auntie.

"Would you stay if Dad came home?" I asked.

"Of course I'd help, Sandy," Auntie said without a pause.

"Are we almost there?" Patsy whined.

"No, dear. Just a few more minutes."

"Will we sit with Daddy?"

"Don't be stupid," Aaron said again.

"No. We'll be far away. But your dad will be able to see you."

"Will he go to the electric chair?" Patsy said. I acted as if the thought had never crossed my mind.

"They don't fry people any more," Aaron said, out of control as he usually was, even when Mom was alive.

"Oh yeah? Then what do they do?" Patsy asked.

"They stick you with a needle and shove drugs in you."

I looked at Auntie Caroline in the rearview mirror; her eyes were wet. But Auntie was tough and I didn't expect tears. None came.

Auntie Caroline decided it was time for a bathroom break, so we pulled off at an Exxon service plaza. Aaron got the men's room key. The lock on the ladies' room had been torn out of the door where there was now just a hole. Auntie and I waited outside the ladies room while Patsy was inside.

Auntie whispered, "You're going to have to be strong, Sandy."

"I know." I was uncomfortable. I didn't choose to be here with Auntie, or with anyone in my family.

"Aaron can't do it. And Patsy is too little." she said.

"Okay," I said, "okay!"

What did she expect me to do? I couldn't make Mom alive again. I couldn't get Dad out of jail.

"We all miss your mother," she said. But there had been months when Auntie and Mom wouldn't speak to each other.

Patsy came out and Auntie went in. Patsy and I walked to the van alone.

"I wish we didn't have to go," Patsy said.

"Dad needs us."

"Auntie isn't like she used to be."

"Why?" I asked.

"Not as nice," said Patsy.

I saw Auntie had come out and she bought pops at a dispenser. Aaron was still inside, probably playing with himself.

We finally got back on the road and rode in silence again. It seemed like hours.

I was surprised when Aaron spoke up. "Were you there where Mom was killed?" he asked Auntie.

"Of course not, why are you asking?"

"Your car was out front of the house," he said. He would know. He would have looked for any opportunity to get a glimpse of Auntie's legs in running shorts.

"I was jogging," Auntie said.

"You were in the woods when Mom was killed." It was like an observation. Not a question. Not an accusation, either. But even Patsy held her breath.

"I don't know when Martha was killed," Auntie said slowly, emphasizing the words as if she were struggling to remember the details.

Aaron wanted Auntie to tell the truth. He didn't want suspicions to spoil his fantasy life with Auntie.

"Rusty and me saw Mom and Dad leave together that morning," said Patsy. Rusty was our dreary-eyed cocker spaniel.

We all sank into a silence.

"It's not a big woods," Aaron said. I had thought about these things, too. And now we were on our way to sit in public and watch my dad. We were all more nervous than I thought.

Auntie kept her eyes on the road. "It's a lot of acres. You can jog and never see anyone you know."

I watched Auntie in the mirror. Her look was a rock. Could I ever be a strong as she was?

"It must have been terrible," Auntie said.

"She wouldn't have died right away. It would have taken a lot of blows," said mister know-it-all in his I'm-so-important mood now. His information came from watching horror films on video. "Mom would have known who it was."

"That's horrible," Auntie said. I think she meant Aaron, who thought words could make you brave.

We were silent again. Aaron slumped. We didn't know what Auntie believed. I admired Auntie. She had opinions and stood up for herself as a woman, just the way I wanted to when I got out of school. And she was usually good to all of us. She wouldn't hurt mom. I had convinced myself of that from the very beginning.

"I heard on TV that a lot murderers are family," said Patsy. She'd been thinking about this. No one, not even Aaron, had anything to say about that.

"Dad wouldn't kill anyone," I said, but I was surprised. It just came out. I hadn't thought about saying it before.

"Of course not," said Auntie. Her voice rang with clarity. With those three words we became a team all of a sudden. We seemed together for Dad on this. Our van was filled with purpose. As we get near the courthouse, we were a little army for Dad. All of us knew we had a role, even though none of us was really sure what exactly that role was. In her amazing way I thought Auntie had taken our few stray parts and made us whole.

This was my first time in this or any courtroom. I was amazed at how much wood there was. They must have cut down an entire forest for justice. There were wooden benches. The walls had wooden panels. The judge and jury boxes were polished wood, too, although the chair seats were upholstered in red leather. I believed we should not sacrifice one tree for this court—or any court, for that matter.

The fluorescent lights on the ceiling glared so intensely that they erased the shadows on faces; the bailiff, court recorder, and judge had an eerie sameness as if they were wearing Halloween masks. We sat in the third row on the left side facing the judge.

Aaron made sure he sat next to Auntie Caroline, probably wanting to grab a feel of her bottom. His fantasies clouded any hope of decency. But Auntie stood up and repositioned us like checkers on a board. Aaron, me, Patsy, Auntie. Hah. She was as far away from Aaron as possible. She had not forgotten our purpose. We looked like fans at a football game.

In his pants pocket Aaron carried Clearasil for his acne. He used it fifteen, maybe twenty times a day. He had gotten it out now, mashing the tube for a little cream. The tube was as empty as you can get without really being empty. The stuff was not working and I thought he was wasting his money. But pimples were his life. His face was splotchy with red and pink mounds; the skin on his back where he couldn't reach looked like the surface of Mars. His thumb and forefinger were as strong as pliers from squeezing blackhead craters.

Aaron was sloppy, too. His glasses slid down his pug nose. He was slack on brushing teeth and the crooked little devils were getting yellow. Aaron thought yellow was cool. He had wanted to be a runaway to New York or Seattle, but that passed. A phase of junior high. He had tried drugs—I'd seen him, but I don't think he was addicted. I thought it was more to rebel against Mom.

Dad's case came up. The bailiff's voice echoed, "Henry Gerhardt Greiner."

After preliminary speeches and lawyers standing and saying "yes, your honor," Dad pleaded not guilty. His voice was easily heard but far from its usual loud, do-it-or-else tone.

After more discussion, the lawyer argued for release with no bail. Auntie leaned forward, I thought to hear better, although the lawyer's voice seemed more than loud enough to me. The lawyer said Dad's medical service to the community was beyond equal. Dad was magnanimous, always caring for others. The lawyer said the weaknesses of the prosecutor's case were obvious. The DNA evidence was easily explained. Dad had a nosebleed that morning and it got on Mom's dress. Finally he pointed out all of Dad's family—us—and friends. All his support. Would any man leave? I barely listened to this, but Aaron listened with the intensity of looking at MTV with no sound.

The judge did not look impressed by Dad's achievements. She denied bail. Auntie Caroline gasped, as did most of the hundred or so other people in the courtroom.

"He lied," Aaron said under his breath to me.

"What?" I said. "Tell me!"

"No—he lied."

"Aaarooaan!" I said, but I realized he was shaking with silent sobs.

"The nosebleed—"

"What is it?" asked Auntie from the end of our line.

"Aaron's crying," Patsy discovered, happy to announce Aaron's baby side to the world. She thought he was crying about the bail. I knew better.

"Be quiet," I said to Patsy.

I watched Dad. I searched for a brief glance as the lawyer droned on. Not one look! Dad was between two guards, who held him by his arms. He could have looked at us. Easily! I willed him to do it, to make it all right. But he did not. Had he forgotten we were there? Impossible!

Aaron held his sobs but tears still trickled down his face. "He didn't have a nosebleed," he said.

As the judge closed the proceedings, Dad stared at his shackled feet.

Aaron curled his upper body on the wooden bench like a possum in danger. I knew he'd been waiting for Dad to look, too. Although Aaron's legs hung down now, his feet were not solidly on the floor. He was a mound of broken bones in a loose skin sac. I still hated him. But he knew something terrible, and for the first time ever, I wanted to touch and comfort him the way Mom did to me when we were small and happy. To tell him Dad was innocent. Not to worry. Dad would be home someday.

Duh. I was struck by how crazy that was. How childish. I was fourteen. Mother wanted me to start taking the pill. Why would I say totally ridiculous things to my brother? He got on my nerves, but he wasn't an idiot!

"Aaron's still crying." Patsy said again, quietly.

"Let him be," I said to Patsy. Patsy stared at me with an odd look I had never seen before. Something in my voice? She turned away and didn't move. "Grow up," I said.

Auntie leaned over Patsy toward Aaron and me. "Aaron," she said, "you okay?"

"Leave him alone," I said. Auntie backed away with a puzzled look, but she didn't interfere.

I finally reached over and touched Aaron's arm, just for a second; it was for the right reason. I was there. He didn't pull away and he glanced ever so briefly at me. I saw the stress in his eyes, shrunken by the lenses of his glasses. Then fear possessed him. I took his trembling hand. He was still staring at the closed door where Dad had been led from the courtroom.

"We'll get through this," I said.

The Cart Boy

illustration by Peter Healy

The Cart Boy

This will never work out," Mr. Rich said, sitting behind his metal desk, thick arms crossed on his massive chest. On the wall were photos of him with his high school football team, with golf clubs and friends, on a family ski trip to Colorado, at the helm of a sloop with all six children and under full sail on Penobscot Bay, and a large print of him at the wheel of his vintage-fifties, two-seater red convertible.

"You aren't worth a damn at hiring, anyway," he said to me.

Even after sixteen years as manager of his independent grocery store, I could never remember a compliment from Mr. Rich. He was a hard-liner who thought the best management strategy was never being pleased with any employee. I'd learned to ignore him whenever possible.

"He'd just be a cart boy," I argued.

"What's this disabled shit?" he said.

"He's got some spastic disorder."

"I hope it's not offensive."

I'd never seen the kid. My sister, a volunteer social worker, had counseled him after he had dropped out of a special ed school. "Don't be a brute," she said. "Give him a chance." She was condescending as always, believing me responsible for my divorce after my wife went West with our children, and disdainful of my reclusive social life over the past few years. "It'll be good PR," she added.

The next week we hired this kid, Marion Passman, whose mama, my sister later confessed, was about to buy him a one-way bus ticket to Arkansas and a father he'd never seen. Marion's job was to retrieve shopping carts from the checkout area and stack them, front into end, near the main entrance.

On his first day of work I watched from my enclosed office. It was raised up from the floor, with a big window so I could look out over the store. Marion walked with startling contortions, his back arched like a strung bow, defying gravity as if he were in a perpetual backward fall. His almost useless right foot jerked up as if he had stepped on a hot fire, then it slammed down like stomping a roach while his left foot pointed delicately forward like a ballerina's. To change direction, he thrashed with pinwheel movement as if balancing on a shaky high wire, left arm stiff with down-pointed fingers, his right bent and twisting.

"He's an eyesore," Mr. Rich said. He was sure Marion would scare customers to Summits, our competitor, where all the checkout girls wore tight sweaters and the stock boys looked like gym instructors. But most of our customers were fascinated, glancing back over their shoulders or peeking between aisles to see Marion. Not one of them complained to me. In fact, they used words like "spunky" and "good worker."

As if to prove my point, the next day I saw from my office perch an always-friendly customer, a Ms. Booker, stare at Marion for a moment before walking up to him and complimenting him on his work. Marion's jerks quickened and he gave a little spasm of a wave as Ms. Booker walked away to come to my office before she checked out.

"He's got so much determination," she said.

"He keeps those carts straight," I said. "Delivery for you today, Ms. Booker?"

"That would be great. And please call me Celine."

Celine lived in one of the many high-rise condos near the store. Rather than carry her groceries, she used the store's "half-mile delivery service," something I'd thought up to try to keep customers from switching to Summits. For six bucks, a bag boy would wheel groceries to a customer's door within thirty minutes of purchase. If the customer wasn't home yet, he left them with the concierge.

It was all going smoothly until Yolanda, a cashier, said it made her nervous having to watch Marion squirm around. "I ain't required to work around no retards," she said.

I told Yolanda to do her job. "Marion's a good worker. Customers like him," I said.

"Ratshit."

"He's better than you," I said.

"I got a friend stocking at Summits. Get me a real job."

She went straight to Mr. Rich to quit.

"I knew there'd be trouble," Mr. Rich said.

"She was useless," I said, "Couldn't tell broccoli from kiwis."

I was sure Marion was not retarded; he just lacked education. After all, he was too busy trying to stay upright to have time to study.

Mr. Rich wasn't convinced of Marion's worth, but made no decision to fire him. "Just keep your eye on him. This ain't a charity operation."

The next few days passed better than I could have expected. Marion grew into his job. He had a system where as soon as someone unloaded a cart he would whisk it to the edge of checkout. He waited until he had collected three or four carts before he took them to the front. He watched for people having trouble separating carts from a stack too, and he'd stumble over to give a hand. Outside, Marion made swings through the parking lot like clockwork, clunking carts into a long train and pushing them up the concrete slope to the store's front door to be brought back into service.

After a month on the job, Marion was walking around with a can of 3-In-One oil. I thought he'd taken it off the shelves, but we didn't carry it and maintenance said they never used it. I watched from my perch. Marion was oiling the carts! It took him a while to get the oilcan tip in place on the wheel, and then he squeezed. When he dribbled oil on the floor, he wiped it up with a paper towel that he kept in his pocket.

"Where'd you get that oil?" Mr. Rich asked Marion.

"I bring'd it."

I told Mr. Rich he ought to have a few more employees like that.

I was pleased that Marion was doing a lot better than Mr. Rich expected. But during the pre-dinner rush on a Friday, Mrs. Tanner slipped on a greasy spot and fell near the grapefruit display. I helped her up. She was bruised but nothing broken. I couldn't tell if she slipped on a Marion oil dribble or the wet puddle from a leak in the automatic vegetable-spray pipe. But, just in case, I took Marion aside and showed him how to put a cloth under where he wanted to oil so nothing would get on the floor. He understood right away and from that time on there was not one fall from a possible oil slick and not one cart in the whole store wobbled or jerked.

The store ran smoothly for a while. Marion fit in as best he could and he was constantly on the move inside and outside. Because he dragged his right foot he had a growing hole on the top front of the rubber part of his shoe. His sock was sticking out, the skin of his toe exposed. At the lunch break I said, "Come on, Marion," and we marched out the front door together walking three blocks toward the center of town. As we walked, people moved off the sidewalk gawking at him as if he had an infectious disease and I wondered if he was used to it, whether it ever bothered him. It was hard to tell. Then we came to a crowd of teenagers who stopped and stared, refusing to give way. Marion rambled out into the street to go around them. God! He didn't have the right reflexes to dodge traffic, and I moved him back on the sidewalk as quickly as I could.

I led Marion into the super-discount "Treat Your Toes" shoe store. "May I help you, sir?" a sales boy said, turning so he didn't have to look at Marion wiggling around.

"Yes, you may," I said. "I want air high-tops with the best tread."

"What size?"

Marion didn't know his size. The sales boy tried to line up a metal foot measurer on Marion, but Marion couldn't hold still.

"I'd think about a seven and a half," the sales boy said in an offhand way, trying to act as if this happened all the time. "We got red, blue, black, silver, gray, and magenta."

"What you want?" I asked Marion.

"Red," Marion stuttered.

"Red," I said, to be sure the shoe kid made no mistakes.

We got the right shoe size after three tries. Marion was a seven. They looked great.

As we walked back to the store, Marion glowed with pride. He couldn't smile well but I could see it in his eyes. Pedestrians now stared in admiration as Marion's shoes propelled him forward.

Slowly, over the next six weeks, Marion began spending more time in the store than at home, often working overtime without pay. One night he missed the last bus, and was waiting outside my office door just before I went home. He wanted to spend the night in the storeroom.

I knew Mr. Rich wouldn't take on that kind of in-store liability. I called for a cab and told Marion I would pay, but the dispatcher was swamped with a Red Sox game so I decided it would be quicker and cheaper to take Marion home myself. I looked up his address in the employee file and checked a city map.

"I serry," he stammered.

"Just point out your place when we get there."

Marion knew all the right turns and we got to the projects just before ten. Marion opened the door to his apartment and whirligigged his way in, knocking the door back against the wall, and I plunged into Marion's home right behind him.

It was a two-room apartment with a bath and half-kitchen, a public housing project left over from the fifties. The bedroom was just an extension of the floor space off to the right.

On a double bed with an uncovered mattress, four pillows—all but one without cover slips—propped up Marion's mother. By the bedside was a wheelchair with a black leather folding seat and glinting bright chrome wheels rimmed in thick rubber tread.

I saw Mom's muscular legs splayed out on the bed; they looked strong.

"What the hell?" she said.

"I'm Harry Nugget."

"He Mr. Boss," Marion chimed in with surprising clarity.

Mom adjusted the half-buttoned man's shirt covering her flat chest. Below she wore a sheer white slip grayed with use and ragged on the hem. I could see by the pubic shadow that it was all she had on, and she made no attempt to cover herself. With her right hand she grabbed the remote control and cut off the television, catching an actor in mid-sentence.

Moving off the bed with the quickness of a squirrel on a limb, she sat easily in the wheelchair, released the brake, and glided the few feet toward me. She stuck out her hand. "I'm disabled. Can't breathe good."

She gripped my hand with the strength of an oyster shucker.

"Excuse the mess. He knocks everything out of place."

Marion probably slept next to the wall where there was a sofa with a pillow and a blanket in a heap on the floor. It was the only piece of furniture other than a small metal-topped table and two wooden kitchen chairs. The mixed smells of boiled cabbage, dried urine, and mildew hung in the air with the acrid taint of marijuana.

"You haven't got much room," I offered.

"Not for that bozo," she said, smiling and showing faintly yellowed teeth with a space where the left upper incisor would have been. "We applied for a two bedroom in the Attica apartments but the waiting list is in the thousands."

"Marion does a good job," I said.

"That's lucky. His father was a no-good. Left me before he was born. Hasn't sent one nickel, either."

"Well, Marion's turned out just fine."

"Pain in the ass most of the time," she mumbled.

I said a few pleasantries and a goodnight. Marion's mother gushed sweetness and urged me to come back for coffee sometime. As I left, she dry-coughed a few times.

We were always busy in the summer months but it wasn't a happy time; even though sales soared, employees complained about the heat and customers' tempers flared. On Thursday, Mr. Rich came brashly into my office with Antonio Silva, the security guy from Ms. Celine Booker's apartment complex. Silva had a problem, Mr. Rich explained.

"Yesterday," Silva began, "Ms. Booker unpacked her bags of groceries your store delivered. In the bottom of one sack she found a mangled rose."

"I don't get it," I said.

"Shut up, Harry. Listen," Mr. Rich said.

"I thought it was trash at first," Silva continued. "But Ms. Booker thought it was a message."

"That's crazy," I said. "Probably from the florist's section. Got stuck on the bottom of a milk carton at checkout."

"But she had a card too, in an envelope unaddressed and unsealed."

"Can I see it?" I asked.

"Ms. Booker is downright scared. She lives in a high-risk neighborhood. She's seeing stalkers, hearing noises, freaks out at the usual hang-up phone calls even more than usual. She's thinking she's going to be violated. She wants protection."

"Our delivery didn't do that!"

“Listen to him, Harry,” Mr. Rich said.

“She’s suffered two attempted rapes within a half mile of the building in the last two years.”

I’d known Silva since high school. Maybe Ms. Booker was scared but I could tell he had the hots for her.

“Can I see the card?” I asked again.

On the front was a misshapen bird, drawn by a cartoonist, a cross between Big Bird and the Roadrunner, with wings and legs splayed out at impossible angles. Inside the card was a yellow happy smiley face that said, “HAVE A GOOD DAY.”

“We got that one,” I said. “It’s not a good seller. Probably got in by accident.”

“Hey. One of the cashiers might remember if it was purchased here,” Silva said.

“Could you check?” Mr. Rich said. Silva stared expectantly at Mr. Rich. “Will fifty bucks an hour do?” Mr. Rich added.

“I can take the afternoon off from the condo. Won’t take long,” Silva said.

Silva loved this detective stuff for Ms. Booker. Throughout the afternoon he interrogated each cashier as they took their breaks and even stayed on to talk to the evening shift. He watched baggers, followed a few deliveries, and concluded that the contact with Ms. Booker was not accidental. I did my own work.

Bingo. “I got it,” Silva said to me in the office, well after six. “The cart boy bought the card.”

“Well, he’s not a rapist,” I said.

Silva wanted to set up a sting operation. Catch Marion in the act. What he really wanted was prolonged time with Ms. Booker.

“We’ll just talk to Marion,” I said again.

Silva wasn’t happy. “If he denies it we’ll never know it was him.”

“It’s no big deal. He’s not dangerous.”

But Silva was like an ivory hunter after elephants. “It’s big for Ms. Booker,” he said.

So I called Marion over the store intercom before Silva could think of a plan.

“Cart boy. Front office, please.”

Marion jerked and flailed until he reached the creaky wooden steps with a pipe railing that led up to the door. Going up seemed three times harder than staying level and he was panting when he entered the office. He maneuvered into a straight-backed wooden chair. I didn't introduce Silva.

"Yes, sir," Marion sputtered.

I held up the rose and the card. Marion trembled.

"Did you put these in Ms. Booker's grocery bags?"

He pointed to the card. He nodded, unable to speak out.

"Why did you do it?" Silva asked.

"She nice lady," Marion said. He managed to say he didn't know about the rose. It was obvious he knew nothing. I asked Silva if he'd heard enough.

I let Marion go back to work and Silva made an appointment for him and me with Ms. Booker for five o'clock the next day. Case solved, perp confronted, slime confessed, Silva summarized to Ms. Booker on the phone. "We'll talk some things over with the little lady about compensation," he said, smiling to me after he hung up. The next day Silva and I arrived at Celine Booker's apartment early.

"Marion?" Celine said when I told her. "The cart boy? I never knew his name."

"He has a crush on you," I said.

"I can't believe it ..."

"You're an attractive woman," Silva said.

"But I only talked to him once. I didn't try to lead—"

"Oh, no, Ms. Booker. It was not your doing," I said immediately. "He wanted to please you. And I'm sure he didn't want to attack you. I'm sure of that."

She thought for a moment. "Of course not. He can barely walk straight. He couldn't harm me," she said.

"I hope you will accept my personal, and the store's, apologies," I said.

Celine was very gracious, refusing to file a complaint. She was totally opposed to even the slightest reprimands. Silva frowned in disbelief. He wanted to jail Marion.

"Don't cause that boy grief," she said emphatically looking at Silva.

"We'll treat him fairly," I said before Silva could answer.

Silva said, "You might ask the store for a tad of compensation. For your inconvenience. It hasn't been easy."

"Definitely not," Celine said.

"He'll never repeat," I said. "I can personally guarantee that."

"You've had more than a modest inconvenience, Celine," Silva persisted. "A threat, even. And I can make it so there's no skin off the kid's nose."

"It doesn't seem right, Tony."

"I won't bother the boy. I know the owner and it won't be no trouble for you at all."

"Only if the boy is not affected."

"It's justice," Silva smiled.

Mr. Rich was already in his office when I arrived for work the next morning.

"Five thousand dollars I shell out because the cart boy's got his thing in a knot over some broad."

"She didn't want trouble."

"Christ, Harry. I got the release. I wrote the check. Silva said it would keep her quiet. You've got to get rid of that kid."

"Marion's done nothing wrong," I said. "It's Silva making trouble 'cause he wants to bag Ms. Booker."

"Look, Harry, we put out five thousand dollars and a promise that he wouldn't bother Ms. Booker again. I can't take the chance he might screw up. What if anything happened to Ms. Booker, cart boy or not? Who are they going to come looking for? Me! And you!"

"He's innocent."

"You're too involved, Harry. You can't get too close to employees. Buying him shoes, for chrissake. Ruins discipline. Spreads resentment." Mr. Rich's face flushed. The little clusters of veins on each side of his nose were turning purple. "Talk to him. Tell him we don't tolerate weird stuff."

"I won't do it!"

"Okay, Harry. You won't do it? I'll do it!" Mr. Rich got up and walked into the back of his office complex, as I went back to my office.

"Cart boy," Mr. Rich called over the loudspeaker a few minutes later. Marion made his way to Mr. Rich's office.

Without Marion we were back to customers without carts when they entered the store, and a tangle of carts near checkout. For an entire month customers questioned Marion's whereabouts, citing how convenient he had made shopping. The baggers would take no responsibility to organize cart retrieval and we were losing carts to homeless rag pickers because carts were left in the parking area too long. Even occasional customers could see the difference in our service. So I added up the cost of cart replacement, noting that the total savings on lost carts was more than Marion's pay. Then I noted that Marion's oiling of the carts extended their life, saving even more money. I placed the report on Mr. Rich's desk as proof of Marion's worth. "Let me hire the kid back," I finally said to Mr. Rich.

"Hire someone else."

"I've tried. The baggers think it's below their dignity. Even the homeless guys looking for day work say the pay is too low."

After a few days of no more applicants, Mr. Rich finally agreed on a trial of having Marion back. I called the number Marion had had someone fill out on his job application, but it had been disconnected and reassigned months ago. So on my way home that night I decided to go by Marion's place.

Within three minutes after I parked, Marion's mother opened the apartment door holding a blue-gray polyester coverlet over her chest and tucked under her armpits. Her legs and feet were uncovered from the knees down. She made no attempt to block my view. A man dressed only in his jockey shorts sat on the edge of the bed next to the wheelchair, a twist of smoke drifting upward from a cigarette in his right hand. He did not look up.

"Where's Marion?"

"Basement," she said, and closed the door.

The laundry room was just to the right as I stepped off the elevator. Marion sat straddling a metal folding chair and staring at an open comic book on a long table for laying out clothes. None of the washers or driers was running. He turned himself and the chair at the same time.

"Marion. What are you doing?"

"Reading," he said with difficulty pointing to the comic book. "I got stay here 'till nine o'clock," his head jerked upward to the wall clock.

"Well, I got good news. Mr. Rich says he wants you back. You can start tomorrow." He paused. Then he raised his shaking arm in a wobbly salute, influenced, I thought, by the military drawings in his comic book. "Yes, Cap'n," he said.

When I arrived at the store before dawn the next morning, Marion was waiting outside the employees' entrance. It was good to see him back.

We were soon moving customers more smoothly. A week after he started I left the store at midmorning to buy an intercom. Mr. Rich wanted to be able to call me to his office without using the overhead speaker. As I was coming back, Marion was out front rounding up the carts. From a distance I paused to admire how surprisingly efficient he was, given how difficult it was for him to walk in a straight line. He pushed a line of eight carts up the ramp to the store and the front cart nudged a loose cart at the top. The cart started rolling slowly—oiled to frictionless perfection—down the ramp, picking up speed. Marion anchored his line of carts by wedging them against the wall. The loose cart headed for Mr. Rich's antique red convertible. With a burst of energy, Marion gained on it. I imagined a two-inch dent in the car door about waist high on the driver's side. Marion put on even more speed, and more flailing too.

Mrs. O'Leary was still driving although she was eighty-two. Her car was parked head-in near Mr. Rich's convertible. She put her foot on the brake, as was required in the new cars, to crank the motor and wrench the gearshift from park to reverse. She used two hands, twisting her body and reaching over the steering wheel, and pressed harder on the brake for leverage. Her foot slipped just as she went into gear, the flat of her heel full on the gas petal. The car lurched back, out of control.

Marion was within ten feet of the cart when Mrs. O'Leary's car hit him, knocked him down, actually bumped up over him like a car going over a speed bump, and then came to a halt against a concrete wall, still dragging him underneath. The errant cart glanced off Mr. Rich's car at an angle, barely leaving a scratch.

Marion was still gasping when I pulled him from beneath the engine block. Unconscious, he lay still—a body without a twitch—gnarled up on the concrete, with little bleeding, just scrapes, an arm bone jutting through the skin, part of his scalp sheared off. I'd never seen him so peaceful, his eyes closed, his mouth relaxed, his lips in a faint curve that could have been his best shot ever at a smile. Someone called for help. I sat beside him, touching his hand for comfort, even after he died.

Lost Papers

illustration by Peter Healy

Lost Papers

It is 1941. Isaac the Jew and Rebecca, his wife of twenty years, stand in line at the checkpoint between Germany and Switzerland for three hours before they reach the barrier.

"Passports," the guard says in German. Isaac hands over his documents.

"You are from … ?"

"Born in Munich," Isaac says.

"You are going to Zurich?"

"No, no. To Basel. I must meet my brother's daughter, now orphaned. She is alone and will be waiting at the train station. Friends have sent her."

"You, woman," the guard says, "where are your papers?"

Rebecca does not look up from her frantic search in her bag. "I cannot find them," she says. She has slipped into her native Polish.

"She will find them," Isaac says.

"Go to the back of the line," the guard says. "Next."

Isaac grabs Rebecca's arm and takes her to the side.

"Incompetent," he whispers.

"I thought they were here," she pleads. "Maybe you have them."

"Why would I have them? He sets down his satchel then empties the contents of her bag on the ground. Unzips, unbuttons, unwraps … but there are no papers.

"I must go to meet Anna," Isaac says. "She will be frightened."

"I cannot stay here," Rebecca says, "One of the women said Gestapo make arrests."

"You must find your papers."

"They were in my bag. Someone has stolen them."

"The papers must be found to cross the border. Stay here. I will be back the day after tomorrow with Anna."

"You don't care that I can't go," she sighed.

He held her shoulders and brought his face close to hers. "I am not the cause of your carelessness. It will soon be over. Anna will be with us."

She cries. "You care more for your brother's illegitimate child than your own wife."

"Hold your tongue," he says. He releases her. "Hide for your safety. Do not be conspicuous."

He goes back to the line and passes into Switzerland without restraint. At the Basel train station he finds Anna sitting alone on a bench against the outside station wall, under an overhang to keep out of the rain.

Anna looks up. "Is that you, Papa?

He takes the child in arms. "Yes, it is me. Your papa." Her likeness to her loving mother pleases him with sweet memories of their time together.

"Mama said you were a small man," she says, looking up at him after he puts her down.

"Your mama was a good woman. Grab your things and we will go to a new life. It is all arranged. Do you have your papers?"

"Yes, Papa." She pats the pocket of her sweater.

"They are not safe there," Isaac says.

He takes the papers from her, opens his satchel, and tucks them in the top slot between his other papers.

It takes a half a day to walk to the border. At the official Swiss booth Isaac shows the agent his papers from his pocket. Then he opens up his case. He hands papers over.

"You are Rebecca?" the Swiss agent asks in French.

Anna laughs. "Non, monsieur. Je m'appelle Anna."

Isaac opens his case again. He finds Anna's papers in the top slot.

"Excuse moi, monsieur," Isaac says with a strained laugh. He holds out the papers to the agent.

"And who is this Rebecca?" the agent says, handing the papers back.

"She is my wife, monsieur."

Isaac trembles and the papers flutter to the ground. Anna helps collect them.

"You must be more careful with your documents," the agent says.

"It is my eyes, monsieur. I lost my glasses and do not see well." But he had kept Rebecca's papers to prevent her from talking to Anna. Rebecca must never know his relation to the girl.

Anna's papers are accepted. They pass into Germany. Isaac begins searching for Rebecca.

"She is old with hair like cobwebs," Isaac says to Anna. "She does not know about your mama or that you are ma petite poupée." He smiles. "She thinks Uncle Aaron was your father. That will be our secret, no?"

"Will we see her soon?"

"She is probably hiding," Isaac says.

After two hours of searching in alleys and behind buildings, Isaac knocks on doors of homes in the village. Maybe someone has taken Rebecca in for the night. They look. But no one has seen a woman called Rebecca.

In the town square the butcher remembers seeing a woman in the street hiding in the shadows near the end of yesterday. But he does not know where she went.

"What will I call her?" Anna asks.

"We will call her mama," Isaac says. "Can you do that?"

"I think so," Anna says, nodding.

The baker has been busy since four in the morning making the dough for fresh loaves and baguettes.

"Yesterday before dawn," the baker says, "the Gestapo herded Jews and people without papers into a truck. I saw her. But no one knows where they were taken."

Anna takes her father's hand and pulls him away. He is dry-eyed, his mouth open, his chapped lips cracked. "Will we find her, Papa?" Anna asks.

"Yes. Of course," he says. He hides his trembling hands in his pockets. "She is here … somewhere."

Inside the Matryoshka

illustration by Betty Harper

Inside the Matryoshka

My one unbreakable rule was to never pick up a hitchhiker. And definitely never at night. But at the far edge of the headlights this girl showed up in the breakdown lane near mile marker 381, kind of humped over as if she didn't even know I was bearing down on her. Not like a hooker, who'd be standing straight with her hand waving shoulder-high and her head tilted like a come-on, or some hidden robber's decoy girl, waving with both arms like the ship was sinking. I slowed with no thought of stopping. She stumbled into the slow lane and crumpled to the ground; I swerved left to keep from killing her. I checked the mirrors, black except the yellow glow-dots of my running lights. I pulled into the breakdown lane, put on flashers, climbed down, and walked back to her. I didn't see any movement in the darkness of the roadside pine forest.

A pickup truck passed on the other side of the highway but didn't even slow, its lights flickering among the trees in the wide median. No Good Samaritans.

She was breathing hard and raspy. I turned her over; her pale skin glowed a faint red in the taillights, increasing to a supernatural yellow hue with the pulse of a flasher. A girl, close to a woman but thin as an antenna. Nose a little too big and lips too skimpy to be pretty. I got her seated up in the cab, half conscious and half sitting, and closed the door quick to keep her from falling out. We were 152 miles from Memphis. Still hadn't seen any more vehicles, or people. I geared up to seventy. I tried to call 911 but got no signal. Couldn't raise anyone on the CB this far out and deep into night. She'd curled up on the seat. She moved with a jerk once, but then seemed to pass out.

I got the dispatcher at the state patrol when I was in range. I began to give my location. With a swipe of her hand on the toggle switch, she cut off the radio. She was awake, and she wasn't stupid.

"Don't you ever touch nothing on this dashboard," I said. "Never." Her dark eyes didn't shift when you looked at them. "I'm calling the cops."

She opened the door, pushing it against the wind like she was strong. She climbed out on the step-up, one hand on the doorframe, the other holding the door open. She'd kill herself at this speed. I braked, but soft-braked, slowly enough not to throw her off. When I was down to fifteen, she jumped.

I stopped, ran back. She was moaning. Her arm and legs bled from scrapes. Her nose was bleeding. I wasn't sure what to do.

She raised herself on all fours, like a little dog, and looked up at me. "No police," she said. She stood, wobbling a little, then lunged toward me and pounded my chest with her fists. I wrapped my arms around her to make her stop and held her for a few seconds before pushing her away at arm's length. She seemed more human up close. "Come on. I got some mercurochrome in the first aid kit." She backed away, shaking her head no, but I picked her up and carried her to the truck.

We were rolling a few minutes later; she was on the seat fast asleep and breathing through her mouth, her nose all crusted with blood. I was thinking about where I should drop her off in Memphis without getting too far off my route.

It was the loneliest time of a trip, the hours before first light. I missed my wife, Madeline, the worst during those times. God bless her. She was at home in Oregon, a good woman; worked as a dispatcher for a trucking firm. Parents ran a motel on the coast road near Gold Beach, now retired. She was the only woman I'd ever had—married her right out of high school—and I was proud of it, too. I was probably the only faithful trucker on that interstate for three hundred miles in either direction. Vile women had tempted me at truck stops a couple times, both in Texas, but with a little prayer God helped me pass them by. Madeline and I had no kids. She was too old now, and it weighed on her in silent times.

The dark outside the cab—black as road tar—made me lonely and I called Madeline on my cell when I was in range. "It's the middle of the night, Clarence. Where are you?" she asked.

"Missing you, babe." She went silent with that bit of sweetness. Talk like that meant a lot to her.

"I got this kid in the cab."

Madeline was still waking up. "A kid?"

"I don't know. Maybe seventeen. She was passed out on the road," I said to Madeleine softly to let the kid sleep. "Then she jumped out of the cab."

I passed a pickup truck going about forty, the bed loaded with chairs, a stove, a refrigerator, a mattress, cardboard packing boxes with the lids flapping, and the trailer hitch sending sparks flying when it scraped the highway.

"Is she hurt?" Madeline asked.

I shook the girl's shoulder to wake her up. I put Madeline on the hands-free speaker.

"Where are you going?" I asked the girl. She was looking at me but said nothing. A car passed going the other way.

"Look," I said, "You either talk or I'm putting you out on the road and calling the state patrol."

"Tatyana," she said, weakly.

"Ask her where she's from," Madeline said over the speaker.

But the girl had closed her eyes and gone limp, like she'd fainted. I wasn't sure it was real.

"She's bleeding," I said to Madeline. "It's all over the seat."

Three blackbirds flapped into the air from a road-killed deer carcass. I swerved. "Gotta go," I said to Madeline as I hung up. I was trying to call the state patrol again when I saw a green exit sign to a town, Parkland, with a rectangular blue hospital sign attached to the bottom.

It wasn't no regular hospital, but a doc-in-the-box operation. I left the girl in the cab and pushed the door buzzer. A muscular woman, close to six feet, 250 pounds with a white lab coat over jeans and a T-shirt, opened the door. "She got insurance?" she asked me. I told her I had nothing to do with the girl. What would I know? She glared. "She's hurt," I said, and the woman signaled with her hand for me to carry the girl from the truck. I laid her on a rolling exam table.

"One hundred and fifty bucks," the woman said. "Cash. We don't take charity."

"You the doc?" I asked.

She started to cover the girl with a sheet.

"I'm leaving," I said.

The woman shrugged. I got in my rig and called Madeline again.

"You've done all you can," Madeline said. "More than most."

Well, that wasn't really true. I could have paid for her treatment. But the doc would take care of her. I thought she had to by law. And they'd find out where the girl came from, and where she was going.

I cranked the motor. The girl came running out the door, the woman in the lab coat running after her. The girl fell and the woman grabbed her, dragging her kicking back into the office. I followed, leaving the truck running with the door open.

The woman was holding the girl down in a waiting room chair, leaning on her shoulders. The girl's nose blood had clotted, but a scrape on her arm still oozed. Another woman in scrubs was on the phone behind a reception desk.

"What are you doing?" I asked.

"She can't pay. And she got no Medicaid."

"You ain't done nothing," I said.

"The doc examined her," she said. "She'll live. She owes."

"It ain't been three minutes?"

"Pay up. Seventy-five dollars will do it."

Fear topped out in the girl's eyes.

I didn't see no diplomas on the wall, or pictures of medical-school buildings with emergency vehicles out front. And I wasn't paying seventy-five dollars for a three-minute exam.

"Come on," I said to the girl.

The big woman moved to stop us; the girl kicked her and I pushed the woman so she fell to the floor on her back, struggling to get up. I grabbed the girl's arm and we headed out the door.

The girl climbed into the truck on her own and we were moving by the time both women were standing at the door, one with a pen and paper, the other peering at us through the early-morning dark. I turned off the lights so they couldn't see the plates. We'd done nothing wrong, but they'd invent something if they could think of it.

We were on the on-ramp to the interstate. The girl's nose was swelling. She grinned like we'd escaped together. I gave her a high five.

"What the hell did you do?" I asked.

"I do nothing now."

"So why you running?"

"I leave place where I work."

"You got no home?"

She shook her head no.

"Where you trying to get to?" I asked.

"Hollywood."

"What for?"

"I sing good."

"Well, just go to Memphis. Lots of singing there."

She coughed, and I saw blood in her hand.

I got Madeline on the line. "I didn't feel good about leaving her," I said.

"You aren't thinking about bringing her home, are you?"

"I got a deadline."

"Leave her at a rest stop. Call the cops." The girl's face scrunched with worry, listening to Madeline. I smiled at her. I wasn't going to leave her at no rest stop. And she had no place to go. "I'll figure something out," I said to Madeline and hung up. The girl smiled.

I drove straight through, napping only two hours near Boise. I fed the kid from the cooler, and she slept in my bunk behind the cab. When she woke, she told me the family she worked for didn't treat her good. She was an oh pear, or something.

I asked her about her family. In Russia, she said. Six brothers and sisters. Mom and dad worked on a farm.

"You got a visa?" I asked.

She threw up all over the seat. Yellow and green with flecks of blood.

"Clean it up," I said, handing her towel from my side door panel. "I ain't stopping till I get out of Idaho." Eighteen hours later I dropped off the trailer—on time.

Madeline was not happy about me bringing home a stranger. But she'd been waiting for me and had fixed a pizza and iced tea like she always did when I got in. “She needs a doctor,” I said to Madeline, telling her about the blood. Madeline was already fixing her ice cream with chocolate sauce.

We took her to a real doctor. Had X-rays and all. The girl had a broke nose, was anemic from her monthlies, malnourished, and her leg scrapes were infected. She had sinusitis and an ear infection. I had to shell out three hundred bucks from my cash reserve account for fuel. I went straight to bed when we got home.

“Tatyana says the man whose family she took care of in Alabama molested her,” Madeline said to me at breakfast in the morning. The girl was still asleep.

“I thought it was Mississippi. That’s where I found her. She ought to have turned him in.”

“She said she tried. But the guy was mayor of the town and the police wouldn’t listen.” Madeline had found purpose. The girl told her she had been heading west for more than a month when I found her.

“Where was her stuff, then?” I asked. “Her backpack? Her plastic garbage bag? It was like she’d left home twenty minutes before I saw her.”

“She doesn’t have a family in Russia except for an aunt she’s seen only a few times,” Madeline said.

“Not what she told me.”

“She’s sweet,” Madeline said, not willing to face up to Tatyana’s not keeping to her stories. “We can’t neglect her.”

“We can’t neglect something don’t belong to us,” I said.

“Be kind,” Madeline said.

Well, Madeline had already taken the girl as family into her mind. And I wasn’t being unkind, but I had a feeling that keeping the girl forever meant we was in for hard times.

Weeks passed. When I was home, Madeline and I almost never ate together any more. At first the girl would go into the kitchen and paw through the pantry or move stuff in the refrigerator to see what might be on the back shelves, then eat in her room. She liked sweets and cheeses, and pizza, and seemed to have no trouble using the oven or the microwave. Then Madeline began cooking for her, taking a tray of food into the girl's room and sitting with her while she ate. When I was on trips, Madeline spent her time trying to give the girl a good American life. She bought her magazines and comic books to help her with her English. But mostly the two of them watched TV—sitcoms and American Idol—in the girl's bedroom, on our big-screen TV that Madeline had moved there. She bought me a used sixteen-inch screen to watch hockey and football in the kitchen. Madeline quit her job and took the girl to the mall almost every day. They sat at tables in the food court and watched people or walked around and stared at the display windows of the jewelry stores. And, as the girl healed up, Madeline bought her clothes that made her look pretty good. She was a lot more woman than I'd thought.

I got back from a trip to Galveston after a swing north with a half-load to Minneapolis. I worried about my precious Madeline. She was a woman who cared a lot and always seemed to be a set-up for never-ending hurt.

Tatyana was in her room with the TV on loud. I sat Madeline down at our round metal-topped kitchen table. She wouldn't look at me except for a passing glance.

"We got to do something," I said. "She's illegal …"

"You don't know that!" Madeline snapped.

"I do. And you do. She can't stay here for the rest of her life."

"She's alone in the world. She's afraid. She can't see the future."

"She wants to go to California. Be a singer."

"She wants to be a doctor."

"And I want to be a ballerina," I said.

"Don't get smart. She told me," Madeline said with a scowl. "She's really a dear soul."

"She lied about her family," I said.

"She made a mistake."

"Well, she goes out at night. Don't think that gets by me."

"She has her friends."

"Have you seen them?"

She got up from the table, went to the girl's room. Why was she so angry?

Two weeks later, at breakfast, before the girl was up, Madeline sat with me at our kitchen table, her jaw set. "I've seen the way you look at Tatti now, Clarence. I don't like it."

I swallowed. "What does that mean, Madeline? Just what does that mean?"

"I'm going back to work. I've got a starting date. You'll be here sometimes … between trips. That worries me." Madeline glared.

I shook my head. "We can't have her alone in the house," I shot back. I never looked at Tatyana funny! "I don't trust her," I said. "She won't tell us the truth about her past."

"I trust her more than I do you," Madeline said. It was the first time I ever remember my sweet Madeline saying anything so mean. I couldn't think of a comeback. And I was hurt.

Fall came; the leaves turned, and the temperature was mild on the Sunday Madeline, Tatyana, and I went to the Presbyterian Church together. Tatyana wore a new, swirl-print blue dress and shoes with heels that made her legs look like she wasn't a kid anymore. We took a pew halfway back in the center, Tatyana between Madeline and me. Tatyana smelled fresh and clean, a mixture of strong, girly soaps and shampoo. She slid next to Madeline to leave two to three inches between me and her, but I still felt how near she was, enough to make me want to stare at her, see how attractive she'd become, and I had to think hard to be sure I kept staring straight ahead, toward the preacher, when my mind was full of her. She weren't a kid no more. She'd slipped into being a woman. I felt Madeline's sideways glances.

When the first hymn started we had only one hymnal in the slot on the pew in front of us. Madeline held it because she had sung in the choir, but she held it so Tatyana and I could see. I moved closer to Tatyana, looking to the page to see the words. I could feel her breathing. I was in the breeze of her singing. Her eyes were crinkled with effort and her tone had the breathy sound of a singer in Memphis or New Orleans. She'd been listening to oldies. Once I touched her hair, soft and silky from combing, when I handed a prayer book to Madeline. It was only an instant but the memory of the touch stayed with me.

When we got home, Tatti went to her room, keeping away from me as much as she could. And over the next few days, it got worse—her avoiding me, not looking at me. Then I was on the road for a week, weaving down the West Coast to Tijuana, then to Dallas, and up through Arkansas to pick up I-40. My thinking got jumbled about Tatti; I wanted to make her happy, make her stop ignoring me when I was home. So I bought her a kitten for two dollars from a litter some farmwoman was selling at a roadside vegetable stand just off a state route near Little Rock. Cuddly little black and white mixed-breed maybe two weeks old.

At home, I took Tatyana to the cab. She crawled into the back to find her present. When she came out, her eyes glowed with pleasure. Madeline held back near the kitchen door, looking at Tatyana but not at me.

Later that evening I talked to Tatyana during a commercial break that I muted while the three of us were watching Dancing with the Stars on the big screen in Tatyana's bedroom. The three of us watching together was a first; the two of them had always watched alone while I took in football and hockey on that sixteen-inch screen in the kitchen. Tatti smiled at me. I think it was the kitty. But it might have been the TV show.

"You still want to go to Hollywood?" I asked.

"She's decided to stay here," Madeline said.

"What you going to do?" I asked Tatyana.

"Be dresser of hair," she said.

"She's going to be a cosmetologist," Madeline said.

"Still got to be legal."

I leaned toward Tatyana. "How'd you get in the States?" I asked.

"That's not a fair question," Madeline said.

"Nothing wrong if there's nothing to be ashamed of."

"I lied my years I have. Big boobs help make them believe." She cupped a hand under each still-adolescent breast and lifted up like delivering two cinnamon buns. She was grinning, the space between her front teeth looking kind of sweet.

"Tatti," Madeline scolded. She was not smiling. In truth, I found it a little crude for an innocent Christian girl but when I looked again at Tatti her eyes were sparkling with mischief that I had never seen before, and I had to smile. But she hadn't answered my question.

From that time on, Tatyana was at home in our house. And she was kinder to me. I helped her get a job as a waitress at a truck stop a few miles away, where they asked no questions and paid wages in cash from the till. I dropped her off and picked her up at work when I was in town. Her English was getting better and she talked about her mother and father in Russia. She was an only child. Her father was a doctor and her mother worked in a factory. I told her what she'd told me before, and what Madeline had said about her family. I asked why she'd lied; she got flustered and wouldn't reply. In bed that night, Madeline insisted that Tatti was the kindest, sweetest child she'd ever known—and would never lie. Just confused.

The next month I picked up a trailer from a transcontinental shipper and decided to go home early, even though I'd arrive after ten. I parked my cab in the yard, backing in so my headlights wouldn't piss off the neighbors, who went to bed at seven right after the evening CNN news. The front window of our house glowed yellow behind a drawn shade; the window in the kitchen glared white from the fluorescent ceiling bulbs. I'd never seen that many lights on this late.

I went into the house through the unlocked front door. There was light under Tatti's bedroom door. I knocked. No sound. I opened the door. She stood nude a few feet from me. Her small breasts were slippery with sweat, perfectly matched with nipples the same faint pink as her smeared lipstick. My heartbeat quickened. She had filled out up top with feminine curves thanks to Madeline's good care, but her legs, still young and slightly knock-kneed, were bent in like willow branches. She made no attempt to hide her privates—fine hair the color brown of tree bark and looking soft. I stared. Finally she moved, her face without the slightest emotion at seeing me, and looked at herself in the cracked fragments of a shattered full-length mirror taped to the back of the bathroom door. The door opened.

A dark-haired boy walked out of the bathroom. He had on a long-sleeved white shirt but was carrying jeans and wore flip-flops with nothing else. His limp dick swayed slightly as he moved. He was grinning.

I grabbed him by the back of the neck. I had more than a hundred pounds on him, and he was a foot shorter than me.

"Hey," he said. "Fuck off, man." But I moved fast and shoved him and his clothes out the front door. Tatyana still stood in front of the mirror pieces. She was admiring what she saw, and smiling.

"Get dressed," I said to her. I went through the room, found everything that I thought belonged to her. She turned to watch but held her ground. I stuffed all her belongings into two pillowcases. I grabbed her, still half-naked in unzipped jeans, by the arm.

"That hurts," she whined.

I shoved her out the front door with her stuffed pillowcases. I didn't see the boy.

"You mean man," she called back to me. She spat on the ground.

"You're a whore," I said. It wasn't just anger. I felt betrayed.

I slammed the door, locking it with the deadbolt. A few seconds later I heard her pounding on the locked back door, twisting the knob. But I ignored her.

I sat in my recliner chair with the TV off for many minutes, till my breathing slowed. I called Madeline at work but she didn't pick up, and I hung up when the phone went to voicemail. Tatyana didn't stop pounding. Damn it, I felt sorry for her. Thought about her being afraid in the dark. Still, to teach her a lesson, I waited till just after midnight before I let her in. She brushed by me without a word and I imagined the feel of her.

"Sinner," I said, as she went back to her bedroom.

Madeline came home after midnight.

"You're still awake?" she asked me. "Tough gig?"

I didn't answer.

"What's up, Clarence? You look exhausted."

"I kicked her out."

"Tatyana? Where is she?"

I shrugged, nodding toward the bedroom. "I put her and her stuff out the door."

"My God," Madeline said.

"She was screwing some sloppy, pimply kid."

"That's impossible." Madeline went to Tatyana's room. I heard yelling and crying. I stayed in my chair but couldn't sleep. I didn't talk to Madeline until the next morning.

"She wasn't screwing that kid," Madeline said. "She told me."

But Madeline couldn't look me in the eye when she said it. Madeline had come to love Tatyana like a daughter. It was what she wanted in life and it blinded her to what was real in the world.

The next day Tatti told Madeline I was a dirty old man. That I was spying on her. My mind was in a pigsty, or something like that. She never wanted to see me again. The following day, Tatti spent the night out and Madeline didn't know where.

"She won't live where she's not wanted," Madeline said to me.

"She did wrong."

"She made a mistake. Letting him in. She didn't have sex with him." But I knew Madeline wouldn't believe any dirty truth about Tatyana; she couldn't think bad about her girl.

"I thought she was better than that," I said.

"She still doesn't like the way you look at her."

"That don't make it an excuse," I said.

"She's afraid you might do something."

"Aw, Maddie." I was angry as hell. But later that day the memory of nude Tatyana touched my heart with a sweet longing coated with pain I couldn't keep out. I didn't feel good about it.

Next morning I left before dawn to pick up a container in San Francisco. It was afternoon before I got to the pier to wait my turn—hours in which I could only think about what had happened. I took a snapshot of Madeline and Tatyana I'd taken when we went to church months ago, and I cut out Madeline with a knife so I could see Tatyana standing alone. I just wish I'd never seen her with that kid. And I was even more ashamed at the excitement she still stirred in me.

I was home by the end of the week. I didn't try to talk to Madeline while I was on the trip, and she didn't call me. When I saw Madeline, she was passed out in my recliner, her mouth open and snoring, an almost-empty bottle of Jim Beam on the floor. I'd never known her to take a drink of alcohol.

Tatyana had moved out. I thought Madeline had finally caught her in a lie, but no, Tatyana had said she didn't want to stay in the house with me. Madeline thought I'd made Tatyana leave, the way I looked at her, accusing her of sex she hadn't had. Tatyana was afraid, Madeline said. She'd gotten a job in a shoe store at the mall on a fake ID Madeline had paid for last month, and she was living with an immigrant family on the south side. Although I wasn't sure Tatti wasn't shacked up with a guy. That's what I said to Madeline. She refused to talk to me and the air was so electric in the house I got a pickup job to Colorado so I could get back on the road and be alone for a while.

When I got back home four days later, the tension hadn't eased.

After weeks of Madeline suffering and hearing her complain, I knew something had to be done, for both our sakes.

I finally cornered Tatti when she went out into the mall for a milkshake on her break. I asked her to consider Madeline's feelings. Invited her to live with us until she could start her schooling for cosmetology. Told her I would never hurt her and that I wanted her back home to be a part of our family. She looked me straight in the eye and laughed. Cruel. I made her feel creepy, she said. "You make me nauseate."

"Come back for Madeline's sake," I said. But her face took on a grimace and her voice was hard with scorn. "Never," she said. "She want to be mother to me. She never be mother."

"She loves you like a friend," I said.

She shook her head in disbelief. "She want no friend. She like make rule to feel good."

Tatyana didn't give a damn about Madeline!

Or me.

I left. It was cruel to say those things after Madeline's kindnesses. And the way Tatyana had treated me bugged me for days. I couldn't let her get away with her lies. The next day, I reported her to the authorities. In writing.

Madeline saw her at the mall off and on but Tatyana wouldn't return her looks, much less talk to her. And Madeline blew up when she discovered what I'd done. Investigators came to the house. Madeline blamed me. Hated me. I was evil. I'd committed worse than murder. She wanted to move out, or me to move out. She didn't give a damn which one and she was determined about divorce. She soon made it final. Without contest. And without any willingness to remember our past good times together. Deportation procedures against Tatyana had started.

I got some money from the house settlement and upgraded my equipment to a top-grade Peterbilt; I have a cab with a cooktop and a sink, a bunk where I can stretch out full length, and a thirty-inch screen flatscreen TV with a satellite hookup. I live in my rig now. I still have that photo of Tatyana taped to the dash but most of the time I think of Madeline … like she was in the old days, though. I carry fishing gear, a stationary bike for exercise. And I've never broken my rule again. Oh, I give rides to friends of friends sometimes to save them bus fare, but never a stranger. No, sir. Never again. And how sad that is. America ain't the same no more. Shit. You can't trust no one. Wouldn't mind going back to the days where you could help a stranger without getting sideswiped.

And I go to church a lot, in different towns mostly, to pray for forgiveness for the feelings I still carry for a Russian girl alien who lied and sinned, and made Madeline and me so starry-eyed so as to mess with our feelings, and hooked my heart without a pinch of caring.

Big Gene

illustration by Peter Healy

Big Gene

In the seventies, in rural Maryland just outside Washington, DC, the Black Mountain Boys, an all-white band, had a regular gig at an all-white truck stop and hired Big Gene, a black piano player who had an eleven-inch thumb-to-pinky stretch that whacked out tenths like octaves. Big Gene played boogie like Pete Johnson and Albert Ammons and could walk down into infinity of R&B with a left hand transplanted from Professor Longhair and James Booker. Sid, the fiddle player and band manger, saw Big Gene as a savior, given the diminishing popularity of his country repertoire. "Play the book," he said to Big Gene, "but make it sound like they'll want to shake their booty."

On Big Gene's first night, the truck stop's owner approached Sid as they were setting up.

"Who the fuck is that?" the owner asked Sid. Big Gene did not look up.

"Piano player," Sid said.

"We don't hire no coloreds."

"You hired us. He plays the piano."

"He ain't playing my piano."

"I didn't know you played piano."

"Don't smartass me."

"He's got his own. One of them electric things."

"Never heard of a black guy could play country."

"He was born in a horse barn after his mama finished a cattle drive," Sid said, trying to suppress a smile.

The owner crossed his arms and eyed the band for a few seconds. "Any trouble and you're out of here," he finally said and walked away. "All of you."

They faced the piano toward the wall and Big Gene played his keyboard instead. When he sat on his fortified piano bench, he anchored more than a few gazes at six feet, two inches, and 374 pounds. Big Gene had no love for country music. For him it was like chopping firewood. And he didn't like playing for angry whites. He liked the white guys in the band who cared more about work and family than race, but they were different from the clientele, who seemed deprived of everything and angry at all they'd been denied.

At the first break the drummer came over to Big Gene. "Shit, man, you can really play that thing," he said, nodding at the keyboard.

"Folks seemed to like it," Big Gene said.

"You been in town long?" the drummer asked.

"About a year. Not much work, though."

"Tell me about it, man," the drummer said. "I've been looking for a better gig. Jump ship in a heartbeat."

"Sid seems solid," Big Gene said.

"The best. I hope this crossover works for him. I don't think I can live through another 'Stand by My Man.' The way we play it, I could take a piss between the ones."

Big Gene felt relief getting away after the first night. The place was hell. It never closed, and at any time of day or night there'd be twenty to forty rigs pulled in on diagonals on the three-plus acres of dirt parking, diesels running on the refrigerated loads, some guys sleeping in the cabs, others running a rag over a radiator chrome strip on a Peterbilt. The air was eerie thick—impending doom, like a war zone. And without exception, inside every rig some serious weapon hid within easy reach.

Big Gene got home after one in the morning. Cloretta waited up, sitting in front of a TV that hadn't been turned on.

"We got to talk, Eugene," Cloretta said. "It's after twelve. You got children."

"It's a steady job, Clorrie."

Big Gene lowered himself into an overstuffed armchair.

"It's disgraceful," she said, her voice quivering. "That's what everyone at church thinks."

Big Gene stayed quiet.

"White trash," she blurted out. "And it's no reputation for a man of God to be chasing after."

"It's just music. Making people happy," he said.

He loved his Cloretta. Exhausted, he glanced away.

"If you've got to play piano, play gospel." Her voice had turned angry.

"I can't make a living in the church."

"Well, I can't teach school forever. It takes too much out of me."

Big Gene took his wife's hand and pulled her to standing.

"I've been thinking. I'm going to sell tapes. I got a guy who'll do it for a percentage of sales."

"You're dreaming," she said.

He hugged her so there wasn't much of her showing. "There's a lot of people making big money in my music now."

"They ain't making it at no all-white truck stop."

"We'll be looking for sales in the music stores, too."

She pulled back so he could see her face. "Just don't be selling your soul. I can't tolerate that, Eugene."

The truck stop was the only nightlife with live music for fifty miles, and it was the only place a lot of locals went to get out of the house in the evenings. Most customers were guys. A few brought wives or sweethearts, but not many. Most of the unescorted girls were walking the line out of a trailer park about a mile away. Once you finished your business, you could clean up, too. Behind the gas station and weakly lit fuel pumps, management had erected a prefab shed where you could shower for half a buck, with a dry towel—you got your driver's license back when you handed the towel back to the attendant—and a one-inch cut from a bar of soap.

The restaurant was a concrete-block building that had been a warehouse. It had grill counter service on one side, and a kitchen specializing in spareribs barbecued, half a chicken fried, and meatloaf with pan gravy and potatoes. White waitresses in short skirts carried four or five plates of food without spilling to bare, Formica-topped tables. In the back was a long bar, a tiled dance floor, and the raised platform for the band.

After a few weeks, Big Gene began to play solid boogie solo piano during the breaks. Soon regulars timed their thirsts to hear Big Gene, and the manager booked the Black Mountain Boys for another three months and called Big Gene Sid's pot of gold.

A tall white guy with skin like sunbaked leather and a Braves baseball cap came regular on Thursdays to sit on an end barstool. He was close enough for Big Gene to hear when he laid out for Sid's solos. One night the leathery tall guy said to the guy next to him, "That nigger's good. He plays like Jerry Lee Lewis."

Big Gene overcame his urge to look. Then the guy yelled to Big Gene. "Hey, man. You know 'Great Balls of Fire'?"

Big Gene grinned. "You know I love it," he said. But he played "The Fat Man." Afterward he came off the stand and approached.

The man looked puzzled. "I mean it, boy. You great," he said with an edgy smile.

"Thank you, sir," Big Gene said.

"You ought to learn 'Great Balls of Fire.' I was telling the man here. You flat-ass sound like Jerry Lee Lewis."

Big Gene waited; the leathery man stared. "Mr. Lewis learned from us coloreds," Big Gene said.

"You're shitting me." The man looked genuinely surprised.

"Yes sir. Mr. Lewis learned from some of the greats, like we all do."

"Goddamn."

"Yes, sir. It's the God's truth," Big Gene said, smiling.

As Big Gene climbed back on stage to start the next set, Sid whispered to him, "What was that all about?"

"That redneck thought I took my playing from Jerry Lee Lewis. I was correcting his misperceptions."

"I'm surprised he didn't shoot you."

"I was a little shocked, too," Big Gene said, grinning.

A few weeks later, during a break, Big Gene rolled out his version of "Great Balls of Fire." He played it on the house piano. The leathery guy stood up and yelled, "I mean, that was flat-out next to best I ever heard!" He waved a power fist in the air to Big Gene.

"What you drink?" the leathery guy asked Big Gene from his barstool.

"He only drink cranberry juice," said the bartender. Big Gene started playing. The leathery guy put two bucks on the counter. "On me," he said. He walked to the piano. The bartender carried a water glass half full of cranberry juice and put it down at the side of Big Gene without comment. Big Gene played on, and when he finished the leathery man stepped up to him.

"How you drink cranberry juice and still play like that? It's like you're high as the moon." The leathery guy sipped beer from a bottle.

Big Gene drank his juice while sitting on the piano stool. The owner—always dressed in a gray silk suit with a no-tie, shiny black shirt buttoned at the neck—came up to Big Gene, took the glass of cranberry juice from him, and placed it on the floor behind the piano.

The leathery guy stiffened. "Hey, Howard, you got a problem?"

"The help can't drink with customers."

"It's cranberry juice. Besides, he's the piano player. He ain't just help."

The owner hesitated as he weighed what was offending a good customer, and how it could hurt business to have some guy drinking with the coloreds.

"We got rules, Parker."

"You got no rules about cranberry juice."

"Don't make it regular. You hear me?" the owner said. He shook his head and walked off.

Big Gene stood.

The leathery guy picked up Big Gene's glass and handed it to him. He was eye level with Big Gene now. "Name's Parker Smith. I'm a carpenter. I do custom cabinets mostly—finishing stuff—but with hard times I been doing on-site construction a lot this last year. I tell you man, I don't like it. But I do it to keep food on the table, know what I'm saying?"

"I hear you," Big Gene said.

"You got children?" Parker asked, leaning his elbow on the top of the piano.

"Boy eleven and a girl eight."

"I got seven kids. Same wife."

The click of hard-heeled boots pounding the floor tiles came toward them—sounding weird like trouble—and Big Gene looked to Parker, who held his gaze for a few seconds. The guy approaching was past his best years, his jeans low on his belly and held together with a tooled leather belt and a brass buckle cast in the shape of a big-rig cab coming at you.

"Hey Parker. You taking up with colored?"

"No man," Parker said. "This is Jerry Lee Lewis. He ain't no colored."

"He look colored."

"He's the fucking piano player."

The belt buckle guy never once looked at Big Gene.

"Don't be looking good, Parker. You got your responsibilities. You gotta be careful what people thinking these days." He walked away.

Parker had his head down. He didn't speak for many seconds. "Don't pay no attention to him," he said to Big Gene. "He's Klan."

Big Gene felt a muscle twitch in his face.

"He thinks 'cause I'm Klan, he's got rights," Parker said.

Big Gene couldn't speak at first. "Really, you a wizard?" he finally asked hesitantly.

"Shit no. Don't get bent wrong."

Big Gene was tight as a high-end piano wire.

"Don't ride your clutch, my man," Parker said, "We ain't against all coloreds."

"That isn't the rumor," Big Gene said.

Parker looked straight at Big Gene, then looked away. "That ain't you, man. You regular."

"Thank you," Big Gene said, but the words didn't come easy.

Cloretta heard from a woman at church that Gene was talking to a Klansman at the truck stop. "It isn't right," she said one night when they were in bed, neither able to sleep.

"It can make a difference," Big Gene said.

"You aren't Dr. King," she said. "It's arrogant to be thinking that way."

Big Gene had thought out what he wanted to tell her. "He's afraid, Clorrie, deep down. Like I'm a moccasin or something. But now he begins to see me like a garden snake that has no teeth and no poison, and that I'm working—snaking around—just like him to stay alive. There isn't much fear left in you after you pick up your first garden snake who doesn't care about hurting you, probably doesn't see much difference between you and a tree stump. Might even appreciate you're not stepping on him."

"Crazy talk," she said, and turned her back to him. He stared at the ceiling. He believed Dr. King would take these opportunities and peace would come one man at a time—not by going to war.

The next afternoon Cloretta greeted him when she got home after school.

"I'm sorry about last night, Eugene."

"It's okay, Clorrie."

"It's just that I don't see why you're making up to him."

Big Gene didn't say anything for a while. "He loves his wife," he said to her. She had started washing dishes at the kitchen sink. "And I love you."

"You are too smooth for your own good," she said over her shoulder.

Big Gene didn't see Parker much in the summer. Parker had a plot of land he leased to plant soy, and with tending his crop and making cabinets, he was pretty tired a night. But on a late summer night after harvest he came by the truck stop after twelve. He parked.

The band had finished locking up their stuff, and Big Gene walked out of the building alone and saw three black guys beating up on a guy behind a red pickup. Big Gene squinted. It was Parker. A skinny kid with a razor ripped Parker's shirt and sliced his chest and now was starting on his thighs. Behind him there was a taller kid holding a shiv like he was waiting to jam it through Parker's ribs into his heart.

Big Gene got to the shiv kid just as he began to move, grabbed him by his shiv arm with his right hand, and squeezed until the shiv fell. Then he grabbed the kid's crotch with his left hand and picked the shiv kid off the ground and held him so his feet didn't touch earth.

"What the fuck?" the razor kid said, backing off.

Big Gene shook the shiv kid and threw him to the ground.

"He Klan, bro." the razor kid said.

"No killing," Big Gene said. Big Gene took the razor from the kid and picked up the shiv from where it had fallen.

"He'd hang you from a fucking tree," said the kid holding Parker.

The kid let Parker go, and Parker slumped down; he'd lost a bucket of blood.

"Cutting a man is not the way to overcome."

"You one weird motherfucker," the kid said as the three backed away, turned, and ran.

Big Gene picked Parker up and carried him toward the restaurant. "You're going to make it," he said to Parker, who was barely conscious. A photo flash went off and blinded Big Gene as he came close to the door.

The manager had brought out a folding chair and Big Gene set Parker down. A few minutes later, when the emergency van turned into the parking lot with lights flashing, Big Gene slipped into the darkness to go to his car.

Next day Big Gene saw a photo of Parker Smith being carried from an assault for treatment—like it was something no one would expect a negro to do—on the front page of the local paper.

Parker's chest carried scars, but his legs healed better. He rarely came to hear Big Gene play any more until one Thursday night in the spring.

Big Gene came off the bandstand after the first set to say hello.

Parker had never mentioned anything about his assault to Big Gene, and he didn't say anything about it that night, either. He said his son, Harry, was in juvenile. It was a big worry for him.

The Black Mountain Boys began to straggle back in from break; Big Gene turned to go back on stage.

"I was wondering," Parker said, "if you'd play the reception at my daughter's wedding in June."

"I can ask Sid."

"No, man. Just you."

Big Gene stared at Parker, whose lips were tight, his brow creased with apprehension.

"Sure," Big Gene said.

"And bring your wife. I'd be proud to have her," Parker said.

"I'll ask, but I don't think she'll come."

"Women like weddings."

"Her mother died waiting for treatment at the hospital. She's bitter. Thinks her mother would be alive if she were white."

"Sweet talk her, man."

Big Gene put on his tuxedo for the wedding gig. Cloretta sat on the bed in her robe and watched as he dressed.

"You're asking for trouble," she said.

"At a wedding?"

"There'll be hate there, Eugene. That man's friends have killed the likes of us."

"I'm sorry you're not going. I'd like you to meet him."

"When hell freezes," she said.

Big Gene sat near the back of the church. The bride had a scrubbed glow to her skin, her eyes avoiding the crowd. At the reception, Parker introduced Big Gene to friends.

"This is the man that saved my ass," Parker said to a man in a light-blue suit and his wife, who wore blue shoes—seemingly trying to match his suit—with four-inch heels and a white satin short dress.

"Pleased to meet you," Big Gene said. The man barely reached his shoulder.

The man reached out his hand, and Big Gene took it. "Any friend of Parker's is a friend of mine."

The wedding photographer snapped pictures.

The organist for the ceremony played the piano for the bride and groom's first dance. But after that, Big Gene played out the time—and the people danced.

Two days later, before Cloretta left for school, she held up the Sunday paper to show the black-and-white picture of Big Gene shaking hands with the man in the blue suit. She read the caption: "Klan Reaches Out."

"It's not right," Cloretta said.

"He doesn't look dangerous," Big Gene said, and smiled.

Cloretta frowned. "They called you a civil rights activist. You shouldn't be shaking his hand. You shoulda whooped his butt."

The next afternoon a man from the National Urban League came to the house to arrange a live interview in Washington a week later. Cloretta was waiting when Big Gene got home from the TV station.

"What did you think?" he asked.

"That man didn't let you talk enough."

"Weren't you just a little bit impressed?"

"You're too full of yourself," she said.

He held her tightly, until she relaxed a little. She was always tense these days.

More than a year passed. Big Gene was selling his own tapes at gigs and at a music store in DC. Cloretta had changed schools to take a higher-paying job in administration. Daughter Sharyll was beginning to look at colleges and had visited the University of Maryland. Son Hal was on the basketball team at school and hoped to be a starter.

One Tuesday night, a thirty-foot cross burned on a knoll behind Cloretta's and Big Gene's AME church. It toppled onto the church school, which burned to the ground.

In the middle of the night, Cloretta wept. Big Gene turned the night-light on and got up. He brought her iced tea from the kitchen. "At least the sanctuary wasn't damaged," he said.

"The school is important!"

He put the iced tea on the floor next to the bed.

"I don't want that," she said.

He picked up the glass and put it on the dresser.

"What's up, baby?"

"Don't you 'baby' me."

He got back in bed but didn't touch her.

She stopped her crying, wiping her eyes with the edge of the sheet. "I can't stand it anymore."

"The church has insurance."

"And we'll rebuild. And be burned. And someone will die. And we'll rebuild again. And no one will be punished."

"There's an outrage …" Big Gene began.

"There will never be a white man jailed or hung for crimes against us."

"It's takes time, Clorrie. I think we're making progress."

"In the name of God, Eugene," Cloretta said, "Where's the fight in you? You're not the man I married."

There had been a time when he had used his size to assault men. He wouldn't do that anymore.

"It's your friend," she said. "He did it."

"That's not fair, Clorrie. I don't think he'd do this."

"You don't think he was involved? He at least knew about it!"

Big Gene didn't know Parker's activities with the Klan, really.

"You're blind, Eugene. They're running over you."

Big Gene paused. "We'll win, Clorrie, but not with hate and anger. That defeats us."

She didn't respond. The depth of her silence hurt him when he said "I love you" and she turned away.

Months later, new construction had started on the church school. Big Gene was home from work, standing with Cloretta on the porch. A cardboard box had been dropped off at the front door.

"Did they say what it was?" Big Gene said.

"I didn't see who delivered."

Big Gene picked it up. It wasn't heavy. He listened. There was no sound.

"Throw it out," Cloretta said, fearing it was a bomb.

Big Gene stripped off the tape and opened the flaps. White satin gleamed. He pulled out a full-length robe, unadorned except for a patch with a white cross and a red background. From the bottom he pulled out a pointed hood, with two eye slits.

"It's a threat," Cloretta said. "They're going to hurt us."

"It means he's left the Klan, Clorrie."

She stuffed the robe back into the box. "Don't let anyone see it."

Big Gene picked up the box and took it into the guest room. Cloretta followed. He took a hanger from the closet.

"Don't," she said.

"It means a lot to me, Clorrie." On the hanger the robe was so long it gathered on the floor.

"In the name of God, Gene. I don't want that in the closet."

"It's a symbol of hope."

"That's crazy talk. I can't stand it."

Big Gene reached into the closet. "I'll store it in the shed."

"Dear Jesus," she said. "Leave it in the closet. It's you I don't want. Not the robe."

By the middle of the decade, Big Gene had finished playing music professionally. He owned a real estate business. Parker Smith died on the job—broke his neck when he fell backward off a second-floor balcony at a home site under construction. Big Gene still lived in the same house. In his guest room closet he had seven Klan robes from former members he'd gotten to know through Parker—robes he showed to visitors, most of whom acted as if Big Gene's mind had shrunk from too many years of loud music. Cloretta never forgave him, and after the divorce she took the kids and moved in with her sister in Minnesota. Later, Big Gene married a secretary he had met at church. She had marched with Dr. King, a Miss Melanie Harper.

In 1978, by popular demand, Big Gene ran for congress.

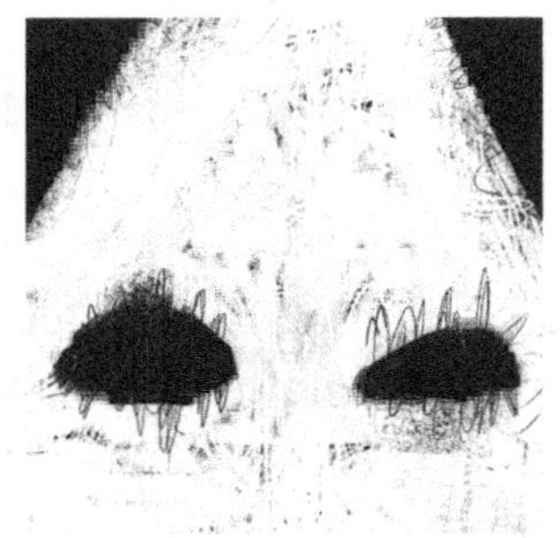

Grief

illustration by Peter Healy

Grief

One Tuesday, an old cardboard shipping box with UPS tracking labels from Florida was left outside Sarah Tanner's door by the building manager. Masking tape fortified the torn edges and black marker blotted out the original California wine company logo. On the top were coffee-stained partial circles from coffee cup rims. Sarah briefly worried that the box might be a threat; she was afraid of everything lately, after her divorce. She cut the carelessly applied transparent tape that sealed the top and folded back the flaps. She rummaged through items from a camping trip: a backpack, water bottles, a toilet kit, extra hiking socks. Every item evoked memories of her fervent affair with Peter Musconi more than twenty-five years ago.

In the bottom of the box was a business envelope with no markings, the flap sealed with Scotch tape. She opened it. A white-gold engagement ring dropped to the floor. A faceted diamond, perfect color, no inclusions, and more than a carat, glittered rare value. Pristine, without blemishes. She picked it up, clutched it in her hand. It's how she remembered the perfection of her affair with Peter Musconi. Pristine.

She'd never seen this ring before but knew it was meant for her. Their love for each other had been interrupted by the suddenness and immediacy of the breakup; Peter believed she'd been unfaithful; unfounded, circumstantial evidence delivered in rumor and innuendo had convinced him.

She sat and put her head back on the armless metal kitchen chair to stare at the blistered paint on the ceiling. Almost everything about Peter, his kindness, his caring, returned to her with edged clarity. And the longing resurfaced—began to consume her again. Tears blurred her vision. It had been easier to ignore thoughts of Peter when she was still dutifully caring for her husband Carl and daughter Carmen. But Carl, a surgeon ready to retire, was living alone after the divorce in his three-room apartment, and Carmen was a medical student in training and lived near the hospital.

The quiet of this post-divorce rented apartment now irritated her. She turned on the radio near the sink. She sat again and leaned forward, resting her forehead on her arms. Many minutes passed before she reached for the phone to call the owner of the name, Richard Conway, on the box's return label.

Richard Conway, a probate lawyer in Florida, was not available for a phone conversation at first. When he finally did respond, he was unfriendly. Mr. Musconi was dying, he said. Leukemia. He had made up a will for him. "He asked me to find this box. I had to crawl below ground to a storage bin beneath his apartment."

She needed to believe that Peter still cared. That he hadn't forgotten. That she had misjudged him. "There was an expensive ring," she ventured.

"I do probate. I barely know him."

"It's probably worth at least ten thousand dollars. Is that a mistake or what?"

Mr. Conway was silent.

"Can I talk to him?"

"He's on a respirator most of the time. He mouths a few words. But he mostly writes on a pad."

"Would you ask him about the ring?" she asked.

"I'm finished with him. The will is finalized."

"Where is he? What hospital?"

"Near Sarasota," he said. He reluctantly looked up the address. "Goodbye," he said abruptly.

In the morning she chose a white blouse, black skirt, and matching jacket to attend the evening faculty meeting without having to come home to change after work. Later that night, she had to meet her daughter, Carmen. A rumor was circulating that Carmen was dating a man her father's age, the chair of psychiatry at the university where Sarah worked as a scientist. Hospital and school policies prohibited faculty dating students in hopes of preventing favoritism that might result in costly legal action. If Carmen persisted, scandal could strangle her career, and her lover's.

Sarah was afraid to intervene, afraid to risk the last of her barely existent parental control. But Carmen no longer accepted her father's calls, and her father had insisted that Sarah talk to her. He was angry and frustrated with Carmen's denials, irate at her irrational behavior.

After the faculty meeting, Sarah took a cab to Carmen's apartment. Carmen was not home, so Sarah dined at a deli alone and then let herself in to wait. Finally, just before midnight, Carmen arrived and immediately expressed resentment at her mother's unwelcome visit; she obviously suspected Sarah's purpose and delayed their talk with hyperactivity and silence, finally spending many minutes behind the closed bathroom door. Sarah waited anxiously, sitting cross-legged on a throw rug, proud at sixty-one that she could still bend like a teenager.

Carmen emerged from the bathroom in pajamas and a robe and settled into a place on the love seat. The lights were off. Carmen preferred the dim light that seeped through the window from the street, under the half-drawn shade.

Sarah asked about Carmen's rotation at the hospital. Carmen—perched on the love seat, her face barely visible, left leg up and right foot positioned to relieve the chronic pain she had from a congenital deformity of the lower spine—did not respond. Sarah never suppressed her worry about the imperfection, even though she'd been told by many that she was blameless, that some handed-down gene or an accident during the pregnancy was not responsible.

Carmen gasped with pain and changed position.

"Can I get you a pillow?" Sarah asked.

"I don't need a pillow, mother. I need to go to bed."

"It's not me, Carmen. I didn't come to irritate you. Your father thinks we need to talk."

"It's not negotiable."

Below the window shade a dim glow from a neon bank sign across the street outlined shapes in the room, but did not throw shadows. Icy rain pelted the windows. The tip of the joint between Carmen's thumb and forefinger glowed as she inhaled.

"We're in love." Carmen said.

Sarah paused. "It can't work, Carmen."

"We're discreet."

"His wife knows!"

"He doesn't love her. I don't think he ever did."

"Married professors can't love students," Sarah said.

"My God, mother. What difference does that make?"

"It's against school policy. It's immoral."

"He's going to separate …"

Sarah leaned back on the floor, put her hands behind her head, and crossed her legs as Carmen stared. Then she worried that Carmen would see her flexibility as a taunt. She sat again with her arms around her knees. "He told the committee it was over," she said. "I heard it at work. They warned him. He denied any wrongdoing. I heard from one committee member they almost recommended his dismissal."

"He has to say that. Until his divorce is final."

Sarah waited. "Your father won't support you if this goes on. He told me to tell you."

Carmen hissed with disgust. "How could you let him do that?"

"I have no say with your father. You won't answer his calls, Carmen. He needed me to tell you."

Carmen scraped the butt dead in an ashtray. She closed her eyes. "You'll support the tuition," she said. "You have to do that."

Sarah hesitated. "I don't have that kind of money, Carmen."

"Make him do it, then. What's different? I'm his daughter."

"You're having an adulterous affair. No one approves. He thinks you're ruining your life."

"And you? What do you think?"

It's crazy, Sarah didn't say. You're blinded by lust for an older man who's attracted to your youth. There is no permanence in that. You're doomed to pain and humiliation. "I think you're making a serious mistake," she said.

"As if you're some expert. What the fuck would you know about love? I'd never want what you and Dad had."

"You know, Carmen, I don't give a damn what you do anymore." But I know more about love than you'll ever know, Sarah thought, remembering Peter Musconi. What she had with Peter was beautiful, spoiled by the misunderstanding that shattered a joy of caring. It was love so special, so electric and binding, between two human beings—a love that Carmen might never know. But Sarah could not tell Carmen now. Carmen would dispute every word, and another argument would only again accent Sarah's failure as a mother.

Carmen rolled to one side to ease the pain of standing. "I'm going to bed," she said.

"I'll sleep here till morning," Sarah said, moving to the love seat.

"Suit yourself," Carmen said.

Sarah could not sleep. Carmen's crack about Sarah knowing nothing about love hurt her more than she would have expected. But why allow Carmen the satisfaction of irritating her at will? Look at the facts. Carmen hadn't developed the life skills Sarah had hoped she would. Oh, she loved Carmen and worried for her, but Carmen was not a superstar in anything. Of course she was pretty enough, being young helped, and her deformity was barely noticeable. But she was consistently cranky and insecure, smart but not brilliant, demanding but never giving. And she had no parental respect. None. Well, Sarah reasoned, I gave so much more than most mothers. She was definitely not responsible for Carmen's mediocrity—that Sarah ultimately blamed on Carl. He had really wanted a boy. Sarah saw the disappointment in his face after the delivery. At first he was kind and attentive to Carmen, and loyal, even if humorless. But as Carmen got older and lost her daddy's-cute-little-girl routine, he increasingly ignored her. He spoke in platitudes and reprimands, chipping away her already-thin veneer of confidence.

Dawn came. Sarah sat up and put her bare feet on the floor. She would go see Peter. He was dying. She wanted to believe his package was a signal of his longing for her over these years, longing she hoped equaled her own. She wanted to know her never-fading passion, although suppressed by time, marriage, and motherhood, was not just a memory of what might have been. She was unconcerned with pretenses now. She'd been desperately lonely for years. If Carmen knew about Peter, saw him, saw the source of Sarah's intensity, caring, hoping, and longing, maybe Carmen would know why love lost had ossified Sarah's heart, forever trapping the marrow of feeling inside. It was not Sarah's fault. But it had dried up any caring they as a family might have had for each other in the early years.

One of Sarah's PhD colleagues knew a spine clinic near where Peter was hospitalized. Sarah made an appointment and insisted Carmen go. They would have three days together. Carmen resisted by reflex, but her pain had turned worse with winter and she liked the idea of warm Florida, where she could get the pills her internist would no longer prescribe and take medically related personal days off from her student duties at the hospital.

The next day Sarah went to Carmen's apartment and they took a cab to La Guardia. A freezing rain iced the wipers and visibility was not good.

Carmen undid her wool coat in the heat of the cab. Sarah thought Carmen looked attractive in a cochineal red dress, the hemline above her knees to show her thin, only slightly defined legs, which gave her a little-girl look. Sarah understood how a middle-aged man could be attracted to Carmen's youthful skin and naturally blond hair.

"Who's this friend?" Carmen asked, as if this was the first time she'd thought of it. Sarah wanted to blurt the joy of her good memories about Peter. Tell her of the crescendo of sharing and caring she had never forgotten.

"I knew him in school," Sarah said. "I spent a year in his lab as a postdoc."

"Really."

"He was a surgeon, but he was doing work in angiogenesis in a mouse model."

Carmen gazed out the window.

Sarah wanted to tell her what she and Peter had talked about: beauty, fulfillment, shared values. How the sound of his breathing in the dark aroused her. She wanted to explain how an ardent suitor she never liked or encouraged in any way had lied to Peter to convince him she was unfaithful.

"Is your pain any better today?" she asked Carmen.

"It doesn't change," Carmen said without looking at her.

When Sarah asked her about her pathology rotation, Carmen shrugged. Sarah said little else. Their flight arrived in Florida four hours late. The motel front desk had already shut down. They rang a bell for the sleepy attendant.

After the visit to the specialist, Sarah took Carmen with her to the hospital. Peter's family was not there; they rarely came, the nurse said. Sarah and Carmen looked down at Peter. His breath rattled in the opening of the tracheotomy tube in his neck.

"Peter," Sarah said.

Monitors at the beside gave uncoordinated beeps for vital functions.

"He's not conscious," Carmen said. Carmen's authoritative medical-student tone irritated Sarah. "Let's go," Carmen added.

"In a minute," Sarah said sharply. This is Peter, she wanted to say, the first man I gave myself to—with passion and warmth and caring I never experienced again. Do you think you're strong enough to carry that with you for a lifetime, my little Carmen? The joy of being loved?

"He's seventy-two?" Carmen asked.

Sarah held Peter's coarse, dry-skinned hand in hers. Tears filled her eyes. Carmen turned away and went to sit in an armless chair near the door. Carmen saw no love. She saw sentimentality and it embarrassed her. Disgusting, really. The sentimentality.

Bringing Carmen had been an enormous mistake. She would never understand; she could never perceive the reality across twenty-five years of time, with Peter unable to communicate.

Sarah remained quiet for many minutes as Carmen read a magazine. Sarah slowly became aware of Peter's presence. Then there was tension in his hand, an attempt to communicate. One time she thought his head turned a fraction of an inch toward her. She squeezed his hand gently. She knew he squeezed back. Carmen never knew.

"Why did you break up?" Carmen asked.

It was what Sarah had wanted. An interest in the past from Carmen. But now it seemed insincere.

"It was a fateful misunderstanding."

"That is so male," Carmen said with disdain.

"He was hurt. We both were." She felt Peter's hand tighten again.

"His pressure is dropping," Carmen said as she stared at a green-line monitor.

Sarah thought through his closed eyelids Peter tried to look at her.

"His pulse is irregular," Carmen said.

"Get the nurse."

"Push the call button, Mother."

"I don't see it."

"It's probably on the floor."

"Please go!" Sarah no longer wanted Carmen in the room. Carmen's crass aloofness seemed cruel. She wished again she had never brought her.

"Damn it," Carmen said.

As the door closed, the tension in Peter's hand increased. She thought he might have smiled.

The pulse monitor alarm went off. In a few seconds a nurse rushed in. Carmen did not return. There was so much Sarah needed to explain; she felt life leaving when Peter's body tensed ever so slightly in waves that must have been more imagined than real, like a breeze caressing a flag, then the flag drooping, motionless. Sarah waited, hoping for more time with Peter, but resuscitation routines were useless.

Sarah took Carmen to the airport that evening. With Peter's death, she needed desperately to tell Carmen every detail of her love for him. Sarah wanted to probe the loss she was suffering. How love could lapse so irreversibly into grief. But Carmen talked continually about her pain and her doctor's appointment, allowing no time for conversation, as if she dreaded words from her mother, any words.

In a motel room Sarah waited alone for the funeral, lying on the bed with little sleep day or night, eating crackers and drinking sodas she collected from the vending machine down the hall. Three days later she attended the brief service at the funeral parlor. The youngest son had come to oversee arrangements.

"Who are you?" the son asked.

Sarah gave him a questioning look. She could see a likeness to Peter, and her grief escalated.

"An old friend. Years ago."

"You dated?"

"Almost two years."

He looked away. He had demons he was hiding, but she could only guess what they might be. She wondered if he loved his father. She doubted he loved anyone.

"He was a wonderful man," she said reflexively.

"What would you know?" he said without turning.

"I knew him well," she said testily. She looked away from the son, from the casket, out an open door to an alley.

"No one ever knew him." He laughed without humor and walked away. He had no consolation for her; he had no grief to compare.

A minister, who did not seem to have known Peter or the family, said prayers. The son gave a short, remote, insecure eulogy to the thirteen people who attended. She could imagine Carmen reluctantly giving the same empty words for her. She left before the reception started.

Waiting to board a flight to return home, Sarah sat at gate A32 next to a gray-haired woman in a print dress with wire-framed bifocal glasses and swollen feet in black, low-heeled shoes. She clutched her bag on her lap.

Sarah, when she closed her eyes, saw the redundant details of Peter's dying parade before her. She needed to talk about him, about them. In death he deserved to be known for the good man he was. Someone needed to know. To know the source of her misery.

"You don't like flying?" Sarah said.

"Why, no, I don't. It's my second time. To visit my only grandchild."

Sarah looked down.

"I flew down to see a friend who died …" Sarah began.

"She's adopted. My daughter-in-law has blocked tubes, or something."

"I hadn't seen my friend ..."

"Did you come far?" the woman asked. She talked loudly, as if she might be hard of hearing.

"I live in New York now. That's why I didn't ..."

"I go to Houston. It takes two stops."

The overhead announcement told standbys that there were no seats available. The woman heard this and opened her purse and looked at her boarding pass. She replaced it.

"He was cremated," Sarah said.

"That's the way now. Isn't it?" the woman said. "But not for me. I want to be whole for the second coming." The woman shook her head as if affirming that cremation was a serious mistake. Then she stood, pointing to a light-green tote bag. "Would you watch that?" she asked. She headed toward the restrooms. Sarah waited until the woman returned before joining her group, which was in the process of boarding.

Her aisle seat was on a two-seat row; in the window seat a tall black youth with a reversed baseball cap sat with his knees angled into her space. She slipped down into the seat. He said nothing. Peter's open coffin was on her mind, his lifeless look so inhuman that the passing of his life seemed even more acute.

The plane leveled off at cruising altitude. The youth ate a banana he pulled out of his pocket, put the skin in the seat-back pocket in front of him.

"You like bananas?" Sarah asked.

He looked at her as if to tell her to go away, and then ignored her. He seemed intent on ignoring her.

"Not really," he said.

Sarah smiled. Surprised.

"Potassium," he said.

"You play basketball?" she asked.

The youth looked at her guardedly. He nodded.

"I had a friend who played basketball. He was tall. A natural when he was young."

The boy turned his head to stare out the window.

"He passed away four days ago."

The boy twisted in his seat. He waved to a passing attendant. "You got a pillow?" he called out.

"I'll see," the attendant said, beginning to open overhead bins.

"Are you tired from a game?" Sarah asked.

The attendant returned with a pillow. The youth tucked it under his head, turning away and closing his eyes.

Sarah extracted an in-flight magazine from the seat pocket in front of her and methodically turned the pages without reading. The youth was asleep and breathing deeply when the snacks were served; in her seat pocket, she saved three packets of peanuts for him to eat when he woke.

Back home, Sarah believed that Peter had waited to die until she arrived at his bedside. She removed the box from her closet, put it on the kitchen table, and removed the items, pausing to stare at each one before she stuffed them back into the box and carried it to the trash chute at the end of the hall. It was bulky and stuck in the opening, and she had to push with her arm almost up to her shoulder into the main drop. When it fell, she felt no different. She had hoped for finality, a sense of a house burned to the ground and then moving on to a new life in a new place. But nothing changed. When she returned she checked the kitchen drawer to be sure the ring was still there.

The next morning she was up earlier than usual to dress and leave. The night had been turbulent with indecision, but before dawn she knew she must tell Carmen it was best to follow her heart. Carmen must not suffer from recoiling love. If Carmen loves, she must love as much as she possibly can and never squelch love for fear of it fading. Of course there would be dangers Sarah could never mention. Carmen wouldn't listen anyway. But Carmen must know, a tethered heart is never freed, and swells with an oppressive sensitivity that becomes ever-present. Sarah would say no more, except that she would sell the ring to help pay this semester's tuition.

Outside the apartment building, as she was about to hail a cab, the homeless man who lived in the neighborhood called to her. He was wedged into the right angle where the building wall met the street.

"You got anything today?" he said, grinning, his eyes looking up.

Sarah found a five-dollar bill in her purse. "My friend died …"

"Oh, no. Shame, it is. Everlasting condolences," he said. A chunk of hardened egg yolk wiggled at the corner of his mouth, caught in his beard. "Dying ain't good for no one, friend or not."

"I hadn't seen him for twenty-five years …"

"Lesson learned there."

He looked content, like a baby about to burp. A neighbor had fed him. He waved to a woman passing, a stranger.

"Hey, you. Spare a little something for a homeless vet?" The woman ignored him.

Sarah kept an eye to the street. Cabs were sparse today.

"I don't think he ever knew …" she began hesitantly.

The derelict wiped his mouth with his frayed sleeve. His eyes closed, his head nodded. She sat beside him on the street, her back to the wall. She wanted her words to come out now. She did not believe he really heard her tell him about Peter, about the missed opportunity of a life vibrant with love. But she spoke with intensity from the heart as if he knew every meaning. And when it was over, she slumped, her mind soothed, her emotions quieted, before forcing herself to stand. When she hailed a taxi, he awoke.

"You have a good day, my dear," he said, raising a limp hand.

She tucked a twenty-dollar bill into his jacket pocket as the taxi pulled up to the curb.

"Bless you," he mumbled.

The Miracle of Madame Villard

illustration by Peter Healy

The Miracle of Madame Villard

Paris, 1793

The hands of the faith healer probed the lump on Jean-Luc's mother's neck. Stone hard it was, and fixed like a burl on a log.

"She will need strained carrot and turnip broth fortified with smushed, dried eucalyptus root," the faith healer said to the father staring at her, rigid with concern.

The mother's eyes burned with owl-like intensity, brimming with much fear and little hope. The father's eyes were glazed and opaque, hiding the memories of his dear wife, Charlotte, mother of his two sons, core of the family, whose once-lovely hands were now callused from her work as a seamstress, her once-warm heart cold as winter with age.

The boy, Jean-Luc, was sixteen and man size. The faith healer had seen him grow clever, learning his father's ironmonger's trade quickly and creating strong, pleasing designs. How his eyes burned with love for his mother.

The faith healer stood and motioned to Jean-Luc and his father to step outside into the alley. The chilled night breeze swirled among the single-room dwellings as low clouds moved swiftly overhead to cover and uncover the bright half-moon in the black sky. To the east, the glow of fires from the riots near the Bastille outlined the rooftops of the city.

"She needs a miracle," the faith healer whispered. She had seen many sick with these throat lumps before. They were hard to feed and often choked to death. "The good Saint Marcouf. He is the saint of neck swellings," she said to the boy and his father.

"How do we pray?" the father asked.

"In the Cathedral near Dieppe," the faith healer said, unable it instruct in a man's contact with his Lord, "where the Saint cured a girl well after the time of Charlemagne. The bones of his hand lie in a glass case, on a velvet pillow the color of ruby. The faithful who have touched have been cured. I have heard it from two pilgrims. I have no doubt of the power of his healings."

"She cannot walk to the north coast," Jean-Luc said.

"There is a public coach still running once a week. It takes three days."

"We have no money for coach fare," Jean-Luc's father said. "No one buys my ironwork now with the revolution."

"Sell at the executions. The rich and poor attend. And vendors make a fortune."

"I can sell my candleholder lamps, Father," Jean-Luc said.

"And I will find work outside the shop," the father said. "I will ask my cousin for work."

Jean-Luc ran back inside and knelt next to his mother. "We will take you to the saint, Mother."

"Jules?" the mother asked.

"I'm Jean-Luc, Mama. Jules has been gone for a year. Remember?"

Jean-Luc's father went to find work the next morning. Jean-Luc fed his mother gruel with a spoon, then left for the Place de la Concorde, where an execution was scheduled. He carried one lamp and tied two to the sash of his tunic.

Already the crowds murmured with excitement. Vendor business was brisk. Workers placed benches for peripheral seating for the wealthy as spectators mingled near the guillotine to secure the best views.

Jean-Luc went near the northwest corner. An aristocratic girl his age paraded in a stately manner along the path, followed by two boys and a girl, all fashionably dressed. The girl's full-length, white silk dress floated around her and the points of pink slippers peeked out from under the hem with each step. How delicate she was. Her high cheekbones spoke of class and privilege. Her brown eyes brooded in the frame of her light, straw-colored hair. Her slender hands were as if fashioned from porcelain.

Jean-Luc approached with his candleholder lamp held out in front of him.

She was afraid. At first her heart stopped, but an instant later, it raced with fear and excitement. She stopped and held out an arm to stop her companions. This huge boy-peasant was capable of breaking her in half, but his confident, healthy smile erased her fear. His black hair danced with joyous curls. His warm, blue eyes seemed cut from a sun-soaked morning sky. Suddenly, she wanted to surrender. She stepped forward, away from her friends, so they would not see her confusion.

"What have we here?" She smiled tentatively at Jean-Luc, then glanced toward her friends before looking back at him. "You. The giant. What in the world are you holding?"

Jean-Luc stared into the chestnut brown of the girl's angelic eyes; he had almost forgotten his purpose and his arm had fallen limp to his side, his hand still holding the lamp. He held up the sample again.

"It is for tapers. Very useful. See how the flame is protected by the curve—"

"It's iron," she said. How his eyes sparkled like gems.

"But sturdy," said Jean-Luc.

"But not brass. And not hand-blown glass, either. Are you giving them away?"

"No. It is for sale. Reasonable, too. My mother is very sick."

"Let me touch it!"

He handed it to her. She took it both hands and held it up.

"Where would you use this?" the girl asked the friend to her right.

"In the stable," her friend giggled.

"Exactly," the girl said. She had angered as she realized the folly of her emotions. This boy had robbed her, against her will, of her required disdain for peasants. And he had flustered her thinking and tarnished the respect of her friends too. "And when do you light a taper among the wild beasts in a stable?" she asked.

"Never. Never a taper in a stable," the girl's friend replied. There was laughter among them all now.

"I made it for a lady's bedroom," Jean-Luc said. The girl's eyes—full of possession as she regained control of her superiority—were quick to engage Jean-Luc's.

"The flame holds steady when you walk from room to room," Jean-Luc said.

"An iron tool for a lady's bedroom," the girl said. "You will die even poorer than you are now."

She smiled to her entourage one by one, holding the lamp away from her as if it might soil her dress.

"It is very reasonable at two deniers," Jean-Luc said. "I'm sure you could find it useful. Give it to a friend."

"A friend! My God." She rolled both eyes to the heavens. "Francis. Give him a sous for the damn thing. He needs the charity."

Francis, so hopelessly in love with the girl even a slug couldn't fail to notice it, stepped up and put his fingers in his waistcoat pocket. He pull out a coin and held it so Jean-Luc could not reach it.

"Thank you, sir," Jean-Luc said. The girl, still carrying his lamp, had turned her back.

"You are a fool," Francis retorted. He pocketed the coin.

"My lamp. You owe me," Jean-Luc said.

"Nothing." Francis said. "It is worthless."

The girl threw the lamp under the wheels of a passing wagon, and she and Francis left with her friends. Jean-Luc retrieved his lamp. It was bent and needed much repair.

Jean-Luc circled the crowded Place without a sale. Late in the afternoon, he headed home past burning government buildings. Acrid smoke trickled into the air above the city and was quickly dissipated by the wind. Sporadic fights erupted throughout the district, and he took side streets to be safe from the violent bands of revolutionaries. The alley of his parents' house was already dark with early evening when he arrived.

The faith healer stood outside the door. Her arms were crossed, her gaze locked on him.

"Your father's been burned. They're bringing him home."

"What happened?"

"Revolutionaries went to the shop. Your father had just returned. They wanted weapons to kill. They found none. They set to burning and left him half-conscious inside."

"Will he be all right?"

"He will not last the night." She looked up the alley.

Two men carried his father on a plank, his arms and legs dangling.

Jean-Luc ran to him and peered down into his face. "Father?" he whispered.

His father's eyes were closed, his face on the left side swollen purple and bleeding. His father said nothing.

The men left his father on his pallet in the house. The faith healer rubbed oils on parts of his charred skin and covered oozing flesh with scraps of gray cloth. Jean-Luc sat crossed-legged by his father's damaged body. His father opened his one good eye.

"Jean-Luc," he said. "Tomorrow. I found work with my distant cousin. The executioner at the Place de Grève. In the morning. You go. Remember. They call him Aiguisé."

"I will go, Father."

"Take care of your mother, son." He closed his eye. "She is a good woman."

Jean-Luc went to his mother, who sat on her stool in the corner facing the wall.

"Papa's dying," Jean-Luc said.

For many seconds she remained motionless and said nothing. "Something smells," she finally said. "Bring me a wet cloth."

Jean-Luc dipped a cloth in a pan of rainwater and brought it to his mother. She held it to her nose.

Jean-Luc sat by his father for the rest of the night. There was no motion when the soul left the body, and Jean-Luc did not know the moment his father died.

The next day, Jean-Luc arrived at the Place de Grève as he had promised. His father's cousin, the executioner called Aiguisé, wore black. He was bald, like many in the family. Aiguisé worked alone on a square platform passing a river whetstone over the guillotine blade that had been lowered three-quarters for the sharpening. He gave no sign that he recognized Jean-Luc.

"Get off!" Aiguisé said. "Stay in the crowd."

"I'm am Auguste Villard's son."

Aiguisé's head turned to stare. "You've grown! Where is your father?"

"He is dead from a fire."

"And you take his place?"

"My mother is very sick. She needs a miracle."

Aiguisé returned to his sharpening. "Your father should never have married a woman not from around here."

"She was very beautiful," Jean-Luc said.

"Mean, boy. Basque, she was. And mad-dog mean."

"She loves God."

"Stop your nonsense."

Aiguisé laid down his whetstone on the neck collar of the guillotine. He showed Jean-Luc the mop, the wooden pail with iron trim, the straw broom with the thick wooden handle, and the gunnysack: "Hold it wide open to catch the head. Then take it to the family, who must wait near the stairs," Aiguisé said.

Jean-Luc practiced holding the sack.

"Wider! And round, not like a slit."

The crowd had grown fifty gawkers deep in a few minutes. Aiguisé gave Jean-Luc the broom.

"My money?" Jean-Luc asked. With four executions planned in three days he would have enough for coach fare.

"When we finish," replied Aiguisé. "Half what was for your father. You are a child."

"I am family."

"Far removed," said Aiguisé. Near the guillotine Jean-Luc swept away leaves, twigs, acorns, ground dust, and the dirt that fell from Aiguisé's boots.

"Sweep the stairs," Aiguisé said, sharpening the blade again. His reputation for a clean cut brought rich purses from the accused.

Two men led a frail woman in a white linen dress. Countess Christine Roquefort. She walked in bitty steps, her ankles shackled, her dress hem dragging over the bloodstained platform planks. The men forced her to kneel in a corner opposite the guillotine. The crowd heckled. She stared defiantly.

A priest approached. From his hand she swatted a Bible that fell face down. The priest turned and left, and the crowd chanted for action. But Aiguisé was not ready, hammering a dowel into one of the triangular supports for more strength.

"Get her offering," Aiguisé said to Jean-Luc over the crowd noise. Jean-Luc propped the broom near the guillotine and walked across the platform to the woman. He went down on one knee. She stared at him with light-blue, wet eyes rimmed with red.

"Let me go," she said.

"God Bless. I take my father's place," he said.

"I married a man of title. Is that a crime?" she sobbed.

"It is God's will," Jean-Luc said echoing the litany of the cathedral.

"God's will is to save me." Her intense stare held fear and determination. "This is your destiny!"

"I am the sweeper," he said.

"You are more than that, boy. It is your judgment! Did you think of that?" The desperate woman glared to convince.

Jean-Luc shuddered with the chill she had given him. She pleaded again, but he could not respond. He rose, astonished at her words.

She reached into the slit in her dress over her bosom to pull out a velvet purse dyed indigo. It had a gold braided drawstring. She held it to her chest just below the neck.

"My God, boy. Help me," she said.

Jean-Luc did not move, speechless.

"Take the money for yourself. Let me go," she said.

Jean-Luc looked away as temptation gripped him. He had no doubt the purse held more money than he had ever seen, and more than enough to take his mother to the miracle.

"If you will not act," she said to Jean-Luc, her voice cracking with stress, "tell the murderer to be swift." She held out the purse.

Jean-Luc took the purse to Aiguisé.

"Barely enough," Aiguisé said. "She could afford more."

"She said to be swift."

"What is swift? They are fools. The blade always falls the same speed. I have no control. It is the sharpness that makes me special."

Aiguisé positioned Jean-Luc near the front of the guillotine, then anchored the woman in the neck collar, securing it with a metal bolt. "Why me?" the woman cried. "You devil!"

Aiguisé stood back to the side. He raised his arm, his other hand on the blade release. The crowd roared. The wind in the trees fragmented the sun's glare and the angled blade shimmered with an almost human excitement.

Aiguisé pulled. The plunge began. Jean-Luc gasped.

He grabbed the broom, stepped forward and shoved the handle between the plunging blade and the Countess's neck. The blade cracked the handle in two and rebounded, slightly slicing into the victim's neck only by an inch. She moaned. Her legs kicked back—her body thrashed. "Finish! Finish!" she yelled.

Aiguisé pummeled Jean-Luc's head twice with his axe handle and Jean-Luc fell to the planks. Aiguisé raised the guillotine blade high enough to clear the wound, and with one stroke of his axe completed the severing of the woman's head.

In the silence, the head lay on its right side. One eyelid twitched. Aiguisé clutched the hair and held up the Countess Roquefort for the crowd to see, shielding the ragged axe cut at the neck with his arm. The crowd cheered. As he struggled to put the head into the sack, the countess's nose hung up on the edge. "Merde," he said. Finally it slipped in.

Aiguisé moved quickly to Jean-Luc and delivered a powerful kick to his stomach. "I'll kill you," he said. He walked to the stairs to lower the sacked head to the family.

Jean-Luc bled from his nose and mouth and his stomach churned, but he crawled to the edge of the platform and fell over the edge before Aiguisé reached him. Hands from the crowd broke his fall and stood him up. "Run," a voice said. The crowd parted. Jean-Luc ran until he was home, Aiguisé's threats still ringing in his ears.

To escape Aiguisé, Jean-Luc left home within an hour and carried his mother on his back as he hurried on the road that led to Saint Marcouf's miracle. Hours later, when the moon set, he found hay bales in a field to keep them warm. The next morning he collected walnuts to eat, and then they were back on the north road again. The burning sun was unshielded by clouds, and soon Jean-Luc's tunic was damp. His mother rode with her arms around his neck, her legs held steady by his arms, her head nodding on the back of his shoulder as she dozed. He stopped often to let her rest.

By mid-afternoon they had crossed two rivers.

"I'm hungry," his mother said, her first words in many hours.

He made her comfortable by the side of the road and went over fields of sunflowers to find wild red raspberries tucked near the cracked and pitted stones of a segment of Roman wall. He filled his sash.

He returned to the road. His mother stood next to a short man who held the lead of a white goat harnessed to a two-wheeled cart. He spread the fingers of his free hand and combed through wild, curly gray hair to no effect. Jean-Luc ran to his mother and to give her the berries. But she ate goat cheese.

"Who are you?" Jean-Luc asked the man.

"Are you Jules?" the man, Emile, asked.

"I am Jean-Luc. And this is my mother, Madame Villard."

"Ah, this woman said Jules would pay for whatever I gave her."

"Jules is my brother. A revolutionary. He has been gone more than a year."

Jean-Luc looked to his mother, who gazed at him. She had a faint smile, and her eyes sparkled with conspiracy.

"We have no money," Jean-Luc said.

Emile poured milk he'd intended for Charlotte back into a pail.

"I must insist, my friend. This is my only income. It cannot be free."

Charlotte finished eating the cheese, and Jean-Luc moved to give her the berries.

"I do not lie, Mister. My father is dead. My mother is sick. See her neck lump? We are on our way to the dathedral near Dieppe for a saint miracle. Do you know the Saint Marcouf?"

Emile turned to Charlotte. "Eat no more," he said. But she had finished.

Jean-Luc looked into the man's cart. Lying in a box protected by a Persian carpet was a lute, the body pierced by two ragged-edged holes, the surface partially burned—strings missing, two pegs bent. In the midst of pots and pans and other containers lay a hurdy-gurdy with the crank twisted and useless.

"What do you do, boy?" Emile asked.

"I am an ironmonger. I learned from my father." He closed his eyes for a few seconds at the thought of his dead father.

"Do you make weapons for revolutionaries?"

"That is not God's will."

Charlotte ate berries. "Good," she said.

"You do not look like thieves," Emile said.

Jean-Luc pointed to the hurdy-gurdy. "If you are going our way, walk with us. At night, when we rest, I can fix the crank as compensation."

"You repair instruments?"

"That one is easy for me."

"Could you do the lute too? I must have a fine instrument to regain my career."

"I do not do woodwork. Only the iron."

"It is the finest of hurdy-gurdies. I saved it from my patron's drawing room before he was beheaded."

"It will be like new."

Emile thought for a moment. "I have no choice," he mumbled.

They walked. Jean-Luc still carried his mother on his back, Emile beside him reached barely to his shoulder height, dipping with each step from a leg injured by horse kick in his youth,. The goat and the cart followed behind.

"Put the woman in the cart. We'll make better time," Emile said after a few miles.

They put down the back gate of the cart. Jean-Luc's mother now faced where they had been; her legs hung down, she steadied herself gripping the sides, and she could lean back against Emile's collection of pots and pans.

The road entered a large forest where cool shadows refreshed the travelers. Emile broke out in song in a clear tenor voice. He used the rhythm of their steps as accompaniment. Birds in the forest broke their wary silence and sang full-throated.

"I am good, no?" Emile said.

"Sing more," Charlotte said.

That night Emile searched for a patch of pine needles in a copse of trees. He tied the goat near grass for grazing. He lit a fire and they ate cheese and drank wine from Emile's bottle. "Not too much," he said. "We'll need some for tomorrow."

Emile took his lute from the goat cart and sang. Charlotte rocked to the melodies. Jean-Luc repaired the hurdy-gurdy without tools and Emile saw immediate economic potential in the strong, sure hands of the boy. Emile needed money for costumes to establish himself as a court musician again.

The fire had died down to glowing ash when John-Luc stretched out near his mother. Sleep did not come, and he stared at the sky believing his father was waiting for them among the glittering stars.

The predawn chill brought shivers to Charlotte, and Jean-Luc carried her until after dawn to warm her. When the sun was well above the trees, Emile handed the goat lead to Jean-Luc and, without stopping, took a brass gong from his sack in the cart and picked up a dry stick. He showed Charlotte how to hit the gong. Then he picked up his lute and sang as he walked. Charlotte banged away with little sense of the rhythm.

"Great," said Emile. "Now we'll practice a little more."

And after many repeats, it did sound better.

Just before noon they came to a village. In the center near the well was the day market of three produce vendors and one hawker of firewood. Emile stopped his group, anchored the goat, and told Charlotte to stand up and hold her gong. He brought the hurdy-gurdy to the back of the goat cart and told Jean-Luc how to turn the handle and press two keys. Emile instructed him to play without letting up when he nodded, and to stop when he nodded again. He stepped from the cart, placed a tin cup at an arm's length from his feet, and clapped, holding his lute under his arm.

Five adults, three children, and two dogs turned to stare.

Emile nodded and the hurdy-gurdy droned. "Charlotte," he called.

Nothing.

"Hit the gong!"

Charlotte responded and gave some rhythm close to what they'd practiced.

Emile played the lute and sang. He swayed. His head bobbed. Then he nodded and stopped singing. The drone stopped.

Bang, bang, bang, went the gong.

"Charlotte."

Bang, bang, bang.

"Charlotte!"

Emile ran to her and took the stick from her hand. The audience stood stock still. He applauded as an example. No one responded. He picked up his cup and held it out. Every one of the crowd turned their backs, and the dogs sank back into the dust.

Emile came back to the cart.

"You've got to stop when I stop," he said to Charlotte.

"I thought she did well," said Jean-Luc.

"Well, she did fine. It was excellent. She just has to stop when I stop. We lose the effect if she doesn't."

"I'll stop," Charlotte said earnestly.

"Let's do it again," Jean-Luc said.

Emile put the cup down. Nodded and started. Same song. And they all stopped together. Emile bowed.

A girl of seven in a brown flax dress stepped over and dropped a single, thin, copper denier into the cup.

"Thank you little darling," Emile said.

When he returned to the cart, he looked warmly at Charlotte and Jean-Luc.

"That was better. We are professionals."

But his eyes said he knew their survival depended on Jean-Luc's repairs.

"We are many days from the saint," Jean-Luc said. His mother was smiling.

"Unhitch the goat," Emile said.

The next afternoon they came to a town near a crossroads with a square and a small church.

"This is ideal for a show," Emile said.

"We have no time for more shows," Jean-Luc said intently. "Already my mother is tiring earlier every day."

"We will need the money, boy. It will not take long."

Emile stood, with Charlotte and Jean-Luc behind, near a well. A crowd of seventeen people formed a semicircle two to three deep. A few listeners dropped coins in the cup. The group was more polished now. Charlotte obviously enjoyed herself, a distinct change from the beginning of her trip. She was also more attentive and lucid, and although the lump in her neck was bigger, she spoke more often, straining to be heard.

A slender girl stood at the crowd edge in an ankle-length brown dress of good quality, but streaked with stains and impregnated with dust. Her slippers were scuffed and worn, and the left one had a hole near the toe. Her long and curly blond hair partly hid her high cheekbones, deep-set blue eyes, and oval face. Her small but expressive mouth was set in a determined line, her thin lips chapped.

When the group stopped playing, she ran forward and scooped up the money cup. Emile reached for her. She dodged around him. "Get her," Emile yelled.

Jean-Luc laid down the hurdy-gurdy and ran. Within fifty yards, he grabbed her dress but she twisted away and ran faster. He tripped and fell. She held the cup with one hand, and with the other hand she picked up the coins and swallowed them one by one as she ran. The effort slowed her and Jean-Luc caught up. This time he tackled her around the waist and brought her to the ground; she kicked and pounded his chest with her hands. He grabbed her wrists and pinned her down, his face inches away from hers. He stared into her angry eyes. She spit at him but he did not let go of her arms.

Emile caught up.

"She swallowed our money," Jean-Luc said.

"Clever. But I have seen it many times in Paris."

"It is lost. We will have nothing to honor the saint."

"It does not vomit well." Emile thought for a few seconds. "But we will take her with us until it passes."

"I hate you," the girl said.

"You are a thief. You should be locked in prison and branded."

"Shall I let her up?" Jean-Luc asked.

"Careful. Hold her tight. We will tie her."

At the cart, Jean-Luc restrained her again as Emile tied her hands behind her back. With leather strips he strapped her arms to her chest, and then placed a spare goat collar with a rope around her neck.

"Lay her down. Sit on her legs," Emile said.

Emile reached into a sack for a bottle half filled with light, amber-colored oil. He steadied the girl's head with his knees, pinched her nose, and forced her mouth open with a stick.

"Pour it in," Emile said to Jean-Luc.

Jean-Luc, still straddling the girl, poured oil into her mouth. She wrenched her lips so the oil seeped out. On the next try, Emile covered her mouth with his hand and pinched her nostrils so she could not breathe. She swallowed.

"Damn. She wasted half of it." Emile said. "Do it again."

When all the oil was used, Jean-Luc lifted the girl to her feet.

"I hate you," she sputtered again.

As they prepared to travel, Charlotte walked to the girl and spoke kindly.

"What shall we call you?" she said.

The girl turned her head away.

They started moving. Emile led the goat. Jean-Luc led the girl on the leash; she kept the rope taut with resistance, even though it hurt her neck. Charlotte rode in the back of the cart, gazing left and right at the birds and trees. After more than an hour the girl slackened the rope between her and Jean-Luc.

"Is that pig your father?" she whispered.

Jean-Luc looked at her for a moment. "That is Emile."

"Is that your mother?" She looked to Charlotte.

"My father is dead," Jean-Luc said.

"How old are you?"

"I am older than you."

"You look young."

"I'm almost seventeen."

"I'm fifteen. Almost sixteen."

They walked for a while.

"Where is your family?" Jean-Luc asked.

"Dead. The carriage went over a cliff into the river. The revolutionaries."

Emile hummed to himself contentedly.

"He is your uncle?" the girl asked.

"I do not know him well," Jean-Luc said.

Emile laughed. "I am our leader."

Charlotte called from the back of the cart, her voice strained from the lump. "Tell us your name, child."

"Yes, ma'am. I'm called Sapphire."

"Sapphire is a gem," Charlotte said.

Sapphire shut her eyes for a moment. "My mama said that," she said. "That I was a gem."

Emile laughed, but not unkindly. "And now you are a thief."

"Only for food. I am hungry."

"That gives you no reason to eat our coins."

"Let the child be!" Charlotte said.

Jean-Luc looked briefly in surprise at his mother; how she had changed since Paris.

"You are too big for a boy," Sapphire whispered to Jean-Luc.

"And you talk too much," he replied.

The fire was embers. The food had been sparse this evening. Charlotte slept on a blanket on her side in fetal position. Emile lay on his back with his hands behind his head, his eyes closed but not asleep.

Jean-Luc slept soundly on his back near Sapphire, who faced away from him on her side. Her hands were tied behind her with the end line knotted around Jean-Luc's wrist. A second rope bound Sapphire's leg to Jean-Luc's ankle. Sapphire could not move without waking Jean-Luc.

It was well after midnight when Sapphire suddenly tried to sit up, falling back on her side. "I gotta go! I'm going to explode," she yelled.

Emile rose. Jean-Luc sat up. Charlotte moaned in her sleep.

Emile poked Charlotte. "Get up! Go with her!" He helped Jean-Luc untie Sapphire.

Charlotte led Sapphire among tree trunks away from view toward a stream.

They heard moans. From the dark Sapphire yelled. "I'm dirty."

"Finish, child. Get it all out," Charlotte said. "I'll wash your dress in the stream."

Jean-Luc and Emile took torches to the site. Charlotte tended Sapphire away from their view. Emile and Jean-Luc sorted out the coins and cleaned them in the stream water.

"I hate shit," Emile said.

The next morning at dawn, Emile, Jean-Luc, and Charlotte prepared for their journey to the saint. Sapphire stood apart in still-damp clothes, her hair tousled, exhausted from her ordeal and little sleep.

Jean-Luc looked sternly at her. "Do not follow. We must travel fast for my mother."

"I would never follow you," Sapphire said.

Charlotte smiled. "Go back to your kin."

"I have no kin."

"Find an orphanage," Emile said. "There are many near the sea."

"I do not want to be an orphan."

Emile laughed. "You cannot change what you are."

"She is not a thief," Jean-Luc said.

"That is not what I meant," Emile said. "Orphans are orphans."

"She is only a child," Charlotte said.

Emile led the goat cart forward. From the back, Charlotte watched as Sapphire stood still. After a quarter of a mile, Charlotte waved. Sapphire stood motionless. Charlotte waved again. This time Sapphire raised her hand head-high, and lowered it slowly. Sapphire had not moved when she vanished from Charlotte's sight.

On the road, Jean-Luc, Charlotte, and Emile passed recruits going toward Paris to join army regiments. They passed revolutionaries eager to attack aristocrats. They saw displaced families wandering with no place to receive them. Just before noon, Emile stopped a farmer's widow with her possessions in a horse-drawn wagon. He had seen tools—an anvil, sturdy tongs, bellows. He spoke to Jean-Luc. "See those tools? You can make repairs."

"We do not have time for repairs," Jean-Luc said.

"We are poor," Emile said. "An extra hour here and there. We will have money for your saint and my lute. We can start earlier in the morning to make up the time."

"You have given us no money," Jean-Luc said.

Emile paused. "I am the treasurer," he said.

Jean-Luc scoffed but saw the tools as useful. Emile bargained a good price. In the next village they sang and played; Jean-Luc spotted a wagon wheel in need of repair, then a broken bucket handle. Emile approached the owners and set prices.

Two days later, on market day in a midsize town, they set up before a lively crowd of twenty or more. Emile started a dance tune. Feet tapped. Hands clapped. The crowd grew as villagers came from all directions. As Emile grinned with their success, Sapphire emerged from a clump of trees at the edge of the square.

She skirted the crowd, staying far away from Jean-Luc, Charlotte, and Emile. She danced, her arms wide, her skirts rippling back and forth, the whites of her legs bright in the sun, her worn slippers stirring clouds of dust. Most of the crowd watched her, not the musicians, and began to sway to her rhythm. In one wild leap she stepped on her dress hem and ripped a fair hole, but she danced on.

The crowd cheered. She skipped and jumped, twirling in the now-tight space between the players and the crowd. Jean-Luc glanced at Emile. Emile's brow creased with concern. Sapphire kicked high. Charlotte banged away at her gong, fascinated by Sapphire, and let out a cry of delight. Emile gave Charlotte a stern look. Sapphire kicked again. Leapt. Kicked again. The crowd laughed with pleasure at her skill and enthusiasm.

Emile signaled the group to stop. Sapphire faced the crowd, feet together, and bowed. Then she ran among the spectators using her skirts held loose in her hands to form a pouch—as a collector. The crowd gave coins. "Bravo! Bravo!" Then she paused before a youth dressed as a country gentleman. He eyed her and dropped a shiny copper among her coins, more money than the musicians would earn in two or three performances. Sapphire held the shiny coin high so Jean-Luc, Charlotte, and especially Emile could see its color glinting in the sun.

"We can't allow that," Emile said.

Charlotte put down her gong and ran to Sapphire to hug her.

"It is our money," Emile said.

Jean-Luc turned to him. "That's true, but she did do the dance."

"We can't afford competition," Emile said.

Charlotte brought Sapphire back to the goat cart.

"I dance good?" Sapphire asked Jean-Luc.

Emile smiled. Jean-Luc put the hurdy-gurdy in the wagon.

"We are a singing group. We do not need dancing during our performance," Emile said.

Charlotte pointed to Sapphire's coins. "See how much money she collected?"

"On our talent," Emile said.

"She danced well," Jean-Luc said.

"Do you think she'd be a good addition to our troupe? Is that what you mean?" Emile countered with sarcasm.

Jean-Luc hesitated. "I did not mean that. Another traveler will slow us down."

Charlotte raised her hand. "A traveler will not slow us. Anyone can walk faster than a goat with a cart."

"But we cannot share what we earn, Mother," Jean-Luc said.

"That is very true," Emile said. "We have not made nearly enough money to buy even a secondhand lute."

Jean-Luc flushed with anger. "We need money for the saint."

"My point exactly." Emile touched his arm and said to Sapphire. "Give me the money, child."

Sapphire shook her head "no."

"I'll take it," Emile said.

Sapphire did not budge.

"It is hers," Charlotte said.

"It can't be all hers," Emile said. "We made the music."

"She pleased the crowd," Jean-Luc said.

Emile frowned and after a thoughtful silence he said, "All right! Keep it." He looked to Jean-Luc. "You think we ought to let her come along? Washed up, she might bring in more generous customers. The men will like her." He turned to Charlotte. "What do you think?"

"She won't eat much," Charlotte said.

"Then it's done," Emile said.

Sapphire did a little hop-step. Charlotte took her hand.

"We must reach the saint soon," Jean-Luc said, but no one was listening.

The next night the troupe made camp in a clearing of woods. A cooking fire burned with fresh logs. Emile mouthed the line of a new song and picked a melody on the few remaining strings of his lute. Charlotte and Jean-Luc rested. Sapphire, wrapped in a shawl, worked to repair the tear in her dress. She had tied the fabric into a crude knot to conceal the hole.

Charlotte stood, turning so she faced away from the others. She shamelessly pulled up her dress, exposing her loose-skinned, wrinkled buttocks. From her waist, she untied a string that held a small cloth sack. She let her skirts down and opened the sack, removing a piece of fine linen, folded over twice and four inches long. She knelt next to Sapphire and unfolded the linen. Five needles gleamed with reflections from the fire.

"They are beautiful," Sapphire said.

"Mama sewed for Marie Antoinette," Jean-Luc said.

Charlotte put on a modest face. "Not for her exactly!" she said proudly.

"Her court," Jean-Luc said.

"Lace on undergarments. And only for two."

"Still, you were famous."

"Pooh," Charlotte said. Still, she was pleased.

Charlotte tried to show Sapphire how to repair her dress, but her stiff fingers with swollen knuckles could not pick up a needle.

Emile turned to Charlotte. "I can help," he said. He went to the goat cart and returned with candle stubs in a pot that he placed on a few embers from the fire. The wax melted. He carried the pot to Charlotte, testing the wax temperature with his finger.

"Excellent for the rheumatism." he said. "Hold out your hand."

Emile guided Charlotte's hand, dipping her knuckles into the wax.

"Oouuuee," Charlotte said happily. She extended and flexed her fingers. She picked up a needle, and with improved facility stitched around the hole in Sapphire's dress to show her the technique.

Sapphire stared intently, and then took the needle and tried her skill.

The next morning, as Charlotte and Sapphire walked toward the men who were hitching the goat to the cart, Charlotte handed Sapphire the linen pouch that contained her needles. "You are very good at your sewing, Sapphire," she said.

"I will gladly carry these for you, Madame," she said, holding out the needles.

"No. They are yours to keep."

Sapphire looked away to hide her tears. She could not speak.

Late the next afternoon, they crested a hill. Jean-Luc pointed to the west. "The cathedral!" They hurried to the arched doors of the entrance, gazing at stone statues of the disciples. Inside, they took the stairs to the stone-lined crypt, descending into the dank and the cold one by one with Emile leading. Jean-Luc carried Charlotte in his arms. Her eyes were closed and she was breathing with difficulty. She had weakened over the last two days of travel.

The walls were scarred with scratches and marks of pilgrims' testimonials. A stack of broken crutches, bandages, splints, clothing, canes, and walking sticks rose almost to the ceiling.

A novice in a white frock on a three-legged stool guarded the low, arched door to the small room of the saint. Light flickered from candles on iron sconces around a case of glass and forged brass. In the case, bones of a human hand lay on a red velvet pillow trimmed with threads of gold. They stood before the youthful novice.

"Let us pass," said Jean-Luc. "We must touch the saint for a miracle."

"Two sous. Many give more," said the novice in a high, prepubescent voice.

"God does not sell miracles," said Sapphire.

The novice shrugged. "Many pray here. Where you can see the saint. It can be sufficient."

"But we are poor," Sapphire said.

"Find your miracle elsewhere," the novice said, shrugging with indifference.

"Give us our earnings, Emile," Sapphire said.

Emile hesitated.

"It is for Mother," she said emphatically. She counted their combined worth. "Nineteen denier."

"Any offering will please God," the novice said. "But bishop allows no exceptions." He sighed. "I will join you in your prayers."

"We must go in," Sapphire said. "She is dying."

The novice began the litany of a tired, brief prayer. Charlotte's raspy breathing filled the silent, tomb-stale air when he finished.

Emile reached into his coat. "I have the money for my lute."

Emile added coins to those Sapphire had in her hand.

Sapphire gave the exact amount to the novice. "May you rot in hell," she said.

"Bless," the novice replied.

Minutes later, in the cove of the Saint Marcouf, Jean-Luc held his mother up to the saint. The novice raised the case and held it to one side. Sapphire took Charlotte's hand.

"Be quick," the novice said.

Emile glared at him.

The hand of Charlotte touched a bone of the saint. Sapphire whispered a prayer. "Praise God," said Jean-Luc. The novice put the case back in place.

An hour later, Jean-Luc sat on a boulder, one of many that lined each side of the path to the cathedral, and held his mother. Emile and Sapphire stood before them. Charlotte opened her eyes and, with effort, reached out to take Sapphire's hand. "You are my child now," she said. When the soul passed from Charlotte, she shivered from foot to head as if the life was stripped from her like skin from a rabbit.

They buried Charlotte in a field within hours. Emile insisted on going to town to sell what he could for the trip back. "I'll meet you tomorrow at the shed where we spent the night," he said.

Sapphire and Jean-Luc found a place near a stream to rest for the night. In the morning, an early mist turned into a drizzle as they walked to where Charlotte was buried. Their steps were tired and listless. Jean-Luc and Sapphire prayed at the unmarked grave until noon.

"There was no miracle," Sapphire said.

"She was close to God," he said, "near the end." He smiled at her. "And she liked you."

Sapphire cried. "I have no one."

"Emile and I will take care of you. Mother would have wanted that."

"Is that what you want?" she asked.

He shrugged, his cheeks and ears tinged with blush.

Then they walked the two miles to the shed without speaking. The door was open.

"I do not smell the goat," Jean-Luc said.

"It is like Emile not to come. He must not be here," Sapphire said.

"He will come. He said so."

Sapphire walked into the shed. Jean-Luc had to bend almost half over to follow.

In the center of the dirt floor were the tools for metalwork, carefully stacked, and the gong Charlotte had played.

"He's been here," said Jean-Luc.

"Why has he left all this?" Sapphire said.

"I think it is for us."

"But why?" She paused. Someone was approaching.

A frail boy of six came through the door with a leather purse in his right hand.

"Who are you?" Jean-Luc asked.

The boy hesitated. "The man with the stick-out hair said I give you this or he make me disappear." The boy held out the purse.

Sapphire opened the purse. "More than fifty denier," she said. "From the treasury."

Jean-Luc began to pack the tools in a sack. He looked at the boy. "What did the man say?"

"He said tell you my father gone … " The boy struggled to get it right. " … my little sister born dead and my mother died too."

The boy shifted his weight nervously from one foot to the other.

Sapphire looked at Jean-Luc. "He's an orphan!"

The boy shook his head from side to side. "I don't want to be an orphan," he said.

Sapphire took the boy's hand. "He can be our family, can't he?" she said to Jean-Luc.

Jean-Luc laughed warmly.

Clouds

illustration by Peter Healy

Clouds

"Put your glasses on," Margaret said to her son. He touched his neck, wet with sweat, and wiped his hand on his T-shirt. The back window was down a few inches for ventilation and gave a steady, breathy growl at highway speeds.

"The glasses, Ben."

He picked up the thick lenses from the seat and, with a couple of missed tries, pulled the temple straps down over his head.

"We'll play a game, Ben," she said. "You want to play a game?"

"Play game," he said. She passed an eighteen-wheeler, leaving plenty of room, and tucked back into the slow lane. It was midmorning, and wavy lines of invisible heat from the road were already distorting the view. Ben rocked back and forth; she let him go on for a while.

"Can you see the clouds?" she asked. There was a line of cars slowed in the fast lane, and bumper to bumper. She kept a good distance to let them sort it out. Ben stopped rocking and was shaking his head from side to side.

"Look up," she said. "In the sky. Clouds are in the sky, Ben. Next to where God lives."

"God live," he said. He strained against the seat belt to lean forward and look up through the windshield.

"Can you see them?"

"See them," he said.

"Well, we'll find one and we'll name it. Tell what it is. There are all sorts of things up in the sky."

"I do good," he said.

"Of course you will."

"I do good," he said again.

"Find one up there. Keep looking. Tell me what it is."

He put his hand on the glass.

"You can't touch them, Ben. They're far away."

He took his hand down. "Far," he said.

"What does it look like, Ben? Does it remind you of something?"

Ben stared. Finally he said: "Weekie."

She didn't respond for a long moment. He was looking at her, grinning.

"She's gone, Ben."

"Gone," he said. He continued to look. "Story?" he said to the cloud.

"She's gone, Ben. She's in heaven with the angels. She won't be here to tell you stories anymore."

"I love you," he said to the cloud. Sorrow altered his usual smile and his eyes were moist.

"It's okay," she said, talking to herself as she often did these days. What if he did believe Weekie was a cloud? There was no harm.

He slept a while. So as not to wake him, she passed the rest stop where they would have exercised. A truck horn blast woke him. She said, "Look, Ben. More clouds."

In less than an hour she drove into the closest city to their small town. She found her ex-husband sitting in the park near the museum, where he usually was in the mornings on the rare days she had to find him. She parked at the curb on a yellow line and honked a few times. He folded his blanket into a long rectangle and wrapped it around his neck. He stuffed gloves and two long scarves into a laundry bag, then put on a woolen ski cap that he pulled down over his ears. She couldn't tell if he was sober. She hadn't seen any bottles near him as he packed up. He came to the car, opened the back door, and climbed in.

"It's Daddy, Ben."

"Daddy," Ben said.

She made no effort to greet her husband. Her intense aversion had turned to dispassionate distaste a couple of years ago. Even from the front seat she could smell the sweet, acrid breath of bad booze and indigestion.

"Hey, my little man," he said.

"Lil' man," Ben said without looking around, and he started rocking backward and forward.

She pulled to the side of a street and took a city map from a folder in the side door pocket. She studied the map on the steering wheel.

"He's no better," her ex-husband said. "He seems worse."

"Weekie died," she said, following a street on the map with her finger. "There's no one." She looked up in time to see her ex-husband shrug in the rearview mirror. She pulled back into traffic.

"You got the money?" he asked.

She didn't answer.

"All three hundred?"

"Three," Ben said.

"I ain't doing this if you ain't got it all," her ex-husband said.

Ben looked up, but they were in the city now and it wasn't easy to find clouds.

"You got it all?"

She paused at stop sign, looking up the street for the office building.

The lawyer was not in today. But the receptionist was a notary.

"Won't a lawyer need to sign?" Margaret asked. The receptionist looked at the papers. "He's already signed," she said. She looked up. "I'll need identification."

She knew her ex-husband wanted the money first, but the presence of the receptionist kept him quiet. She handed over his expired driver's license—she kept for him so he wouldn't lose it—and the receptionist studied the picture intently for a few seconds and then looked at him. "Sign here," she said. Her ex-husband wrote his name. Then she let go of Ben's hand and signed below her ex-husband's scrawl.

Outside, he grabbed her arm.

"Don't touch me," she said. She backed away and reached into her purse. She gave him the money and waited as he counted.

"I'll drop you at the bus station," she said.

He seemed more subdued now that he had the money. She thought he was probably on his way to the Carolina coast for a while before he headed South for the winter. But she could never be sure.

She let him out at the bus station. He said nothing as he left. She turned off the motor. She took Ben's suitcase from the trunk and opened it on the backseat. She got a clean shirt and changed it for the already-damp one he had on. She left the suitcase on the backseat. As she slid in the front, she checked her folder again. She had the signed papers with her now, thank God, and the health records from the doctors and the hospital. She strapped Ben back into his seat. She drove, following the route signs out of the city, where she rarely came for business or pleasure. In twenty-five minutes she was back on the freeway.

"Look again for clouds, Ben. See what you can see."

Ben stared and after a while he said, "See."

"That's good, Ben."

"I did good."

"Yes."

She paused before she said, "Always look for clouds, Ben, and think about me coming to visit."

"Whizit," he said.

"'Visit' means come to see you. Come to be with you." But she knew she could rarely get off work to make this long drive.

She drove well under the speed limit for another two hours. The signs marking the distance to Gowanda were now spaced every few miles. Ben had been looking out the side window; for the last few miles his attention had still been on the sky.

"Cloud," Ben said excitedly.

She glanced up. "It looks like a cow."

"Mommie!" he said.

She laughed. "Mommie doesn't look like a cow," she said. But she was deeply touched.

She patted the side of his head with the palm of her hand while keeping her eyes on the road. She put her hand back on the wheel.

She wished she could feel better about his new accomplishment. But he'd forget her soon enough, and she'd be lost in the sky with Weekie. Her heart ached so that she frowned and took her eyes off the road for an instant to look at him. When she looked back to the road, she could just make out the sign for Gowanda—thirty-four miles.

She tried not to think of the relief she hoped would come when he had caregivers. But an unformed dream of future normalcy had invaded her heart and mind, and it brought on the ever-present pain of guilt.

She pulled into a rest stop and took him into a stall in the ladies' restroom. After he finished, she bought him goldfish crackers from a vending machine and opened the bag for him when they were back in the car.

He finished the goldfish, and she gave him a Mars bar with the wrapper off. He ate it slowly but took big bites. She wiped stray chocolate off his hands and mouth with a tissue from a box she kept under the seat behind her feet.

"What is it, Ben?"

He pointed to the sky. He turned. "Mommie." He grinned.

She followed the signs. The road was two lanes now. She wanted to stop the car and take him in her arms, envelop him with a hug he'd never forget. But it would only confuse him, scare him. She saw the three-story institute, its main building with a clock tower and a wing on each side, like open arms, the grounds not well tended. She pulled up a long drive that curved to the front entrance. She could see paint peeling on the windowsills, and the brick walls pocked with holes from lost mortar and crumbled bricks. A door to the side of the main double door had two pieces of white typing paper tacked side by side at eye level and "Reception" written in black marker.

"I did good?" Ben asked as she unbuckled his seat belt.

"Yes, Ben. You did real good."

Reddog

illustration by Peter Healy

illustration by Peter Healy

Reddog

On Christmas Day, my second year in prison for murder, my mother stopped coming to visit. She doesn't call and I can't get in touch with her. In August, she missed my twenty-fifth birthday. A couple months later, my sister came and said, "Mother doesn't want to think about it anymore. Try to understand."

I did try.

Eventually my sister quit coming; she had a lot on her mind with her van full of kids and no husband. So I go a year with no visitors, and when I get dragged to administration to face an assistant to the warden, I'm half-crazy.

"A graduate student working in criminal justice wants to include you in her experiments," he said. "Your choice. Two or three times a month. Goes on your record as good behavior."

Sessions would be out of maximum security. Like a mini vacation.

"Hey. What's with the experiments?" I asked. "She stick you with drugs, stuff like that?"

"Just talk."

"Hey, Captain. She a looker?"

"Don't get your fantasies revved up. She's a pro."

"You be there?"

"Just you and her. And high security."

"Maybe I get out of max sooner?" I asked. You get a cell in the main building and you could talk to guys, set things up.

"Can't promise." He walked around the table, stuck a ballpoint pen in my cuffed hand, and showed me where to sign. "Consent papers."

You needed a magnifying glass to read the print on the last two pages. "I don't know about signing anything," I said.

"It's permission to talk, record, use information," he said.

"I thought this was research," I said. I hated do-gooders and I didn't need rehabilitation. I needed parole, miraculous DNA evidence, a new trial.

"I don't give a shit what you do. I'm here because the warden says to cover our ass legally. It's routine. No one's trying to screw you. No one cares."

"She ain't a lawyer, is she? She ain't trying to retry the case or something."

"She's a student. We checked. She was a paralegal before she went back to grad school. She's demonstrated against the death penalty. Arrested once, but never charged. She won't violate your rights, if that's what you're thinking. You don't have rights."

I signed her papers with a bump-and-a-line so no one could ever read my name.

The researcher, a Ms. Pearlstein, shows up the next day for our first session; she wants to see how things might go. I'm cool, out of maximum security in the south extension, but still with two guards, one inside and one outside the door, and me chained hand and foot.

She was maybe five feet two, wore these thick glasses made the dark of her eyes look like raisins, and her voice had this whine like an echo of metal cut with a circular saw. She was sitting on a folding chair with her skinny legs crossed, her head tilted down. She asked me a few questions, like how I felt about prison, and if I was guilty. I told her prison was like heaven and I wasn't guilty.

"What you studying?" I asked.

She wanted to talk about the crime and my punishment. What did I care? I was feeling like an eagle soaring. And I'd tell her anything to keep this going, get out of max.

"Accidents happen," I said.

"It was no accident," she said.

"You're good-looking," I said, smiling.

She didn't smile back. "I'm not here to talk about me."

"You got a boyfriend?"

She sighed. "I have essential questions to ask."

"You the boss, babe."

She frowned, then glared at me like she could see into my brain. "I want to know everything that happened that day. How you felt. What you were thinking," she said.

"It's in the trial stuff, baby."

"You may call me Ms. Pearlstein. I know the trial transcripts well. Trials deal with evasions of the truth." She still gave me her hard look.

I waited. Then I said, "Hey, little lady. You think I lied? That what's scratching your ass?"

"I am not the 'little lady.'"

I laughed. "You Ms. Pearlstein," I said.

"I don't know if you lied. I want to know what you and Hershel Cracken were thinking, moment by moment."

"Talk to Reddog. He's the guy give you the story."

Everyone called Hershel Cracken "Reddog," and he was waiting on a lethal at Huntsville; I was in this place for life.

"I've been talking to Hershel, too," Ms. Pearlstein said.

"He ain't called Hershel!"

"How do you feel about him?"

"We're buddies," I said.

"No! His execution."

"Hey. You reap just what you sow."

She glared again. "Are you religious?"

She was writing again, and I was staring at her when a thought came to me like being run over by an eighteen-wheeler.

"You working for the 'Dog? Appeal stuff? That what you here for?"

"I am not working for Hershel. I work for justice. And I will try to find out any detail that might help in an appeal. Something that might contradict testimony and raise a reasonable doubt."

"That ain't research," I said.

"It is very much a part of my research. It's about criminal justice." She looked in her stack of papers and pulled out a sheet. "What you say is used for science. How prisoners think. I'll analyze our sessions for response quality." She talked loudly and slowly, as if I didn't speak English. "Part of our work is truth in meaning. Our sessions are analyzed by independent graders. You can see it in this representation."

She adjusted the sheet of paper with colored bars on it so I could see better. "The red bars represent silence, green bars are for meaningful talk, and black bars are for diversions from the truth. Everyone's graph is different. My work relates responses to personalities and various crimes. I specialize in murder."

That was real rat shit. And that's what I told her. I raised my hand to her, my chains rattling.

"Sean brought it on himself," I said. "We didn't do nothing."

"I don't believe that at all," she said. "Sean was murdered. It's clear from the transcripts, the autopsy, and the witnesses, before and after."

I looked right at her. "You do guys?" I asked.

She jerked back like I might have slapped her.

"Let's review the rules," she said coldly, "I'm a professional. I won't respond to personal questions."

"Hey. You my woman," I said. She must have done guys; if she was a dyke, she'd probably need to come out with it. But she was shaking, not looking at me. She was deciding whether to pack up her stuff. Her shoulders slumped.

"Can't you be human?" she said.

"I'm swelled up human for you, baby," I said, looking to see if she got my meaning.

"Just answer the questions!" Then, from her folder, she took out a loose sheet of paper with lines and boxes on it and put it down on the table.

"What are you in for?" she asked.

"B and E."

"Your record says murder two."

"People get confused. Screw up the truth," I laughed.

"That's a lie. An outright lie."

"Why ask?"

She paused. "It's routine. Demographics. I want to hear it from you."

"I stole a bicycle," I said.

She stood up. She wasn't higher than my armpit if I'd been standing unchained.

"I expected you to cooperate!" she said. "You're nothing but lies."

"You only been here twenty minutes," I said, but she was hurrying to get out. "You coming back?"

"Why should I?" she said over her shoulder.

"You the chief," I said. "Me the Indian."

She had her stuff together and she turned to me. Her face was red. "You are one miserable human being. If I come back, I expect you to treat me with respect. I am an educated woman and a researcher. You are a murderer. I don't want you talking down to me again."

"I ain't no murderer," I said.

Back in my cell, I had this anger, like I wanted to put my fist through the wall. I did fifty push-ups and a hundred squats. Then I was sitting on the bed laughing, thinking to myself, and I figured I'd put her crooked little face right up there on the wall, head high, where I could see her while standing over the toilet for a piss. I had a marking pen. I drew pictures on the wall I copied from magazines—of airplanes, tattoos I'd like, guns, motorcycles, cars. So I draw her face with a small circle about half the real size of her. I point the chin a little. Her nose is almost nothing, so I put two dots for her nose holes. Then I scratch in hair that looks almost like a wig, step back, and laugh at how close I've come to the real Pearlstein. Then I draw in circles and curves for her eyes—close together, looking off to one side like she did most of the time in the session—and after two eyebrow arches, I put thick glasses on. For her mouth, I use a thin line, mean looking. She looked fragile next to my big drawing of a Harley Fatboy, copied straight out of Motorcycle Cruiser. Like a child who wasn't telling it like it was.

As it turned out, my next session with Pearlstein was only two days later. She looked different, less dry and peely than I remembered, more like some guy's ugly baby sister. I guessed she was twenty-five, but her hair looked a lot older, gray like cobwebs and in tight old-lady curls. At least she'd combed her hair, so it didn't look as if she were in a tornado.

Her picture was still on my wall and it didn't need changing; I had her eyes right—close together and small, like she was peeking out of her skull through half-inch drill holes. I'd been laughing at my picture.

Cocky little bitch. I wasn't angry no more, but I was surprised she showed up, like she was hot for our sessions more than she let on.

The guards always chained me to the same iron ring sunk in one of the concrete floor blocks, but she was farther away from me today. She must have asked for the new spot; the guards didn't give a damn about where she sat as long as I couldn't reach her. The dented metal table between us was about as long as she was tall, with its legs bolted to the floor. She was looking at her papers, so I rattled my chains. The inside guard looked over at me. I was feeling good, so good. Here in all this space, and there was sunlight coming between the iron bars in the window that laid out long boxes of yellowed light on the gray-white linoleum floor. Sweet, sweet! Ain't no sunshine in maximum.

She wrote on her pad for a while.

"You a real doc?" I asked her.

"Does it make a difference?" She still stared at her pad. Her voice was a little squeaky.

"You ain't one, or you would have said so."

She shifted in her chair. "Please try to keep to the subject."

"You my subject, sweetie pie."

"Ms. Pearlstein," she said angrily.

"You got a first name. Like Virginity?"

"Where were you when you first saw Sean McGarity?"

"Maybe you called Chastity. Chastity Pearlstein!"

"Answer my question.""I love the way your lips wiggle," I said.

She slammed her folder on the table. "I don't like smartasses. I've got too much to do." She nodded to the guard and picked up her papers and her tape recorder. She'd spent less than five minutes with me. That was no session!

"Up yours," I said, but she was already out the door. The guard pointed at me, his first finger straight out like the barrel of a gun. The bastard. The guard closed the door and called for transfer. In a few seconds I'd be on my way back to maximum.

The room got silent except for the A/C fan. I rested my chained hands on the table. There was a tap on the door. Soft, like a woman. The inside guard turned the key in the lock, and Pearlstein came back in and stared at me as if I was dog shit on her shoe. She whispered to the guard, her jaw clenched. She came back to the table.

"I'll forget your antics," she said.

"Why you pissed?" I asked.

She paused. "I care too much about what I do sometimes."

"Lighten up," I said.

"I don't need your advice. When did you first see Sean?"

I kept my mouth shut.

Her lips were in a hard line. "Are you refusing to talk?" she asked. "Why can't you answer simple questions?"

"You think I'm going to change my story. Well, I ain't changing my story."

"Damn it. I want to find out what the real story is—the story beneath what's been told."

"Reddog's guilty. I ain't guilty," I said. "That's the truth."

"You were both convicted."

"He got what was coming."

"He got murder one because you plea bargained."

"That ain't research talk," I said.

"You have given me so many black bars for my research. You can't tell the truth about anything!"

We sat in silence while she stared at her notes.

"I'll tell you the truth. You my honey."

"I am not your honey!"

She uncrossed her legs and put both feet solid on the floor.

"You'll never get Reddog off," I said.

"Think what you want," she said. She was straightening her papers by holding the edges and tapping the stack bottom on the table. Her index finger twitched.

"You can't blow his conviction," I said.

"How could you possibly know?"

"You can ask more questions."

"I'm wasting my time."

"For Reddog, or research?" I asked, but she didn't answer. Her mind was locked on Reddog like a fly on cow shit. The research gig might be legit, but it wasn't what she'd give her virginity for. She wanted the 'Dog alive. The guard unlocked the door for her, sliding the dead bolt. She walked out. Within minutes the transfer guys were taking me back to max.

In my cell, I took my marking pen and changed my drawing of her head. I added a stick drawing of her body with arms and legs, and then I put a line between where her thighs might be, a line like a stick jammed up her twat. It was crude, but I felt better.

Each day, I wondered if I would get out for a session. Security guys had scrotal squeeze about advanced notice giving cons the edge for escape attempts. For guys in max with no outside contacts, it didn't seem to make no difference.

After five days I was moved back to the session room about two hours before lunch. Pearlstein sat straight in her chair with both feet on the floor. She looked more like a girl now; I mean she had her little tits poking up under a red sweater. Her glasses were bent, sitting a little crooked on her face, and she kept taking hold of the corner of the frame and sliding them up her nose.

She started right in with questions.

"I see your mother hasn't been coming to visit."

"Aren't you the little detective," I said.

"You don't care about your mother?" she asked.

"She's a fat slob. I didn't choose her. No one would have chosen her."

"What's she do?"

"She goes out of the house once a month to pick up her welfare and ADC checks."

Pearlstein did a lot of busy writing.

"You ain't making bars," I said.

"My associates do the graphs on a computer at school."

"Well, my mother ain't worth a shit. Put that on a graph."

"Did you feel that way when she was still visiting?"

"She wasn't no good then, either."

She waited before she spoke again. When she looked up, she had wrinkles on her brow and she squinted at me.

"Hey. You giving conjugals to the 'Dog?" I asked.

"You're crude."

"But I ain't stupid," I said. "The research is like a decoy in a bank robbery."

"I never said you were stupid," she said, swallowing hard.

"But that's what you think!" My heart pounded and I strained at my wrist cuffs.

"You'll never know what I'm thinking. Never in a thousand years."

"I don't have to take shit from no student trainee," I said. "You ain't even a real doc!"

She shoved her chair back and looked up. "Okay," she said. "Calm down. It was not the right thing to say." She went back to her pad, writing fast. I tried making my mind blank, squeezing her out. It was a prison thing to do, to be sure nothing ever got to you. But I was still breathing hard and fast. I stared at her, the way she was hunched over, her hair over her ears, hiding most of her face. Her pencil stuck up between her first finger and her bird-finger, and it made these little circles as she wrote. I hadn't seen anything like that since grade school. There was a lot about Ms. Pearlstein that came out slow, and only if you looked hard.

After a few minutes she began picking up her stuff but stayed seated. "Think about it, Billie," she said. "Talking about it doesn't make any difference now. There will never be a retrial for you. But you could save a man from dying."

"You ain't leaving?" I said.

"I want justice, Billie. It's so easy." She looked small but solid. She wasn't backing down on anything.

"I understand what you're saying," I said.

"Do you, Billie? Do you know what justice is? The difference between right and wrong?"

"I been to school."

"It's more than that, Billie. It's what's inside."

"What you really needing, baby?"

"You were driving the truck when Sean went down. I know that. The world knows that. But if you said it, we might have an appeal."

"The kid asked for it," I said.

"You know what the world believes? It was gay bashing. You'll never change that. But you could keep a man alive."

"Reddog tied the kid to the truck. He hugged the kid to make him feel good." She looked more interested than I had ever seen. "He grabbed the kid's crotch and stroked him, until the kid laughed and said 'That's all me.'"

"But you were driving!"

I shut up.

"Think about it, Billie. The truth won't hurt you now."

"Sean wasn't my kind of guy," I said. He'd been out of the closet since the day he was born. He wore tan slacks with that slick-soft cloth that never wrinkles, and a white girly shirt unbuttoned at the top so the no-hair skin on his chest showed halfway down to his belly button. He ran his fingers through his hair to keep it sticking up for that I-just-got-out-of-bed look. He stroked this little, light mustache, with hairs that looked like he stole them from a caterpillar and pasted them on one by one. The kid drank screwdrivers!

"But you were the one who accelerated the truck to more than sixty miles an hour, dragging the helpless boy until his clothes and skin were gone, his face smashed! Say it!"

"Reddog's guilty."

"You were driving!"

"Fuck off."

She held her breath, her hands clenched in bloodless fists. She turned slowly, all of her belongings cradled in her arms.

"You coming back?" I called to her.

Alone in my cell with my black marker, I covered her body with a dress so that line in her twat was blotted out. She looked better with a dress on. And I hadn't been feeling good about hurting her with a stick like that. But I drew shackles around each foot, with chains hanging down, every link showing as if it might drag her off the wall.

It was three days later when Pearlstein came back, two hours earlier than she ever did before, just after breakfast. I'd cooled down a bit, and I'd been thinking about our last session. She was doing what she had to do. I was determined not to take it to heart. Especially the truth part; she didn't tell the whole truth, either.

She was already in the room when the guards brought me in.

"Hi," I said.

She didn't say nothing, just sat, her chair pushed back from the table. Her skinny legs were crossed and her knobby kneecaps stuck up like baby turtle shells on a log when you're out shooting squirrels. She doodled on her pad.

"You want to talk?" she finally asked.

"Don't make no difference to me," I said. I stared. Her dress was green, the shade of summer grass, and it made her hair look the color of rain clouds. Her skin was as white as a shower-stall wall, and she had a few pimple-crater scars on her cheeks. One was still reddish and big enough to hurt when she touched it. She had holes in her ears for earrings. I wondered what Pearlstein wore on the outside. Studs? Those long, dangling earrings that'd shimmy when she moved her head? Pussy counselors took off their jewelry for sessions, so I'd never know what she wore.

"It really wasn't me," I finally said. "If that's what you want to know."

"Even your mother doesn't believe that." She crossed her legs and pulled her dress down, covering her knee.

"What did my mother say?"

"She said you worshipped Reddog. Couldn't sit still when he was away. That you were a good boy until you met him."

"We were just buddies."

"Reddog said you were the one."

"Look," I said. "Reddog set the kid up! I didn't set the kid up!"

"Why did you do that?"

I thought out what she wanted to hear. "We didn't find no babes in Jolly's bar, but Sean comes in, light on his feet, looking for guys. The 'Dog thought he'd have some laughs."

"So Reddog approached Sean?"

I was about to say the kid was grinning at Reddog and he waved the kid over to him, but before I could get the words out, Pearlstein called the guard over from where he stood near the door. Her skin was even paler now than usual, and sweat glinted on her brow.

"You want to hear about it?" I asked. But Ms. Pearlstein stood up. She had to go to the bathroom. God, how I wished I had a cigarette, but tobacco was banned.

She was gone a long time before she came back and sat down, and

I waited, thinking she'd ask a question. Nothing. Like she'd forgotten what we were talking about. The time was ticking on, the hour getting shorter.

"I'm not feeling good," she said.

"You look like a ghost," I said.

"It's probably some flu."

She shut off the recorder and put a rubber band around her rolled-up sheets of scribbles. She wasn't allowed to bring a briefcase into secure rooms.

"Don't go," I said.

"Maybe tomorrow."

It was funny, but I hoped she felt better.

"A glass of water," I said to the guard.

He didn't move.

"She's sick," I said. "Grab her some water?"

He signaled to the outside guard, who brought water in a paper cup.

"She's wasting her time with you," the inside guard said to me, soft and mean.

She drank the water, looking down. Within minutes she was back looking at me.

"You better?" I asked.

She didn't answer. She turned on the recorder. Shuffled some papers and looked at the electric clock on the wall.

"I can't understand why Sean went with you," Pearlstein said in a raspy voice, like she might have been vomiting.

"You really okay?"

"I'm better. I thought you were the sweet-talking guy," she said. "Reddog was the strong silent type."

"You got that right," I said with pride.

"But it was Reddog, then, who talked Sean into going with you?"

"That's right."

Reddog might not have been a big talker, but he had a molasses-sweet voice that turned heads. And he was the best-looking man in five states. People took to him, remembered him like a good chunk of hot pecan pie with ice cream. And this kid Sean fell for Reddog after one look.

"He was in love with the 'Dog. Couldn't keep his eyes off him."

I waited. For the first time she wasn't doodling or squiggling. Her right hand was pressed flat on her stomach.

"Reddog drove when you left the bar?" she asked.

"The kid in the middle between me and the 'Dog. I remembered the kid's knee was shoved against my thigh because of the gearshift on the floor, but the kid's hand was on the 'Dog's thigh."

"'Cool wheels,' the kid said.

"'Where you get shitty talk like that,' Reddog said. 'Cool wheels'? You queer or something?' Then the kid laughed."

"How did you get Sean behind the truck?"

"Reddog smooth talking," I said. "Reddog made it sound like weight training, you had to push yourself to get better, keep tight and fit."

Pearlstein raised her pencil to me, holding it like a cop's nightstick. "When Sean got behind the truck, didn't you drive Reddog's truck?"

"You keep asking that. This ain't cross-examination."

"I can understand that it started out as a game. But it wasn't a game when the driver jammed that accelerator to the floor."

The kid was exactly what Reddog said he hated: wimpy look, whiny voice, sissy shoes, pale lips, pukey mustache. But Reddog enjoyed setting the kid up for showing him what a queer he was. And he liked touching him. Teasing him.

"How did Sean fall down?"

Pearlstein's tape had stopped spinning. It needed a turning but I said nothing. Pearlstein was quiet, the smooth top of her pencil clenched between her teeth.

"I think you were jealous, Billie."

I laughed. "Of Sean? You got your head up your ass."

"Did you try to save Sean?"

"Sure," I said, thinking hard. "I did everything." I looked right at Pearlstein. "He was gasping. His right eye was puffy and almost shut; the other eyelid was half-open, his eyeball rolled up so it showed only white. I pushed on the kid's chest, CPR stuff from the army. Blood all over me."

"I never heard this. Did Reddog do anything?" Pearlstein asked.

"Nothing!"

"Who said to bury him?" Pearlstein asked.

"'We've got to get rid of him,' Reddog said."

"Not you?"

"Not me!"

I looked at Pearlstein to see if she believed me, but she had her eyes down looking at her paper. Her pencil wiggled a little, then went still.

"You know about Reddog's trial?" she asked.

"I heard." We were caught before the kid settled in his grave. Four people saw us leave Jolly's.

"It took the jury two hours to convict him," she said.

The cops hated Reddog, and they wanted the world to think the Texas justice system was lubed to smooth running with I'll-fix-your-ass grease. The prosecutors ate up my plea bargain.

"You think the jury was wrong about Reddog?" Pearlstein asked.

"They got off on giving him the max," I said.

Her eyelids drooped. Her pencil was still now.

"What story he tell you?" I asked.

Pearlstein looked at me. "Not that."

"Would I lie to you?"

"You weren't driving when Sean went down?"

"What'd I tell you?" I said. I must have shouted or something close to it, because she squinted. And the truth was, I was driving when Sean went down. Reddog was leaning his head out the window, calling to the little fucker from the passenger side, telling him he was doing great. The little shit. I shoved the accelerator, the engine straining to do the hundred and twenty it had done for me plenty of times.

"You think I'd lie?" I asked.

She shuffled her papers into a pile. I was strangely calm.

"You're the one who should be waiting for execution," she said. Pearlstein gathered up her tape recorder and paper stack without a word.

"Time's not up," I said. The way she was grabbing things up looked like she wasn't thinking about coming back.

She didn't look to me.

"Okay, I was driving, but it didn't make any difference. Reddog was guilty." She was looking around, then found her pencil.

"He tied the knot. Put the kid behind the truck," I said.

Anger blazed in her eyes. I thought she was going to spit at me.

"I was driving when the kid went down! You can tell them that."

She was writing on the outside of a folder without putting her stuff down. "And you sped up. Faster than any human could run."

"Yeah. You can tell them that, too."

She was breathing hard.

"What more do you want?" I asked.

"I don't know," she said. "The governor has refused a stay. But I'll try. It may be too late."

"You coming back?"

She reached the door. She turned her steady gaze to me. In the shadows, her eyes were the size of bore holes in a pistol.

Back in my cell, the evil, hard lines of her drawing bugged me. I wet a few squares of toilet paper and tried to wash her off the wall, but the swipes just blurred the lines, and the terrible shape of her still would not fade. I took the two-inch metal handle off the toilet flusher and hacked at the wall, at the drawing, crumbling the painted cement block inch by inch until she was gone, just a pile of crumbled wall dust at my feet.

I sat on my bunk. I looked at the pile of dust and trash as if she were still there. I could never draw her again, and for a crazy moment I wondered if I could put her back together—glue, or tape, or something. But she was destroyed. Hell, it was just a drawing. And I had every right to be pissed at her. She was the one who'd lied to me about experiments. All that talk about truth. Truth don't mean nothing!

I had to sweep out the cell at clean-up the next morning. Damned if the guard didn't deny workout sessions in the exercise yard for a week for destroying the wall. Christ, it was only the top part of the concrete, not a hole or anything.

The 'Dog was put down with appeal denied. Word spread through the prison, even in maximum security, as if there were no walls. And I waited, thinking maybe the research might start up again. But the days went by for more than three months. The patch of destroyed wall never changed until some maintenance guy slapped some plaster on it while I was getting eye care in the infirmary. Pearlstein didn't show, and the lost picture I'd drawn on the wall stayed with me only in my mind, trapped in its own cell.

A few weeks later, my mind started playing tricks on me. It happens to cons. One night I heard the 'Dog. He was behind a closed door at the end of the hall. His voice was soft, and I couldn't make out the words. Then it was gone. Days later, in the middle of the night, the lights on low illumination, I heard him taking a piss. I knew I couldn't see him, and I didn't try. The next night, he came, standing in the shadows just outside the bars, maybe five feet back near the opposite wall. Just an outline, but I knew he was wearing a tank top, tight jeans. I knew, too, the shape of his lats, the curve of his delts and biceps. He stood there, motionless, silent, and then he was gone before I could think to call out to him.

The War of the Flies

illustration by Peter Healy

The War of the Flies

The summer when I was eight, the dead flies were so thick on Grandma's porch that Mom swept them into piles and shoveled them into large plastic trash bags.

"They're a danger. Think of the disease," Mom said.

It was our once-a-year visit to Grandma. The flies arrived one at a time at first.

"I didn't invite them," said Grandma.

"They're here for some reason. Flies are attracted to something," Mom said.

"Well, it's not that I'm dirty."

Grandma went into her workroom at the back of the house to weave throw rugs on her antique loom—whish, whish, bang, squeak, squeak. Whish, whish, bang, squeak, squeak. Mom stayed in the kitchen scrubbing sinks and floors with Lysol. "Your grandmother is mean and stubborn," she said.

I thought it was Mom who was mean and stubborn, not letting me spend my summer time with Dad in Alaska, but I didn't say so.

Grandma lived in Calliope, New York, a four-hour train ride from New York City through farming country. Her house was just out of town near the river at the edge of a bog. From my bedroom window I looked out on the two-thousand-acre farm owned by Obadiah Waddle, whose wife had died. He had a few dairy cows, lots of laying chickens, and grew mostly cash crops like soybeans. He never said much but he let me ride with him on his tractor and taught me to milk a cow. Grandma frequently took him tuna-fish casseroles covered with crushed Ritz crackers in a Pyrex bowl to heat up in the oven. Sometimes she stayed to share dinner with Mr. Waddle almost until bedtime, while Mom and I ate alone.

Grandma thought we were only as good as the food we put in our stomachs. She fed me meats and sweets to make me grow and keep me pleasant. For Mom, Grandma cooked brussels sprouts, beans, acorn squash, and fried baloney with pickle relish.

"Baloney is a good source of protein," Grandma said when Mom complained.

"It's the floor scraps they sweep up at the meat factory," Mom said.

"You'll never live long enough to enjoy your social security," Grandma said.

Mom said fried baloney was the reason she could never stay here for more than two weeks.

Grandpa had been a Methodist preacher before he had his stroke two years ago, and ever since then he had been in the second-floor bedroom. The stroke had made him loud and mean. "Took the good side of his brain," Grandma said. Now Grandpa thought the heathen had attacked Calliope and he feared evil. He called Mom—his only child—the "witch of the antichrist." And he frequently confused me with David and complimented me on my bravery with Goliath.

Grandpa's bowels didn't stop up too good, and that set Grandma and Mom to clean him two or three times a day. That left bad smells in the house and foul moods in Mom and Grandma.

"Father's mess attracts flies," Mom said.

"Nothing of the sort. I keep him clean as a whistle," said Grandma.

Grandma didn't talk to Mom much after that.

We'd been there two days when I killed the first fly after three swats with one of the flyswatters—the old-fashioned, metal-screen-mesh kind with cloth binding around the edge and a wire handle—that hung on nails near the doors. By about sunset I needed only one swat per fly. Still I wasn't keeping up, so Grandma borrowed strips of sticky paper from Mr. Waddle next door that we hung from the light fixtures in the kitchen and pantry. Then Grandma called Mrs. Rather in the next house down the road. Mrs. Rather had flies, too. Grandma felt better knowing she wasn't dirtier than her neighbor, and Grandpa, as family, wasn't the only fly attraction.

The next morning, stuck flies blackened the papers.

"Mercy be," said Grandma. We hung up more flypaper and by early afternoon it was black again with flies. I was getting good with my swats now, killing two and three flies with one swing.

"I wish Dad was here," I said to Grandma when Mom was upstairs. "He'd know what to do."

"Yep. He'd get 'em," said Grandma. Mom and Dad were in a custody fight over me and Dad hadn't been allowed to visit in more than a year.

Dad sent me a postcard from Nome, Alaska. I saw it in the mailbox at home before Mom could take it out and save it for me until I was older. On the front was a picture of a man in a winter coat with fur trim around the hood. Of course that wasn't Dad. He worked on a pipeline. They had moose, caribou, and bear, he wrote.

The flies were getting worse.

"Each filthy little bastard carries hordes of diseases," Mom said.

"Can you see the diseases?" I asked. Mom was a sixth-grade science teacher at a private school. Her job made her know everything about the mysteries of disease.

"Of course not. They're microscopic." She gave me that look that she used with Dad sometimes. Like we were too slow to understand.

Grandma kept a five-inch magnifying glass to read the phone book. Under the lens the flies were as large as jellybeans: their heads round circles, their legs fuzzy, their wings transparent as Saran wrap. I wondered where the bugs hid.

On the fifth day, dead flies layered the porch and we swept them up to shovel into bags. Mom drove forty miles to get surgical masks: mine half-covered my eyes, and Grandpa tore his off again and again; we gave up on his disease prevention. We lined all the doors we didn't use with tape, but the flies crept in through the heating ducts.

Mom called PestKill the Surefire Exterminator.

"He's useless," Grandma said about PestKill. "His garage went bankrupt."

The pest killer came with a tank strapped to his back and a wand with a nozzle. He sprayed in the basement and attic. Mom followed to be sure he didn't miss a spot.

With my magnifying glass I noticed that flies never died on their backs, at least that I could tell. They seemed to just fall over on their sides, their legs pulled up, their bodies often arched. I showed one to Grandma.

"Do flies hurt?" I asked.

"No, Bobby."

"But they're all stiff and twisted."

"Rig-a-tortoise. Happens when we die."

The same morning a health department guy parked his green pickup truck in the driveway. "The bog and farm next door are thick with larvae," he said.

"We ain't never had larvae before," Grandma said.

"From chicken manure for fertilizer. Cows, too. Maybe you should move out for a week or so."

"We got an invalid upstairs," Grandma said.

The health guy said he was sorry and they would hire a crop duster to spray.

"It'll poison the river," Mom said. She was an environmentalist. She belonged to the Sierra Club and bought Ranger Rick magazine for me.

"We've got to do something," said the health man.

That afternoon a red-and-white crop duster plane swooped down to level out across the bog and Mr. Waddle's fields, then pulled up and did a roll to come back the other way. That was what I wanted to do when I grew up. Mom shook her fist. "Polluter," she yelled.

"Could we go flying sometime?" I asked Mom.

"That's stupid. You're sounding like your father."

I turned away but Mom grabbed me and squeezed me from behind. She said she was sorry and she loved me and I wasn't like Dad at all.

The next day it wasn't much better but it wasn't any worse. Mom wanted the sheriff to jail Mr. Waddle for causing an apocalypse with his chicken shit. She looked in the phone book for the number.

"There's no proof," Grandma said.

"You're so irritating," Mom said, but she closed the phone book without calling.

In the evening Grandpa soiled himself and the flies descended. Grandma screamed. Mom sprayed insect kill and Grandma and I washed Grandpa off with towels and water from a bucket. It took a long time.

Mom refused to surrender to the flies. It wasn't in Mom's blood to give up when she had a cause. That was what Dad used to say to me after they'd had a fight.

Two days later the live flies were gone. We still found lots of dead ones behind the sofa and in the curtains. Flyswatters hung idle on their nails and we took down the strips. No more crop dusters or health men in pickup trucks.

"That's weird," Mom said.

"Praise the Lord," Grandma said.

"Cool," I added.

"I'm baking," Grandpa yelled from above, loud enough for us to hear downstairs. I was sent up to open two windows as wide as I could.

"Don't ever let a snake roam in your garden, Judas."

"I won't ever let a snake into my garden, Grandpa. Never!"

"That's a good Christian boy. Wish my kin was like you," he said.

Mom turned silent and kept to herself in her bedroom. I think she was mad, but not the insane kind. Well, maybe a little. She had found purpose in her war with the flies but now the enemy refused to fly around anymore. She felt defeated at the surrender; there was no glory, no purpose, no lesson learned to be taught to the multitudes.

Grandma started cooking again, singing to herself, beating eggs and opening and closing the oven door. For meals, we'd had microwaved packaged food for days. Now grandma chopped raw vegetables and plucked a fresh-killed chicken. She made a special dinner for me to take next door to Mr. Waddle. I might get a tractor ride.

"What's that?" Mom asked.

"Tuna-fish casserole for Mr. Waddle."

Mom grabbed my shoulders and the dish fell out of my hands to the floor; the glass shattered. I wiggled away.

"Don't feed that criminal," Mom said.

Grandma came in from the other room. "Wasn't Mr. Waddle's fault."

"That's your trouble, Mother. You never stand up for what's right."

"Oh, yeah?"

The bag was getting dark brown spots from the casserole soaking into the paper, but Grandma kept quiet.

"He can't eat that," I said.

"I'll get him something else." Grandma said.

"It's your mess," Mom said to me.

"We'll clean it up when we get back," Grandma whispered to me.

Mr. Waddle and Grandma hugged when we took him the chicken.

"How you doing, Bobby?" Mr. Waddle asked.

"Okay."

"Doesn't sound so okay."

"He misses his father, don't you Bobby?"

"Yes'm."

"Why is Evelyn so mad?" Mr. Waddle asked.

"Bobby wants to see his Dad."

Mr. Waddle put his food down and said we ought to pray. We all kneeled next to his sofa.

"Dear Lord, in thy mercy, let this young man see his father again, a father he loves …" And when he finished Grandma said "Amen," and kissed me on the top of the head. Ick!

"Could I talk to my Dad?" I asked Grandma.

"You don't talk to your Dad?" Mr. Waddle asked.

"His mother won't let him, " Grandma said.

Mr. Waddle looked and Grandma. "I don't see why I couldn't give him a call."

"I know the number," Grandma said. She looked to the palm of her hand where she'd jotted it down with a ballpoint pen.

Dad told me how big moose were dangerous but independent. He wanted me to come visit, and after we finished talking, Dad talked to Grandma a long time about legal stuff.

Back in Grandma's house, I hugged Mom.

"You look happy, my little man," she said.

And I was, but I didn't tell her until the next day that Grandma and I had planned a trip while we were at Mr. Waddle's. To Alaska!

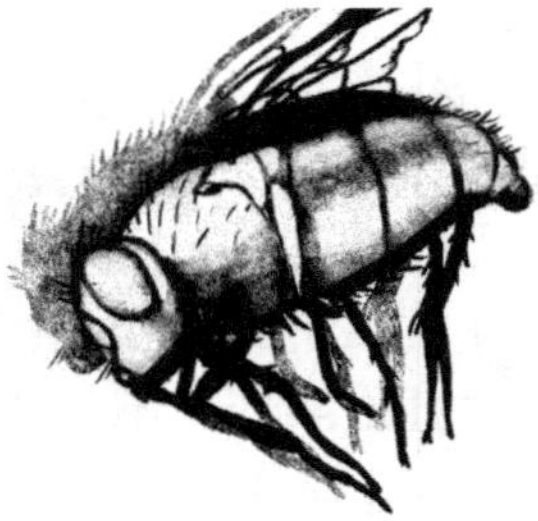

Crossing Over

illustration by Peter Healy

Crossing Over

My name is Agnes Swaggert, and I work in this nursing home for next to nothing. I do good things for old folks like Mr. Wiggins, who has been with us for two months. He lost his hair to radiation, his eyesight to Cadillacs , and his voice to a trach. He moans nonstop, drools and spits, shits five times a day so the sheets got to be changed. I don't think he ever sleeps.

I go to sit for a moment at the nurses' station, put my arms on the counter. I got scars on my right arm, and I set to thinking, as I often do when I feel like this. Them scars make me think about my kin—Grandma mostly. Mr. Wiggins moans but I pay him no mind. Mr. Wiggins will be number fifty-nine.

Funny how I can see every one of them. I think goodly about each one, being as I knew them so well. Like being down front in the movie theater and the lights go on and you turn around and there they are lined up, row after row. Sometimes I think I'm a mother duck, all of them waddling behind me, crossing over the road to the other side. Mr. Wiggins is whining real good now, so I think about Grandma. What a woman she was. I'd be guessing I liked her more than momma or daddy.

It was my granny who taught me, after momma had left for work and it was bedtime.

"What is that, grandma?" I said to her one night.

"Your mother will never teach you."

"No. No. What's in your hand?" I had expected she had a peppermint stick hidden for me. But it was only a cigarette. She lit up, took out the cigarette from her lips, and picked a piece of tobacco from her tongue.

"When can I smoke?" I asked.

"When you're old enough to know what's right and wrong."

"I know what's right and wrong," I said.

"You don't nohow. Your momma ain't teaching you the ways of Lord."

"She told me, Grandma! She told me how Jesus had this fish and when lots of people come, he kept cutting up the fish and he fed a whole crowd. And then they wanted bread, and Jesus had this loaf that when you sliced it, it just kept coming until everyone weren't hungry no more."

"It's the suffering, precious," she said. "That's where the real learning is. Jesus taught us to suffer unto me. It's the suffer part your momma don't know nothing about. She's godless and I ain't going to tell you about it so don't ask."

"You mean 'cause Daddy left?"

"I don't know as I blame your mother, what with her troubles and all. You too young to understand."

"She taught me, Grandma. She did!"

"We must know ourselves," Grandma said. "Jesus went into the dark and it was hot and dry and he stayed there for a long time like none of us could. And when they put them spikes through his hands and feet, he never cried out once. Never!"

"I know," I said, but I really wasn't sure.

"You don't know nothing," she said. "I can make you into a real woman."

"I'd like that," I said.

"Hold out your arm," Grandma said.

I did as she commanded, putting out my arm, pulling back my nightie sleeve.

"Sit up on the edge of the bed," she said.

I shifted my legs so they hung over the side.

"Don't you flinch," she said. She took two strong draws on a cigarette till it was glowing and she put the tip on the white part of my arm and pressed down. The pain went shooting up, not like lightning, but like when you get a finger shut in the door. I sat there looking at Grandma and never flinched, never cried. Grandma counted.

"One. Two. Three. Four. Five." Then she pulled the cigarette away. "That was real good," she said. "Real good. Now we do one more time tonight."

And over the next month I got to know how Jesus, our Savior, handled the pain, 'cause he was like God's son and it made him special. I got to where Grandma could count five or six times. "Real good," she said, "I's proud of you. You is a good learner."

Well, old Mr. Wiggins is alone again now. I wait till after the night shift comes on. The only nurse is on the second floor. I can hear when she moves; it's so quiet at night except for Mr. Wiggins's whiny moan. Loud he is tonight, bless his soul. Past being able to suffer like a real Christian. He moaning like a heathen now.

I don't need my medicine syringe for this. I just take away the breathing machine, hold my hand over his mouth, and pinch his nose. I got sterile gloves on, of course. He's in restraints and at first he wiggles like a fish out of water on a dry dock. Then in three minutes it's over. I put the breathing machine back on.

"God bless you," I say to Mr. Wiggins as he is crossing over. "God bless you."

I go out and clean up Mrs. Sampson. She's got bladder problems.

"How you making it?" I say to her.

She tries to smile. I like that. Even though she's suffering, it's like she ain't giving in.

"Could you get me some water, Agnes?" she says.

I look at her. "Don't you fret, dear. I bring the water soon as I drop Mr. Wiggins's dirty sheets by the laundry."

"Hurry," she said.

I can tell you this, I heard the first sound of whine in her voice, the first sign of her not taking her suffering like the good Christian woman she used to be.

Father Ryan

illustration by Peter Healy

Father Ryan

The wind gust between the walkway and the airplane door chilled Father Ryan as he waited for Bishop Henley to move into the cabin. Father Ryan's hand swept across his rustled thick head of light-brown hair as the flight attendant smiled and turned to open a can of tomato juice in the galley.

Inside, the cabin was warm and humid. The Bishop pushed ahead for his assigned window seat in first class.

"Are you sure you wouldn't like the aisle, sir?" Father Ryan said, with a touch of sincere sympathy for the bishop's large frame in cramped circumstances. But there was more than a little sarcasm, too. The Bishop liked to look down with a divine sweep of gaze over his ecumenical territory as they took off, a move Father Ryan described often, to the delight of all who knew the Bishop.

The Bishop did not answer. Being around Father Ryan consistently engulfed him in an intense, resentful smoldering. The Bishop thanked God for this duty of taking Father Ryan from Boston to his new parish in Idaho, and he pushed aside any guilt at being delighted to never have to speak to him again, except maybe at conferences. Being rid of this priest gave him hopeful expectations of a tranquil future. After much prayer, the Bishop believed that his dislike for Father Ryan was not just their personality clashes, but an appropriate distaste for his loose, too-friendly demeanor with the parishioners. That, the Bishop was sure, had been the source of the complaint from the young married woman, whom the Bishop did not trust but could not ignore. During the Bishop's interview with the complainant, she had been unable to hide surprise and pleasure—and a touch of mischievousness—in her eyes at the moment when the Bishop expected anger and accusation.

She did not claim assault, or even touching. "Suggestive," she said. "He hinted," she added. Was she a prevaricator? Probably. But with all the recent sex scandals among the clergy, he could not let this explode. He'd seen enough of danger in his thirty-five years of service to the Lord to know when it lurked.

The situation still stressed the Bishop. He was particularly confused by Father Ryan's response to his admonition over the young woman's—was her name Helen? —complaint. Initially Father Ryan seemed perplexed, unable to mount a defense, and then the Bishop saw a switch to defiance with a definite touch of pride and that ever-present glint of humor. After that confrontation, Father Ryan refused to even address the complaint with the Bishop, much less defend himself, as if he considered it trivial and unworthy of self-recrimination.

Father Ryan's bag slipped into the overhead easily. The first-class seat yielded pleasantly to his flesh.

"Are you really comfortable, sir?" he said to the Bishop. "You seem tense."

The Bishop watched the ground crew disconnect hoses and truck baggage. He resented Father Ryan's so public observation on his temperament and physical condition. Wasn't it as always? Or was that fair? Could Father Ryan be innocently sincere? Erroneous thinking there. Father Ryan was definitely cursed with a well-developed sense of satire that had not a smidgen of sincerity. The Bishop tried to appear unconcerned. No one of his status should be ruffled by such a routine administrative problem as Father Ryan. He sighed silently.

After the preflight preparations, the plane began its takeoff roll; Father Ryan leaned back to enjoy the thrust of the engines, the ebullient disconnection from the earth. Father Ryan noticed the Bishop's hands gripping the armrest, and knew the Bishop was praying by rote for safety and survival, and probably not including any of his colleagues, especially Father Ryan.

Father Ryan believed the Bishop's attitudes and accusations toward him were unfounded. And even though Father Ryan would never let on, they had kindled the greatest humiliation in him. He was celibate, proudly so, and his dedication to Christ and the Church had never wavered.

Father Ryan had instantly forgiven Helen. It was a refined name, Helen. He had come to think of her as Helen of Troy the entire time he knew her. She was, in a quirky way, beautiful. Married, but standing on the fortifications of Troy for all the enemy to see, with unshakable self-confidence in her allure. She was justly proud.

Father Ryan still felt the right approach had been to not appear defensive or accusatory in front of the Bishop. That would have yielded a loss of dignity, and a resultant suspicion of the truth of Helen's claims. So he did not defend himself. In fact, he had been complimentary of Helen, refusing to admit to himself that he enjoyed her company. In all honesty, he had angered at first over Helen's misunderstanding of his intentions. But he had immediately decided she deserved the benefit of the doubt concerning her desire to complain, which, he reasoned, was reflexive and not personal. After all, she had enjoyed the talks and the confessions. She had said that. And she had known he was celibate. Teased him once about it. But he'd done nothing and was innocent of provocation in the judgment of his maker, and that was enough. He found solace in his well of forgiveness for her spiteful visit to the Bishop. She deserved forgiveness; she was hardworking, and he was sure she feared God.

Father Ryan accepted the relocation without protest to higher authority—divine or administrative. And he forgave the Bishop for his actions, too, which were probably inevitable under the circumstances.

They had reached cruising altitude. The flight attendant in first class had a lovely shape, Father Ryan thought. Just lovely. He imagined her name was Janice. As she bent over to serve the other passengers, he savored—dear God, he did savor—the lovely curve of her backside. Not a sin, he thought immediately. Admiration is not a sin. And priests had a right to be human at times. He had always believed that.

He sneezed. His allergies were in full bloom.

She walked toward the back of the plane. She did not look at him as he waited for her to reach his row. She looked to others across the aisle. He touched her thigh, about halfway between the knee and the pelvis, a thigh with implied softness under the tight fabric. He touched just enough to get her attention.

"Excuse me, do you have a tissue?" he asked.

Her face flushed and contorted into harsh lines. "Don't touch me," she said.

Father Ryan stared. "I wanted …"

"You touched me. Don't do it again."

Father Ryan wiped his nose with the back of his hand. "I have allergies."

"Ask. But don't touch," she repeated with renewed emphasis. She moved, making a show of pleasantness to those in the next row, ignoring the priests.

"That's embarrassing," the Bishop said to Father Ryan. He sighed audibly. "Dear God. Why doesn't it surprise me?"

"A misunderstanding, sir," Father Ryan said, with less authority than he had wanted. The Bishop turned away to look out with his divine glare over the state of Pennsylvania.

An hour later Janice inched the service cart down the aisle. Father Ryan watched the grace of her skill at smiling and handing—and pleasing. She anchored her cart in the aisle near his row, and started with those passengers opposite him. She dropped a drink can, and it bounced off a seat armrest onto the floor and spewed liquid. She bent over, her backside less than a foot from him. He reached to the cart for napkins to help her clean up. Clutching a small stack of napkins, his hand started its path from the cart to the floor and the back of it accidentally made contact with Janice's backside. He knew immediately the implications of the accident and in his surprise he dropped the napkins. She stood up, her hand moving with the light speed of a heavenly ray, the open palm poised to hit him. But she stopped and clasped her hands, the restrictions of her professional training overriding her feelings, and her face turned tense as if she might cry.

"I can report this, you know," she said.

"I was reaching for the napkins." Father Ryan said, afraid he had delayed too long with his explanation to comfort. She seemed rebuked now. But her features remained rigid.

"It's okay," Father Ryan said, "I understand." He tried to smile, but his frown of concern remained.

The chief flight attendant arrived. Janice whispered in his ear. "One more time and I'll put you in handcuffs," the chief flight attendant said. "I have the authority."

"There is no need to threaten," the Bishop said, irritated to be defending Father Ryan yet again under the halo of the Church. "I can assure you Father meant no harm."

The chief flight attendant considered this for a few seconds. He glanced at Janice with suspicion. The frown on his face suggested that this was not Janice's first such altercation. "Of course," he said. "Let's just forget it."

Janice deliberately avoided eye contact with Father Ryan. He smiled. He noticed her badge said her name was Ester. She didn't strike him as an Ester. He was determined to always think of her as a Janice. Especially now that her lovely eyes carried the spark of interest. Now, Janice stared at Father Ryan with an almost apologetic, motherly benevolence before she followed the male chief flight attendant up the aisle.

Father Ryan read St. Thomas Aquinas mechanically, his eyes revisiting the words on the page as his mind dwelled on his words and glances with Janice. The Bishop looked out the window. After an hour, Father Ryan put down his book.

"I seem to be having a run of bad luck," Father Ryan whispered, leaning toward the Bishop and holding the flat of his hand near his mouth to assure the Bishop that this was confidential and to prevent any passengers from hearing. Father Ryan waited, but the Bishop did not turn his head.

"I pray about it. But sometimes it seems unjust." Father Ryan paused. "The accusations. Am I a victim of divine punishment?"

The Bishop finally looked at him, with a noncommittal stare.

"Sorry, sir," Father Ryan said. "It's just that these things test my faith at times. Not now. This is minor, of course. But with the greater injustices, I do wonder at times. Does God care?"

The Bishop stared out the window again to marvel at the Mississippi, the aortic lifeline. He was well aware of it from occasional visits to the heathen of the Louisiana diocese. When the Bishop made no attempt to respond, Father Ryan picked up his book and opened to a random page.

Janice rolled the service cart into first class from the galley. The Bishop had red wine. Father Ryan declined. Janice smiled and handed him salted peanuts. "You'll be leaving us in Salt Lake City?" she said sweetly.

"Yes," said the Bishop before Father Ryan could answer, turning again to the window.

Janice handed Father Ryan two paper napkins. "For your allergies, Father. You might want to put them in your pocket." She quickly rolled the cart down the aisle.

Father Ryan glanced at the second napkin with a torn edge. In ballpoint pen Janice had written a phone number.

The Bishop had not seen. Thank God. Father Ryan stuffed the napkins into his side pocket and put his head back.

Father Ryan did not believe he was a man of the world, but he knew Janice's gesture for what it must be. She had misunderstood him, probably not cognizant of his devotion to his vows. Protestants often seemed unaware of such things. But it was worse. She failed to respect his piety. She assumed a licentious intent. And that was unfair. His distress agitated him, and he made his way down the aisle to the rear restroom. He splashed water on his face, rubbed his neck to relieve the tension.

Back in his seat, some of his composure returned slowly over the next hour. He reflected, with his earphones delivering Pachelbel. Was there something about him that had precipitated such behavior in Janice? He never provoked. Surely not. He had dedicated his life to Christ. No one could mistake that. And that eliminated provocation. And he was not one of those priests who, with clandestine unconcern, ignored celibacy. Look at the French. The Italians. He was not among them.

He drummed his fingers on the seat arms. He found his gaze darting here and there, without purpose. He removed his earpieces and stuffed them with his iPod in the seat pocket in front of him. The music had begun to grate on his ears. Finally he put down the tray table, crossed his arms, and lowered his head. Doubt swept through him. Did I look to that woman with lust in my heart?

When he raised his head, the Bishop was staring at him, his eyes hard with distrust.

"You're incorrigible," the Bishop said.

Father Ryan looked away, close to tormented that the lust might be in him forever, like the Blood of the Lamb after Eucharist.

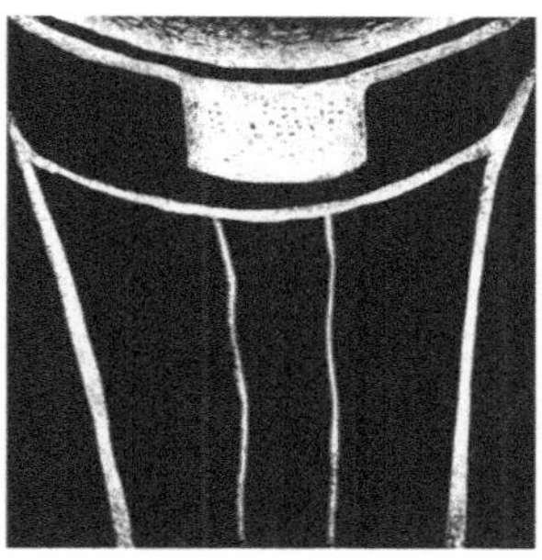

Facing Grace with Gloria

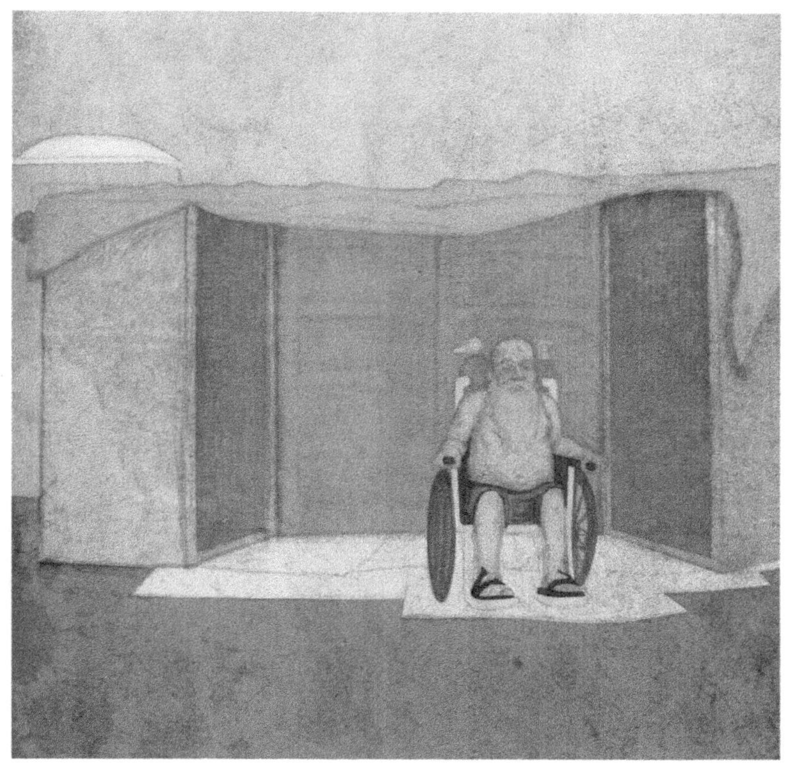

illustration by Peter Healy

Facing Grace with Gloria

I was sleeping in this mission after being discharged from the psych ward at DC General, and some hophead stole my cash from my veteran's disability checks that had piled up while I was so rudely and unjustly incarcerated. So I dropped by my best buddy, Arthur, who lived in two side-tilted dumpsters at the edge of inner Washington, DC.

"You got any cash?" I asked.

"Nothing."

"I want to visit my mother."

"She write to you?"

"Not yet. But she needs me. Came to me when I was inside."

Mother was in Eureka, California. At least her spirit was, and her ashes were, too, in an urn in my older sister's bungalow; I hoped they were out of reach of her two young children by her second husband. My sister refused to see me, but Mother cared that I came to visit. I slept in a cardboard lean-to near Route 101, and I could feel Mother in the air, even when it rained.

"I need money," I said.

"Work the monument," Arthur said.

"That'll take weeks."

"Hey. You might get lucky."

I cleaned up best I could in the restroom of a discount trade mart and headed on down to the Potomac River.

I put my cardboard sign up on an intact discarded painter's easel: "Crash site. Tours. Flight 63. $1.00. Kids free." I waited.

A few folks dribbled by, but they gave me wide berths and blank stares. After an hour three ladies came up—I'm blessed, from my mother's side, with a right-on feeling about people—and I knew at least two of these broads were trouble: cranky oldies who were dressed, one in brown and the other in gray, like spinster twins, in ankle-length dresses with long sleeves, probably from a Midwestern town too small to have a library. These were women who cut their own hair without looking in a mirror. But the third was a girl, maybe nineteen or twenty years old. She had even-edged shoulder-length hair and a round face like one of those angel paintings by Italians you see in the gallery near the toilets in the museum on a free night. She wore this short skirt that didn't cover her cute little knees—all puckered with dimples and curves like little midgets laughing. And she moved as if she had no weight. Her name was Gloria.

They paid their three bucks; I'll give them that. I took them to a riverside grove of trees that hid the shrine that was a waist-high pyramid of round and oval rocks worn smooth and cemented together. Some rocks were gray or brown, but others were dried-blood red or almost white. A few glittered with mica. On top, I had supported with loose stones a plastic yellow flower with a red center and green leaves on the stem.

"The plane came down right over there." I pointed to the river, very wide at this point. We were in comfortable shade now, about seventy-five yards from the bridge.

"You saw it crash?" Brown said.

"Yep."

The gray lady scowled. "Liar! We had loved ones on that flight. It went down nine miles from here."

"I take exception," I said firmly. "Plane came down late fall." I told them about the pregnant woman and all the little children.

"We must insist you discontinue this scam."

I took out two pictures of the crash and rescue from my pocket. Each was a newspaper clipping laminated with drugstore plastic and trimmed to fit the hand. But they ignored my photos.

"What exactly is that?" asked Brown, nodding at the shrine.

"A shrine to a man who sacrificed himself for another," I said with the genuine pride Arthur had taught me. "You want to take a free picture? You'll never see another one like it."

"Using a tragedy to make money," said Gray. "Disgraceful."

"We're in Washington for a settlement," Brown said. "We were appalled by your sign."

"You must stop," Gray sputtered.

"I've already settled," said the girl.

Wow! This might be luck.

"A shrine to honor a real hero," I said, pulsing to the potential, looking directly to the girl, watching those eyes for the faintest touch of sympathy for the dead. I saw the flash of caring!

The other two glared on.

"You're lying to people," said the girl.

"I was there! A little upstream," I admitted. "But I saw it."

"You're sick," the girl said, not with hate, but sad. Real sad. And her eyes shifted—washed with a cringe of fear I often see—as if I was a lunatic. Well, the last shrink I saw thought I was bipolar. She was a medical student and I said, "It's schizophrenia, doc! We're like Mensa, Harvard Divinity, and Yale Law. Not lazy and not crazy. A disease of the genes!" But the doc shook her head and said I had a lot to learn. You can see my conundrum. Gloria had cash to give but she had no respect for me, and I just wasn't clear on how to tap her reserve, but I was clear that this wasn't the group to pass our best moneymaker, the red-painted shoebox with the slot in the top for donations to the families' "relief fund."

I followed them back to the bridge. My heart sank as they walked away. At the other side of the bridge, the girl said something to the two oldies, broke away, and returned to me as the others walked on.

Some driving need had overtaken her; I could see it in her walk. Up close, she stared as if I were some mysterious gift wrapped up in twice-used Christmas paper. I was panting with the possibilities for a trip to Eureka. And she was so pretty! She brought a flood of happiness like too many suds in a bubble bath.

"You really were at the crash," she said. "One of the flight attendants was pregnant. She told me herself. But no one knew."

I let her believe.

"What month?" she asked.

"February."

"Day?"

"Fourth."

"I mean day of the week."

"Monday." All that was in the clippings. "I was there!" I said with conviction. "Me and my buddy were sleeping in a crevice under the bridge. It's been filled in now."

"Oh, no!" She started sobbing. "You weren't really there." She slipped down into a crossed-legged position like a monk. I couldn't bend like that so I stood and tilted over a little bit. Nothing came into my head, so I let her weep it out.

"I know that bridge. There was no place for people to sleep. I know every inch. I thought you might have really been there, in spite of all these lies."

I tried to hold back, but something about this sweet, innocent thing reminded me of Mother and told me it was time to paint a little truth. It wasn't easy.

"I wasn't there," I said. "Only Arthur, my buddy, was there. But he's real sick and waiting on word from a class action suit on Agent Orange. So I'm the only one to honor the hero. He told me every detail."

I decided not to tell her that Arthur, who glued the rocks onto government property, believed he'd seen the miracle face of God the night of the crash and did these shrine tours for free for years, passing a hat for donations, of course. He began charging when his cough-spit turned red and he really needed doctor cash.

She didn't look surprised. Just disappointed. "I wish you had been there," she said. "I want to know about the man. Can I talk to Arthur?"

This was where experience counted.

"Arthur is a loner. Keeps his peace, mostly," I said, my head down, not looking at her.

"Is he here? In the city?"

"He's on the edge."

"I want to talk to him."

"I can't take the time," I said turning away. "I've got to stay the day."

She grabbed my coat sleeve near the patch. "I'll pay. I've got money."

"No way."

"Please take me?"

She reached in her purse and peeled off two tens from a roll of bills—a big roll of big bills.

Owwee! But I shrugged with disinterest. She added two more.

It's cash from the crash, I thought. Probably more than she needs.

Then she peeled off two, three, four … biggies!

"Okay!" I said. "But the cab's on you."

I grabbed the flower and my laminated shots, slipped my sign into my plastic trash bag, grabbed my easel, and we were on our way.

The cabbie dropped us off two blocks from Arthur's abode, saying he didn't drive into the valley of sure death for anyone.

"We can walk," Gloria said brightly. A sweet girl totally unafraid and unaware that this wasn't Main Street, USA. Sure enough, on the way I saw human movement in the shadows of an abandoned warehouse, and I grabbed her arm and hustled her along so she never knew.

Near the landfill, she stared in wonder at Arthur's two discarded dumpsters tipped on their sides, angled like the open jaws of a dinosaur skeleton's head, covered with tarps and cardboard sheets held down with rocks and bits of concrete. He had a discarded Porta Potty, with no door, out back. He was asleep, sitting up in his aluminum chair, with tubes curving under his arm and over his chest and plastic wraps over his oxygen tanks.

"That's him," I told my new friend.

"Is he alive?"

Arthur coughed in his half-sleep. Then he gave up a wet one.

"Don't stand too close. You get hit with the spit."

She moved back a step.

"Arthur," I said. "Meet and greet. You got company."

Arthur shook his head so his gray-streaked beard wagged like a broom. He was wearing only shorts and torn sandals with straps and soles smoothed by some long-gone hippie. Sweat glistened on his forehead.

Although he was half-blind, I waved my cash behind Gloria as she stared at him, trying to get him on board my Gloria train. Arthur didn't have my instincts for the big deal.

"You were at the crash? Air Florida 63?" she gushed. Arthur missed my cash wave behind her head.

"Why do you ask?"

"My father was on that flight. Flight 63."

Arthur finally saw me and gave me a glare. I put away the cash. "Sorry about your dad," I said.

"I'm having a little trouble understanding your purpose," Arthur said.

"I saw the shrine. I thought you saw the crash!"

"A hero," Arthur said.

"Tell me. I want to know!"

Arthur coughed as if to get the story spirited into his voice. He pushed up in his chair and leaned forward slightly. He'd told it before. The DC bard, he was. This was going to be great!

"It was just before midnight, wet snow coming down almost like rain. The jet had iced wings and lost altitude after takeoff. The pilot tried to land on river ice to miss people on the ground. The plane slid on its belly and stopped. Survivors crawled out the exits and slid into the frozen river, grasping for anything—but there was only ice. The plane sank, slow at first, then faster. Like the Titanic."

"In the Atlantic," I said.

Arthur ignored me. "Poor souls lost, some bodies never found."

"What about the man?" she asked.

"The rescue chopper arrived and let down a line with a clamp. It wasn't a chair or anything fancy. The man grabbed the line and could have saved himself but he turned to a woman—a stranger, I learned later—holding onto a piece of ice about fifty feet away. The man shoved the line toward her but the chopper downdraft blew the line away. The man pointed at the line; it stopped in midair. With a slow motion of his hand he willed that line to move to her. 'Strap it around your chest!' he yelled, 'under your arms! Snap the clamp!' The chopper people pulled that woman into the aircraft, a spotlight still fixed on this man, who was glowing like a lightbulb filament. I watched him. The rotor air wash splashed water on the ice and he couldn't hold and he went under. The chopper flew off."

"A miracle," I said.

"A tragedy," Arthur added wisely.

"Could you see him?" the girl asked Arthur.

"Yeah. I was maybe two hundred feet away."

"Was he old?"

"What do you mean, 'old'?"

"Fifty?"

"Yeah. I could see his face. About fifty."

"Could you see his hair?"

"Like the color?"

"Was he bald?"

"Bald. I could see he was bald," Arthur said.

The girl eyed Arthur as if he had just parted the Red Sea. I thought that was a good sign for closing the deal, sort of just payment for the true scoop.

"He was a big man," Arthur said.

"With big shoulders?"

"It was hard to know with him in the water. But I could tell by his neck he was large."

"He was a big man!" she said as if in a dream. Then the kid started crying.

"Your father?"

She nodded.

"A son of God."

"He died for a stranger," I said. "A real hero!"

"To do that for another human being," Arthur said. "A man blessed with the grace of God." I thought Arthur had gone too far bringing the grace of God into it.

She wiped her nose with the short sleeve of her blouse. "I didn't know my father well. My folks were divorced and I lived with my mother. She says it couldn't have been my father who saved that woman."

Arthur let go with a lung-turner of a cough. His face turned red. The bald dome on top of his head flushed. "That's the story," he finally said.

The girl dug in her bag. She wanted to give Arthur five of her big bills. Behind her back I gave Arthur a one-man high five. Crazy Arthur said "no." He'd never accept anything from the daughter of him, he said. Goddamn! Arthur had always been a little slow to embrace opportunity, but this was ridiculous.

Gloria sat motionless for a while. Her wad must have had a thousand dollars. Just a little of that would make an easy round-trip bus ride to Eureka, if added to what I had. I felt like bawling. When she had collected herself, she thanked Arthur again, said she was grateful to know.

"Walk her down to that motel near the expressway. They'll call her a cab," Arthur instructed.

I protested, but Arthur had fallen asleep again.

We were on our way: me, and Gloria, and her cash.

"What's Arthur's last name?" Like she might send him a thank-you note or a little gift in the mail.

I wasn't feeling up to chatting. "I'm not sure. O'Leary, maybe. I forget."

"Will he die?"

"I ain't a doctor. But he looks dead already."

We walked without talking. She had a new spring in her stride. She was smiling to herself, as if someone had given her warm cocoa on a cold night. I hate children, but if I had to have one, I'd have chosen Gloria.

We were close to the motel. She stopped, opened her bag, and asked if I needed more. Maybe not all was lost. I could make it to Eureka, and maybe get Arthur out of the VA clinic to a real doctor, too.

"That's a lot of dough," I said, eyeing her stash.

"You've been so kind." She offered me at least five hundred.

I was fighting with myself inside. More money than I'd seen in years. Maybe I wouldn't tell Arthur; he would never know, and I deserved it after all I'd been through to set it up. Ideas were bouncing around in my head like ping-pong balls in a rotating lottery cage. One crazy idea kept popping up! If she did pay, she would soon wonder if Arthur's story was true and whether it was really her dad or not.

"It's yours," she said.

I shook my head no in a moment of insanity. I just wasn't up to erasing Arthur's graffiti from this girl's blackboard.

The sun was gone, rubbed out by a rain cloud, and the roar of an eighteen-wheeler downshifting blasted us from the overpass of the expressway. I saw her to the motel lobby sliding door; it was stuck on closed and I pried it open for her. I turned quickly. There was no need for long good-byes.

The Perennial Student

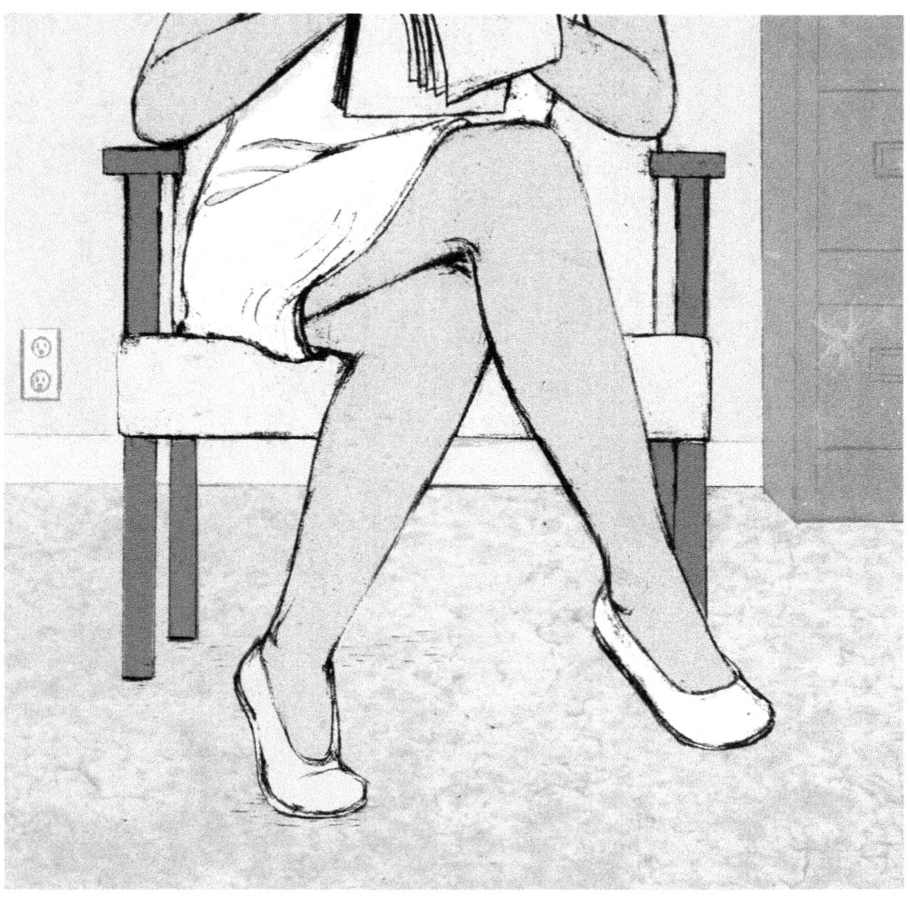

illustration by Peter Healy

The Perennial Student

Associate professor William Possum was looking for student Denise Witherspoon, an attractive, slightly overweight, moderately intelligent woman who was destroying his class. Denise had caused five angry letters, two dropouts, and a formal complaint that said Denise "made an evening of anticipated learning a dreadful experience."

And it had gone further than the classroom. Possum's mentor and department chair, Alice Cherry, had made it clear she was "damned tired" of the "deteriorating" situation.

"She's impossible," Possum had countered, describing Denise's undeserved pride and unjust criticisms of her fellow students. Finally, in frustration, Possum argued that Denise should be dismissed. "Let's give her her money back," he said.

He was shocked at Cherry's lack of understanding. Students paid good money and were entitled to their education, Cherry said. "This is an administrative problem. Talk to her!"

Possum had to talk to Denise alone before she got to the classroom. He waited inside the entrance hall of the ivy-coated building that housed the departments of English and computer science. He had a direct view of the front, although he made sure those coming in could not make out his features in the shadow of the backlit, life-size statue of the school's founder.

Possum saw Denise entering through the left side of the twelve-foot oak doors. How innocent she looked. "Denise," he called, "over here." She squinted toward the sound of his voice.

"Will?" she asked. All his other students respectfully called him Mr. Possum.

"Yes. Over here. Behind the statue. I need to talk to you."

He had practiced word choice and phrasing. Now was the moment he'd been dreading. He guided Denise to the quietest corner of the foyer, next to a seven-foot corn plant and away from the flow of students arriving for the seven o'clock classes. He looked at her directly. The hot summer air seemed to press them together.

"Look, Denise. You have really made a contribution to the class."

"Oh, thank you," she interrupted. "That's so cool."

"Writing is sensitive business …" he started again.

"Only when you let it all hang out."

"It's not particularly an issue of hanging out."

"You got to tell it like it is. Tell the truth."

He tasted the first sourness of defeat. How could this mundane woman with her formidable convictions make him feel so hopeless?

"I did not mean that we should not tell the truth. It is a question of adjusting to the sensitivity of the writer."

"I know sensitivity. You teach us real good." She smiled. "It's all about no pain, no gain."

Was she mocking him with her stare of excessive interest? He worried someone might overhear. My God, how she made him flounder under this silly corn plant, as awkward as an armadillo in a swimming pool.

"Each creative composition is so personal, it makes a writer vulnerable," he said.

She nodded in full agreement.

He decided to be direct. "I must ask you to be considerate of other class members in your comments."

She recoiled slightly, frowning. "Shutting me down?"

"No. Not 'shutting you down.' Just soften your comments."

She looked away. "You've had complaints, haven't you? Well, it's not fair for them to come down on me. They're not good writers."

"Just go a little easier on the approach."

"It's the men, isn't?" she asked.

Possum swallowed. "No. It's not just the men."

Discrimination, he wondered? Was she thinking of filing a complaint? His tongue stuck to the dry roof of his mouth. Where was his carefully planned congenial discourse that would lead to an open exchange of ideas on common ground?

"I wish you—I mean we …," she seemed uncomfortable with her thought.

"Just try. Okay?"

Without a word she hustled away, the strap of her large carryall swaddled in the cleavage of her breasts. There were still ten minutes before class. She did not go up the spiral staircase that led to the classroom. She went to the restroom. She closed the door without looking at him. Even though to see him she would have had to move her head with a breakneck quick twist to the right, he saw significance in the fact that she didn't look.

He worried that their talk had been too short. He had wished for the slightest apology. And why go to the restroom? To relieve herself? She'd just arrived! Or had she been devastated? Of course not! Not Denise. And he had been extremely gentle. But he pictured her in an emotional crisis, huddled in a stall with the sliding metal bolt on the door in the locked position.

In the classroom, Possum chatted with the other students and waited a few extra minutes beyond the hour for Denise to return. Finally he began without her. Ten minutes after class started, she entered. She looked transformed—proud, demure, vulnerable, injured. She walked erect around the table to a chair, holding her carryall and notepad. All the students' gazes were on her. No one spoke. Her lids were swollen. Her eyes rippled with the pinkness of a good cry. Her sweeping gaze of the room locked on Possum, unyielding. My pain is caused by him, she did not need to say aloud. William Possum, cruel associate professor of English.

Possum got the class going again. Denise sat motionless and silent as the first two students read. The discussions were lively and informative. Possum relaxed a little. He may have lost a skirmish, but he felt he had won the war. Everyone, even Denise, had benefited. And Possum refused to worry about Denise's psyche. Denise was resilient. Even if in learning about herself she had been hurt a little, which Possum doubted, it wasn't as if she were going out to hang herself from a telephone pole. Maybe Alice Cherry had given him valuable advice.

Possum placed Denise's work on the bottom of the stack and silently prayed she would pass on her turn to read. Her writing was terrible, without exception. She had no concept of revision; a first write was a final product for her. She presented fragments of ideas that were totally unrelated as a finished story. She loved to describe her work as spontaneous, insisting that a lack of continuity was avant-garde. When asked what an incomprehensible paragraph meant, she'd say it was a "stream of consciousness," and believed it jacked up the reader's need to discover his or her own creativity. She ignored constructive criticism or argued that the critic couldn't understand. In essence, critics were stupid.

But even worse, her tidbits about humanity were crude and offensive. She was fond of dildos, intercourse in impossible positions, snuff sex, and the like. Dreadful, Possum thought. When she read her work, the class sank into a silence of the tomb.

After two hours, he came to the last manuscript for the evening. "Denise. Would you like to read?"

"Oh, yes."

Possum struggled to find some theme in her four-thousand-word manuscript. Incestuous longings acted out in amazing detail.

Possum interrupted before Denise finished. "Time's up." He thanked Denise for her contribution.

"Hey. I'll finish next class," she said.

Possum blamed himself. His inability to control Denise exposed his lack of teaching proficiency; she had become a turning point in his career. He believed that a full professor could handle Denise. She demanded both experience and the professorial talent that led to promotions. She was one of the difficult challenges that everyone must meet on life's road to a full professorship, and he refused to let her defeat him. He didn't cherish another conference with Alice Cherry, but he saw political advantage in keeping her involved. So he reluctantly asked her again for help.

"Maybe you need to explore the dynamics of your students," Cherry said.

"Dynamics?" Why did Cherry, a chairperson, give him such vague instructions?

"What makes them tick. Why you react as you do."

"Where do I do that?"

"Look to a professional. Someone with insight. Roger Ownings, maybe."

So Possum invited Roger Ownings, a sociology teacher, for a beer and pizza at the university pub. Roger was a longtime acquaintance and man about town. "I've got a few things to talk about," Possum had said.

"I must say," Roger said after listening to Possum's overview of the problem, "you seem fascinated by this Denise."

Possum blushed and wished he had gone to a reputable psychologist or a psychiatrist, although that would have required a two-hour drive to a bigger town. Clearly Roger was untrained in these matters. And Cherry didn't know that Roger lusted after every good-looking female student in his classes. Thoroughly unprofessional. But Possum must do what Cherry required, so he told Roger the details of how Denise managed to humiliate and anger his students.

Roger listened. "You have a like for her, William. I can hear it."

Possum suppressed his need to damn Roger's advice. Try to see his point! he thought. But Roger was wrong.

"I do not have a like for her," Possum said. "She ignores her lack of talent with total belief in her superiority. She has never taken one suggestion for improvement in her writing. She's really irritating."

"Well said, Possum. You're crazy for her."

"Stop it." Possum wished he could leave gracefully. He had never realized how unlikable Roger was. "She has this cocky attitude. The worst I've ever seen."

"Correct me if I'm wrong," said Roger. "but I bet she's young, well built, and smiles widely with good teeth."

"She's overweight. She has absolutely no class. And she grins!" Denise loved to wear jean skirts to class, her soft flesh bulging over her waistband like bread dough expanding over the edge of a baking pan. Her form-fitting shirts displayed overripe breasts spilling over the limits of a bra that struggled to contain them. Her nipples were always visible through the sheer elastic fabric, and their erectile activity, Possum believed, was positive proof of her unchecked passion. He was constantly wondering when they would pop out again with determination and suggestion, flooding him with embarrassment he could not suppress.

"What does she say?" Roger asked.

"She crucifies the language," Possum said in his lecturing tone. "Uses the F-word whenever she wants. And she is full of misinterpretations. She believes men who say 'hello' really mean 'Hi, let's procreate.'"

"Let yourself go," Roger said. "It's 'fuck,' William, not 'procreate.'"

Possum sipped his beer, the liquid surface rippling from his tremor of anger. Roger refused to understand that Denise was destroying his career.

"Why don't you just date her? Tell her to quit coming to class so you can have a legitimate friendship," Roger said.

Possum leaned back, aghast. "That's the worst advice. I can't date students. She's ten years younger. I'm up for promotion."

"She's not a real student. Not an undergraduate. This is adult education. Noncredit."

"I'm not attracted to students," Possum insisted.

"You could get to know her outside of class. You don't have to marry her."

"She's not my type."

"It might be worth a try. You're our most eligible bachelor."

"You're way off here, Roger. Way off."

They sipped their beers in silence. A tune on the jukebox started and finished.

"Great-looking babes don't have problems in sociology. We get the unfortunate uglies with no appeal."

"You haven't listened to a word I've said."

"Got to go, my man. But listen to old Roger. Give her a chance."

"Roger," Possum said, "everything is not about sex."

"You're wrong, William. Without sex the sun would never rise."

The next day, Alice Cherry called an emergency meeting. An adult student, Maybelle Rather, had come to discuss Possum's teaching skills, and Cherry wanted Possum there.

Maybelle, who matriculated under the senior citizen discount rate, sat in Cherry's office, her back as straight as a ruler. "I can't stand any more of her acid comments. Your class is a shambles, Mr. Possum; there is no organization. You return our stories two weeks late. And you refuse to curb that Denise person. She is beyond human courtesy. I don't see how you can let her go on."

Possum shuddered. "Please don't give up," he urged. "I'll talk to her again. See if I can't get her to temper her approach."

Maybelle looked doubtful.

"Learning should be fun," Cherry said vaguely, but Possum could tell she was angry.

"There is no enjoyment when that woman is around. And she never misses a class!" Maybelle closed the door with a firm hand. Alice Cherry turned to Possum.

"Why can't you solve these student problems?"

"I talked to Denise." He told her how it worked for most of one session. But that by the next session, she was right back to her insulting ways.

"What about Roger Ownings?"

Possum nodded. "He thought I should set up private meetings. Tutorials." He felt a twinge of guilt at his euphemism for Roger's suggestion of a date. "As an alternative to coming to class."

"Do it here in the department during the day. And keep me informed."

"Could someone else do it? Elsie or Harold?"

"You do it, William. You teach creative writing."

Denise was ecstatic about personal tutoring. Possum had been careful on the phone. He told her the class had continued to complain and, to please everyone, he thought that he should arrange special teaching sessions for her. He didn't fully agree with the class's assessment, he said, but it seemed practical and, in addition, he could give her intensified instruction to help her writing. She agreed to sessions at eleven in the morning on Wednesdays.

She came dressed in a demure, white, sleeveless dress and white flats. Her legs were bare and her skin glowed with perspiration. She had tied her hair back with a red ribbon. Possum thought the effect was a little childish and gave her the air of a farmyard maid.

"I think this is going to work out fine," Possum said.

"I want to write something really great."

"You're coming right along."

"The class is doing super. I mean, after our little talk and all. They're getting better."

"It's your education that is important to me," Possum said.

"You know, Will, you're a great teacher. You have what I like. With you everything is so … so big." She laughed.

Possum smiled through his apprehension of her crass double entendre. "Thanks. I think I know what you mean."

"Why did you say that? 'You think you know what I mean.'"

"I wasn't sure about the 'big' idea." He smiled weakly.

She moaned. It was as if he'd rubbed a brass vessel and some hostile genie had emerged in a vapor cloud. She pouted. She put on a petulant ingenue sort of look. "I know I'm not polished. No one knows what it's like."

"You're …"

"It's like I'm talking to stones or something."

"You do just fine," he said, but he feared to encourage her too much.

She looked on the verge of genuine tears. Suddenly Possum felt his resistance collapsing.

"That's pure shit," she said.

"No, Denise. You're making progress."

"The class zeros out. Whacko. They think I'm some fucking freak."

Possum handed her a Kleenex from his desk drawer. A few large tears rolled down her cheeks. Now he felt responsible for her pain.

"Why don't you read now," he said.

"You really want it?" she sniveled.

"Yes," he said. "Read to me."

She crossed her legs and her skirt slipped up her thigh. Slowly and deliberately she began to pulsate the free foot up and down.

"Read it all the way through. As we do in class."

She read, holding the manuscript in front of her and occasionally glancing over at Possum, who sat rigidly.

She had written a set of loosely connected scenes for the session. As she read, Possum took notes on a yellow lined legal pad. He dared not interrupt.

After twenty minutes she stopped abruptly. Considering her never-ending sewer of sexual exploits, Possum wasn't sure whether she had finished.

"It's good?" she asked after a long pause.

Possum swallowed and stared out the window for a second. "I like the character …"

"Buster?"

"No. The third one. Evan."

"You mean Sean."

"Yes, Sean. But I did think the rape of a nine-year-old was jarring. I didn't see his motivation. If it were my story, I'd make the rape victim older and not so empty, change it so it's not an act of random violence."

"But Will, men are brutal. It's universal, like you're always talking about."

"I believe it's important to use universal themes. But the good story shows a character by a logical progression of acts and thoughts." He prayed she might be receptive to instruction.

"He had a thought. He wanted to ram it to her."

Possum shifted; the chair seemed too small for him.

"Maybe the victim could be fleshed out a little, too. More detail and something about her feelings."

"She's a victim. Not a perp."

He felt he was on a steeply sloped tin roof in the rain and his rubber-soled shoes were slipping. "Well, enhancing the reader's knowledge about characters can make their victimization even more dramatic."

"You think this is all shit, don't you?"

"Not at all," Possum said quickly.

"Don't lie, Will. The class said the same thing. It's all just shit."

"You have a wonderful gift for detail."

"Don't dig for something good."

"You shouldn't feel down. Every writer has self-doubt."

"Why don't you just shove it up your ass."

"Denise, I didn't mean …"

"I'm tired of fucking flatheads telling me what's good and what isn't."

"Please, Denise …"

"Fuck you." She was flushed. She picked up her manuscript that had fallen to the floor. Possum tried to help but she pushed him away.

"Denise …"

"I trusted you. You twerp."

She put her mechanical pencil in her purse, extended her middle finger, and stalked out.

"Please, Denise …"

That evening, it took Possum until bedtime to calm down. He analyzed every detail of the session as if he were searching through his office jar of mixed jellybeans for the red ones. But he could not locate where he went wrong.

The next day he didn't hear from Denise, and each hour he agonized over his responsibility. Should he try to contact her? He decided not. She was too unreasonable.

Denise did not show at the four additional Wednesday sessions she was entitled to. He waited the entire hour each time. She didn't call. Possum had perceived no teaching success at their last meeting, but he felt he had achieved a resolution to her disruptive class habits. Not a crisp resolution. But at least a final one.

He told Alice Cherry that Denise had dropped out. His creative writing class emerged into less chaos, as if the students savored the contrast of their tranquil, Denise-deficient sessions. Then the summer session was finally over.

Three weeks later, Alice Cherry called Possum to her office. "I don't like to have to tell you this, but your promotion was turned down by the committee."

Possum thought he'd been prepared for it, but the reality turned his interior into a vacuum. It was seconds before he could reply.

"Did that creative writing class thing have anything to do with it?"

"No. Not just that. All your evaluations are terrible. I get complaints about your classes raging out of control. Your publications are nonexistent. I don't think you'll ever make it."

Cherry's attack was too strong. She must have some other reason for not supporting him.

"I'll never give up," he said forcefully.

"And William …"

"Yes?"

"Here is a list of the registrants for the upcoming creative writing class." She handed him a sheet with a column of names. "Get a grip on this one, okay?"

Now he was thinking Denise had sunk him. She was a teacher's worst nightmare.

Possum scanned the list, numb with the reality of his failure. Seventeen students. Alphabetically listed. His gaze froze at the very bottom, stuck on the name "Witherspoon, Denise." My God!

Of course he was not totally surprised. She always signed up for everything. But how odd he felt, and he turned his head quickly away from Cherry. With his eyes closed, he searched the absurdity of this sea of dread that Denise's name brought on. And over that vast expanse soared an albatross of expectation. He could not deny it; he was glad Denise was coming back.

He looked at Cherry, who stared at him relentlessly. She had seen his albatross before. Would she ever let him be a professor of English?

"Do you want that Denise person in your class?" Cherry asked.

He considered his response carefully. "I can handle her," he said.

The Activist

illustration by Peter Healy

The Activist

"I ain't going to stand for it," Mama said. She said this often.

She held a small dead human about as long as an ear of corn. Even though the head was too big, the hands too small, you could tell it might have been somebody.

"Push down," Mama said.

My sister moaned. With a gush of blood the afterbirth slid onto the bed. Her skin was white as wood ash.

"I don't feel good," she said.

"Shut up, Pearl Anne," Mama said. "Shut up and grow up."

"I'm seventeen."

"You're acting like a two-year-old."

"I'm going to throw up," Pearl Anne said.

I wasn't feeling so hot, either.

"Go get some towels, Ether Mae. Help get Pearl Anne cleaned up."

I didn't move. Pearl Anne got herself into this fix, not me. I'd never had a boy put his thing in me. Pearl Anne said it felt funny but not so good that she couldn't do without it. So she'd decided to quit. She wanted more respect. She quit too late.

Now Mama moaned and held this dead thing. "My grandchild," she said. "Didn't I tell you get some towels?"

"Don't want to." I backed away a little.

"You'll get the stick. You're too old to have me telling you what to do." I was eleven.

I found some rags and two towels and got them wet under the faucet in the sink, then squeezed the water out.

"Goddamn it. Wring them out. You're dripping all over the floor," Mama screamed.

"What's that doctor's name wouldn't treat you, Pearl Anne?"

Pearl Anne put her hand to her mouth and wiped away some vomit chunks. "Lady doctor."

I started wiping up blood from the bed. I picked up the afterbirth, holding it between two towels so I wouldn't have to touch it, but I could still feel the warmth. I dropped it in the toilet and flushed it down. I got Pearl Anne on the potty. She still had lots of blood that came out in chunks like sliced cow's liver. Her belly skin was pale with blue veins snaking around.

While I worked to get the blood off Pearl Anne, Mama sat at the kitchen table. She had a shoebox. She took a face cloth, pink with a white border, and laid it in the bottom. Then she put Pearl Anne's dead thing inside. She took a piece of Saran wrap and covered the top so you could still see Pearl Anne's dead thing's little face and hands and its legs all drawn up. Mama put the top on the box and took a black felt-tip Magic Marker and smeared in tight strokes with lines next to each other so the entire box top was black.

"What's that, Mama?"

"A coffin."

I thought she was a little crazy from losing her only grandchild. "It's a shoebox," I mumbled.

She whacked me across the side of my head half-hard, but still serious.

"Don't want no disrespect for the dead. This is kin."

"What kin?"

"Your nephew."

I stared hard but didn't feel any kinship.

Mama pushed me ahead of her into the bedroom. Pearl Anne's bed was wet and still stained with blood.

"She's got blood in her crotch," Mama yelled.

"I ain't doing that," I said. So we decided to put Pearl Anne in the bathtub. The water heater wasn't working right and I had to heat water on the stove. Mama and I got Pearl Anne in the tub.

"I'm going to faint. I'm going to faint," Pearl Anne whined loud and ornery.

After we washed her, I helped her out of the tub and Mama led her to my bed. She fell asleep. Snoring.

"Come with me," Mama said.

"What about Pearl Anne?"

"Only one thing wrong with her: she can't say no."

Mama climbed into the pickup on the driver's side, setting the little shoebox on the seat. After I got in she said, "Don't let it slide onto the floor."

I put my hand on the box and turned it so it was long against the back of the seat. I imagined the ink stain on my fingers.

Mama drove dead stop to forty-five to dead stop. She blasted the horn at people walking in the road, at old people driving too slow. She breathed scratchy and deep. Her blazing eyes reflected light from the windshield as if her eye globes were marbles, and her hands gripped the wheel so hard her scruffy red fingers were white at the joints.

"Where we going?" I asked.

"Watch the coffin. You'll see soon enough."

We drove over the Chattahoochee River Bridge, past the old mill with the missing roof and broken windows, then the abandoned railway station. The We Care health clinic was at the mini mall just ahead.

Mama stopped a block away where a pay telephone was tacked to the wall of the 7-Eleven store. She dialed 911 and the local TV station. Mama got back in the truck and sighed. "I bet they won't come."

"Why you do that, Mama?"

"Shut your mouth. We doing what's right for our family." She grabbed my hair and yanked my head so my face was looking right at her. "You got to fight for every bit of justice in this world. Don't ever make me say that to you again."

"Let go."

"You don't deserve to be a Crawford."

I wished I wasn't a Crawford. Or a kid. Or living in that double-wide trailer with Pearl Anne and Mama. But I kept my mouth zipped tight.

Mama got the truck started, and in thirty seconds she double-parked in front of the clinic even though there were other spots open. "You grab the coffin," she said.

We got out of the truck and marched into the clinic. Doctor's names were spelled out in white plastic letters on a black felt board. A star marked the "physician of the day," a woman doctor.

"Follow me." Mama yanked my arm so hard I almost dropped the box.

We marched right by the receptionist into the back.

The woman doctor stood writing at a chest-high counter. Both the doctor and the nurse looked at us.

"You the doctor?" Mama said to the woman. She said "dock-tooor." Mean-like.

"Doctor Paterson."

"A real doctor?"

Mama pushed me forward.

"Yes."

"You got all the training or are you in training?"

"I'm a special fellow—"

"Ah! If you was all trained, my grandchild would be with us today."

"You've got your facts—"

"Give me that box," Mama screamed at me.

I shoved the box forward thinking Mama would take it.

"Take off the lid" she said instead.

I could see magic marker all over my fingers and had a sinking feeling it would never come off.

"Turn that lid upside down." Mama grabbed the box so the doctor could see through the Saran wrap. "This child is dead because of you."

The doctor stared like the grandchild might breathe fire or rise from the dead. I could see her hands tremble.

"My daughter, Ms. Pearl Anne Crawford, seen you day before yesterday. You told her go to the welfare hospital."

The nurse sitting behind a desk tried to speak up but her mouth was working like a dying fish on a dry dock in the hot sun. "We can't take Medicaid," the doctor said. "I checked her. She was all right."

"She weren't all right. Her baby died."

"She was fine. This girl was with her." The doctor pointed down at me scary, like God from the stained glass window in my Mama's Church of the Apocalypse.

I started to say Pearl Anne was fine when the doctor saw her but Mama bumped me with an elbow before I could finish.

"I referred her to the County Hospital," the doctor said.

Mama hated the County Hospital worse than she hated sinners. "We ain't never going to that hellhole," Mama went on. "You made my daughter grieve."

I thought of Pearl Anne snoring on my bed.

The nurse whispered to the doctor. "I'm calling the cops."

"That's good. We need some arrests here," Mama said.

A man and woman from 911 rushed from the lobby through the inner door carrying bags and metal tubes and a little tank. "Emergency?"

"Goddamn right there's an emergency." Mama peeked out the open door looking for the TV crew.

"Where?"

"Give me that coffin, Ether Mae." I handed over the coffin. My nephew now was on his side, his arms still out and touching the cardboard like he might be trying to get out. Mama twisted the coffin so the 911 people could see.

"Dead."

"It's a fetus," the 911 woman said.

"Kilt. Refused treatment. Put that in your report. By her." Mama pointed an accusing finger at the doctor, who was shaking all over now and looking angry with Mama.

"Weren't her fault, Mama." The doctor had treated Pearl Anne really kind.

Mama hit me so hard I dropped the coffin. The Saran wrap came off one side and my nephew rolled out on the floor, ashamed, I thought, of being naked and paraded around by Mama.

"You dropped our kin." She hit me again. Softer, but it still hurt.

Mama peered out to see about the TV people. But cops with black uniforms and caps with shiny plastic bills came in, a white guy tall as an apple tree and a skinny little black lady.

"What's the matter?" the big cop said.

The nurse spoke up quick. "It's her." She pointed to Mama. "Brought a dead fetus and says we're responsible. Threatening us."

"I didn't threaten no one. I want them arrested."

"For what?" the woman cop asked.

"Killing my grandchild. Making my daughter grieve. Going against the will of God!"

I could tell there were a lot of feelings whizzing around that room, but no sympathy, not for Mama. The 911 people looked at Mama as if she were a lunatic. The nurse and receptionist thought, "white trash." The doctor still shook with anger. Both cops stared at Mama, wondering why they ever went to cop school and planning what to do next.

"Can you take that baby?" the big cop asked the 911 guys.

"I can't take a dead fetus we ain't treated."

"Against regulations to keep it here," the nurse said.

"You ain't doing nothing with my grandchild."

"Did you treat this woman's daughter, doctor?" the lady cop asked.

The doctor gripped the edge of the counter with both hands. "I checked her but didn't charge her."

"No-pays!" the receptionist said. I scooped up my nephew with the side of the coffin box and settled him inside. His head was twisted on his neck a little like he might have been hurt.

"The baby was alive," continued the doctor. "It moved."

"Nothing wrong?" the cop asked.

"Blood pressure up a little. I suggested the County Hospital."

"We can't accept Medicaid," the receptionist said.

"Look here, Dr. Smart Girl," Mama spat, "we ain't never going to the County."

"That's where we work," said the 911 woman.

"Well, let me tell you. The devil's got you. My husband, Horace Crawford, God rest his soul, sat with blood pressure and diabetes and his heart failed so bad you could see it thumping in his chest. He went to your County Hospital; I was sitting beside him, waiting for nine hours. Every time I walked up to the counter they told me they'd get to him as soon as they could. Well, they got to him. But by then he was as a cold as a slab of hog hanging in a chill room."

"That's too bad," said the 911 woman.

"Criminal," said Mama. And she was crying tears. Pearl Anne said crying was when Mama was at her best. The people here didn't know what to think. The 911 guys looked like they'd just seen the ghost of my papa.

"He wouldn't have been cold. Takes a long time to get cold," the 911 man said.

"He was dead. Dead cold," Mama said in a voice so controlled and angry the 911 man looked out the door to avoid the hatred in her stare.

The police told 911 to get on, and they sat Mama down in a chair in the waiting room. "I know you're distressed," said the woman cop, "but you're out of line here. My partner wants to book you."

"I ain't done nothing."

"Disturbing the peace. But I told him to let you go."

"They kilt my grandchild."

"They did what was right. Now you get on."

I sat in a waiting room chair holding the coffin on my lap. Mama was thinking about what she could do.

"I ain't moving until you arrest them."

"I mean it. Move along or you go to jail."

"Go to the truck, Ether Mae."

"And take that dead thing with you," spat the nurse.

"Watch your words," the woman cop warned the nurse as I started out.

A few minutes later, the cops shoved Mama out the door.

As soon as we got home, Mama went to pray at the Church of the Apocalypse and talk to her friends about a demonstration at the clinic, probably burning candles and a protest fire. "You keep your nephew safe," she said as she left, and I sat at the kitchen table looking through the Saran wrap at my kin. He seemed like he was trying to catch his breath so I took off the Saran wrap. He liked that, I thought. I smiled at him, 'cause he was so small and helpless. "You came at the wrong time," I said. "For you," I added. I thought for a moment. "But sure was the right time for Mama." I thought he might have smiled a little.

Pearl Anne was still asleep in my room. I just sat with my nephew for a while. He seemed so nice all balled up and laying on his back on the pink-and-white facecloth little blanket. I got thinking about respect—him being dropped in the clinic and falling out of his coffin and all.

About being gawked at naked under his Saran wrap. And I thought, it ain't right. "You only got me," I said to him. I knew he was dead, but he heard. I was sure of it. "You need help."

I turned my little nephew in his coffin so he was comfortable on his side. I got four stones the size of chicken eggs from the garden and put one in each corner. Then I put the Saran wrap back on top. The lid was torn, but I made it whole with Scotch tape. With the same roll of tape, I sealed the coffin lid on tight and put it in a plastic grocery sack.

I walked, holding the coffin flat so the rocks wouldn't move, to the Chattahoochee River. I'd heard Chattahoochee was some Indian god. Probably had long pigtails and feathers stuck in his hair. Even though the Indians I'd seen never smiled much, I thought little nephew would be happier with them than he would with us. I walked to where the highway crossed over, along the guardrail to the center of the flat bridge, and let the bag with my nephew in his coffin fall into the water.

Plop. The coffin floated away from the bridge and disappeared where the river and the sky were the same shade of dark.

I closed my eyes. I could see my little smiling nephew sitting in my papa's lap at the right hand of God. Those Chattahoochee Indians had taken him home.

Curse of a Lonely Heart

illustration by Peter Healy

Curse of a Lonely Heart

In college I had been attracted to my roommate, Peter Townsend. But after fifteen years of marriage to Amanda, my thoughts of Peter had faded—until I heard a rumor that he would interview for chair of the department of psychiatry at the university where I was a professor of botany. I called to invite him to our house for a dinner while he was in town. I told Amanda.

"Goddamn it, Tony. I don't like him."

"You could try," I said. There'd been a few minutes at my twentieth college reunion when I thought Amanda could never get enough of Peter.

"You made a move. He turned you down," I said.

"I've never 'made a move' on any man."

"That's a little disingenuous," I said. I was surprised at my anger. We had so little between us. And I truly didn't care if she slept with every man she met, as long as she was confidential about it.

"Only if you grill. We can eat outside," Amanda said.

"Do a sit-down dinner," I said. Amanda was a proud cook of exacting proportions, frequently adjusted temperatures, and rigid freshness. Peter deserved the best.

She finally agreed and insisted we invite another faculty couple, Ester (in social science) and Henry (in molecular biology), and Amanda's sister Madeleine, who was to balance the table as Peter's dinner partner. Madeleine was in library science, thirty-five years old and never married. She was attractive but with a porcelain-figurine look to her face and a frightened-rabbit personality that I did not think was to Peter's taste. But I said nothing to Amanda.

We gathered together on a Thursday night. I had insisted that Peter be presented as the honored guest, and he fit easily into the role as if he expected nothing less. The dinner was below Amanda's usual standards of excellence—she complained that she'd lacked time during the week—and she glared frequently at Peter as if her failures were his fault.

Ester started the dinner conversation. "Why would you be interested in a chair here?" she asked.

"Opportunity," Peter said.

"Not to improve negotiations at home? That's how you medical doctors squeeze those high clinical salaries, isn't it?"

"Peter is not that kind of faculty," I said.

"How would you know, Tony? The department here is close to broke. The previous chair left under a cloud of harassment accusations."

"The department has an excellent reputation," I said.

Amanda came in from the kitchen wearing oven mitts and carrying a hot ceramic dish filled with a bubbling parsnip puree.

"Are you considering other positions?" Amanda asked Peter.

"As they come up," Peter said.

For the next two courses the conversation came in spurts and we drank wine in the silences. But just before dessert, Madeline told a story about her schnauzer falling into the bathtub, and Ester expressed concern about the poor quality of students applying for admission this year. Even Amanda seemed warmed up and chattier, telling of her recent trip to the Bahamas with her boss, the university chancellor, for a conference. Henry, silent throughout with his own thoughts, finally said yes when asked if he wanted another piece of flourless chocolate cake.

After dinner we straggled to the living room. I directed Peter to our most comfortable overstuffed chair. Amanda, Madeleine, and I sat in side chairs, and Ester and Henry took the sofa near the fire, seating that honored Peter at the heart of a half-circle. Two open bottles of red wine were on the coffee table, and there was a plate of marzipan that Amanda had beaten and molded into bananas, grapes, and lemons. A shaded floor lamp in the corner and the flames from the log fire gave us a low-intensity but pleasing light. We were all smiling.

"I can't believe you're not married," murmured Ester to Peter, swaying on the sofa as if in a lifeboat, her cheeks flushed. In the last hour she'd stared at Peter continuously, ignoring Henry. Peter rarely looked at her. "Are you gay?" she finally asked.

Peter turned his head and stared. "Not that I've yet realized," he finally said, good-naturedly. In college, nude, he had been a dream of a man. I remembered after a shower, water running over his defined figure, his abdominal muscles without a trace of fat. He was still a man's man.

"You're attracted to men but never act?" Ester persisted. She was a woman who clung to girlish guile as she approached middle age.

"Not at all," said Peter.

"Every man has gay thoughts," Amanda said.

Her authoritative tone irritated me, and I glared at her to be quiet. "Not true," I said—I was sure Peter's thoughts were heterosexual. Amanda and I often disagreed in our unusual moments of discussion. For the most part, we spent our time in the house in separate rooms. We had settled into a marriage with rare intimacy, and I had a circle of friends she didn't ask about.

"What do you think, Peter?" Amanda asked. "Every man has a touch of gay?"

I could tell the teasing about masculinity had begun to irritate Peter, and he was trying not to show it.

"I know the pain of love lost," Peter said. "I will never marry again."

"Undoubtedly with gay thoughts," Ester said. Her probing had been a flirtation that fell flat. Peter seemed unaware.

"A woman trifled with my affections," Peter said. "I have not recovered."

"It's so easy to blame it on the woman," Amanda said.

"She made mistakes," Peter said, "but I never blamed her."

"Oh, that is so male. She made the mistakes!" Ester said.

"Don't presume what you don't know," Peter said.

"Tell us the details. Let us decide about love and affection," Amanda said.

"What man knows the meaning of love?" Ester said.

"I want to hear," Madeleine said.

Henry looked interested, too. He was the kind of guy who would fantasize himself in freeze-frame poses with Peter's woman.

"Well, let me take a break and then I'll tell you," Peter said. He went up the stairs to the second-floor bathroom while we huddled around the wine.

"That was rude," Madeleine whispered to Amanda. She could not suppress a dreamy adolescent gaze when looking at Peter.

"Grow up, Maddie," Amanda said. "He's a monster."

"I think he's a good guy," Henry said.

"Shut up, Henry," Ester said. "He's fucking sexist."

Henry stared at the fingers of his right hand that he splayed for no reason. He'd repeated the gesture frequently since we'd left the dining room. "That's not fair, honey."

"You've got a rock for a brain," Ester said. She filled her wine glass.

"Look," I said, "Peter is our guest. It's not fair to put him on the spot."

"Loosen up, Tony," Ester replied.

Peter came down the stairs and sat again near the center point of our half-circle, sinking down in the soft chair. Everyone could see he was eager to tell his tale.

He began …

The third year after I was appointed full professor in psychiatry, a medical school student—I'll call her Cathy—came to do research. Her project was clinical fluff, some idea that hypnosis at age regression levels could be used to pinpoint triggers of recurrent depression. Cathy saw patients in all faculty practices, but she spent more time with me than anyone else. Looking back on it, there was probably an unrecognized attraction from the very beginning. I found her competent and always available, and was careful to treat her no better or worse than any other student.

She was a small girl with light-brown hair, a round face with slightly pinched features, and penetrating pale-blue eyes. Her lopsided smile, more right than left—quickly became endearing—one of her best features. She was a runner with a svelte figure and dressed in professional silk blouses and colorful skirts with provocative hemlines.

As was routine after students completed a service rotation, she was invited to the annual department outdoor barbecue. In a social setting, I found her animated intelligence charming, and since she was technically no longer a student, I asked her for a date. She asked about my divorce—I'd been a bachelor for fourteen years—and she thought my maturity was attractive.

In a few weeks we couldn't bear to be away from each other. It was a mutual attraction of a lifetime. At the end of internship, she accepted a pediatric residency in New Haven. I, of course, could not move from my position at the university in DC, and we vowed to spend every weekend together until she could finish her two years of training. As it turned out, she could rarely leave her clinical responsibilities, and I traveled to her. In the second year, our weekends together became more infrequent. I would arrive un-greeted at the airport and take a taxi to sit alone in her cramped apartment on a bone-crunching futon. When she finally left the hospital, she was too exhausted to make love.

In two years she managed only two trips to Washington, but I did take her to New York and Boston a few times. She began to talk of a formal wedding. In public, she referred to us as engaged and wore a plain gold ring when we went out that disappeared by the time we settled back in our hotel room.

But in truth, there were times when I felt like a stranger. My lifelong policy had always been honesty, and I told Cathy of the strain of traveling so far for so few unpredictable hours of watching her sleep. And I always added—repeatedly—how much I needed her. We can work it out, she said.

Just before we broke up, it was late autumn and the leaves were off the trees. The only flight available for the weekend made two stops and was two hours late. It was past eleven when we got to her apartment complex.

Cathy slowed in the parking lot. A van with dark tinted-windows was crowded into her space between two smaller cars.

She parked on the street and I rolled my suitcase to the apartment and carried it up three flights of stairs. I went to shower. Cathy slipped into a T-shirt and shorts and turned to making her dinner. I had eaten during my layover.

She made a sandwich for herself and was eating at the metal-topped kitchen table. I sat across from her in my underwear, having a glass of wine. We heard a knock on the door, and Cathy put down her sandwich.

"Don't answer it," she whispered, signaling me to be quiet.

A man's hoarse voice called her name, and the knocking got faster and louder.

I got my pants from the closet and fumbled in my hurry to get them on.

"Go away," Cathy called out.

The man began pounding the door.

"Cathy!" he yelled. The pounding increased.

"He'll go away," she said softly.

She seemed to be right. Footsteps retreated down the wooden floor of the hallway. She released her grip on my arm and I led her into the living room. She collapsed into an overstuffed chair, her limbs shaking.

I sat on the sofa opposite her. My breathing began to slow.

"You know him?" I asked.

"I've seen him once," she said.

I was about to ask for details when the two hooked prongs of a tire iron splintered through the upper panel of the door. My gaze locked on hers in disbelief.

"Caaaaathy," the attacker moaned. Then after another blow, "I know he's in there."

"Go away," Cathy said. "I'll call the police." But her last few words were buried in a crash of iron on wood.

Cathy turned off the floor lamp in the living room, as if a dim light might slow him down.

"Get knives," I whispered as we backed into the kitchen. She opened drawers and found a bread knife the length of a rat; she pointed to a small paring knife for me that would have been useless. Her look had shifted from scared to terrified.

We retreated to the bedroom; the explosive sounds followed. Whap, groan, whap, whap. I wondered if the attacker had a gun.

"He's going to kill us," I said.

"Dear God," she said. I locked the bedroom door, twisting the pouty-lip dime-sized center circle in the handle.

Cathy cowered on the bed, her knifepoint straight up. I searched in her closet for a gun, or an axe, or even a ski pole. I came up with a metal clothes hanger and unwound the wire; maybe I could blind him.

The pounding got faster again. Cathy dialed 911 on the bedside phone. "We're being attacked," she screamed. She had to repeat the address twice. I wedged the back of a chair under the bedroom door handle and pulled Cathy off the bed and as far away from the door as possible. We crouched, weapons ready.

The attacker crashed into the apartment, bumping against the living room furniture. He started with his tire iron on the bedroom door; Cathy was wheezing. In less than a minute he was through the door, shoving the chair barrier aside easily with one arm. I couldn't see his face in the dark.

"Get in the bathroom," I yelled to Cathy.

We clambered to the bathroom, which was no bigger than a hall closet. I flipped the light switch as Cathy climbed over the toilet into the tub so I could get the door closed. I pushed the center lock pin in the door handle. The attacker's tire iron splintered the door panel and came within inches of my face. I stumbled, knocking Cathy down.

The attacker kicked out the door panel and reached in and twisted the handle from the inside. When the door opened, he froze and stared first at me and then at Cathy. He was almost six feet tall, with narrow shoulders and a beginning potbelly. He looked about thirty. He wore glasses, a T-shirt, and tan cotton pants. His scruffy running shoes had untied laces, and he wore a wide belt that held an automatic pistol.

Cathy had one leg over the edge of the tub; he stared at her thigh. She pointed the knife at him, twisting the shower curtain to cover herself. I gripped the showerhead with one hand and waved my clothes hanger.

He rested the curve of his tire iron on the bathroom tiles and we had a few seconds to think. He was now strangely subdued.

"So this is the boyfriend?" he said, looking to me as if I were some inferior cut of beef just served at an overpriced restaurant.

"Fiancé," said Cathy.

"I should kill him," the attacker said. His voice was breathy and mean.

He backed into the bedroom, pointing the pistol at me with his right hand and holding the tire iron with his left. Cathy sobbed. "Get out," she said. Then, this guy, whose name turned out to be Kyle, sat on the bed and wept, moaning.

I let out a giddy laugh when I realized I wouldn't die. Cathy walked to the bed and tried to take the gun from Kyle, who pushed her away.

Two cops arrived and asked questions to Cathy and Kyle—because of their youth—as if they were betrothed and I was the stranger. I tried to maintain a dignity, but I was fighting humiliation at being ignored as some elderly nobody.

After ten minutes the male cop arrested Kyle, taking him to the station. The woman cop stayed behind to write the formal report. I pretended disinterest.

Cathy told her story. She had met Kyle on a rare night off when she was lonely and went to a party for singles. They talked for a few minutes. "You're everything I ever wanted in a woman," Kyle had said. At that point, she told him she was engaged and to leave her alone. After the party Kyle became more determined, and he started calling her five, six times a day. As the cop finished writing, I stared at Cathy in disbelief. Why hadn't she been honest and told me? The cop finally left.

The door to the apartment was useless. Cathy found a sheet, and with lots of thumbtacks we covered the holes. Then I backed the sofa and tilted it on end so that it blocked most of the opening.

We got in bed and propped pillows against the headboard. We sat in silence.

"Who really is this Kyle?" I finally asked. She was still breathing fast. He was a computer programmer whose hobby was making kites in the shapes of dragons, snakes, and carnivorous dinosaurs. That was all she knew.

"You dated?" I asked.

"Never," she said. "I didn't lie. He was at one party."

Despite her denial, the thought of Kyle and Cathy as a couple overwhelmed me. Women went to singles parties to pick up guys, right? I sulked.

"Forget him. I've wanted to see you so much," she said.

"Look. I'm angry. Okay? I mean, I come to visit my fiancée, and her boyfriend tears down the door and wants to kill me."

"He isn't my boyfriend. Can't you just hold me?"

I flushed. "I didn't diddle with other girls."

She began crying.

"Did you screw?" I asked.

"What a terrible thing to say," interrupted Amanda.

"Chauvinist. You hadn't even committed," Ester said.

"What did she reply?" I asked.

She said: "Of course not." She turned away from me. And we fell into silence.

The electric clock on the night table had an irritating drone and a click as the second hand staggered around the iridescent dial. I kept at least eighteen inches between us.

I stayed silent, my breathing strained. I listened to the night sounds of the normal people living around us. Bathwater running. A toilet flush. A yell in the parking lot. A car starting up. I felt as if I didn't belong.

At one point she touched me gently on the side of my face and I moved farther away. At six thirty, first light slipped into the room under the window shade. Cathy got up to make coffee.

In the daylight, the sofa propped on end against the door looked ridiculous. The sheet we had tacked up barely covered the opening and was so transparent I could see the apartment door across the hall.

I told Cathy I would leave that afternoon. A day early.

"I'm afraid," she said. "I can't get the door fixed until Monday."

Without a word, I went out back to a trash heap behind the complex and picked out a few mismatched boards. Then, using some nails I found in her utility closet and a rock I retrieved from the edge of the parking lot, I nailed a barrier over the door, board by board, inch by inch. She could go in and out through the window to the fire escape.

"Can't you just love me?" she asked.

I had no conversation in me. I turned away and quickly packed. When I left for the airport by taxi, Cathy stayed in the bedroom behind the closed door.

Years later, she married a doctor.

I never saw her again.

We sat in silence for a while. Amanda was the first to speak.

"You should have believed her. She loved you."

"She should have told me about Kyle," Peter said. "She had some deep-seated reason for not telling me. It was a matter of trust."

"Why don't you look into yourself for all that deep-seated crap," Ester said. "You rejected her. You ought to be jailed." Ester threw a closed fist into the air.

"You were a jerk," Amanda said.

"She sacrificed so much for you," Ester said, her voice rippling in anger. "This Cathy. She's a saint."

"I'll agree she wasn't evil," said Peter. "But she made a mistake going to that party, and she couldn't admit to it."

"There is nothing more precious than a woman's love," Madeleine said softly.

Henry looked up in disgust to where the ceiling met the wall. Ester squeezed her lids shut to avoid looking at Madeleine, whose moist eyes glinted in sympathy for Peter.

"Don't tell us you never dated other women," Ester said. "All those years."

"My only liaisons were necessities of my profession. They were hardly dates."

"You're unbelievable," Amanda said.

Peter flushed. He stood and walked to the door. I stood to dissuade him, but Amanda pulled me back down and shushed me. The silence was hostile. Peter said nothing, putting on his coat and closing the front door without looking back.

I looked around. Everyone, except Madeline, seemed relieved he was gone.

"We should have been a little more gracious to him," Madeleine said to Amanda. "He has so much more depth than I imagined."

"He's an asshole," Amanda said.

"I thought him sensitive," I said.

Ester put her glass on the coffee table with a thud. "That's what I've never liked about you, Tony," she said. "The way you treat women."

Amanda laughed.

"Don't turn on me," I said. "Peter's a good friend. He was right to question that girl's feelings for him."

"What he did to the girl was inexcusable," Ester said.

Madeleine frowned.

"She made the choice. He was the one always going to her. He sacrificed." My voice was loud. "No one should tolerate her deceit."

"You're obnoxious, Tony," Ester said. "I've always thought that. I'm glad the wine let me say it."

"Is that what you think?" I asked Amanda. "I'm out of line here?"

She paused. "You're wrong, Tony," she said.

I stood. I would not be insulted in my own home. I climbed the stairs and shut the door to my room. I stood in the dark, listening as the guests argued for a while, then said their goodbyes. I took off my clothes without turning on the light and left them rumpled on a chair. I went to bed in my underwear and stared at the ceiling.

An hour later, Amanda opened the door to my room. She sat down gingerly on the edge of my single bed near the foot and looked to the dark window. She was quiet for many minutes.

"We're sad, you and I," she finally said.

"Speak for yourself," I said. I wondered at the sincerity of her coming to me like this. She was very close to my leg. There was a blanket between us, but I could feel her presence. She laid the palm of her hand above my knee, her fingers spread slightly apart, but when I didn't respond she took it away. I could see only the indistinct outline of the side of her face in the dark. I stayed quiet.

After a few more minutes, she left. She closed the door with extended gentleness so no sound was made.

Sleep had still not come when the morning light seeped through the window under the shade. The bedcovers had slipped off. I was still on my back, my hands on my chest with fingers interlaced, my feet touching. I was alone.

On the Road to Yazoo City

illustration by Peter Healy

On the Road to Yazoo City

My life at twenty-one was never in tune—like a D-string on an antique Gibson with a peg that wouldn't hold. I'm walking up this two-lane side road about ten miles west of Canton and north of Jackson, where I have just come from. Haven't seen a car in maybe an hour, the straps of my pack digging into my shoulders, the sun burning my eyes because I lost my shades leaning over a riverbank to fill my water jug, and dragging the guitar case 'cause it's just too heavy to lift off the ground. Pure shit. But I got to make it work. I'm flat broke.

About half a mile down the road I see this man on a bike, pedaling like to die and holding straight on the faded centerline. I flag him down and drop my backpack. He stops the bike, straddling the bar and breathing hard.

"Mister!" I say. "You point me to Yazoo city?"

He points to his mouth and pulls a little broken piece of slate and a piece of chalk from his pocket.

"Why?" he writes in block letters on the slate.

I guess it is a Mississippi kind of question. Someone asks you something. You ask them back something different. Then you spend a lot time being sure you don't tell them what you know they want to know.

"Gig," I say. I'm not about to give him the scoop. Truth is I was feeling so bad about this sweet girl—damn near a virgin—in Biloxi, I got drunk and missed a whole week of gigs with a band I'd been working with for two months. Manager left a note in the F-hole of my archtop acoustic. "No job. No more. Try Yazoo."

The guy's eyes light up when I say "gig," as if he dreams of being me someday. He points straight ahead, smiling, and he draws an X on his slate and circles the right upper branch.

"Yazoo City?" I ask again to be sure.

He grins a grin-with-gaps and gives me a thumbs-up. Before I get my stuff mounted again, he's back on the road, pedaling like mad now.

I plod toward the crossroads, about to drop. In Jackson, I'd missed the once-a-week bus to Yazoo City, then spent my last money on a meal of crackers and Coke out of the vending machines. A woman who mops the toilets told me I could walk the distance in a few hours. There's some good information for you. I'm close to six hours of walking now, and I ain't seen nothing, much less Yazoo City.

Sun's about halfway down on the afternoon. Up ahead I see a crossroad; I imagine this is what the mute guy had been drawing because there's a paved road going off to the right.

I go about half a mile, and this little girl comes out of a cabin that's got a washing machine on the porch and a rusted Ford pickup—vintage mid-forties—jacked up on concrete blocks in the yard. She runs out to me.

"You want some gum?" she says, taking a wad out of her mouth.

"Pass on that one, baby," I say.

"Where you going?"

She's got a way of asking the tough questions up front. "I ain't sure," I say, thinking in the broad sense. I have a direction, but no purpose.

"What's in that?" she says, pointing to the guitar.

"Guitar. You know what a guitar is?"

She nodded once. "Play."

I'm zonked, so I put things down and stretch out on the roadside gravel. "Two strings busted, baby. Don't play good." But I dig an "A" harp from my back pocket. "I play you a tune, you like?" She doesn't say anything, but I play her a tune, "Oh, Susanna." She doesn't look real excited, so I play "The Saints Go Marching In."

"You like it?"

She shrugs, which, in my state, I take as a real downer.

"Look, here's another." I sing with this one. "Empty Bed Blues." And I'm about to cry, thinking about my woman. When I'm finished, her eyes seem to have a little more interest.

"My gal left me," I explain to her. "She was a waitress in Biloxi. Madeline's her name. Dear God, I love that girl. And I thought we would be together forever because she said 'I love you, too.' But two weeks later, she said my life was 'unstable,' that's exactly the word she used, and then she went to Atlanta to 'sort things out' at her mother's house. Unstable! Can you imagine that?"

The girl is still just staring at me. "Me blow that thing?" she asks.

I'm thinking I don't want the spit or nothing. But she looks about to cry so I explain. "Sorry, honey. You got gum and these harps is really personal. It's like a toothbrush." Well, that was something I hadn't had in a few days, and I don't think she'd seen one for a while, either.

I'm thinking about just putting my head back and sleeping a while, maybe the night, by the side of the road. It's not like traffic's a problem keeping me awake. She grabs the harmonica and starts running like the wind. It's my Big River, twenty-four bucks new, and I take out after her. She runs into the house and I run in right behind her, mad as hell but admiring that she's willing to go for what she wants.

Inside, the shack is a big room with a stove and a refrigerator with the door open. Stuff inside the fridge looks hot. I hear moaning, and the little girl pokes her head out the door of the room off to the right and stares at me.

Now there's yelling. I go into the room.

Goddamn. There's a woman on the bed, on a bare mattress, with a pillow behind her head, and she's got her dress up and her knees up and I'm looking straight into her private parts that are bulging. I see this little football of hair, and then she stops yelling and the hair goes back in.

She's breathing hard, and all of sudden I am, too. She whispers, "Get me some water in a bucket. Bring me the blanket from the couch." And the kid walks out, calm, like this happens every day. I'm ready to get back to my guitar and backpack, and get moving.

She begins a moan, and then stops. "Excuse me, ma'am," I say, thinking I might tell her her daughter, or at least this girl, stole my harmonica.

Then she moans short and starts screaming, and I back to the door. I see the football of hair growing larger. I wonder where the water is.

But I'm not knowing at all what to do with it. At least the blanket seems like a good idea, to wrap the kid in if it gets here.

"It's coming," she screams.

It's damned obvious it's coming, and I am scared shitless.

"It's coming," she screams again.

And I'm looking at this woman's parts and thinking about all the times I dreamed about being down in there and believing I'll never be thinking that again.

"It's coming," she screams, and damn if it doesn't come in a flush of piss and blood and shit. It's half out, and she's trying to sit up like a crunch and help it, but she falls back. I step up and try to grab its head, but it's slippery as snot, so I get it by the shoulders trying to figure out a way for a pull, and here it comes itself, sliding down the bed and if I don't stop the little devil, it'll go right on into the iron pipe cross the foot of the bed. The first thing I see is it's a boy—a soul brother—and I feel a little better about knowing it and I touch him on the head.

I seen enough TV to know you hold him up, and I take one hand on each leg. I think I have to whack him on the bottom, but I don't have a free hand. Thank the dear Lord he just cries on his own. I look down, and the woman is crying and smiling and mumbling "thank you, Jesus" over and over, and she's bleeding now so blood is running off the end of the bed in a little stream. The cord is still dangling, and she tells me to hand her the little guy.

The girl comes in and puts the blanket on the woman's crotch, and after the woman's got the little boy, I'm thinking about how to get out of there.

"Get me the knife, Pearl," the woman says.

Out goes the kid. "Ain't here," she yells back.

The woman sits and just chews on the cord until the end drops. Then she makes a little tie like ribbon candy.

She moans again. But not for long.

"I'm sorry, ma'am."

She don't say nothing.

"It was like an accident."

She's still silent.

"I was just walking by. On the road to Yazoo City."

"This ain't the road to Yazoo City," she manages to whisper. She moans again. "Could you sit a spell?"

I don't answer, and after a minute I pull up the only chair in the room. The baby is cradled on her chest, stuff like wax all over it with flecks of blood on his closed eyes. But he seems content.

The afterbirth comes after a mild moan. Then the blood pretty much stops. The little girl plops the water bucket down, but I don't move. The woman holds out her hand and I take it, her fingers soft and tired feeling.

"What about your husband?" I ask.

"He don't cotton to birthing," she whispers.

I sit there maybe five minutes.

"You got a sweetheart?" she asks.

"Had one," I say. "She left me. I ain't feeling too good about women right now."

"Man needs a good woman," she whispers.

I close my eyes and feel the woman's fingers weave into mine, holding tight. I'm afraid to let go, afraid she might drift off somewhere like a dandelion seed, and I'll be alone. After another five minutes or so, I let go. The feel of her hand lingers on my skin in a way I won't forget.

"You get the doctor," she says.

"I don't know the doctor."

"Phone at the store. Mile past the crossroads."

"Back up the road?'

"Yeah, take the fork to Canton."

"Okay," I say.

I walk out to the big room. On the sink is another piece of broken slate with some smudged writing on it. I go to pick it up, thinking it might have some information about the doctor, but the little girl grabs it.

"I gotta find the doctor," I say, pointing to the slate.

She looks at me with a blank stare. She ain't the best communicator. I'm wondering about the harp. Getting it back. But then I think what the hell, maybe it'll do her more good than it did me.

"Let the good times roll," I say, and give her a little wave. She doesn't move and her stare is still fixed on me.

I get back to the roadside, look around a little, but my backpack and guitar are gone. Every last thing I have in the world.

Jesus, I think, angry as hell, maybe I should track down the thief. That guitar is big bucks. I'd beat the hell out of him. Then I'm thinking about my promise about the doctor—I can't go back on a promise—so I start moving again. After a while I'm surprised. Walking is a lot easier without lugging that damn guitar. I'm trying to be positive. I'm feeling lighter, like a balloon that broke away from being tied down. I'm thinking this is a sign. A new direction. Screw the gigs. Maybe I could try a career in fast food.

Just as I'm about to make the turn toward the phone place, the guy on the bike pedals up and whips out his slate. He writes a question mark. He's got more schooling than I thought. He's wearing my Chicago Cubs baseball cap, too, the one I had in my pack. He points up the road the way I come. He's grinning at me like he just slipped an ace into a losing hand of poker.

"It's a boy," I say. He jumps up and down a couple times, still straddling the bike, and waves his arms over his head.

"Good-looking, too," I say.

He wipes the slate with the heel of his hand. I see he's wearing two of my fingerpicks. Damn! For a second, I want to strangle him.

"OK?" he writes. He cups his hands in front of his chest like breasts, I guess as a sign to tell me he's asking about the woman.

"You got to get the doctor," I tell him, but he starts shaking his head, pointing to his mouth.

"Okay," I say, "Okay!"

He wipes the slate clean again and writes, "U OK?"

I'm feeling light on possessions and I need to find some money for a burger and fries. I know I could sell my metronome that I still got in my pocket. Maybe sweet-talk a loan for a couple days.

"I'm cool," I say.

He puts the slate back in his pocket and slaps me on the shoulder like I'm his best friend. He makes the peace sign with his hand, and looks worried. That's too much my-buddy stuff for a guy that just ripped off my guitar. I have the thought to mangle him on the spot. But I can't stop seeing in my mind his woman and my Madeline, all at once. Maybe he's doing it for his family. So I slap him on the back, friendly.

"I like your groove," I say, with more meaning than I thought I had in me.

He gets ready to crank up his bike.

"Hey, my man," I say pointing down the road. "Is that the way to Atlanta?"

He writes another question mark on his slate with "Yazoo" after it.

"My woman in Atlanta," I say.

He points the other way toward Atlanta. His grin is so wide I can see where his back teeth are missing.

Captain Withers's Wife

illustration by Peter Healy

Captain Withers's Wife

In 1963, on an American base in France, Amy Withers loaded her husband's hair-trigger automatic pistol, called the military police, wrapped her newborn baby in a hand-knitted beige afghan with a purple border, and waited at the front window of her commonplace bungalow. A policeman arrived, parked his car near the curb, and walked toward the house. She opened the front window from above and shot four rounds into the air.

The policeman backed away. "We got a call …"

"I called," Amy yelled. "I want the commander."

The policeman swore. "You need a shrink," he mumbled.

"I heard that, you creep." She shot another round into the air.

Amy grabbed the baby, left the afghan on the floor. She opened the door and shoved the baby out, grabbing his clothing over his spine and supporting his bottom with the right hand still holding the gun.

"I'm afraid I'll hurt him."

"I'm not calling the commander!" He crouched behind the car, his gun drawn.

Amy closed the door and went to the window. Her next bullet made a hole in the rear-door window of the police car.

The policeman crawled into the front seat from the passenger side, keeping his head down. He called for backup. A second car arrived with a superior officer. From a safe distance and with a bullhorn, the new officer demanded Amy's surrender. When Amy didn't respond, he zigzagged toward the front door of the house with a weapon under his flak vest. Crouching, he knocked.

The door opened six inches and the automatic came out. He couldn't see the woman.

"Give me the baby," he said, standing up.

"I want the commander."

"The commander can't come."

"Captain Withers has left me without a dime."

The superior officer grabbed for the gun. Amy lurched back and shot above his head. He flattened against the wall at the side of the door and reached for his pistol. Amy came out, the baby cradled in her arm, and pointed the automatic at the superior officer's left eye. He removed his hand from the vest and showed her his palm.

"Look," said Amy pushing the child forward so he could see without moving. "You know my husband. Blond. Blue eyed. Does this look like my husband?"

The kid was really small. The eyes were darker than any he could ever remember in a baby. And the thin hair swept on top of the pink scalp like a wave breaking on the shore was black, not blond.

"It's on your conscience if anything happens," Amy pressed.

The officer relaxed a little. "Mothers can't kill their children."

"Just call the commander. Use my name. He knows me."

She slammed the door shut with her foot and went back to wait in front of her window where she could watch all the activity on the street. The baby cried when she wrapped him in the afghan and put him on the floor.

"Hush," she said. "You got me into this mess."

She reloaded.

By the time the superior officer returned to his command center, he had decided to contact the commander. He did not like the commander, who was only a full colonel temporarily appointed as commander until a general could be found. The superior officer half-smiled at the opportunity to annoy the commander with leadership trivia. The call went out from base communications, and within thirty minutes the commander—who was divorced and liked to party—was found in a private room at the officers' club.

"We got a dependent with a gun threatening to kill her baby," the senior officer said over a static-filled line.

"Take her in. You can't let it get out of control," the commander barked.

"It's Amy Withers. That's what she said to tell you."

The pause at the commander's end of the line was brief but definitive. "She's crazy. Call the doc. Send her to the loony bin."

"I should wait for the doc? Do nothing?"

"You deaf?" The commander rang off.

The superior officer smirked to himself.

When the call about Amy came, the doctor—in his bungalow of the type specially assigned to high-ranking officers of major and above—was sitting on the edge of a bed massaging his wife's nude back. She was face-down, the bottom part of her body under a sheet, her bent arms splayed out on each side of the pillow supporting her shaved head, flawlessly done daily by her best girlfriend, whose head she shaved in return.

"Don't answer it," his wife said in the habitually cold, detached words that he had learned to ignore over the last ten years of marriage. At least when they had been stationed in Minnesota, she had enjoyed horseback riding and private yoga instruction. But now she rarely ventured beyond the perimeter fence that surrounded the base, reluctantly playing bridge in the cramped living rooms of older women who dealt cards with a flask of gin cradled on the floor between their ankles.

"I'm on call, J.D.," he said, reaching for the phone. She slapped his arm and he paused. The phone rang again.

"You didn't tell me you were on call." She believed the twice-weekly massage he gave her for back pain would, if divided into parts, lose its therapeutic continuity. "Don't go."

The phone rang again.

"I hate this place," she said, but he heard "I hate you." Maybe he hadn't been around enough early in their marriage, or maybe he should have left her with her mother in Florida when he was assigned overseas, but was he really to blame? After internship she insisted he go into general practice in the military when he had been accepted for a residency in psychiatry. Her headaches—and sudden bouts of fatigue in moments of affection—had all but extinguished his desire for her. And last month she vacationed with her friend at Mont Blanc without him.

When he answered the phone she stood up with her back to him, covering herself with a towel, and went to the bathroom to dress.

The doctor climbed into the commander's limousine, parked a safe distance from the front of Amy Withers's house. The commander was a lanky, swarthy man with a high voice whose appearance on a scene of domestic unrest was unusual and puzzling. "She's crazy, doc. You need to give her a tranquilizer or something. Commit her so we can fly her back emergency," the commander said as the doctor closed the door.

"Who is it?" the doctor asked. The base was small. Everyone knew everyone.

"Withers's wife."

The doctor's heart beat hard and fast. Amy Withers. Just her name made him feel her presence. She had strong, efficient limbs and a face of natural beauty, a smell of freshness, and a hushed way of speaking. More than a year ago she had walked into his office, distraught. Her husband played around. She blamed herself for failing to re-create her mother and father's almost perfect marriage. To help her cope, the doctor increased her appointments to twice a week; soon he knew everything about her. She began to stop talking in mid-sentence and stare out the window, her eyes moist from lost dreams and her body rigid with longing for an omen of hope. The silences were so intense that he was, in the beginning, afraid to intrude, but when he sensed her need and finally asked his softly worded questions about what she believed, what she wanted in life, what her dreams told her, he was captivated by her openness. She was unable to lie about her world or herself, even by omission. One time she stared and he did not look away, their eyes filled with each other, and he could only recover his composure by thumbing through his appointment calendar for no reason, his heart quickened with joy and dread.

Toward the end, she came as often as every other day. Even though anticipation of her arrival crowded his mind and only the sight of her dampened his longing, he was meticulously professional at every session. He hid his reverence when she was near as best he could, and he kept the sessions to exactly thirty minutes, unfailingly mentioning at the end of their time how much progress she had made. Then, without warning, ten minutes into the final session, he was consumed by an urge to compliment her, to tell her how he admired her resilience, how he loved the indescribable blue of her eyes, how he had come to measure the timing of his breathing to the exact intake of her own air. He stood silently to face the window, his back to her.

"Are you sick?" Amy had asked. He terminated the session immediately, making an excuse about an emergency. That afternoon, speaking to the receptionist, he made sure that all future treatments for Amy Withers would be referred to a colleague.

Amy never spoke to him again. On the few occasions when he would see her in the waiting room, or at the base commissary, she would avoid his gaze. He waved to her once, but she turned away. Soon she stopped coming to the clinic.

The doctor squirmed on the limousine's leather seat.

The commander straightened his career service ribbons, from habit. The doctor seemed oddly distracted, as if unaware of the severity of the problem. "Look, Doc. You got to talk to her," the commander said.

"Storm the place," the doctor said.

"She's good with the gun. She could have killed the MP."

The doctor desperately sought a solution that would avoid contact. "You talk to her, then," the he said.

"I'm through talking to her. She's nuts."

"What's she want?"

"Money! She can fly back on a government plane as a dependent. And she's on standby. But Withers has cut her off. She wants me to garnish his salary to guarantee her income. Make up back pay. She's thought about it. I don't even know if I can garnish a captain's salary without legal proceedings."

"Do what she wants. Withers is a cheating son of a bitch."

"I'm working on it. But she says she's afraid she'll kill the kid."

"Her baby?" A baby was news to the doctor, and confusion made him avoid the commander's stare.

The commander frowned. "I can't afford a wrong guess on what she might or might not do," he said, waving his hand in dismissal. "You got something to knock her out?"

A call came in over the radio and the limousine driver lowered the window separating the front seat from the back. Staff members at headquarters had not found the administrator who could solve garnishment problems, the driver said. Yes, they were hurrying! The commander reached across the doctor for the door handle and shoved him out of the car. "Commit her!"

"You need a plan," the doctor said.

"Goddamn it. You keep her calm. I'll be back in touch."

From the street, the doctor searched the front of the house for signs of Amy. The sun had set, but he could see the front window was open a crack. He could not see her or a weapon.

On the narrow path, he tried to stride confidently toward the house, stumbling once on a crack in the concrete obscured by the dark. He reminded himself that the woman he remembered would not shoot him. The front door opened. He paused at the threshold. He saw the standard living room of all base housing—a couch next to the wall with a framed picture of an American flag over it. A small lamp glowed on a side table.

"Hello," he called as he stepped up on the stoop. Amy was behind the door, out of the line of fire. Could she hear him? There was growing noise from the vehicles arriving in front of the house and the chatter of neighbors who had been evacuated; they huddled near a canvas-backed supply truck that provided coffee and pastries, the engine running, the headlights creating long shadows on the street and sidewalks.

"Mrs. Withers?" The doctor entered cautiously. She closed the door behind them.

"My God. Why would they send you?"

"The commander thinks you're crazy."

"I don't need a doctor. Especially you!"

"The commander wants you hospitalized. I was on call."

She was not insane. Her dark-blue eyes still shone with the rational determination he had always admired.

"I need money to go home."

"The commander's working on it."

"That bastard."

"We could wait at the hospital," he said.

"So I won't kill my child?"

"Does it have milk?"

She slumped onto the two-seater sofa, the gun on the cushion next to her. He stayed near the closed door. She put her head in her hands, her fingers buried in her golden hair, her elbows on her bare knees, the hem of her wrinkled dress carelessly resting at mid-thigh. She did not cry.

"It's only a baby. But I hate it enough."

He pulled up a straight-backed government-issue wood chair.

"We've been eating at Mary Wheeler's house," Amy said. "My father died in April and mother's alone on social security. And my husband has cut me off."

"He has to support you."

She leaned back, her hands loosely by her sides, her head extended with her chin up slightly. The front of her dress gaped where a button was lost.

"No one likes your husband. But he can't be so bad that he won't support his child."

She exhaled. "It's not his."

"Oh, Amy. Does he know?"

"Of course he knows."

"Did you tell the commander?"

"I didn't need to tell the commander."

"If he knew, I'm sure he could find some way to get you support."

"What's he going to do? He sent you."

"He's working on it. He wants me to calm you."

"He wants to get rid of me."

The doctor felt sympathy at first, then betrayal. How often he had thought of her since her therapeutic sessions, always in an aura of her dedicated longing for him. He assumed an unstated lifetime of dedication to each other that those silent sessions had implied.

"How could you?" the doctor said.

"Don't judge me," Amy retorted, "I was alone on a week-long religious retreat. I needed someone. The commander said he loved me. I was a fool to believe him."

She sat up straight, both feet on the floor, a space between her back and the sofa so that her hair cascaded behind her when she used both hands to gather it off her shoulders.

"I'm sure the commander will do something," he said, leaning forward, his forearms on his thighs, his eyes fixed on the reflection of the lamp on his black patent-leather shoes.

"I've tried for weeks. He won't even see me."

"Well, he was working on it when I came in."

"And he wants to commit me!"

The doctor had his hands together, fingers interlocked. His knuckles had turned white. "I'll wait with you," he said.

She leaned back again. The gun slipped from the cushion to the floor, discharging a muffled shot into the wall behind the sofa toward the kitchen. She brought it closer to her carelessly with her foot and picked it up. "Don't even think about trying to make a move. I'm a good shot."

He had not thought about it. He was not a hero.

"You're partly to blame," she said. "Those sessions."

The shot had unnerved him; his mouth was dry. He looked to the baby on the floor near the window. It dozed, spit dribbling down the side of its face.

"Weren't they helpful?" he asked hoarsely.

She didn't speak, turning her gaze to him. He looked away.

"You cared," she said softly.

"I was glad to help," he answered.

"No. You wanted me. I needed that."

He had longed for her over these many months, and he had fought against his need to act, to risk contacting her, to tell her why he terminated that last session.

"I won't shoot the child," she said. "I could never do that."

"You're not a murderer," he said.

"I'm afraid for him," she said. "No love makes the innocent dry up and blow away … it's like murder … in a way."

The baby cried and fell silent again.

"Should we take a look?" he asked.

"He's all right!" she said. The baby did turn quiet, lying unaware, with a trace of a contented smile.

"We can work this out safely in the hospital," he said.

"With me sedated so I won't know who I am?" she said.

He could see her thoughts on her face. Screw you and your plans to restrain me. You are a repulsive icon for unstated promises never kept, implied expectations never fulfilled. Could you ever seize a moment? No! I hated you for that. "I'm not leaving until I get support," she said. The tension in her legs caused her knees to flutter.

She shifted her automatic from one hand to the other. The doctor stayed seated on the chair, his mind a jumble of memories and emotions. He was again obsessed by her presence, aware of how alert she made him feel even when she was consumed by anger. The doctor walked to the window. The silence now in the room, intensified by the sound of the bustle outside, held fear and uncertainty, so different from their therapeutic sessions that had pulsed with longing and potential. The difference hurt.

Amy and the doctor waited in the dim lighting of the living room and didn't speak for a while. Then the doctor went to the bathroom. Amy changed the baby's diaper. Then they sat again, he in his chair, she lying on her sofa, legs up, the automatic on her breasts rising and falling with her breathing.

"It can't be long now," he said. He forced himself into his professional mode. He would not try to disarm her. It would only result in disaster. He hoped to rationalize with her—without threats and violence—for a stay in the hospital to resolve her fears, and to satisfy the commander. "You're not what you pretend," he said. "Life has pushed you to the limits."

She said nothing.

"All those hours we had together. I know who you are, what you suffered. Don't destroy what you can be."

Her eyes were closed but she was wide awake.

"It's being here in a foreign country," he said. "No support. No one to turn to. You held on more than most of us could." He knew things could only get worse for Amy, but he tried to remain upbeat.

The baby whimpered again, but only for a few seconds. The doctor's stomach growled and he could feel the beat of his heart.

"I loved you," he said. He looked away, surprised at the sound of his own words. He wanted to bring her to the pain of his reality.

She sat straight up with her feet on the floor, the gun resting in the valley made by her dress between her legs.

"You never loved me," she said. "You teased me. You sucked me into fantasies I could never have imagined on my own!"

"No!" he said. "I cared."

"Your wife fills you with hate."

"I was always thinking of you."

"Everyone knows you hate her. You have a void, doctor, a deep void, and I was something that made you know you were still alive. That is not love!"

"I'm a professional, Amy. I was helping."

"Those long silences. That wasn't being a doctor. And it wasn't just to help me!"

He couldn't look at her.

"Look at me. Tell me how you love me, now. That you'll take me away. Make everything all right."

He had loved her. "I'll take you to the hospital," he said. "I promise you I will make it all right."

"Liar. You won't take me, support me."

"It was love. I didn't do it to fill a void."

"Where were you all those months? Even now you're here because you were on call. If you love me, say it. Say it with meaning!"

He hesitated. "I love you," he said, but he was afraid of her now, unsure of what she, and he, had become.

"Liar!" she said again.

"What more can I do?" Even to himself, he seemed to be pleading.

"Be honest. You letch."

He walked to the window. There were even more vehicles now.

"Get out," she said. "You will never accept me. Married or divorced. Child or childless. It was enough for you to sit there and enjoy the potential. You're sick."

"I'll wait until the commander comes back. I'll help you negotiate."

"I'll always be Amy Withers, vulnerable patient."

"You need support. That's only fair," he said.

"I've waited too long."

"I'll help, Amy. Let me help." He tried to smile, and when she didn't respond he returned to his chair.

"Don't go out of your way," she said. And she positioned herself on the sofa so it was obvious she was through talking.

To his staff, the commander said he was tired of dealing with a pilot's hysterical wife and couldn't see placing himself, a base commander, in a position of danger, no matter how low-risk the danger might be. In truth he could not face Amy's career-smashing truths and accusing glare. He sent his adjutant, a tall, deep-spoken man whom he found industrious if not overly intelligent. The adjutant calmly knocked on the door.

Amy jumped up from the couch and opened the door cautiously, making sure the commander was alone. It was not the commander, but she let the adjutant in, closing the door and backing away. The adjutant did not salute when the doctor stood. Amy waved with her pistol when the adjutant tried to move; he stopped. The three of them stood in a lopsided triangle facing each other.

"Where's the commander?" Amy asked.

"I'm fully empowered to deal."

"You've brought the papers? Cash?"

"Yes. I've brought papers for application for an exclusive account at the American bank on base. Money can easily be transferred to the States. You sign and I'll take the papers by tomorrow to establish your account for deposit."

"What money?"

"Part of your husband's salary."

"Half of my husband's salary! Guaranteed. Notarized."

"I don't know what percentage they're working on, but fifty percent sounds reasonable. I'll pass it on."

"And cash to make up for the last six months deposited. I've been cheated."

"The judge advocate is working on a settlement. Your husband has been contacted in Beirut and will be back the day after tomorrow."

"He'll never agree."

"The commander will convince him."

"And no money now?"

"You can live in the hospital. No charge. Maybe the commander can establish a line of credit at the commissary."

The doctor moved closer to the two. "Be straight with her, lieutenant. Don't bullshit."

"Hey. It's only until the legal stuff is worked out. You know the system, Doc. Christ, it's a nightmare."

"She wants what is rightfully hers," the doctor said.

"I know her pain," said the adjutant to the doctor.

"No you don't!" Amy said. "You don't know what it is to be abandoned."

"We all know Withers is not the perfect husband," the adjutant said.

Amy moaned.

"This woman has been wronged, Lieutenant."

"We've gone the limit on this one, doc. A lot further than I think we should have, to tell the truth," the adjutant said.

"You've done nothing," Amy said.

The adjutant shook his head. She picked up the baby in the afghan, the automatic still in her hand. The adjutant moved toward her. She waved the gun at him. "Stay back." The child cried.

Amy shoved the baby toward him. He made no move to take it.

"You take care of him. You love him. Raise him to be a confident, resourceful human being." She pushed back the afghan from the baby's face so the adjutant could see.

The child certainly didn't look like Withers. He paused, looking puzzled.

"Let her go," the doctor said. "Take the baby."

"I plan to," said the adjutant. He reached out with his right palm and pushed the baby and Amy back, and turned to the door to call for help.

The shot rang out as he gripped the doorknob, before he opened the door.

"Oh, God. Dear God," Amy cried.

The doctor reached out, leaning toward her. The barrel of the gun, discolored now with the infant's gushing blood, waved without purpose at odd angles as Amy struggled to remove her son from the bloody afghan.

"Oh, God," she cried. "He was so innocent."

"You've killed him," the adjutant said.

"I didn't kill him," she screamed. "The gun went off." She slumped to the floor on her knees, laying the little corpse on the couch, still trying to get the child's legs free from the tangled afghan. The gun barrel jerked toward the doctor and discharged again. A sharp pain pierced the doctor, and his legs gave way. He crumpled to the floor, watching her gaze shift from terror to the wild calmness of despair, then she put the gun to her temple and squeezed the trigger. As she fell forward face-down, her arm draped across the doctor's chest. She took only a few more breaths; he reached out, the flat of his hand on her ribs, and felt the last beat of her heart. Unable to move his legs, he waited for the adjutant to uncover his eyes. "Get an ambulance," the doctor said.

The doctor allowed his wife to see him in his hospital room three days later. He'd been operated on and had been assured that his injuries were not life threatening. But he had needed time to think before talking to her.

She stood at the bedside and took his hand in hers without lifting it off the sheet.

"You're letting your hair grow again," he said. It had some length and had been teased to the stiffness of synthetic carpet.

"My friends don't like it. But I'm glad you noticed."

They suffered a silence without looking at each other.

"It must have been terrible," she said, "Your patient! Everyone says she was crazy from the day she arrived."

He couldn't speak of Amy. She wasn't crazy, even at the end.

"What did you think of her?" she asked.

"She had a lousy marriage. No one would help," he finally managed.

"You liked her?"

He weighed versions of the truth. "I did."

She let go of his hand without moving. "Did you love her?"

He hesitated. "No," he said avoiding her stare.

"There's a rumor she saw you almost every day for weeks at a time."

"She was sick," he said. "She needed help."

"I really don't care if you were screwing her. But I do care if people think you were."

"I wasn't screwing her. It wasn't like that. She was my patient."

His wife rubbed her eye with her knuckle to wipe out some speck of irritation. She sat on the edge of the bed. "Does it hurt? My sitting here?"

"No. I'll never have feeling again. Or movement."

"The doctor told me," she said.

"I'll be in a wheelchair forever. At least with full disability. It was in the line of duty."

"I've made arrangements. We can go to Mother's house. I can have a special room for you on the first floor with wheelchair access."

"We can live close to normal," he said. "I may still be able to have a limited practice."

"You'll do no such thing. You're my disabled husband. We'll do for you. I've ordered bookshelves for your room. A radio-television-stereo combination. And I'll be going back to work. I've already been accepted for a legal secretary job at a firm I knew well before we were married. With the government check, we'll get along just fine." She was almost exuberant, eager to get on to a new life. She seemed released from some oppressive, crushing restraint.

"All that in just three days?" he asked.

"To tell the truth, I'd been thinking about it for a while. Going back to work. You're being hurt like this just moved it up a year."

"I'm almost surely impotent," he said. "Can you stand an invalid husband?"

"Nonsense talk," she said, moving off the bed. She bent and hugged him, and then kissed him on the forehead.

"I'll be back tomorrow. I've arranged for early return for both of us on medevac. The movers will pack at the end of the week. I've sold the car for more than it's worth."

She shut the door. He was glad she was gone. When he closed his eyes, Amy Withers was on her couch with her hair pulled back, her blue eyes deep as tiny oceans. He couldn't erase this memory, especially detailed in silent times, and his chest tightened with a dull pain unrelated to his injuries.

His wife returned with a shiny chrome urinal that she hung on the side bedrail. "The nurse asked me," she said. She blew him a kiss as she left. He had never seen her blow kisses—to him or any man.

From his bed, looking out the small hospital-room window, he could see only treetops and the clouds that obscured the blue French sky.

The Thirteen Nudes of Ernest Goings

illustration by David Riley

illlustration by David Riley

The Thirteen Nudes of Ernest Goings

Amanda Goings parked her station wagon in the unpaved drive to her mother's two-story, white, green-trimmed clapboard house. Its pitched roof had for many years kept snows from long Maine winters from collecting and crushing the Goings family. The curtains parted on a window to the right of the door. The interior lights were turned off and it was too dark to see, but Amanda waved to let her mother know she'd be back in a few minutes to take her to the luncheon. The curtain fell back in place.

Amanda walked fifty yards to the stone wall at the edge of the property, her rubber-soled shoes unsteady on the sheets of wet leaves under the maples and the walnut tree. She came to a ragged break that had been there since her childhood. For thirty-two years, the wall had been the divider between the Goings family's property and the neighboring property recently purchased by her father.

She climbed the knoll and passed through a line of cedars. She stumbled near the top, her turned-in foot and withered left leg, the result of a birth defect, failing to support her adequately. On the downhill slope, invisible from her mother's house and the road, was a barn, the only structure that remained on the property. She swore as she always did when she saw the two rectangular roof skylights that mirrored northern light from gray overhead clouds. She thought the expensive renovation of the barn a waste of money—split levels floored with slate and twelve-inch antique floorboards, directional track lighting, and an open-loft living facility adjacent to a studio with rows of vertical racks for the drying and storage of paintings.

She knocked at the door to the right of the original swinging doors that had been sealed and left as authentic-residual decoration. She heard nothing.

"Goddamn it," she yelled. "Answer the door!" Her father was probably up. It was eleven o'clock, but his hours had been erratic since he had begun living alone in the barn.

"I'm busy," he called back from the silent interior.

She took out a letter-size fold-over brochure from her inside coat pocket.

"The promotion is in from New York."

"Leave it," he said. She heard the twang of a guitar string, the pitch mounting as a peg was screwed tighter. Then she heard the six disparate notes of an unharmonious chord. He had no ear for music. And he practiced often now, his foot tapping behind the beat of sixties rockers he played on a cassette recorder.

She opened the lid to a dark-green painted-tin mailbox, slipped the brochure in, and let the lid drop.

The Cottontail Inn conference room dining facility had only four windows on one sidewall. These gave little light, and the rheostats on the faux carriage lamps along the wall had to be cranked up to highest intensity. The room was set with circular tables draped with white cloth, and many of the seated women of the Rockton Garden Club had to turn their chairs to see Amanda on the small speaker's stage at the end of the room. A tubular reading light glowed on the podium next to the gooseneck mic. Amanda tilted up on her toes to see. She tapped the microphone with the middle finger of her right hand. The members had finished their chicken entrée, but still took a few seconds to direct their attention to Amanda.

"Welcome," Amanda said. She thanked Mertha Williams, the club president, for the success of the luncheon and the club. "The Ernest Goings Foundation has always been pleased to sponsor these quarterly meetings of the Garden Club," she continued, "and today's door prize is Ernest's new book of full-color reproductions of his most popular paintings, Barn Doors in Lincoln County. Mother, would you draw the winning slip?"

As her mother came forward, Amanda stood as tall as she could on her good leg to make a presence when she greeted her mother. This provincial crowd underappreciated Amanda, and some still thought her father really managed his art career. But it was Amanda's shrewd business skills that had anchored her father's success over the last ten years. She was not some nepotistic hanger-on.

Amanda's mother, Margaret, selected one slip of paper from among many in a shoebox that was traditional for these drawings and brought forward by a volunteer. Margaret said nothing, and handed the winning slip to Amanda before returning to her seat.

And the winner? Tall and thin Fabia Worthington, who approached the podium without joy. She didn't like Ernest Goings's bucolic, hyperrealistic paintings; she adored Renoir. Amanda held the book prize above her head for a few seconds for all to see before handing it to Fabia, who flipped through the pages. "No nudes?" she asked. The audience laughed.

Amanda leaned closer to the microphone. "Fabia is kind to remind us that Ernest will show his new series of figure paintings next Thursday at the Slade Gallery in Boston on Newbury Street. Please join us." Then she walked back to her mother and her mother's friends, Julia and Sally, at a prominently placed table for four. Mertha gave the financial report and assigned committees for the spring garden show. Dessert was served.

"My goodness, Margaret," Sally whispered. "Thirteen nudes!"

"Ernest was always good at figure drawing," Margaret said. She had always been awed by his talent.

"Maine landscapes made him famous," Julia said smiling. "He should sow the seeds from plants that won last year's awards."

"It's his love of nature that makes his scenes come alive," Amanda said.

"Who knows what makes a painting good?" Sally said.

"He's always had a special gift," Margaret said.

"His art has touched millions," Amanda added.

"Not nudes," Sally said.

"They're portraits of a girl," Amanda said firmly.

"You can't judge the nudes," Julia said to Amanda. "You're all business."

"She is definitely a woman," Sally said. "You can see that." Sally picked up one of the brochures that had been placed at every table, showing a minute photo of one of the paintings; she waved it at Amanda. Julia nodded.

Amanda watched her mother closely. Margaret's eyes had lost focus, and she pushed her lower lip behind her upper teeth to control the trembling.

"I wouldn't trust my husband in the barn alone with a woman, clothed or unclothed," Julia said to Margaret. "How did you let him get away with it?"

"The mother was with the model," Margaret said emphatically.

"That's not what I heard," Julia said.

"Don't be catty," Amanda said. "She was only fifteen. Artists and models have strict professional standards."

Eunice, an indigent mother, had brought her daughter, Hester, for the early modeling sessions until she found domestic work. After that, Hester went to the barn alone, disappearing over the ridge out of view.

"I'm sure it was her gift of holding still that attracted Ernest," Sally said sarcastically.

"That's not appropriate," said Amanda. These women were the foulest, most malevolent weeds of this community, and they made Amanda want to get out of rural Maine. She had an MBA—and national acclaim—and job offers in DC, Atlanta, and Oregon.

"You're too sensitive, Amanda," Julia said.

Amanda touched the arm of her mother for comfort. Her mother had slumped in her chair, her eyes closed, no doubt hoping for a biting response to come to her to silence Sally and Julia.

"You're not still cooking for Ernest's sales, are you?" Julia asked Margaret.

Margaret leaned forward and clasped one hand in the other in her lap under the table to hide her tremor. "It wouldn't be a Goings opening without our traditions," she said, bringing up her chin slightly. She baked sugar cookies shaped liked painters' palettes, with thumbholes and tan and brown chocolate chips along the edges that melted during cooking to suggest oil paints squeezed from a tube. She stacked the cookies on china platters on a linen-covered card table near the reception table at the door, far away from the catered opaque-eyed salmon, the bacon-wrapped warmed scallops, and the wedged sandwiches bulging with cold sprouts.

"It's a disgrace. After all you've done for him," Julia said.

Sally said. "He's treated you like dirt."

"Oh, Ernest loves it," Margaret said looking off into the distance. "And I do it for his fans. They expect it after all these years." Her voice was now shaky and her neck veins pulsing.

"Don't be a slave," Julia said. "It's embarrassing."

As Amanda stood, her chair scraped the bare wooden floors. She gripped her mother's arm. "We've got work to do," she said. She led her mother out of the inn.

When Amanda and Margaret reached home, Margaret refused Amanda's suggestion for coffee. She would not take her pills.

"They don't know art," Margaret said.

"They thrive on the salacious remark, Mother. No matter what the topic."

"He shouldn't have used the barn."

"It must have been innocent."

"No one believes that," Margaret said, and she lay face down on the sofa, weeping.

"They're not your friends, Mother," Amanda said. "Forget them."

—

Amanda ran the many branches of the Goings business in her small, private, but well-appointed office at the family-owned gallery and art store in Rockton. She was reviewing the pricing for the show in Boston. Paintings sold at record prices in five or six figures, and Amanda turned enviable profits by negotiating the lowest commission for each painting.

It was Saturday, and Christina, who worked gallery sales on weekends, knocked on the office door.

"Eunice Cummings is here," she said. "She won't leave."

Eunice was the model, Hester's, mother.

Amanda looked at an appointment book. "I could see her Tuesday afternoon at three."

But the door opened, and Eunice pushed Christina aside and walked in. "Got no time, Tuesday," she said.

"She wouldn't leave," Christina apologized.

Eunice stood in front of Amanda's desk, her hands in the pockets of her hand-knitted gray-green wool sweater, speechless. Her round face, spotted with facial hair on her chin and lip, had a grayish cast. Her brown eyes looked down, her lips pursed.

"What can I do for you, Eunice?" Eunice was thin and her jeans hung loose. She wore a light-green down jacket stitched in large squares, and a maroon woolen ski cap pulled down over her ears.

"Mrs. Pritchard said she'd get her son to take me and Hester to the opening in Boston," Eunice said.

The wealthy and stylish patrons on Newbury Street would probably hand Eunice a toilet brush and a mop when she walked into Slade Gallery. But the shows were open to the public. Amanda nodded. "You'll enjoy it," she said.

"I don't think so."

"Is there something specific you want, Eunice?"

"Hester wants her due," Eunice said.

Amanda leaned back in her swivel chair, her feet, in running shoes, dangling.

"He promised her ten percent of them paintings," Eunice said.

Amanda stared.

"He said he was going to treat her right."

Amanda breathed deeply. "Slow down, Eunice." Amanda swiveled a quarter turn in her chair, pushing with her leg. "Hester was paid the standard modeling fee. I've seen the cancelled checks."

"He showed her indecent, to my mind," Eunice said.

"You signed for the permission."

"Not for what is in that foldout."

"We don't pay a percentage of sales to a model," Amanda said. But previous models had always been clothed, old, sturdy people who wore hats to block the sun or catch the rain, and always at a distance, on the porch of a farmhouse or on a dock with commercial fishing boats in the background.

"I got a lawyer. An esquire. He's going to write you a letter. I just come to see if you'd do right without us paying him all that money."

Ten percent was at least three hundred thousand dollars. Eunice remained standing, waiting for an answer.

"He told her lies," Eunice continued.

Amanda's father was capable of avoiding truth, usually by prolonged, miserable silences.

"He said he loved her."

"You heard him?"

"Hester don't lie."

Eunice stared unblinkingly, and a tear trickled down her face to the left of her nose.

Amanda had to be practical. "I'd be careful about spreading rumors, Eunice."

Eunice didn't hesitate. "Ain't never been one to talk bad about folks. Never."

"Well, don't get your hopes up. We are not paying a percentage of sales." Eunice's gaze went distant, somewhere behind Amanda. She was trembling with frustration. When words failed, she left the office breathing hard and fast.

Amanda dismissed Christina. Her heart was still pounding, and she sat with her head back, her eyes closed. After a few minutes, she called artists she knew well and confirmed their hourly rates for models, never with residual compensations. Then she itemized every check and cash withdrawal marked for modeling fees. Hester had definitely been paid more than required by common practice. For the last sessions, it seemed sometimes she was given, by Ernest, excessive compensation for time spent, and without a reason noted in the "for" column.

Amanda knocked on the front door of the barn-studio, and when there was no answer, she tried the knob. It was unlocked. Her father rarely answered the studio door, and never when he was painting. A thirty-six-by-fifty-two inch canvas primed with a burnt umber wash was mounted, and totally dry, on his easel. He was at his workbench stretching canvas over handmade stretchers. Two canvases, freshly gessoed, were propped against the wall. He prepared daily, but he hadn't finished a painting since he stopped painting Hester. Amanda closed the door.

"We need to talk," Amanda said.

"Well, hello to you," he said.

"Cut that off," Amanda said, nodding at the boom box on the workbench.

He looked briefly to Amanda then back to his work, irritated, as if Amanda were an inferior model begging for work.

Amanda pushed the "off" switch on the player.

"Eunice Cummings came to me today. She expects ten percent of sales of the Hester portraits."

"She's deranged," he said, looking away from her and picking up ridged canvas pliers from a workbench. He gripped the edge of the linen canvas.

"You never promised?"

"I never talked to her after the first few sessions. She stopped coming." He fastened the canvas, seven sharp hits from a pneumatic staple gun.

"She says you told Hester."

He looked sharply at her. "Don't bring Hester into it." He leaned the canvas on edge against the leg under the table.

"You painted her!"

He walked to a large picture window to look out, his hands clasped behind his head. "Hester is off limits, Amanda. None of your business."

She moved to where he could not ignore her.

"Eunice has a lawyer. Hester is my business."

"Eunice is lying." His breathing was shallow. "She took the modeling fees."

"Everyone in town thinks something happened in the barn."

He walked two steps away from Amanda. She could see only his backside.

"Don't accuse me."

"I'm asking for the truth."

"You're prying."

Amanda grabbed his arm but he refused to turn. "What did you do?"

"Don't be a bitch. I painted a girl. And I did it well."

She let go and moved back, still facing him.

"We've handed out the brochure. Nudes, everyone said. Not child figure studies."

"Those sessions were hard work, Amanda. I spent more than a year finally doing something more than rocks and curtains blowing through an open window."

"You painted a fifteen-year-old girl alone with you in a barn. We all wonder about that."

"I captured that beautiful balance between innocence and sexuality. Nobody alive has done what I've done."

Paintings were a product to Amanda. She never studied her father's paintings. She had no idea what an artist or an art critic would think.

He walked to the small refrigerator near a sink set in a small countertop. He bent over and took a soda. He turned to Amanda, sweeping with his free hand long, uneven strands of gray hair with dark streaks from his face. His blues eyes, now more like faded watercolor than the rich, cobalt-oil-paint blue of his youth, fixed on the wall above and behind Amanda. He drank from the can.

"A scandal could end your career," she said.

"Hester will never accuse. Trust me. She's not the type." He smiled.

"Our fame and fortune are at stake here."

He grimaced, shaking his head. "Manage the business, Amanda. That's what you're good at." Then he stepped on the trashcan foot pedal; the lid opened, and he tossed in the can. "I'm an artist. Hester was a model. No one needs to know more."

"I'm not sure I can bury this."

"We're already in the money. Marty's presold four of the nudes. They're exceptional."

"Not if the circumstances are clouded by suspicion."

"Great art is great art. It moves people in different ways."

He looked at her as if she were a gnarled, downed tree limb that needed to be removed from the yard. What did he want in a daughter?

"Well. Don't ignore Mother at the reception," Amanda said, buttoning her coat. "You at least owe her that."

She let herself out the door.

Hester Cummings did seasonal counterwork at the cold-serve lobster-roll shack in Wiscasset. She left work and met Amanda outside on a path a few feet from the low highway bridge spanning the Sheepscot River. She had kept Amanda waiting for half an hour.

"Are you still modeling?" Amanda asked when they stood together. Hester was close to five feet five, and Amanda tilted her head back slightly to see Hester's vacant face with uneasy eyes.

"The lawyer said I shouldn't talk to you," Hester said.

"To me? Or anyone?"

"He said you'd be the one asking me questions." Hester stared at Amanda, her hands, palm in, tucked in the back pockets of her tight jeans skirt. She had put on weight.

"But you're talking to me."

"I didn't like him too good."

When Hester smiled a little, Amanda smiled too. Amanda's smile was her best feature. She felt cheated on good features. Her hair was scraggly and a dull brown, and a childhood pox had pitted her skin with scars. But her smile made people relax, and speak more freely.

"Did my father promise more than a modeling fee, Hester?"

"He said I meant a lot to him."

"Did he say he loved you?"

Hester hesitated. "Yes, ma'am."

"He doesn't paint you anymore. You okay with that?"

"He got done with his series."

"You still see him?"

Hester looked away.

"And you think he'll do you right?"

"Course he will. When he can." She straightened and her head went back defiantly. She glared down at Amanda.

For a while, Amanda looked at a lobster boat coming to dock. Then she looked back at Hester. "Do you love him?"

Hester squeezed her eyes shut for a few seconds as if to cry, but didn't answer.

"Did he say he'd pay you ten percent?"

"That's what he said I was worth."

Amanda leaned a few inches closer. "It's hard to believe, Hester. We've never promised that to a model."

Hester looked away again. "You wouldn't know about modeling. You ain't that pretty."

They stood in silence. Although Hester had matured early to a soft, almost plump fertility, she stood with her head slightly down, her toes turned in, her arms hanging awkwardly like a child. And, despite what she thought, being young was her only asset. She must have thrived on the attention from posing. How real posing must have made her feel; Ernest's constant stares for discovery made her needy and wondrous, submissive and hungry. Was Hester in love with her father? Or was she just curious about men?

"I loved a man," Amanda said. "I couldn't be without him."

"I heard about him. He left you."

"In a way. He killed himself," Amanda said. When Amanda was in the MBA program in Boston, she had loved the brilliant but sullen Jimmy Headman. His lovemaking still haunted her. She had not found anyone like him.

"Loving hurts a lot, don't it? I mean, like it isn't all feeling good."

"He went to take care of his demented mother in Canada."

"Look. I ain't saying no more," Hester said. "Lawyer said you'd try to trick me."

She turned toward the shack.

"I won't trick you," Amanda said wearily.

"You're tough as nails, Miss Amanda. No one can trust you."

Amanda shook her head as Hester turned and walked away. "Most people don't feel that way," she said when Hester couldn't hear.

Amanda waited until Hester disappeared back into the shack, then she turned to gaze at the water. Colorful buoys marking submerged lobster traps bobbed on the wind-whipped surface. The water was dark grey.

Early on the day of the opening, Amanda parked in the drive of her mother's house. It was biting cold in the mornings now, and the two oaks on each side of her parents' house had dropped the last of their brown shriveled leaves. Amanda helped her mother load groceries, linens and the folding card table into the car. Her mother shivered in a light green dress and a skimpy raincoat that she thought was her most attractive outfit since she'd lost thirteen pounds.

Amanda drove. They traveled in silence through small towns until they got to Brunswick. They stopped at a Dunkin' Donuts for coffee and doughnuts that they ate in the car.

"Did you talk to him?" Margaret picked small bits of a plain cake donought with her thumb and forefinger. She would eat less than a third – throw the rest away.

Amanda did not answer. Her father took up too much precious space in their lives that he didn't deserve.

"He was improper?" Margaret persisted.

"He's such an asshole. He's never been open about anything."

Margaret put her donut and half-filled small coffee cup into a bag.

"You talked to the girl," Margaret said.

"She loves him," Amanda replied. "But I can't prove she screwed him."

"I'm in the way of their happy life together?"

"She's filled with need and wonder, Mother. I doubt she thinks about you."

Amanda placed her trash in the bag and climbed out of the car to deposit it in a barrel. She got back in and started the car without replying.

"Don't you think she's retarded?" Margaret said.

"She's shy, mother. And afraid. But she's not evil. I feel sorry for her."

They were soon on the I-95 south for Boston. Margaret sat with her hands flat on her thighs staring ahead at the traffic.

"He should never have painted her," Margaret said after they passed the tollbooth.

"He gave her a sense of self she'd never known," Amanda said. "And probably will never know again."

"I called Angus Partridge. Sex with a minor is illegal whether it gave her a sense of self or not."

Amanda passed an eighteen-wheeler. She liked to keep exactly five miles an hour above the speed limit. Amanda didn't care if her mother was talking to Angus about divorce proceedings, but she dreaded the battle. Margaret stared ahead as if some rock wall would emerge on the highway and end their lives.

"I don't think he's finished one canvas since he stopped painting that girl," Margaret said softly.

"He thinks the success of the show will override the suspicions," Amanda said. "And if he did have sex with her, I doubt Hester would ever testify, or that he'd ever be successfully prosecuted even if charged." But even if the show were a success and Ernest went on unscathed by opinions, the marriage was over. Amanda felt a new resolve to never marry.

Amanda steered the car into the fast lane. Maybe a quick settlement with Eunice would be necessary to cut off the publicity as soon as possible.

"He's only good at barn doors," Margaret said.

Amanda meter-parked on the street in Boston and helped her mother carry ingredients and utensils to the gallery. The front door to the showroom was locked – the gallery was closed two days for instillation of the new show – and Amanda used her key to enter the side door. In the kitchen, Margaret stored cookie dough in the refrigerator, turned on one of three baking ovens to preheat, and washed two bowls for cheese straws. They had a few hours before the caterers arrived at five-thirty.

"I want to see the show before I bake," Margaret said.

"I'll meet you in the gallery," Amanda said, and she walked to the small room she used as an office during shows. She took a manila folder out of her briefcase and carried it to the showroom to confirm inventory.

Her mother had turned on the lights. Amanda had seen only a few of the paintings; her visits to the barn were for business, and the few canvasses she had seen were partially finished. Now the nudes were prominently mounted in gold leaf frames with traditional Goings's landscapes in between.

"Mama?" Amanda said.

Her mother slumped on a side chair, staring. She pointed to a life-size frontal view of Hester gazing wide-eyed from the canvas. Hester's buttocks splayed over the edge a porcelain sink, her hands on the edge for support. Both feet were spread apart and flat on the floor. She dominated the space with detail – every hair seemed recreated, flecks on her blue irises were plain and disturbing, the healed acne scars of her facial skin, uncompromised. Her nudity exposed a strange asymmetry of the nipples on her large breasts. Her pelvis was too wide for beauty, and her sturdy legs ended in thick ankles. Her facial expression seemed unaware that anyone would look at her. He had captured the childishness of her figure, and an almost prepubescent softness of her face, but the overall impression was not that she was child – or nude.Rather, it showed the excessive time and passion of the artist to create such minutia.

"It's lewd," her mother said. "It's like he licked every inch of that girl's skin."

Amanda agreed, but said nothing. The adjacent paintings were half and three-quarter studio figures, smaller and less offensive. Then there were two outdoor poses in spring settings, one where Hester lay face up in grass with her hands behind her head; in the other, she squatted to pick up a flower.

Amanda moved and stopped in front of a life-size portrait of Hester sitting on a wooden bench in front of a piano – a quarter-turn view – her arms back, her left leg extended to the floor. Her right leg was bent at the knee with her foot on the bench, a suggestive glimpse of her privates nestled between pink thigh-flesh. Amanda moaned; such detail seemed so unnecessary.

"I hate him," her mother said. "He wanted her."

Amanda gripped her mother's shoulders from the back and pushed her to standing.

"Forget him. Finish the baking," Amanda said. She still hoped the meticulous images would awe the patrons enough to ignore her father's obsession, which, Amanda was now convinced, was more lust than love.

"He's making a fool of himself. And he's your father," her mother said.

"They might be art, Mother."

"They're filthy," her mother said.

Amanda followed her mother into the kitchen, opened the refrigerator, took a bowl and placed it in her mother's hands. "I've got work with Marty."

Amanda walked down the short hall to one of three office doors. She knocked.

Marty, the gallery owner, greeted her from behind his desk, but did not smile. "Ready?" he asked.

Amanda took a folder for documents from a leather briefcase and placed it on the desk. Marty glanced at each paper.

"Will this ruin his career?" Amanda asked as he read. "My mother thinks it's artistic suicide."

"I tried. I joked with him, said they looked like Mexican porn on velvet. He said I was a shitty agent."

"It's all profit for you, Marty."

"Who cares if they're immoral? They'll sell, Amanda. Go into private collections. Look at Balthus."

Marty moved out from behind his desk. He was bald and wore a pinstriped business suit and a white shirt open at the neck.

Together they went out the gallery side door and walked two blocks to a lawyer's office, which was up a flight of stairs above a woman's clothing store, and notarized the sales agreements.

"I'm going home," said Marty when they were back at the door. "Pick you up at the motel?"

"We'll dress here." They had two hours before the caterers and personnel arrived. More than three hours before the opening.

Amanda let herself into the gallery and went into the kitchen. She placed her briefcase on the floor. She called out to her mother, who did not answer. The smell of baking cookies forced memories of summer vacation days home from boarding school, her mother hosting her father's openings, and a joyful celebration in an outrageously expensive restaurant to celebrate her father's growing success.

She walked out, the door closing behind her.

"Mother!" she called.

Silence.

She walked to the gallery. Her mother sat in a wooden armchair in the empty expanse of the show space, her feet splayed before her, her arms draped over the sides, her head back with her eyes closed.

Amanda felt her mother's pulse.

"Go away," he mother moaned. Amanda turned on the lights. She gasped.

An open plastic bottle of Liquid-Plumr lay on its side in an opaque pool that corroded the varnish on the oak floors. Two brushes and a kitchen fork on a kitchen towel were nearby.

"My God, Mother. "

"It's the stuff to unclog drains," she said, her eyes still closed. "I got tired."

Every Hester detail was scraped clean from the sinkportrait.

"He's beyond saving himself," her mother said.

Amanda paused. Margaret had left the background of the painting meticulously preserved, accenting Ernest Goings' talent for settings. The remaining nudes seemed even more out of place now. For minutes, Amanda did not move.

"That poor child."

"We can't judge," Amanda said.

"We might keep him out of jail."

Amanda scanned the remaining nudes. She had never felt about paintings. Feelings corroded a manager's business acumen in the art world. But she knew what her mother felt. There was more than bad judgment on these canvasses. There was revelation.

Amanda bent over and handed a brush to her mother. "Start on the last three over there," she said. "We'll meet in the middle."

Amanda found another paintbrush and a spatula in the kitchen, and two bottles of caustic under the sink. Back in the gallery, her broad brushstrokes dissolved paint on contact. She did not preserve settings.

They worked in silence for almost an hour, scraping off what remained of Hester until she was gone from every portrait. Margaret gasped when Marty came into the gallery. Amanda collected her tools and set them on a chair.

"Goddamn it," Marty said, his face creased with lines, his eyes dark and threatening. "You've really fucked up."

The odor of burnt cookies seeped into the gallery from the kitchen. Amanda suppressed a smile.

"Oh dear ..." Margaret sighed sarcastically. "The cookies."

"Burnt to an inedible crisp ..." Amanda said.

"What will the guest have to enjoy?" Margaret said.

"It's a crime," Marty said. He stood with his feet planted, the fingers in his clenched fists turning white.

"It's a family matter," Amanda said. "Back off."

Technically, the paintings were Marty's property during the sale.

"You're going to put me in jail? Put Mother on the chain gang?"

"Insurance will be tricky, Amanda."

"It's an act of God." Amanda laughed. True, Marty was not a pleasant man, overweight with his handsome features sliding away, but he worked hard with dependable honesty. She looked at him. He was frowning.

"I have expenses," Marty said.

"You've made more than two million off Ernest Goings," Amanda said.

"I've got my girls to educate."

"Hang loose, Marty. I'll cover your losses."

Marty sighed and stared at the two women streaked with dissolving paint: one with a skinny but muscular body with a deformed leg and the hard face of a woman who knows pain, her brown eyes glinting with excitement; the other teetering on old age, but breathing fast and grinning with the broad innocence of a child. For years, he had disliked Ernest Goings and ignored the family whenever he could, but he felt no anger.

Amanda took her mother's hand to leave.

"The pans. My purse," her mother said.

"Get out of Boston," Marty said. "This has to be reported."

Amanda and Margaret went to the kitchen to collect their things, the double-hinged door closing behind them.

The doorbell rang persistently. Marty unlocked the gallery front door. Eunice stood in a green cotton dress, printed with white and yellow daises that buttoned down the front. One brown lace in her white running shoes had come untied. Next to her, Hester wore black jeans tight enough to stretch the buttonhole at the waist, and a too big, thrift-store white blouse with an Alice-in-Wonderland frilly trim. She teetered in silver stiletto-heeled pumps. Her ankles were swollen.

"We're closed," Marty said.

"This here is the model," Eunice said. "We can't do the regular time …"

"I'm sorry," Marty interjected.

" … our ride got to leave early."

Eunice wedged her way in through the door opening and dragged Hester behind her.

"We got our rights," Eunice said.

Marty held out his arm to block them. Eunice pushed his arm away and after a slight hesitiation he didn't resist.

Eunice strode by and Hester wobbled, hurrying to keep up. They stopped in mid gallery.

Amanda came alone from the kitchen and Marty pointed to Eunice and Hester. Hester took small steps to stand alone in front of the portrait Margaret had mutilated first. She whimpered.

After more than a minute, Hester touched her forefinger to the edge of the hole in the canvas. Then, with a flat palm, she intently stroked the air where her image had been, as if she could wipe off the reality of the hole and restore the illusion. She choked and let her hand fall to her side.

"I was important to him," Hester said.

Amanda cringed.

"I wasn't just a picture," Hester said. She sat on the floor, cross-legged. The waist button on her jeans had popped open. One shoe fell off and lay on its side, the heel angled up. Hester still stared at the hole where she had once been so meticulously rendered.

Amanda walked back to the kitchen. Margaret held her purse and her utensils.

"It was the child, wasn't it?" Margaret said. "Was her mother with her?"

"She's destroyed."

Amanda led her out the side door to the car, and in half an hour they were driving directly to Margaret's sister's house in New Hampshire, arriving well after midnight to stay the night.

"I'll send your things," Amanda said to her mother the next morning.

"What about the house?"

"Don't go back. I'll come for you in a few weeks."

"And Ernest?"

"He'll probably press charges, Mother."

Amanda drove straight to the Rockton office. She taped an "Out of Business" sign to the window. She secured valuables, mailed deposits, disconnected phones, paid bills. She went to the bank to certify a check for Marty's commission. She closed business accounts, took her due, and transferred money for her mother's private accounts. She had accepted a position as CFO of a commercial gallery in Oregon.

In her final hour in Rockton, Amanda placed all the documentation of Hester's modeling and payments with promotional photos of the destroyed portraits, in protective sleeves, in a business envelope for mailing. She dialed Portland police.

"I'm reporting abuse of a minor."

"You the victim?"

She faltered. "No," she said. She took a deep breath. "I'm the daughter."

"You got evidence?"

"Talk to the victim. I think she's pregnant."

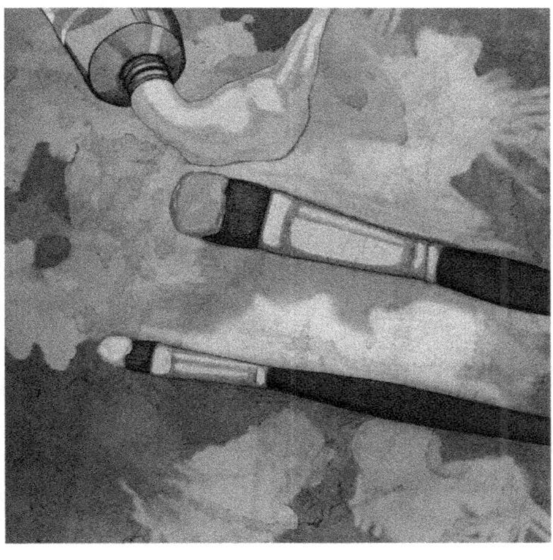

SISTER CARRIE

A Novella

illustration by Peter Healy

illustration by Peter Healy

Sister Carrie

CHAPTER 1

2003
Piedmont of North Carolina

Inside the cemetery bordered by a waist-high iron fence, crowded with modest stone markers and wooden crosses, some draped with plastic flowers, two fresh graves waited side by side, flanked by the caskets of the mother and father of the Broward family. Carrie Broward, a tall, muscular girl with pretty facial features and short-cut straw-blond hair, stepped forward from the sparse crowd. Jessie Broward, her older sister, a full-figured woman with a close resemblance to her sister but with pecan-shell-brown hair, followed to lay flowers on their parents' caskets. The other Broward siblings, Henry and Martha, stood a few feet away, heads bowed and eyes closed.

At the cemetery's edge, a young Arab driver in a dark suit and tie leaned against one of the two freshly washed hearses, spotless but dull from decades of use. His eyes did not leave the sisters. A minister delivered a final prayer for the deceased. The gnarled fingers of an old woman sitting on a three-legged stool painfully searched the frets of her weary guitar for the strummed chords of "Just a Closer Walk with Thee." The service concluded, the mourners drifted toward the church, and the undertaker directed workers to lift the straps of the first coffin for its descent into the earth.

The next morning, the four Broward children gathered to divide their parents' possessions at the modest, century-old, family farmhouse with a tilted for-sale sign on a stick at the end of the dirt drive.

"I am not taking on responsibility for a seventeen-year-old," Henry said, pausing mid-brushstroke and turning from the window frame he was painting.

"Quiet, she'll hear you," Martha said from the kitchen, throwing a cracked and chipped casserole dish into a metal trash can with a crash of splintering glass, and turning back to scrub glassware in the sink.

Jessie went to the front door to look for Carrie. "She's carrying stuff out of the tool shed."

"Don't let her throw out any power tools," Henry said.

"I've only got a one-bedroom apartment," Jessie said, picking up a broom and sweeping.

"Well, she can't stay here alone. You'd have to move out here," Martha said.

"It's forty miles."

"Get a job closer."

"There's no jobs here. No people."

"I can't afford it," Henry said. "Her living with us. Marie is trying to get into college."

Carrie came in the front door. Jessie stopped sweeping the fireplace hearth.

"Can I keep this?" Carrie asked. She held up a child's oak chair less than two and a half feet high, with a hoop back and spindle slats.

"It's junk," Henry said.

"It's was mother's when she was a little girl," Carrie said. "She told me."

"Bullshit."

"Leave it in the shed," Martha said. "Sell it with the house."

"I want it for my kids," Carrie said. She set the chair defiantly near the front door and went back to the shed to finish cleaning.

"That is exactly why I won't take her," Martha said. "Obstinate. Disrespectful. I have no responsibility to live with that for the rest of my life." A stemmed glass splintered as she threw it in the trash.

They worked in tense silence for a few minutes.

"You're the one, Jessie. You're closest to her," Henry said.

"She'd at least be able to stay close to where she was born," Martha added. "She doesn't have the smarts to make it in a big city."

"Move into a bigger apartment, for Christ's sake," Henry said to Jessie.

"And who will pay for that?" Jessie said.

Silence.

"Well?"

Martha went somewhere into the back of the kitchen, out of view. Henry stared out the window and kept working.

"I'm not taking her on," Jessie said. "I can't afford it."

"Sell what's left after today," Martha said, coming back and wiping her hands on a dish towel.

"There's nothing of value," Jessie said. "You've taken everything."

"I'll try to send an allowance," Martha said.

"How much?"

"I can't afford more than a few dollars a month. Jake won't give anything extra to me. I'll have to take it out of my house budget."

"Then I get what's in the bank accounts," Jessie said.

"No way," Henry said. "I'll be the executor."

"It's the only way I can take her on," Jessie said.

Martha picked up a box full of dishes and started toward her truck. She looked to Henry. "You've got more money than all of us put together," she said.

"I've got family responsibilities," Henry said.

"And a big boat," Martha retorted.

"I make just above poverty wage," Jessie said. "Hourly. Nothing guaranteed."

Martha reentered. "Give her the money, Henry. It can't be much anyway."

Henry paused. "Only part. And only if Carrie is living with her."

By late afternoon, cars and a van were packed, and Martha left for Michigan and Henry for Arizona. As Jessie locked up the house, she pretended not to see that Carrie had tucked the child's chair under some blankets in the back of her car.

For weeks after the funeral, from her bedroom, Jessie heard quiet sobs coming from Carrie, who was sleeping on the sofa bed in the living room. Carrie missed their parents and the farm, but she rarely spoke of them. And with time, the crying disappeared. Carrie got a job in a movie theater working at the concession stand. She liked helping the patrons and considered her job a career to conquer. And she stayed busy. When Jessie returned from her work as an assistant for an optometrist, she'd usually find Carrie polishing, scrubbing, and cleaning the apartment. For recreation Carrie chatted on the Internet on Jessie's computer, or watched movies or late-night reruns of I Love Lucy on TV.

Jessie loved Carrie as best she could—better than she did Martha and Henry, for that matter—and convinced herself she liked having Carrie around, but she couldn't bury the burden of inherited parenthood. It wasn't personal. Jessie really didn't have room for a teenage girl, or anybody, in her apartment, and she felt trapped. Worst of all, there was no relief. Henry and Martha still refused to consider taking Carrie in, even on a rotating schedule, and Jessie had no support. No money had been sent by either Henry or Martha.

The reality haunted Jessie now. Carrie had dropped out of high school to work the farm, selling produce roadside and in town markets. She would never go back to school, and college had never been considered. As Carrie settled in, Jessie's dream of a loving husband and a happy brood of children of her own faded. So Jessie prayed and thought, thought and prayed, and finally accepted that her new responsibilities of mothering Carrie would never go away. She determined to bring up Carrie with their parents' Christian principles, and keep her innocent from worldly sins.

CHAPTER 2

One Tuesday, almost four months after the funeral, Jessie waited at the apartment front door to take Carrie to work at the movieplex. Carrie, who was in Jessie's cramped bedroom with the door open, typed laboriously on Jessie's computer with her index fingers. Mom's child's rocking chair—the aged, scratched, and dented oak oiled and polished by Carrie—sat against the wall squeezed between the bed and the computer stand.

"Hurry, it's raining," Jessie called.

"I can take the bus," Carrie called back.

"I can't be late. Shut it off."

"He wants to meet me!" Carrie exclaimed as the screen displayed a chat-room return.

"Who?"

"Zamel."

"Zamel? What's with Zamel?"

"He says he saw me at the funeral."

Jessie entered the room. "You don't know him."

"He's single. He lives alone. He fixes computers and works part time for the funeral home."

"You can't tell crap on the Internet. He might be a rapist, or a serial killer."

"He's not."

"A terrorist, even!"

"He loves animals. He wants a puppy. He misses his mother in Iran."

"Don't promise him anything."

"He wants to meet me at the mall."

"No!"

"He wants to meet you, too."

"That will never happen."

Carrie typed a reply and turned off the computer. "You didn't say yes, did you?" Jessie said.

"I can do what I want."

"Not until you're eighteen. And maybe not then."

Carrie grabbed a jacket from the bed as Jessie slipped into her rain gear and opened the door.

"You are not going to see that boy!" Jessie said as they walked to the car.

CHAPTER 3

Two days later, Jessie and Carrie sat at a white-painted metal table for four in the second-floor mall food court. Jessie wore jeans and a sweatshirt; Carrie had on tight slacks and a lace-trimmed blouse low cut to show cleavage, and orange plastic hoop earrings dangling from her ears.

"I hope he's not late," Carrie said for the second time.

"We're twenty minutes early," Jessie replied. She had no idea how to handle this infatuation that seemed to make Carrie contrary to everything she said. She picked up a picture of the guy that Carrie had printed from the Net. "I can't see his face," she said. It was fuzzy like a picture from a store surveillance camera.

Carrie jumped up. "There he is!"

Zamel rose inching above the meshing top stair of the escalator. He was six inches shorter than Carrie and built like he was prepubescent, but he wore adult clothes—a black short-sleeved shirt, tan Sansabelt slacks, and white running shoes. His black hair shined, his white teeth gleamed when he smiled, contrasting with his dark skin. Carrie ran and took his hand but he glanced at Jessie and then, gently and shyly, pulled his hand away. Jessie wasn't ready to acknowledge him yet and remained impassive; still, he nodded to her as he and Carrie approached.

Zamel pulled out a chair for Carrie and then stood before Jessie, who was almost at eye level with him while sitting, and staring at him relentlessly.

"It is a pleasure to meet you," Zamel said.

"Really?"

"Carrie has told me all about you. You are like a mother to her."

"I'm her sister. She lives with me."

"She's told me. I'm so sorry to hear about your dear parents. So sudden."

Jessie shook her head in disbelief. "You might as well sit down."

"It would be my pleasure to buy you a drink. I know Carrie loves Dr. Pepper with lots of ice."

Jessie paused, concerned that she was not Christian enough to be ashamed of her impulse to order something expensive. "Chocolate milkshake," she said.

"My favorite also." Zamel left for drinks.

Carrie beamed. "Isn't he wonderful? So polite."

"He's darker than I thought."

"He's Persian."

"Like Persia is in Africa somewhere. He's not one of us."

Carrie turned her head away in anger.

"Break it off now," Jessie said. "Don't let it get complicated."

"Be nice to him, Jessie. For me."

Jessie begrudgingly admired the way Zamel placed the milkshake before her, first carefully laying a brown paper napkin, and another one to the side, removing the straws from their paper wrappers, careful to never touch them, handing them to her and then serving Carrie. He had a cup of water for himself.

"Thanks," Jessie said to Zamel, glancing quickly at Carrie to convince her she wasn't satisfied in any way by the performance.

"Pleased to have the opportunity," Zamel said.

"Are you legal?" Jessie asked.

"I have student visa. I take classes at Stringer Community College. I hope to apply for a green card."

"You have family?"

"Yes. In Iran."

"You saw Carrie at the funeral?"

"I was there. Yes."

"You tracked her down?"

"Not exactly. I found her on the Internet. I work with computers."

Jessie squinted, her brow creased.

Carrie clasped Zamel's arm. "Leave us, Jessie," she pleaded.

"I don't think so."

"You promised."

"I never …"

"P … l … e … a … s … e!"

Carrie and Zamel wore identical forlorn looks that made Jessie suspicious of predesigned agendas. She sighed inwardly and walked toward the Sears store entrance, looking back over her shoulder at the two of them, now talking intently.

Two hours later Jessie led Carrie by the arm from the mall to her Ford Focus. Zamel waited near the doors of the mall exit, grinning. What exactly had gone on?

"He is so cool," Carrie said.

They walked to opposite sides of the car. Jessie paused before unlocking the doors.

"That's it. No more, Carrie. He's not right for you."

Carrie tensed. They got in the car. Jessie put the key in the ignition. "We're going to the museum next Sunday," Carrie said.

In the name of God! Jessie thought. She had hoped this would be the end. Not the beginning. Not Carrie falling for some Internet guy. And she cringed inwardly at Carrie's blatant disregard for her authority.

"Absolutely not!" she said. "Tell him no."

"I can take the bus. He doesn't have a car."

Jessie started the engine. "It's over. I mean it." She backed out of the parking space. Carrie stared determinedly out the side window hoping to get a last glimpse of Zamel.

CHAPTER 4

Sunday was a free day at the museum. Jessie waited with Carrie outside the front door. Zamel walked briskly from the bus stop carrying a bunch of flowers, the stems wrapped in a paper towel: daisies, bluebonnets, Queen Anne's lace, a few dandelions, a white blossom, a few pussy willows. He'd probably found them in a field.

He bowed to a smiling Carrie, then presented the flowers to Jessie. They had clearly cooked this up in their Internet chats. Jessie's eyes moistened but she quickly recovered, with a stern look. She struggled to hide pleasure that was impossible to explain and out of proportion to the gift of the scraggy bouquet.

"Do you like them?" Zamel asked.

"They're all right."

"For a beautiful lady."

"Monkey babble." Jessie pulled her keys from her jacket pocket. "Wait here," she said and walked to her parked car.

She opened the trunk and carefully positioned the flowers. She freed a bloom in danger of being crushed by the closing lid. She locked the car and smiled reluctantly to herself, making sure Zamel and Carrie could not see that she was inexplicably pleased in a way she had not felt for a long time.

Jessie followed Carrie and Zamel through the turnstiles into the lobby. Zamel picked up a guide map at an information kiosk and traced a route with his finger to Carrie. As they went off, Jessie followed yards behind, keeping them in sight, up the grand staircase to the galleries.

Jessie browsed alone in the main gallery, careful to position herself so she could see Carrie and Zamel, side by side, in an adjacent gallery. A Victorian reproduction of a life-size bronze statue of a nude male Greek—in full extension throwing a discus—caught her eye. The genitalia were worn shiny smooth from the touches of art patrons. After a quick feel, Jessie pulled back her hand and furtively glanced over to make sure that Carrie and Zamel were not watching. She couldn't tell. She quickly gazed at a marble Madonna and child statue. When she looked again Carrie and Zamel could not contain their smiles. Jessie blushed with humiliation.

She moved along quickly, so flustered she couldn't concentrate on the art … and now she didn't feel confident enough to look for Carrie and Zamel, who had disappeared. She paused to calm down and collect her thoughts. She had every right to touch that statue. It wasn't a sin. Thousands of others had. She was here to protect Carrie. Don't get distracted! When she saw Carrie and Zamel cross a corridor a few minutes later, she headed toward them; Zamel left when he saw her coming.

"What's wrong with him?" she asked Carrie.

"He wants to be alone with me and he's afraid to hurt your feelings."

But Jessie wondered if he might have been offended by the touch. Something in his religion maybe. Sexist probably! She took Carrie's arm. "This isn't working …"

"It's wonderful." Carrie pulled away.

"Please let's leave," Carrie said to her.

Zamel arrived. "It is wonderful painting, don't you think?" he said, pointing vaguely to a wall covered with paintings. "Maybe you join us later for a look at the mummy?"

"What mummy?"

"I think in the Egyptian display in the basement."

Jessie shook her head in disbelief. "You're too smooth for your own good."

"I do not mean to offend, Miss Jessie."

"You can't offend me. I don't listen."

"I just meant ..."

"Please, Jessie, just for a little while," Carrie said again.

"Where will you go?"

"Just around here."

"Maybe in sculpture?" Zamel said.

"Don't leave modern art," Jessie said, thinking specifically about the nudes in sculpture. With just paintings on the wall and only one skinny stick-sculpture of a saint in the gallery center there was little to hide behind in modern art, and little to identify in the abstract imagery that might be erotic to the young.

"As you wish," Zamel said to Jessie.

"I'll be around. You just won't see me."

CHAPTER 5

An hour later, Jessie sat alone at a small table for two in the museum cafeteria. Two plates of mostly eaten pastries were on a brown plastic tray with a half-full cup of mocha coffee and an empty Diet Sprite bottle. Jessie stared without focus, her lips tight with frustration.

There were many people and few seats. A man grabbed the back of the other chair at her table. He was only a few years older than her twenty-five, balding, with a stubble of beard growth and a full mustache.

Tinted glasses shrouded his eyes. His hands were strong, with sure movements.

"Can I sit here?" he asked.

She shrugged without looking at him. "There are other tables."

"I'd like to."

She saw his determination, deliberately surveying him from top to as much as she could see. He seemed scruffy but not dangerous.

"Suit yourself."

He sat. "Harold Lester," he said. He held out his hand.

She waved him off. "I'm not in the mood."

"I know you from church."

"I've never seen you."

"No. When we were in high school."

"I went to church on Easter and Christmas in those days." She stared for a few seconds. "I don't remember you."

"I looked different then," he said.

"I would hope so."

Next to them a family settled in at a table the mother had been saving; the parents yelled at the boisterous children to be quiet. Harold sipped his coffee.

"You still live on the farm?" Harold said.

"I'm from the planet Elagron, in the nebular galaxy," Jessie said.

"An alien who likes art? Don't find many of those."

"I'm chaperoning my sister," she said testily.

"The mean one?"

"Not Martha. The young one."

"In the cafeteria?"

"She's in modern art."

"She's a cube?"

Jessie looked away, barely hiding a smile.

They avoided each other's gazes and sank into silence while the family next to them argued loudly. Harold got up. Jessie thought he would leave and she was aware of a slight regret she couldn't explain; she'd not liked being alone, and in spite of herself, liked having him around. He returned with more coffee and a chocolate chip cookie wrapped in cellophane that he set on her tray.

Jessie placed the cookie on the table and shoved it toward him. "I don't want that." She was still irritated with herself for not wanting him to go away. He was definitely not attractive, and she didn't trust what he said about school and church. But he seemed interested in her.

Harold sat. "You going to stay here all day?" he asked.

"Look. My sister's in love with this guy who's trying to put the make on her at this very moment. I don't plan to let anything happen. I mean anything!"

"She still underage?"

"She's almost seventeen. But she's my little sister."

"Let nature do its thing."

"She met the guy online. He's foreign. He's small, and dark. And he's a bozo."

"I've got a sister. She married a black guy—like from Africa. Two happy peas in a pod."

"That's different."

Harold had no response for a few seconds. "Relax," he said. "Not much can happen in a crowded art gallery."

"You don't know. They're cooking up something right now. I guarantee it."

"Why did you leave them alone?"

"What do you care?" She was sorry she'd left them alone now. "It doesn't make me feel better, your saying that."

The wall clock showed five to four. She stood and shouldered her bag. "Time to go."

Harold stacked trash on the tray without standing. "Leave mine," Jessie said. "They pick up."

Harold cleared the table. "Enjoyed talking to you."

Jessie walked off. She still didn't remember him. Probably he lied, or had been so nerdy no one remembered him. He had a used-too-many-times look that meant he didn't think enough of himself to try to be attractive and memorable. Besides, she really cared for an attractive, successful, strong-willed man who had thrilled her once or twice a week for more than a year now. He was her boss, and he was married, but he wanted her, which made her like her image in the bathroom mirror, and helped her not think about adultery, which she'd come to believe could not exist where true love dwelled.

She looked back but Harold Lester wasn't following.

CHAPTER 6

In minutes Jessie was in the modern gallery. Carrie and Zamel held hands standing in front of an unframed all-black rectangular painting. As Jessie approached, Carrie left him to face Jessie alone. Zamel stayed within easy hearing distance.

"Zamel wants to get married," Carrie said.

Jessie gasped. "You've only had one date."

"We talk all the time on the Net. He knows of a garage apartment next to his cousin and her husband in Butner. There's a bus. I could keep my job. Clean your place once a week."

Zamel closed in. "Miss Jessie. I must express my interest in Miss Carrie."

He had a dreamy, if not a little forlorn, look. "Go away," Jessie said. She fought the idea that he might be sincere.

"Maybe you would like to talk woman to woman for a while?" Zamel asked.

Jessie changed her mind about getting rid of Zamel. It was time to set things straight. "Stay here," she said to Carrie. She grabbed Zamel by the arm, overcame his resistance, and forced him to walk beside her into the next gallery behind a sarcophagus—out of view of Carrie. Zamel tilted his head back to look at her.

"Stay away from my sister," Jessie said.

"I will not do that. She is the object of my affections."

"She is a child."

"She is a woman to make any man a good wife."

"She's never been with a man. She doesn't know …"

"She has told me many times she is chaste."

"Chaste?"

"I too have withheld relations."

Jessie was at a loss for words for many seconds. "We are leaving. Don't follow. And never speak to my sister again."

"I cannot do that."

"You've got no choice."

Jessie found Carrie staring at a Renaissance painting of a half-nude Venus embraced by Mars. Venus's eyes were focused to infinity, as if she were angrily dissecting a distant galaxy. "Let's go," Jessie said.

"No, Jessie."

"It's sex. He wants your sex!"

Jessie dragged a defiant Carrie by the arm into another room farther away from Zamel. Carrie twisted away. Zamel approached.

"He's an alien," Jessie said in a low voice to Carrie's ear.

"He's American," Carrie replied.

"He is not American! You are his green-card solution. Did you think of that?"

Carrie looked puzzled, not knowing exactly what a green card was.

Zamel approached and stepped up in front of Jessie. "She is not my green card!"

"Do you have one?"

"I told you, I will apply."

"There! An American wife might help! Deny that! And what will you do?"

"I go to school. I switch to Piedmont Community College for my degree."

"He's had almost a year of college," Carrie said defensively.

Jessie's clenched hands gripped the sides of her skirt. "There is nothing on God's green earth that will ever make you acceptable. Nothing!" she said to Zamel.

Carrie straightened. "Stop." She paused. Took a deep breath. "I've told him yes."

Zamel moved to close the gap between him and Carrie and took her hand. "I am very happy.," he said.

"I'm going to unplug the computer," Jessie said.

"I want a family," Carrie said.

"You're not married yet!"

Zamel's smile had not changed. "We will have a wonderful family."

Jessie shoved Zamel back and pulled Carrie out of earshot. "I will never, never allow you to marry this Zamel whatever-his-name-is. Never!"

Carrie ran to Zamel, who stood now in the open arch between the galleries. She kissed him on the cheek and whispered, "She's silly sometimes. Everything will be all right. I know her. She barks but never bites."

Jessie reached them quickly. She grabbed Carrie's arm, dragging her toward the exit. Zamel followed at a distance.

"It's over!" Jessie said. She forced Carrie out of the gallery double doors, between parked cars. Zamel watched from the museum exit, his face now dark with concern.

CHAPTER 7

The Reverend Luther Coffey opened the door to his office in the administrative/recreational wing, just behind the twin-steeple red-brick Baptist church. Jessie and Carrie entered. He directed them to upholstered chairs in front of his polished mahogany desk.

The Reverend, at thirty-five, envied the youth of Carrie and Jessie. He wore his white clergy collar like a Catholic priest. He had brushed his short-cut hair twice before they entered. He wore glasses with thin gold-wire frames to project authority—authority he did not feel here with the sisters, who aroused him in ways he could not suppress.

"Jessie! Rarely I see you these days," he said.

He lowered himself into his leather swivel chair as if sitting on a throne. Through his apprehension of being insignificant, he forced a smile, his lips together.

Jessie made no attempt to greet him. "I brought Carrie to talk to you."

He looked to Carrie. "Jessie told me you want to marry."

"Yes, sir."

Jessie interrupted immediately. "I've told her it's wrong from the beginning."

"Have you known him long?" he asked Carrie, although he knew it had only been weeks.

Jessie answered. "They've had two dates."

"Don't start …" Carrie began.

"It's the truth, isn't it? Or have you been sneaking around that I don't know about?"

Carrie looked down, too angry to find words.

Jessie shook her head. "I've tried. God, how I've tried."

The Reverend spoke up. "Let her speak for herself, Jessie."

Carrie leaned forward intently. "Will you marry us?"

He already had an answer ready. "It's too early to think about that. You and your friend—are you engaged?"

"Yes, sir."

"She doesn't have a ring," Jessie said.

"I don't need a ring," Carrie said. "Do I?" she asked the Reverend.

"A ring is a symbol of a deep commitment," the Reverend said.

"He doesn't have the money now," Carrie said. "He promised he'll have it later."

"See! He doesn't have commitment," Jessie said.

"That's a lie," Carrie said.

"Rings cost money," Jessie said. "Where would that jerk get the money?"

"A ring doesn't have to be expensive," Carrie said.

"There's more to it than that," the Reverend said. He had roughly outlined his approach in his mind before they arrived and he started on his plan. "You could come for sessions with this boy. There are things to be explored, decisions to be made. Then you could start planning for the future together."

"He'll never come for sessions," Jessie said emphatically.

"You don't know what he'll do," Carrie said.

"Is he of the faith?" the Reverend asked. Jessie's concern impressed him. She had taken over the motherly role for Carrie quickly and efficiently. He admired that. Liked her for it.

"No, sir," Carrie said.

"He's Muslim," Jessie said. "Not even Christian."

The Reverend addressed Carrie. "Do you think he can be saved? Could you help him convert?"

Carrie avoided his gaze.

"Ask him, my child," the Reverend said to Carrie. "He might be the major convert of the season."

"I don't see baptism for this guy, now or ever," Jessie said. "His name's Zamel. Does that sound like a Christ disciple?"

The Reverend smiled at Jessie, then spoke to Carrie. "I could talk to him. Man to man. Ask things your father might have asked. Bring up the possibility of conversion."

"He'll meet with you. He said he would," Carrie said.

Jessie glared at Carrie. "He'll never show."

"He's not like that," Carrie said.

"Let's give him chance, Jessie," the Reverend said. He looked at Carrie. "Wednesday afternoon at two?"

"He works."

"Thursday evening, then. At seven?"

Jessie looked dubious. "You want them both?"

He hadn't considered including Carrie, or Jessie. It was not a good idea. "Maybe Zamel alone," he said. "Then you later," he added, looking at Carrie.

Jessie drove intently, staring ahead. Carrie looked out the side window. "The Reverend will never marry you to someone outside the faith. It would be his sin—and yours," Jessie said.

Carrie stayed silent until they were almost home. "I'm not going to change my mind."

Jessie winced at her growing loss of control. Carrie no longer had her open innocence to all things serious; she was snarled in love. It was as if she were adopted or something. Not like the sisters they had always been. Jessie appealed for help. "Pray. Ask God."

Carrie's face tightened.

Jessie angered. "I'm speaking to you!"

Carrie still said nothing, even in the time it took for Jessie to nose into a space at the apartment complex.

CHAPTER 8

Jessie entered the Reverend's church consultation office with Zamel, her hand gripping his upper arm. The Reverend sat behind his desk and did not stand.

"This is the guy," Jessie said.

"I am Zamel." Zamel reached awkwardly across the desk to shake the Reverend's hand.

"Welcome," the Reverend said.

"It is my honor, sir."

"Sit down." Jessie sat, too.

"I thought he was to come alone?" the Reverend asked Jessie.

"I wanted to come alone," Zamel said.

"There you go," Jessie said. "No respect."

"It's what we agreed," the Reverend said.

"I thought it best," Jessie said defensively, offended at the Reverend's rebuke.

The Reverend never registered Jessie's hostility. "You would like to marry our Carrie?" he said to Zamel.

"We are very compatible."

"You are not Christian?"

"No sir, I am not. But I have many family and friends who have married Christians. Our religions are highly compatible."

The Reverend frowned. "You speak like an intelligent man. How can you believe mixing religions can be good?"

"We are in love, sir."

Jessie spoke to both Zamel and the Reverend. "Carrie doesn't know what love is."

"I beg to differ, Miss Jessie. She is not a child," Zamel said.

"But she is Christian. I think that is Jessie's point," the Reverend said.

"She is acceptable to me," Zamel countered.

"We would welcome you in the church," the Reverend said.

"I would be pleased to consider it," Zamel said.

"Before you get married?" Jessie asked.

"Yes, ma'am. If it's possible."

"You would need to attend our classes for converts," the Reverend said. "They're excellent."

"It's not a one-shot deal," Jessie said. "It takes time."

"Of course I will give it consideration," Zamel said. "I will always do what is best for my Carrie."

The Reverend reached into a drawer for an appointment book and then extended a printed sheet of paper to Zamel. "Wednesday nights. Seven to ten. I can have you in the class next week."

Zamel took the paper and read.

The Reverend continued. "You can sign at the bottom. The tuition is payable in installments. Twenty dollars for the registration fee up front."

Zamel took the paper and picked up the pen that the Reverend had pushed toward him on the desk. But he did not sign. "I must wait for my payday."

"The fee is required," said the Reverend.

"Yes, sir. Of course."

The Reverend considered. "Your payday will be fine," he said, "but you'll have to pay the initial installment and the registration fee, too, before starting."

Zamel signed and then stood. "Is that all, sir?"

Jessie spoke to Zamel. "Go to the car. I want to talk to the Reverend."

When the door closed, Jessie took a seat again. The Reverend came from behind the desk, pulled a chair close to Jessie, and sat.

"I never knew you charged for conversion classes," Jessie said.

The Reverend smiled. "We never charge. But I thought I'd test his commitment."

"He'll never pay."

"I won't marry them unless he's Christian. He's a polite young man but I find mixed marriages appallingly unsuccessful. And I've always liked Carrie. I want to discourage him."

"You promise? You'll never marry them, Christian or not?" Jessie said.

"Trust me. He'll never convert." The Reverend smiled.

They both stood. The Reverend took Jessie's hand in both of his. Jessie flinched almost imperceptibly at the intimacy of the gesture.

"Thank you for coming," the Reverend said with excessive intensity. "I'll pray for Carrie. You should, too."

The Reverend still held Jessie's hand in his. She looked uncomfortable and pulled it away quickly, then headed for the door.

CHAPTER 9

Two weeks later, Jessie came back to the apartment a little early after work, worried about Carrie and her plans. A waist-high, taped and sealed packing box half-blocked the door. Carrie was packing an open suitcase on her sofa bed. Jessie walked straight to Carrie. A silver wedding band on Carrie's finger caught the afternoon light from the bedroom window. Jessie froze, waiting for an explanation. "Talk to me!" she finally said.

Carrie kept packing, refusing to look.

"After all I've done for you. The sacrifices. The worry." Jessie glared. "What about Mom and Dad? They wouldn't approve. They'd hate him."

Carrie paused. Her jaw clenched.

"In God's name, you owe it to their memory," Jessie continued.

"Stop it!"

"Just wearing a ring doesn't make you married, you know. You got to have a church wedding with a real minister."

Carrie closed the top of the suitcase and faced Jessie. "It's all legal. It's Muslim."

"My God. You've always dreamed of a church wedding."

"Zamel loves me. You'll never have that. Not with Patrick."

"I don't want a foreigner for a brother-in-law." Jessie cried without wanting to.

After a few seconds, Carrie smiled hesitantly, hoping Jessie's face would show pleasure—that she would accept and share Zamel and her happiness.

Jessie refused to respond. She couldn't stop sobbing. Carrie went back to packing.

"I hope you'll be happy," Jessie finally managed, but she couldn't hide the sarcasm in her voice.

A rusted pickup truck driven by a male Arab pulled into a parking space in front of the apartment. Zamel got out of the passenger side and walked slowly to Carrie; she hugged him. He reacted hesitantly at first, then embraced her. He walked over to Jessie and took both her hands in his. She reluctantly allowed him to come face to face with her.

"I am indeed fortunate to have such a beautiful sister," he said.

How irritating, this happiness on his face. "That's garbage," she said. "You know it. Besides, I'll never be your sister."

"She's a sister-in-law, Zamel," Carrie said.

"I know!" Zamel said brusquely. He carried out the smaller box and Carrie followed with the suitcase. They returned for the big box, and positioned themselves one on each side. Jessie refused to help.

"You'll come visit?" Carrie asked Jessie.

"I don't think so."

Carrie looked away. She still wanted Jessie's blessing.

Zamel lifted the box and with his eyes directed Carrie to help. "You are always welcome at our place. You are family," he said over his shoulder to Jessie. They joggled the box through the door and carried it down the walk.

Jessie followed them out the door but stopped at the top of the steps. She wanted no clue for them that might expose how empty she felt. How abandoned. She went back inside before they were even near the truck. She closed the door, leaned against the wall, and cried.

CHAPTER 10

Zamel's place was a two-car garage rented to live in but with almost no conversions for comfort—no interior walls, and the only light seeping in through a small rectangular glass window on a side door and the single long slits of frosted glass on each of the two sliding front doors. A sink, a knee-high refrigerator on the floor, and a four-burner stove clustered in the rear corner. The only furniture in the room was an aluminum-tube folding chair with plastic woven strips on the back and seat, and a small wooden table. A TV set sat on the floor near the single electrical outlet, and a box-spring mattress on a metal frame was to the side. Indelible oil stains from years of leaky engines stained the bare concrete floor. There was a toilet and a shower that was a showerhead attached to a garden hose, tied loosely to metal tracks that supported the retractable door. Shower water drained over the sloping floor to a central drain.

On their wedding night, Carrie made a cheese and mayonnaise sandwich for each of them. She lit a candle, melted the bottom end, placed it in a saucer, and set it on a packing box. They sat on the floor near the stove holding their plates. After dinner, she expertly tucked stained white sheets on the mattress. It was twilight. She washed the plates in the sink and dried them with a clean but ragged towel and stacked them below the sink where the pipes were. Without a word she took off her T-shirt, folded it, and put it on her closed suitcase. She placed her bra on top of the shirt. She unbuttoned the top of her jeans, slipped out of her pink sneakers, and undressed with a reticent lack of haste, worried at her lack of knowing how to please.

"We must bathe," Zamel said, reaching into a Walmart bag and handing her a just-bought-today towel. "You go first," he said.

A toilet near the front corner of the garage was set directly on the cement. Behind it, she twisted the faucet handle on a T-valve to start the flow of water into the hose that led to the showerhead. After a few seconds, water splashed on her shoulder. She showered and dried, and walked to the bed. Zamel was undressed. He covered his manhood with a wadded shirt.

As Zamel showered, Carrie sat on the edge of the bed, her arms wrapped around her knees, the towel around her shoulders. She watched Zamel dry, and held her breath as he walked to her with the towel in his hand. He turned off the bare lightbulb dangling from the ceiling over the sink. The only weak light came from the cloudless sky through the frosted windows.

"Zamel," she said softly.

He positioned her over the bed, her knees on the floor, her elbows on a pillow on the mattress, her face inches from the sheets, and he took her standing up. She gave a painful gasp. He was finished in seconds. When she realized he was complete, she fell forward on the bed and rolled over.

"Hold me, Zamel," she said.

His face was a shadow. "I could not contain it," he said. He sat on the bed and put his head in his hands.

"I love you," she said.

He moved rapidly into the shadows on the other side of the garage. It was dark now, the night light from outside providing barely enough illumination to maneuver.

Carrie lay on her back with a blanket over her. She heard Zamel's breathing, but could only see his blurred silhouette in the chair.

"Zamel," she said softly. She waited. "That was very good."

She held her breath in the silence.

He spoke, and she started breathing again. "You make me happy," he said. "You are a very good wife."

Carrie ignored the rodent scurrying outside the wall near the head of the bed. She was too happy to care, and she enjoyed her pleasure before falling asleep when Zamel came to bed to lie beside her … and hold her.

CHAPTER 11

Even as a new bride, Carrie worked her movie job six days a week. She Windexed the display cases for packaged candy twice a day, inside and out. She made frequent small batches of popcorn to keep her customers supplied with the freshest. She mopped her space before and after her shift, and greeted returning customers as friends.

At home Carrie made her marriage compatible. She scrubbed the garage, bought curtains for the side door, got storage bins for their clothes and possessions. She got a small stand for the eighteen-inch TV and bought, with her savings, a futon for two. Zamel joined her when he was home in the evenings, sitting next to her. At times he took her hand in his as they watched sitcoms and talent shows, and she felt his always-chilled hand turn warm in hers. At night, he made love to her, exploring her in ways she would relive for days. She kept their sheets clean and washed the blanket twice a week. She learned to cook what he liked from his cousin's wife, Fatima, who lived in the house next door. On the nights Zamel never came home and she was alone, she learned to weave mats on a hand loom Fatima no longer used because the children were so daily and she lived in clouds of exhaustion and suffered from loneliness and her shame of withdrawal from her wifely duties after her second child was born breech and with difficulties.

Jessie didn't see Carrie at all during this time, and Carrie and Zamel had no home phone. Jessie missed Carrie's company, and Carrie had never invited her to Zamel's place. Jessie's loneliness intensified her curiosity about Carrie's life, so one day on her afternoon off she went to see Wonderwoman II at the movieplex. Carrie was behind her counter. Jessie whispered to her when she thought no one could hear: "I miss you," she confessed. "What's up with Zamel?"

"He's busy." Carried smiled. She was chronically content.

"You guys must be rich. Two jobs and all."

"His mother's in Iran. We send our money to her so she can come to America."

Carrie gave Jessie a large popcorn without charge. Butter, too.

"Maybe we could hit the mall sometime?" Jessie asked.

"I can't now, Jessie. I've got to be home for Zamel. He comes home at all hours."

"I'm your sister!"

"Maybe later, after we're settled a little more."

"He doesn't love you."

Carrie busied herself straightening the candy bar display.

Jessie held back her anger. Carrie was taking marriage too seriously if she was turning her back on the only family who cared about her now. And creepy Zamel was obviously a slavemaster. She doubted this marriage would last the year. She took her popcorn. Carrie stood up, still smiling. God, she missed her baby sister talking about her ups and downs; there had been a loving closeness over the years, especially when she had moved in and Jessie took on Carrie's troubles as her own.

CHAPTER 12

A month passed. Jessie's loneliness and worry persisted. Finally she determined to visit Carrie; it was, after all, her obligation to care for her sister. She needed to know what had happened. Was Carrie happy? Who were her friends? Would she and Zamel work out?

Jessie parked her car in front of Carrie's two-car garage, set back a few yards from the street. The garage looked flimsy, standing alone on the lot; the house to the left was now merely a concrete-block foundation smothered with packed, hardened ashes from a fire years ago. The only entrance to the garage was an undersized door on the side, as the two front sliding doors had been nailed immobile with wooden two-by-fours crisscrossing the outside.

To the right of the garage, the small porch of a one-story house was littered with bicycles and toys and a rusted, ancient barber's chair.

From the back of her car Jessie took out Carrie's rocking chair and approached the side door. Carrie opened it a crack as she approached. Only half of Carrie's face was visible.

"You home alone?"

Through the narrow opening, only dark was behind Carrie, with no details visible. The frown on Carrie's face was stark and unfriendly. "It's a mess," Carrie said.

Jessie waited for the door to open, holding the chair. "I thought you might want this."

Carrie opened the door a little more, then changed her mind and narrowed the opening. "We aren't ready …"

"Here. Take the chair," Jessie insisted.

Carrie hesitated, opened the door again, and took the chair.

Jessie hoped to see her sister's living conditions, but only glimpsed the bleak darkness of an interior with little natural light.

"Some other time, Jessie. It's early. Zamel's not dressed."

Jessie backed away, her curiosity not satisfied. "Sure," she said, trying to sound lighthearted. "Hey, take care. Call me."

Carrie closed the door without a word.

Jessie slammed her car door, cranked the engine. Someone yelled. Zamel ran from the garage shirtless, waving his arms, then putting his hands through the armholes of a short-sleeved shirt and pulling it on over his head. As he approached, Jessie rolled down the window.

Zamel leaned down to see better. "Miss Jessie. It's kind for you to come. To bring Carrie's chair."

"No problem."

"I wanted to talk."

"You're never quiet, Zamel."

"I might need your help. For my work."

"It's not Christian, but I don't want to help you with your work."

"You don't have to do anything."

"That makes me very happy."

"I must be honest," Zamel said. "I wanted to see about … maybe I could—I mean Carrie and me … say, borrow your car sometime. I need for Carrie and me to shop. Maybe for an afternoon?"

"Absolutely not."

"Just for a short time. And maybe I won't need it," he said.

"No."

"Later. Would you maybe shift your mind? For Carrie?"

Jessie rolled up the window. Zamel frowned as she drove off. Jessie could see him in her rearview mirror until the car turned the corner at the end of the street and slipped between the trees that lined the two-lane county road.

CHAPTER 13

The night Carrie planned to tell Zamel she was pregnant, he did not come home when expected. They still had no phone at home. Zamel's cell phone was always clipped to his Sansabelt waistband. Carrie checked with Zamel's cousin's wife Fatima next door, but she had no news.

After eleven, Zamel burst thought the door, followed by two dark-skinned men his age. "Go to the back," he said to Carrie.

"Are you all right?" she asked. The tension the three men brought into her home made her afraid.

Zamel did not answer. The two men sat on the bed and Zamel pointed Carrie to the back of the garage, behind the two hanging sheets. Carrie complied, closing the opening between the sheets behind her, and sat on a pallet on the floor and listened to a mix of Arabic and English words from the other room: a friend had been arrested, a stolen car had been driven through a glass window into the student center at the college, a bomb had fizzled. She'd heard part of it on the TV news. Even in silences, she could feel the despair in each of them.

Over the next hour the men's words became earnest and repetitive, with frequent corrections and arguments. When they left, Zamel went to Carrie, still huddled on a blanket she'd spread on the floor. He reached down to help her up. "Will everything be all right?" she asked.

"Go to bed!" he said.

She wanted to stay with him. "I need you tonight," she said.

"I'm spent from my work," he said pulling her up from the blanket. "Go to bed!" He sat in one of the folding chairs. "I will sleep here."

She stood still for a moment, wanting to tell him her news. His eyes were closed, his head back, and he was still breathing hard and fast. She backed away from him, turned, and went to bed, laying on her back and staring into the dark.

She waited three days to tell him about the baby. They were watching TV on the futon. "I'm pregnant," she said.

He held her with real joy. "I pray to Allah for a boy," he said.

CHAPTER 14

The Reverend Luther Coffey asked Jessie to dinner. The restaurant table had a red tablecloth, a candle, and silver-plated utensils. He asked about Carrie.

"I'm not sure, but I think she was trying to look happy when I saw her the last time," Jessie said.

The Reverend enjoyed Jessie's intensity about everything. And he loved her wholesome look. "You think it will last?" he asked.

"It's hard to tell about marriages. Maybe there is something there."

"I doubt it. You can't trust foreigners."

"Sometimes he does things that make me wonder if he really cares for her. He wanted to borrow my car."

"Sounds typical. Put you on the spot like that," he said. "He's as smooth as they come. I've seen a lot of them. Desperate for intimacy. Ready to make their stay in a new country as permanent as they possibly can."

"I only saw her for a few seconds. She wasn't glad to see me, but at least she didn't seem frightened of Zamel."

"You thought she might be?"

"Who knows. He's sexist. I imagine they all beat their wives."

"We can't let her heart be broken," he said. "She's too good a person to let that happen."

"I've tried everything!" Jessie said defensively.

"Visit her often. Point out her misery."

"She won't want me. I was hurt when she turned me away."

"She may not know it, but I'm sure she wants to see you." He straightened the silver on each side of his plate, lining it up exactly parallel.

"You didn't see her face when I went to her place," Jessie said.

He paused. "It's the Christian thing to do," he said.

After dinner in the restaurant parking lot, the Reverend opened his car passenger door for Jessie. "Did you have a good time?" he asked.

She didn't answer right away. "I did," she said, slightly unsure of what she had expected of the evening. He was on the edge of boring sometimes, but he cared about Carrie, and she appreciated that.

The Reverend pulled into a motel parking lot off the main street on the way to Jessie's apartment and killed the engine.

Jessie looked at him. "What's up?"

"I thought maybe we could spend some time alone together."

"Here?"

"Someplace private. Someplace where the wrong people won't see."

"See what?"

"Us talking together."

"We just went to dinner. We talked at dinner." Jessie frowned. "Please take me home."

"Couldn't we talk here then? In the car? We don't have to get out."

"Instead of going inside a motel?"

He couldn't say what he felt. She seemed unaware of the longing he was suffering.

"I want to go home," she said.

He mustered his courage. "You mean a lot to me, Jessie."

"Not in a motel. Go home. Take a cold shower."

"It's not like that." But it was a little like that. "We can go somewhere else. I just don't want the congregation gossiping."

She set her jaw and looked away. He started the car, flustered at her refusal. "You've totally misunderstood—"

"I'm a better person than you suppose, Reverend."

"You're a good woman, Jessie. I never meant anything else."

She shook her head in disbelief. "A motel! You, of all people."

CHAPTER 15

Patrick—a tall, thin man with an angular face, sharp features, and blue eyes, wearing a white long-sleeved shirt and a rep tie—pulled up his jockey shorts and stepped into a pair of gray slacks. He fastened his genuine alligator belt, turned to a mirrored cabinet over a metal sink, and, taking a comb from his back pocket, slowly, almost tenderly, combed his red hair.

"It's still good, ain't it?" Patrick said to Jessie with pride. It was the energy he delivered during sex that satisfied him. The strength of his hands on the breasts; his gripping of the arms, holding his subject almost in air upon entry. He retrieved his tasseled Italian-leather shoes (polished to a mirror shine) from under his optometrist's exam chair.

Jessie lay awkwardly on her side on the examining chair, which was reclined to the maximum but still had an angle between the seat and the back.

"You okay?" Patrick said.

"It hurts," Jessie said. She bent her legs to relieve sharp pains in the vagina.

She slid gingerly off the table. She was nude except for her panties, which were nestled around her right ankle. She pulled them up and stepped into her pastel-pink uniform pants, finished buttoning her white uniform blouse.

"It didn't hurt last time, did it?" he asked.

"That was different,"

"What's wrong?

"This chair hurts me every time," she said. "Sometimes I can't move right for days."

Patrick pulled a paper towel from a wall dispenser and wiped his hands.

"Can't we go somewhere else?" she said.

Patrick was slipping his arms into his white knee-length professional coat. An ophthalmoscope fell out of the side pocket and clattered to the floor. He swore.

"Did you hear me?" Jessie said. "This is important."

"Like a motel? You know I can't take the chance now."

"Not a motel. Someplace romantic."

"Not the right time. Too risky."

"When, then?"

"The kids love Christmas. I've got to wait till after Christmas."

"You'll tell her about divorce?"

"I promised, didn't I?"

"That was so long ago."

"Here is best. After work. Locked down."

"Could we get a place of our own even before the divorce?"

"Quit complaining, Jessie."

"I'm tired of being convenient on an exam chair that hurts."

"We can do it on the floor. I can shove the slit lamp out of the way."

"That's humiliating."

He was busy pocketing his wallet and his keys, stuffing a few papers and charts into a leather briefcase.

"Do you love me?" Jessie asked.

He shuffled through some charts. "That's hurtful, Jessie. After all this time. How could you ask that?"

"It's not a complicated question. Do you love me? Yes or no?"

"Of course I do. You're everything to me."

"Have you ever hinted you're leaving? Do you talk to her about it?"

He laughed. "God, no. She'd explode."

"Why not tell her now? If you love me?"

Patrick adjusted the exam chair to its normal upright position, ready for tomorrow's patient load. "Stop whining." he said.

"I need respect, Patrick? Just one little pea pod of old-fashioned respect? I'm not a whore off the streets."

Patrick's face reddened. The constant probing irritated him. "I'm tired of this shit."

Jessie's heart pounded. Her mind swirled with accusations mixed with demands for an expression of love. "You're tired? You're tired of making love to me? Is that what you mean?"

"Don't twist my words."

"Say what you mean."

"Stop bitching, Jessie."

"I need to know. I need to know you love me. I can't go on without that."

He latched his briefcase. "You aren't worth this crap."

The sense of her being used broke through, although she knew it had been lurking inside her for months. "I hate you," she said.

He hit her full-face with the flat of his hand. She fell to the floor. He backed away, breathing heavily.

She rose on her knees, groping for the exam chair for support. "Is this the real you?" She felt her face with her fingers.

He stood rigid with anger. Why would this barely competent, impudent assistant turn into a nagging bitch after all he'd given her? Who else would have fucked her? Christ, she looked like the farmer's daughter she was. "You're fired. You've never been any good."

"You're sick," she said. Obviously he didn't love her now, but to preserve her self-respect she tried to believe he had needed her at the time they started as lovers. And he had made her feel alive for a while, anyway. Now she feared the humiliation that her trust in his love had been so wrong.

He refused to speak, trying to get control of himself, trying not to hit her again.

She could not look at him, afraid to confirm that he cared nothing for her. She stood unsteadily, walked to the door, and undid the lock. She walked into the dark office past the reception desk. She grabbed her shoulder bag that had been stuffed out of sight under a counter. She closed the outer door with deliberation and the least amount of sound she could manage.

CHAPTER 16

Dark storm clouds made the night sky dimmer than usual in the garage. Carrie arranged her table on an upturned cardboard packing box. She had made two peanut butter and grape jelly sandwiches on white bread, each on its own paper towel. Sliced wedges of tomato were carefully arranged on a saucer next to a clear glass saltshaker. Two Ball jars were partially filled with orange soda. A single white frosted cupcake, with a red candle stuck in the top, was at one side. She lit the candle with a paper match from a fold-over pack. The flame burned evenly in the still air. Zamel sat cross-legged on the floor. He picked up the sandwich. She sat on the edge of the bed and watched lovingly as he ate.

"Don't stare," he said, "It's rude."

"It's fun being married," she said. "You too?"

Zamel continued eating.

"Well?"

Zamel put down his half-eaten sandwich and salted a tomato slice.

"Say something sweet," she said. "It's our anniversary."

Zamel looked surprised at first but frowned to cover any show of emotion. He ate another tomato slice.

"I know you love me," she said, without a bit of rancor at his aloofness.

Zamel's face remained impassive.

"You're silly," she said. "You are a silly little boy."

Zamel frowned at first at what he took as a rebuke. But when he looked at her he knew she was incapable of intentional hurt. He rendered a faint, contained smile, and his look softened.

"Come on. Say it," she teased.

Zamel laughed. He took her in his arms. He whispered in her ear. "You are the best happening of my entire life."

"Say it, you silly goose."

He laughed and kissed her with growing passion.

"Say you love me!"

He kissed her again, and she knew that he couldn't say those three easy words he thought might diminish him in the world, even though no one would ever know. And it didn't matter.

CHAPTER 17

At the movieplex, Jessie paid for a ticket and passed the ticket taker at the turnstile before she saw Carrie, working alone, filling the roaster pan with popcorn seeds. A few patrons passed by as Jessie walked up slowly to the counter. "Hey, girl," she said.

"Still with butter?" Carrie smiled.

"On a diet. Broke up with Patrick. Got to start looking good."

"He's a jerk."

Carrie handed Jessie a large tub of popcorn. As always, no payment was expected. But Jessie knew Carrie would put money in the till for it after she left.

"I'm looking for work," Jessie said.

Carrie looked radiant. Her skin glowed; her hair was lustrous. She served another customer candy and a Coke. Jessie moved to one side and ate her popcorn until the customer left.

"You guys must be rich. Two jobs and all," Jessie said. "Zamel's mother is coming from Iran. We send money for her." "Your place large enough?"

Carrie hesitated, unable to look Jessie in the eye. "I wanted to tell you. We're going to have a baby."

"Oh, no!"

"Zamel wants a boy."

"And you? What do you want?" Jessie asked.

"A boy would be nice. Like Zamel."

"Can you afford it? It costs, like, thousands to have a kid."

"His mama will help."

"His mama will suck up everything you have."

Carrie opened the transparent door and fluffed the popcorn with a scoop. "We're happy," she said.

"I don't believe that, Carrie. You're living like welfare."

Even in the bustle of the lobby, the silence between them turned awkward. Carrie undid the top button of her shirt, and with the back of her hand showed an almond-size citrine on a silver chain.

Jessie tried to seem unimpressed. "Zamel?" she asked.

"It was his sister's. She died." Carrie buttoned up. She took a paper towel from a roll and wiped the counter intently although it was already spotless. "You'll miss your show," Carrie said. She turned away from Jessie to another customer and smiled.

Jessie fought off the pain of Carrie's sudden disinterest. She hadn't expected a baby so soon. She should have responded with a little more enthusiasm.

"Call me sometime," Jessie said as she walked away.

Carrie waved, barely looking at her. When Jessie was out of Carrie's sight, she turned toward the exit and dumped her popcorn in a trash can. After a little fuss with the manager she got a refund on her ticket and left.

CHAPTER 18

After three weeks of job hunting, Jessie landed a sales job in furniture. A big store all on one level with track lighting and clustered displays.

To avoid having to look at herself, she walked around the cheval floor mirror plopped in the center of a bedroom display in the back section of the store. She hated her too-tight pants and white open-necked blouse with plastic buttons on the front and an oval patch above the left breast pocket stitched with "Gripper's Furniture." She had to carry a sign on a short stick that said: "How can I help you?"

She saw Harold Lester enter the store; he walked straight toward her. "New job?" he asked. He'd shaved off his facial hair and gotten a haircut since she'd seen him, many months ago now, at the museum.

"Go away," she said.

He took out a leather fold-over wallet from his pocket and flashed official identification too fast for her to read it.

"So you're a cop?"

"More like an investigator."

"FBI?"

"I work with them at times."

"And all that BS about old school friends? Church?"

He shrugged. "You like this work?" he asked.

"Temporary. It's barely enough to pay the rent." She positioned the sign in front of Harold and pointed to it. "A dining room suite maybe? I got walnut traditional at 50 percent off."

He shook his head. "I need to ask some questions about this Zamel guy."

"You want a bedroom suite?"

"Come on, Jessie, I'm serious."

"Ms. Broward to you." She wasn't angry, really, just disappointed that he'd lied to her about school. "If he's done something wrong, arrest him. At least that would get him away from my sister."

"There's no proof."

"Of what?"

"Of wrong."

"Is he legal?"

"On a student visa."

"Well, he works a lot of jobs."

"You admire him?"

"I don't like him. Too smooth. Sneaky like. But my sister trusts him. They're going to have a baby." Jessie placed her sign on a checkout counter.

"Do you know his friends?" he said.

"My sister doesn't even want me to visit."

"Does she ever mention his friends?"

"I don't talk to her. She doesn't have a phone."

"He has a cell phone."

"I don't think he lets her use it."

"And she's never mentioned his friends. You went there at least once. Talked to her."

"I said ten sentences to her max at the house."

Jessie picked up a sale brochure and handed it to Harold, who did not take it. "Buy a recliner," she said. "Thirty percent off until the end of the week. I get full-price commission on sale items this week only."

"Nothing today."

"You'll be sorry."

"Hard to believe I'll feel sorry about not buying a recliner," he said as he left.

CHAPTER 19

Jessie took a sick day off from the furniture store. She parked her car on the street and walked up the drive to Carrie's garage home. She hesitated and then, with a deep sigh, summoned the determination to knock on the door. It opened; Carrie appeared. It was dark inside again and impossible to see details behind her.

"Hi," Jessie said.

"I didn't know you were coming," Carrie said.

"You don't have a phone. How could I leave a message?"

"Zamel always keeps it with him for business."

"So what am I supposed to do?" Jessie asked. "Not come?"

"It's okay," Carrie said.

Jessie choked up. "It's not been easy, Carrie, without Patrick."

"You miss him?"

"I don't have anyone now." She didn't miss Patrick. It was just that he had left an uncomfortable void in her life.

Carrie had not opened the door more than a few inches. Zamel did not like visitors when he wasn't in the garage. But she missed Jessie; in spite of herself, her heart filled with pleasure at seeing her. "Not busy. Come in. You can meet Zamel's mother."

Mother! Jessie had no idea Mother had arrived. Why had Carrie turned so secretive with marriage? Was she ashamed she'd be criticized? Ridiculed? Well, Jessie had only told Carrie the truth, and never tried to persuade her with anything else. Who could fault that? Jessie followed Carrie inside.

Bed sheets were fastened to metal garage ceiling supports so the garage space was roughly divided in two. Carrie led her past two pallets, each with a blanket folded at the foot but no sheets, that were spread out on the floor about five feet apart. Carrie held a hanging sheet aside for Jessie to enter the other section. There was a double bed and a mattress on a frame, with no headboard. A woman in a dark dress and a roosari over her head sat on the floor on a small woven red-and-dark-blue carpet, peeling turnips with a serrated knife.

Jessie leaned over to within a few inches of Mother. She spoke loudly and slowly, moving her lips excessively to exaggerate her diction. "I am Jessie. Do you like America?" she asked.

The woman looked away quickly, smiling insecurely, "Am … air … ka … peachy."

"Really," Jessie said. "Nice you came." It was meaner than she had meant.

"Mother has nine children," Carrie said.

"Nine?"

Mother kept looking down, pretending the conversation was not about her.

"When are you due?" Jessie asked Carrie.

"Mother says by the end of next month."

"What does the doctor say?"

Carrie pointed to the bed. "That's where mother sleeps." Carrie took Jessie's hand and led her back through the slit in the hanging sheets.

Carrie showed her plastic boxes stacked behind a sheet draped near the door. "I use this for storage."

She pointed to the two pallets. "Zamel and me sleep here."

"Looks painful, being pregnant and all and sleeping on the floor."

"Once you get used to it, it's not so bad."

Sad you need to explain away your miserable surroundings, Jessie thought, but she held back a retort.

They went back out to where Mother sat. Carrie directed Jessie a short distance to the sink next to the decades-old four-burner electric stove, with a chipped porcelain oven door. A small knee-high counter refrigerator sat on the floor, a brown extension cord creeping along the wall to an outlet. Carrie opened the refrigerator and handed Jessie a soda.

"Mountain Dew is Mother's favorite," Carrie said. She took a glass from the sink and filled it with tap water.

Jessie grabbed Carrie's arm. "I want to talk to you outside." She muscled Carrie out the door onto the drive. Mother did not look up as they left.

A man rode a mower on the lawn of the house next door. Jessie spoke loudly over the noise. "This is stupid."

"You shouldn't have come," Carrie said. Jessie had made her feel unworthy.

Jessie handed back the unopened Mountain Dew. "I don't want this."

Carrie put the it in her dress pocket, still holding her water glass. The mower was farther away, the noise less loud.

"I am so much happier than I ever was," Carrie said in a normal voice.

"You mean happier without me?" Jessie asked. "With Zamel?"

"It's not about getting away from you."

Jessie tensed, clenching her jaw, her hands in fists. Carrie's initial discomfort at having Jessie there confirmed that she had removed Jessie from her life.

The mower was close again.

"You're living like white trash," Jessie said. "It's embarrassing." She paused intently. "You need a doctor."

"You don't know what I need." But Carrie's face softened as her anger waned; she could never stay angry long. The mower waned, too. "Zamel's a good man," she said. "I'm lucky to have him."

Jessie knew she had overreacted; she felt slightly guilty and more conciliatory now. "He's not one of us, Carrie. It's not normal."

Carrie angered again. It wasn't right for Jessie to talk like that. "Don't come back. It's you who is not one of us." The mower noise crescendoed.

"That goddamn mower. Who the hell is that?" Jessie asked.

"George. Zamel's cousin." Carrie said.

"The whole family! How do you stand it?" Jessie shook her head, unable to comprehend.

Carrie wiped tears from her eyes with the back of her hand, then walked back to the garage.

Jessie had failed with Carrie. She had wanted her back, wanted them to be family again.

Jessie walked toward her car. George finished mowing the small patch of grass and drove the mower next to her; he idled the blade.

Jessie was unsure what he intended, and stopped. She saw a woman's face in the window of the house. George shut off the mower. He waved toward the house. "That is Fatima, my wife." Fatima came out of the front door and stood on the step, her hands on her hips. Two children joined her. She spoke to them in an angry tone with foreign words.

"I'm Carrie's sister."

George stared at Jessie. Fatima came out of the house and stood a few feet from Jessie and George, the children stopped shoulder to shoulder a few feet behind her.

"Do you speak English?" Jessie said to George. George was impassive. "You are Zamel's cousin, aren't you?"

"My wife is cousin to the mayor of Hutchings, South Carolina."

La-di-da.

The woman turned to return to the house, roughly shoving the children's shoulders to hurry them along.; the humid air around Jessie felt dense with the woman's hostility.

"Be good to my sister," Jessie said.

"She is like family. We do not want you here."

When Jessie got in her car, George pulled the cord to start the motor. The engine roared.

Jessie's heart was empty. She'd lost what had been between Carrie and her. It wasn't as abrupt as an amputation, more like an oozing hemorrhage, so slow that she really wasn't sure what had left and when it had gone. Had she failed as a surrogate mother? She hadn't succeeded; she would always carry that burden. But worst of all, she'd lost the will to be happy. She had slumped into just getting through each day without a single ray of excitement about the future.

CHAPTER 20

Carrie, now in her final month of pregnancy, washed dishes by hand standing at the sink in the garage apartment. Zamel's mother sat away from Carrie on the bed with a plastic container on her knees, snapping beans. Carrie jerked with surprise and an instant of fear when Zamel and his two comrades, Habib and Tahmin, entered through the side door of the garage. Zamel's mother continued with her work, unperturbed.

The distress on Zamel's face pained her heart. "What's happened?"

"Nothing. Go to the back."

"Tell me what's wrong."

"Be quiet. Take Mother."

The two women went behind the hanging sheets that separated the two areas. Tahmin sat on the bed; Habib squatted on the floor. Zamel pulled up the only chair to a folding card table and sat. They said nothing for more than a minute, Habib breathing deeply. Tahmin placed a laptop computer on the table. "See if it works," he said. Zamel plugged in the power after taking the TV plug from the wall socket. The computer screen lit after a few seconds.

Zamel laughed humorously. "It turns on."

"Does it have enough whatever?"

Zamel navigated for a few seconds. "Not enough memory. And the software is not here. I will look in all the files. But I don't think it's there."

"How could I know?" Habib said.

"Is it his computer? You're sure?" Tahmin asked Habib.

"It was on his desk, in a briefcase. Why wouldn't it be his?" Habib answered.

Tahmin swore. "Look again," Tahmin said to Zamel.

"I cannot test it thoroughly now," Zamel said. "It will take hours to be sure."

"You will have to go back to find another," Tahmin said to Habib.

Habib shrugged. "Let him do it," he said nodding to Zamel.

"He cannot raise suspicion where he works," Tahmin said.

Carrie stuck her head between the sheets. Her face was intent with concern and curiosity. "Do you want something to drink?" she said.

"Leave us," Zamel said.

Habib stood and walked to Carrie. He briefly touched her cheek with the back of his hand. He grinned. "You are woman for the gods."

"Don't touch her," Zamel said. Habib backed away.

"We have things to do," Tahmin said.

Habib gave a short, cruel laugh as Carrie retreated behind the sheets.

Zamel glanced to the computer. "I will test it tonight. Wait until I know for sure if we can use it." Tahmin and Habib moved to the door.

"You must never come here again," Zamel said.

"We will come when we must," Habib said. Zamel stayed motionless until they were gone.

Carrie rushed out from behind the sheets. Mother stayed seated and could be seen as a shadow through the sheet barrier. "Tell me, Zamel," Carrie said.

"You must never know. Even I do not know the details."

Carrie went behind the screen and leaned against the wall in despair at being excluded.

Zamel's mother sat on a pallet and continued with her beans; the snaps were loud now. Mother purposely did not look at Carrie. Carrie suspected that Mother knew more than she let on, but since Mother did not talk to her in any language, there was no way to be sure.

CHAPTER 21

Weeks later, Jessie sat at same table in the mall that she and Carrie had sat at while waiting for Zamel more than a year before. The food court was busy but not crowded. She had a large cup of black coffee in front of her and a paper boat containing a few last French fries.

She stared vacantly toward the escalators. Harold Lester emerged and walked toward her. She looked away, hoping to discourage him. She hadn't seen him since he had come to the furniture store.

"This food will make you die young," he said.

"You a doctor?"

"I care about your health."

"So you can make me spy on my brother-in-law?"

He pulled out a chair and sat down.

"Please don't sit there," Jessie said. She drank cold coffee and tried to appear offended, but she was curious as to why he was still following her.

"Why so hostile?" Harold said, staying where he was.

Jessie shrugged. "I don't like all this sneaky stuff."

"I could take you out to dinner." He smiled.

How ridiculous the idea was. There were times like this that made her want to hide under a rock to avoid him.

"Would that be okay?" he said. "Dinner?"

"Say what you have to say here," she said.

"I wouldn't talk business at dinner," he said.

"You got enough to grab him yet?"

"No."

Harold leaned back and stretched out his legs. "You went out to your sister's again. What did she say?"

"She said very specifically, 'Don't talk to bald old men with mustaches.'"

"She give a reason?"

"They're jerks."

"Anything else."

"And serious health risks."

"Nothing new about Zamel?"

"Not one thought to report. He wasn't there." Jessie saw a security guard near the elevator. "Sometimes I think you're stalking me," she said, waving to the guard for help. She'd file a complaint.

Harold turned so the guard could see him, and held up his hand in a friendly greeting. The guard stopped and smiled. Harold gave a thumbs up. The guard walked in the opposite direction.

"What did all that mean?" Jessie said.

"I'm not a threat," Harold said.

"Then why do you keep coming around unannounced?"

He smiled. "You're more likable than you want to be, sometimes."

"I'll bet I'm a lot less likeable than you think I am." Jessie stood, picking up her bag. "What's Zamel done wrong?"

"Nothing I know of exactly. He's suspected."

"A terrorist?"

"I can't prove it."

"Then why are you here?"

"It's my job."

"You're creepy." Jessie walked away.

Harold caught up. He handed her a card. "Call me if you need me. If you think of anything important."

"I think I'll tell Zamel about you."

He smiled. "You think I would be here if he didn't know?"

"Well, I'll tell him anyway? To scare him away from my sister. Maybe she could grow up normal."

She walked away, not sure where she was going, but making an effort to appear purposeful.

She did not know what Harold did, really. Internal security? Police? FBI? Her best guess was that he worked as an immigration official. She doubted Zamel was still legally in the country. But Harold didn't seem tame enough for immigration. And Zamel might be a terrorist. They were popping up everywhere since 9/11.

Jessie called the number on the card Harold gave her, hoping to find out who he worked for. But it went directly to him and she hung up when he answered.

CHAPTER 22

The same evening, Jessie went up the stairs to her apartment and found Carrie sitting on the floor next to the apartment door. She leaned against it, her knees up, her infant wrapped in a blanket in her arms. When she saw Jessie, Carrie stopped nursing and discreetly buttoned her shirt.

Jessie knelt to see the baby better. "What's up? You okay?" Jessie pulled back the blanket. She still did not approve of mixed-marriage offspring, but she was drawn in by the fragile beauty of this newborn. The baby burped. "You want to come in?" Jessie said.

"Is it all right?" Carrie asked tentatively.

"Why wouldn't it be all right? You're not planning to move in, are you?" The hurt on Carrie's face made Jessie want to take back her remark.

Carrie sat on a two-seater sofa and laid the baby beside her, moving a pillow to prevent it from sliding off.

"Zamel kick you out?" Jessie asked.

"That's so mean," Carrie said.

"Well, tell me."

"He takes good care of me, Jessie."

"And his mother? She taking good care of you, too?"

"She may be going back to Iran … I think so … her visa's up. But she needs money. Zamel's taken on another job. He's never home."

"How do you put up with it?"

"He loves me."

"He can't love you."

"Doctor Patrick didn't love you."

"That's different."

"Zamel cares."

Jessie couldn't hide her irritation, and Carrie's reference to Patrick shamed her when she thought how she had succumbed to his lust, in the clutch of sin. Carrie was right, there had been no love with Patrick like Carrie seemed to have with Zamel. Jessie felt a pang of jealousy.

"Zamel will leave," Jessie said. "You'll be alone with the baby."

"He will not. He's trying to get his green card."

Now Jessie wanted to hurt. "Did you know there's an investigator following him? He's been asking me questions about Zamel for months. He's got government identification. He won't say exactly, but I think he's immigration." She looked away and paused before she met Carrie's gaze again. "Maybe he's looking for terrorists. Zamel looks like one."

"He's not a terrorist!" Carrie said. But Jessie heard the hesitancy of doubt in Carrie's voice. Carrie might suspect, too.

"Something's happened," Jessie said.

"Has not."

"He bring you here?"

"I took the bus."

"When's the last time you saw him?" Jessie asked.

"A week."

"You really did hope to move in here, didn't you?"

"I just wanted to see you." Carrie looked away suddenly, her face tense and anxious with exhaustion.

The awkward silence isolated each in her own world. The baby gave a little cry. Carrie rocked the child gently.

"Is it Zamel's mother?" Jessie asked.

"She loves Golshan, Jessie."

"Does she speak English yet?"

"She doesn't try. She won't turn on the TV to learn."

"Does she talk to you?"

Carrie adjusted the baby in her arms. She sobbed. "I'm so lonely."

Jessie sat beside Carrie on the sofa. Touched her hand.

Carrie touched the baby's mouth with her finger, and she cried softly for a few seconds. "Oh, Jessie, he can't tell me things. I get so lonely when he's gone."

"What about his cousin next door? His wife? They talk to you?"

"She doesn't like me. He won't speak to me."

Jessie leaned back on the sofa and put her head back. "I don't have enough room here for the two of you."

"I could never leave Zamel," Carrie said.

"He's left you, without a word."

"He always comes back. He needs me, Jessie. He's not a strong man sometimes." Jessie paused with her eyes closed. "But he's stubborn. He doesn't believe in himself sometimes. But he's kind to me."

"He's out for himself, Carrie. Anyone can see that."

They sat in silence for many minutes, Carrie rocking the baby now. Carrie touched Jessie's arm. "It's too late to go back," Carrie said. "Could we at least stay tonight?"

Jessie pulled the blanket to one side to look at the baby. She touched her index finger to a little hand that clamped down, a tiny but strong grasp that sparked a wave of emotions—attraction, caring, and a deep sadness. Jessie, with her gaze, let Carrie know they could stay the night. She held back on mentioning that she wanted them back to stay as long as they wanted.

Jessie brought in blankets and pillows to fashion a makeshift crib. Carrie lay on the sofa, her head back, her eyes closed … but not asleep. Her hand protected the baby beside her. The baby whimpered. Carrie stood and cradled the baby in her arms. "Hold her," Carrie said to Jessie. Jessie took the baby. Carrie went into the bathroom and shut the door.

The baby whimpered again and started to cry. Jessie, her face impassive, tightened her grip on the child and swung from side to side.

The child stopped crying, the face relaxed.

The baby soon slept, her face toward Jessie. The child's beauty was unique; she had the fine features and glowing skin of a Persian princess. Jessie felt an unchecked love for the child, and its unexpected intensity made her uncomfortable.

Carrie returned and reached for the baby. For an instant Jessie did not to want to let go.

"What is her name again?" Jessie asked.

"Golshan."

After Carrie and Golshan were settled, Jessie went to the kitchenette to prepare something to eat. Three hard knocks on the door startled her. Golshan cried. Jessie went to the door, silently tiptoeing on the carpet. She was breathing hard. She touched nothing but placed her ear against the panel. Someone beat a fist against the door again, five times. She pulled back.

"Zamel?" Carrie said from the couch. Silence. Both women listened.

"Who is it?" Jessie finally asked.

"It's me," the voice said.

"It's Zamel," Carrie said. Jessie opened the door.

Zamel pushed his way in. "Get your belongings, wife."

"Calm down," Jessie said. Carrie would not move.

Zamel stuffed baby things into Carrie's tote bag and grabbed her arm, pulling her up. "Get Golshan."

Jessie faced Zamel. "Leave them alone." She feared for Carrie now, and for Golshan.

"It's okay, Jessie," Carrie said, standing and wrapping Golshan in a blanket.

Zamel shoved Carrie and the baby out the door and followed, carrying the bag.

"You left her. You creep," Jessie said.

"Jessie, I warn you, do not interfere." His eyes were hard with anger.

Jessie stood in the apartment doorway as they disappeared down the stairs at the end of the hall.

Zamel said nothing in the borrowed truck he took Carrie and Golshan home in.

"I was just lonely," Carrie said, but Zamel did not reply. When they entered the garage apartment, Mother took Golshan. Zamel took Carrie's hand and led her behind the hanging sheets where he made tender love to her and held her until she slept, the first peaceful sleep she'd had in months.

CHAPTER 23

After the breakup with Patrick, and with the new job at the furniture store that made her dread work, Jessie started going regularly to church again. She'd heard nothing from Carrie or Zamel. She was afraid a visit to the garage might put Carrie and Golshan in danger. Carrie had not contacted Jessie since her return to the garage; she seemed determined to exclude Jessie from their lives. And she recalled frequently, in detail, the touch and feel of Golshan—pleasant memories of loving the open innocence and unconditional acceptance of a newborn.

The Sunday morning sunrays pierced the branches of the oaks in the church yard, blanketing the front of the church and its steeple with variegated shadows patched with intense reflections from the white paint. The Reverend Luther Coffey, his back to the sun, greeted parishioners as they left the service. "Thank you so much for coming," he said with fragile sincerity to an elderly woman. "I'm so glad you're feeling better."

Jessie bypassed the line and circled away from the Reverend. He excused himself from the next in line and walked quickly to her, touching her arm to make her stop. "Could we talk?"

"There is nothing to talk about."

"About Carrie."

How could Jessie know his true motives? Should she agree or leave? After all, he had wanted to take her to a motel! But she'd come to believe he was too inexperienced with women to want more than talk, though. Even though she insisted to herself that he meant no offense, she still worried she might have led him on in some way.

"Please," he said. "I will be only a minute."

Jessie waited at the edge of the walkway that led from the church. Her Sunday-go-to-meeting low-heeled shoes hurt her feet. She wanted to be home, to kick them off.

In a few minutes, the Reverend approached her and pointed to a bench on the church lawn. "We could sit over there," he said.

When they sat, Jessie blatantly kept a good distance between them.

"I haven't seen Carrie in church," the Reverend said. "Has she lost faith?"

"She doesn't have a car. Butner is a long way without a car."

"Could you bring her to church sometime?"

"Look, I don't run her life. She does what she wants."

Jessie started to stand but the Reverend prevented her with his hand. "It's her husband, Zamel. He wants to convert."

Jessie shook her head in disbelief. "It can't be true."

"He paid the fee," the Reverend said. "He asked me questions about commitment. Baptism. Where we go in the hereafter. He bought a Bible. It's like a miracle."

"You can't believe him."

"He paid the fee."

"You took the fee? From him? I never thought you'd charge him, or anyone, for joining the church."

"I didn't know what to do. He seemed so sincere. I didn't want him to mistrust me."

"It was wrong. He'll mistrust you anyway when he finds out. The church never charges for admission."

The Reverend didn't look at her. "I'll refund it when he gets started. That will be the right thing to do." He thought for a few seconds. "Maybe you could talk to Carrie. Convince her to start coming to church with Zamel."

"Why don't you visit Carrie?"

"We could go together."

Jessie laughed. "I don't think so."

"Why not?"

"It should be a church call."

The Reverend squinted slightly. "You two not getting along?"

"You go. Make the church seem to want her."

The Reverend reached for her hand but she drew away. "I could do that with you," he said earnestly.

"It's not right. Mixing God's business by taking me with you."

"You're her sister. It's not a date."

"Who can tell with you?"

The pain of her remark showed on his face. "That's unfair," he said, with a touch of contrition. Jessie stood.

"Can I call you next week?" he asked.

She hesitated. He was sincere. Now she was convinced the motel incident was definitely a misguided mistake by a man inexperienced with women in every way.

"I would prefer not," she said.

CHAPTER 24

Jessie couldn't stop thinking about Zamel's new commitment to the church. She didn't believe he would follow through and was suspicious that he had actually paid money to begin conversion. She took a sick day off from the furniture store and went to see Carrie at home.

Carrie sat outside the garage, her back against the garage door, her knees up, nursing Golshan. Jessie parked; as she approached, Carrie kept her head down and Jessie squatted to see her face. Carrie was crying.

"What's up?" Jessie asked.

Carrie finished nursing and buttoned her shirt.

"Look at me!" Jessie insisted.

Carrie's eyes were frightened. She seemed trapped in indecision, the way Jessie remembered seeing her in their youth. Carrie could not take control of her life when she was this anxious. She retreated into herself, frozen in thought like a frightened rabbit in a bright headlight.

"Come with me," Jessie said.

"Golshan. I can't."

"Bring her."

"I'll leave her with Mother."

"Bring her."

Carrie finally followed Jessie. They sat in the car. Golshan slept peacefully.

"I'm taking you home," Jessie said. "Enough of this."

"I don't want that," Carrie said.

"What's wrong?"

Carrie cried for a minute or more before she could find words. "Mother's going back to Iran. I think she wants to take Golshan with her. Her 'sweet grandchild.'"

"She's told you this?"

"No. She still speaks only a few words I can understand. Zamel told me."

"How do you know she's leaving?"

"She has long talks with Zamel's cousin's wife next door. Mother takes Golshan with her. When I am at work, Golshan stays there like family."

"What does Zamel say?"

"He says his mother would never take Golshan away."

"And you believe him?"

"I don't know. I don't think he sees what I see," Carrie said.

"Do you think he wants Golshan to grow up in Iran?"

Carrie hesitated. "I don't think so."

"Did you ask him?"

Carrie didn't speak.

Jessie started the car. "I'm taking you away."

Carrie opened the door. "No. I cannot leave Zamel." She had her feet on the ground.

Jessie cut the motor. "That's crazy. Get back in," she said. "Let me hold Golshan."

Carrie handed Golshan to Jessie and settled again in the seat, closing the door. Jessie felt the warmth of the child on her breast. She pressed her cheek against Golshan's head, felt the infinite softness of the black hair. "Zamel's in trouble, Carrie. The authorities have contacted me again asking questions."

Carrie sobbed.

"What do you really know about Zamel?" Jessie asked.

Carrie did not respond for a minute. "He wouldn't do anything wrong."

"You don't believe that."

"He is not a bad person," Carrie said. "I know that."

"Would you know if he's in deep trouble?"

Carrie looked away as if threatened by the question.

"You can't let it hurt Golshan," Jessie said.

Carrie faced the truth. Her face hardened. Then she took Golshan from Jessie. She opened the car door, and walked back to the garage without looking back.

Carrie loved Zamel. It was obvious. Jessie would pray that Carrie's loyalty and caring and unwavering decency would not destroy her life… and Golshan's.

CHAPTER 25

Harold Lester approached a uniformed Jessie in the furniture store, standing near a canopy bed with her sign. For the first time she was relieved to see him.

"Have you heard from Zamel?" he asked. "You went out to see your sister."

"I didn't discuss Zamel," she said.

"Come on. Did she tell you he hasn't been home in more than a week, and he hasn't been to his job in three days?"

Jessie didn't look at him.

"Something's going on, Jessie. We need to know what it is."

"He's joining the church."

"Really?"

"He's taking classes to convert."

"Anything else?"

"What else do you expect?"

"Anything that would tell us where he is and what he's up to."

"My sister thinks he is not bad. That he would do nothing wrong."

Harold laughed. "And she'd be the last to know, wouldn't she?"

"He loves her," Jessie said. "I'm sure of that."

"Do you think that's enough to divert wrongdoing?"

"I don't know. I hope so."

Harold looked serious. "He was trained in Afghanistan, Jessie. Explosives. Computers. That's a lot of dedication. It can't all be innocent."

CHAPTER 26

Jessie awoke to a pounding on the front door, slipped on her slippers, and felt her way in her nightgown into the living room in the semi-darkness.

"Who is it?"

"I have a message," a voice said.

"Who are you?" Jessie whispered.

"A friend of Zamel."

The voice did not sound threatening, but still Jessie was afraid. "Please open," the voice said. "It is urgent."

"Tell me."

"I cannot speak it through the door."

Jessie undid the bolt and chain. A small dark youth wearing a hoodie slipped in. "It is Zamel. He must talk to you. He cannot come here. You are being watched. I am to write instructions for you so that you will not be followed."

"Where are Carrie and Golshan?" Jessie asked.

"His wife is with him."

"His daughter, too?"

"I do not know."

Jessie gave him a pencil and notepaper. Sitting at the kitchen table, the youth detailed how to find Zamel and Carrie.

Jessie dressed, went to her car, drove four blocks, then pulled into a side street, turned off the motor and lights and waited, searching for anyone who might be following. After fifteen minutes only two cars passed. She started driving again. She followed directions for a circuitous route into Raleigh, to a multistory public parking garage. She found a spot on the fourth level, then took the elevator to the fifth level and waited near the stair exit. In minutes, Zamel emerged from the shadows.

She followed him out of the garage, onto a side street. He walked more than a quarter of a mile to an all-night diner. He motioned for her to go down the alley at the side of the diner while he watched the street. Behind the building, hidden by a dumpster, Carrie huddled, cradling Golshan in her arms. Carrie cried when she saw Jessie. Jessie kissed her and sat down, pulling the edge of the blanket back to see if Golshan was really there. Zamel joined them and squatted, his body tense, his eyes searching the darkness nervously.

"We are leaving," Zamel said. "Carrie wanted to see you. To say goodbye."

"Where are you going?"

"I cannot say. We will start a new life."

"In Iran?"

"Not Iran."

"To do more bad things?"

"No. Nothing bad. To make a good life."

"We don't want to be away from you, Jessie," Carrie said.

"This is true," Zamel said. "But we must go."

"The authorities will follow," Jessie said. "They know all about you."

"They are not the only ones we abandon now. Men I've worked with will not approve of our leaving."

"Who?"

"Ones who are more capable of finding us than the authorities."

Jessie looked to Carrie. "Are you in danger?"

Carrie looked away and stood as Zamel rose. "We've got to keep moving," Carrie said.

"To where?"

"I have friend who can help," Zamel said. "We will go there and he will help us find somewhere safe."

"How? Do you have a car?"

"We will find a way."

"Where is it?"

"It is many miles," Zamel said.

"We can do it, Jessie," Carrie said.

"I have money," Zamel said, "but we must avoid the public authorities. They will be looking."

"And you don't know how you will get there," Jessie said. She could not take her eyes off Golshan.

Neither Carrie nor Zamel spoke as they prepared to leave. Golshan slept peacefully, unaware of her parents' urgency and stress.

Jessie loved them, all three. Her heart ached. "I will take you," she said, "wherever you need to go."

Carrie and Zamel stared at her with surprise. Neither had prepared to ask, and neither had ever expected her to offer. They'd come to say goodbye.

Jessie took control. "I'll get the car. Tell me where it's safe to pick you up."

Five hours later Jessie said goodbye to them in a residential neighborhood in the suburbs of Washington, DC. She did not know where they would go from there. She hugged Carrie and kissed Golshan. She turned to embrace Zamel but, embarrassed, he backed away. Jessie moved closer and took Zamel in her arms. "Take good care of them, Zamel. I love you all."

Zamel embraced her and put his head on her chest, his head under her chin.

"We love you …" Carrie said.

Zamel held Jessie's hand. "I am forever grateful …"

"Don't," Jessie said.

"But you have been …"

"You're family, Zamel." She grasped his shoulders. "No thank-yous are ever needed."

And they were gone.

Jessie drove back to her apartment and called in sick the next morning. Harold Lester knocked on her door not much later.

"Where is he, Jessie? Something's about to go down. I need to know."

"I don't know," she said, keeping the door opening narrow so he would not come in.

"You got past us last night. We know you bought gas in Virginia with a credit card."

"He's innocent."

"That's not a judgment you can make."

"I can and I will."

"Where did you take them?"

"He's not evil. He's husband to my sister and father of my only niece."

"And you shouldn't have any hesitation about telling us where he is."

Jessie sighed. "I don't know and there is no way I can find out."

"I can't believe that."

"Believe what you want. I would never betray them."

"That could be obstruction—"

Jessie closed the door, sliding the dead bolt in place.

CHAPTER 27

Jessie was fired from the furniture store for lack of enthusiasm and took a secretarial job at the Reverend Coffey's church. A year and four months later they were married, and a few weeks after that the Reverend accepted a church position in Wilmington.

Jessie had never heard or expected a word from Carrie and Zamel. But one morning, at a modest bungalow near the beach, she walked to the mailbox before leaving for work. She flipped through the letters to find a manila envelope with no return address, forwarded from Atlanta. The handwriting was not familiar. The smudged postmark was unreadable. Inside she found a color photo of a four-year-old girl on her way up the walk to a century-old house with a wraparound porch and a hanging sign that said "Betty Potter's Pre-Kindergarten." The girl wore a white dress trimmed in lace that covered her dark legs to just above the knee, white socks, and white Mary Janes. She carried a shiny black plastic book bag that looked empty. She was grinning at the camera, her brown eyes gleaming with excitement and confidence. A woman was coming down the walk from the house toward her, her arms out, welcoming.

A sticky note said, "First day. Love you."

"Honey," Jessie yelled to the back of the house.

The Reverend Coffey emerged in a T-shirt and drawstring pajama bottoms holding a diapered infant in his arms.

"Look," Jessie said, holding up the photo, her eyes moist. "They're safe."

Other Books by William H. Coles

McDowell
Guardian of Deceit
The Surgeon's Wife
The Spirit of Want
Sister Carrie
Facing Grace with Gloria and Other Stories
The Necklace and Other Stories
Creating Literary Stories: A Fiction Writers Guide
Story in Literary Fiction: A Manual for Writers
Literary Fiction as an Art Form: A Text for Writers
The Short Fiction of William H. Coles 2001-2011
The Illustrated Fiction of William H. Coles 2000-2012

www.ingramcontent.com/pod-product-compliance
Lightning Source LLC
Chambersburg PA
CBHW071958110726
47910CB00005B/1578

* 9 7 8 0 9 9 6 1 9 0 3 9 8 *